NORA ROBERTS

AT SUNRISE

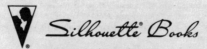

Silhouette Books

Published by Silhouette Books
America's Publisher of Contemporary Romance

SILHOUETTE BOOKS

At Sunrise

ISBN-13: 978-1-335-98412-8

Recycling programs
for this product may
not exist in your area.

Copyright © 2018 by Harlequin Books S.A.

The publisher acknowledges the copyright holder
of the individual works as follows:

Summer Desserts
Copyright © 1985 by Nora Roberts

Temptation
Copyright © 1987 by Nora Roberts

This edition published by arrangement with Harlequin Books S.A.

For questions and comments about the quality of this book, please contact us at CustomerService@Harlequin.com.

® and TM are trademarks of Harlequin Books S.A., used under license. Trademarks indicated with ® are registered in the United States Patent and Trademark Office, the Canadian Intellectual Property Office and in other countries.

Visit Silhouette Books at www.Harlequin.com

Printed in U.S.A.

CONTENTS

SUMMER DESSERTS

To Marianne Shock,
for the cheerful and clever last-minute help.

Chapter 1

Her name was Summer. It was a name that conjured visions of hot petaled flowers, sudden storms and long, restless nights. It also brought images of sun-warmed meadows and naps in the shade. It suited her.

As she stood, hands poised, body tensed, eyes alert, there wasn't a sound in the room. No one, absolutely no one, took their eyes off her. She might move slowly, but there wasn't a person there who wanted to chance missing a gesture, a motion. All attention, all concentration, was riveted upon that one slim, solitary figure. Strains of Chopin floated romantically through the air. The light slanted and shot through her neatly bound hair—rich, warm brown with hints and tints of gold. Two emerald studs winked at her ears.

Her skin was a bit flushed so that a rose tinge accented already prominent cheekbones and the elegant bone structure that comes only from breeding. Excitement, intense concentration, deepened the amber flecks that were sprinkled in the hazel of her eyes. The same excitement and concentration had her soft, molded lips forming a pout.

She was all in white, plain, unadorned white, but she drew the eye as irresistibly as a butterfly in full, dazzling flight. She wouldn't speak, yet everyone in the room strained forward as if to catch the slightest sound.

The room was warm, the smells exotic, the atmosphere taut with anticipation.

Summer might have been alone for all the attention she paid to those around her. There was only one goal, one end. Perfection. She'd never settled for less.

With infinite care she lifted the final diamond-shape and pressed the angelica onto the Savarin to complete the design she'd created. The hours she'd already spent preparing and baking the huge, elaborate dessert were forgotten, as was the heat, the tired leg muscles, the aching arms. The final touch, the *appearance* of a Summer Lyndon creation, was of the utmost importance. Yes, it would taste perfect, smell perfect, even slice perfectly. But if it didn't look perfect, none of that mattered.

With the care of an artist completing a masterpiece, she lifted her brush to give the fruits and almonds a light, delicate coating of apricot glaze.

Still, no one spoke.

Asking no assistance—indeed, she wouldn't have tolerated any—Summer began to fill the center of the Savarin with the rich cream whose recipe she guarded jealously.

Hands steady, head erect, Summer stepped back to give her creation one last critical study. This was the ultimate test, for her eye was keener than any other's when it came to her own work. She folded her arms across her body. Her face was without expression. In the huge kitchen, the ping of a pin dropped on the tile would have reverberated like a gunshot.

Slowly her lips curved, her eyes glittered. Success. Summer lifted one arm and gestured rather dramatically. "Take it away," she ordered.

As two assistants began to roll the glittering concoction from the room, applause broke out.

Summer accepted the accolade as her due. There was a place for modesty, she knew, and she knew it didn't apply to her Savarin. It was, to put it mildly, magnificent. Magnificence was what the Italian duke had wanted for his daughter's engagement party, and magnificence was what he'd paid for. Summer had simply delivered.

"Mademoiselle." Foulfount, the Frenchman whose specialty was shellfish, took Summer by both shoulders. His eyes were round and damp with appreciation. *"Incroyable."* Enthusiastically, he kissed both her cheeks while his thick, clever fingers squeezed her skin as they might a fresh-baked loaf of bread. Summer broke out in her first grin in hours.

"Merci." Someone had opened a celebratory bottle of wine. Summer took two glasses, handing one to the French chef. "To the next time we work together, *mon ami.*"

She tossed back the wine, took off her chef's hat, then breezed out of the kitchen. In the enormous marble-floored, chandeliered dining room, her Savarin was even now being served and admired. Her last thought before leaving was—thank God someone else had to clean up the mess.

Two hours later, she had her shoes off and her eyes closed. A gruesome murder mystery lay open on her lap as her plane cruised over the Atlantic. She was going home. She'd spent almost three full days in Milan for the sole purpose of creating that one dish. It wasn't an unusual experience for her. Summer had baked *Charlotte Malakoff* in Madrid, flamed *Crêpes Fourée* in Athens and molded *île Flottante* in Istanbul. For her expenses, and a stunning fee, Summer Lyndon would create a dessert that would live in the memory long after the last bite, drop or crumb was consumed.

Have wisk, will travel, she thought vaguely and smiled through a yawn.

She considered herself a specialist, not unlike a skilled surgeon. Indeed, she'd studied, apprenticed and practiced as long as many respected members of the medical profession. Five years after passing the stringent requirements to become a Cordon Bleu chef in Paris, the city where cooking is its own art, Summer had a reputation for being as temperamental as any artist, for having the mind of a computer when it came to remembering recipes and for having the hands of an angel.

Summer half dozed in her first-class seat and fought off a desperate craving for a slice of pepperoni pizza.

She knew the flight time would go faster if she could read or sleep her way through it. She decided to mix the two, taking the light nap first. Summer was a woman who prized her sleep almost as highly as she prized her recipe for chocolate mousse.

On her return to Philadelphia, her schedule would be hectic at best. There was the bombe to prepare for the governor's charity banquet, the annual meeting of the Gourmet Society, the demonstration she'd agreed to do for public television…and that meeting, she remembered drowsily.

What had that bird-voiced woman said over the phone? Summer wondered. Drake—no, Blake—Cocharan. Blake Cocharan III of the Cocharan hotel chain. Excellent hotels, Summer thought without any real interest. She'd patronized a number of them in various corners of the world. Mr. Cocharan the Third had a business proposition for her.

Summer assumed that he wanted her to create some special dessert exclusively for his chain of hotels, something they could attach the Cocharan name to. She wasn't averse to the notion—under the proper circumstances. And for the proper fee. Naturally she'd have to investigate the entire Cocharan enterprise carefully before she agreed to involve her skill or her name with it. If any one of their hotels was of inferior quality…

With a yawn, Summer decided to think about it later—after she'd met with The Third personality. Blake Cocharan III, she thought again with a sleepily amused smile. Plump, balding, probably dyspeptic. Italian shoes, Swiss watch, French shirts, German car—and no doubt he'd consider himself unflaggingly American. The image she created hung in her mind a moment, and, bored with it, she yawned again—then sighed as the idea of pizza once again invaded her thoughts. Summer tilted her seat back farther and determinedly willed herself to sleep.

Blake Cocharan III sat in the plush rear seat of the gunmetal-gray limo and meticulously went over the report on the newest Cocharan House being constructed in Saint Croix. He was a man who could scoop up a mess of scattered details and align them in perfect, systematic order. Chaos was simply a form of order waiting to be unjumbled with logic. Blake was a very logical man. Point A invariably led to point B, and from there to C. No matter how confused the maze, with patience and logic, one could find the route.

Because of his talent for doing just that, Blake, at thirty-five, had almost complete control of the Cocharan empire. He'd inherited his wealth and, as a result, rarely thought of it. But he'd earned his position, and valued it. Quality was a Cocharan tradition. Nothing but the finest would do for any Cocharan House, from the linen on the beds to the mortar in the foundations.

His report on Summer Lyndon told him she was the best.

Setting aside the Saint Croix packet, Blake slipped another file from the slim briefcase by his feet. A single ring, oval-faced, gold and scrolled, gleamed dully on his hand. Summer Lyndon, he mused, flipping the file open...

Twenty-eight, graduate Sorbonne, certified Cordon Bleu chef. Father, Rothschild Lyndon, respected member of British Parliament. Mother, Monique Dubois Lyndon, former star of the French cinema. Parents amicably divorced for twenty-three years. Summer Lyndon had spent her formative years between London and Paris before her mother had married an American hardware tycoon, based in Philadelphia. Summer had then returned to Paris to complete her education and currently had living quarters both there and in Philadelphia. Her mother had since married a third time, a paper baron on this round, and her father was separated from his second wife, a successful barrister.

All of Blake's probing had produced the same basic answer. Summer Lyndon was the best dessert chef on either side of the Atlantic. She was also a superb all-around chef with an instinctive knowledge of quality, a flair for creativity and the ability to improvise in a crisis. On the other hand, she was reputed to be dictatorial, temperamental and brutally frank. These qualities, however, hadn't alienated her from heads of state, aristocracy or celebrities.

She might insist on having Chopin piped into the kitchen while she cooked, or summarily refuse to work at all if the lighting wasn't to her liking, but her mousse alone was enough to make a strong man beg to grant her slightest wish.

Blake wasn't a man to beg for anything...but he wanted Summer Lyndon for Cocharan House. He never doubted he could persuade her to agree to precisely what he had in mind.

A formidable woman, he imagined, respecting that. He had no patience with weak wills or soft brains—particularly in people who worked for him. Not many women had risen to the position, or the reputation, that Summer Lyndon held. Women might traditionally be cooks, but men were traditionally chefs.

He imagined her thick waisted from sampling her own creations. Strong hands, he thought idly. Her skin was probably a bit pasty from all those hours indoors in kitchens. A no-nonsense woman, he was sure, with an uncompromising view on what was edible and why. Organized, logical and cultured—perhaps a bit plain due to her preoccupation with food rather than fashion.

Blake imagined that they would deal with each other very well. With a glance at his watch, Blake noted with satisfaction that he was right on time for the meeting.

The limo cruised to a halt beside the curb. "I'll be no more than an hour," Blake told the driver as he climbed out.

"Yes, sir." The driver checked his watch. When Mr. Cocharan said an hour, you could depend on it.

Blake glanced up at the fourth floor as he crossed to the well-kept old building. The windows were open, he noted. Warm spring air poured in, while music—a melody he couldn't quite catch over the sounds of traffic—poured out. When Blake went in, he learned that the single elevator was out of order. He walked up four flights.

After Blake knocked, the door was opened by a small woman with a stunning face who was dressed in a T-shirt and slim black jeans. The maid on her way out for a day off? Blake wondered idly. She didn't look strong enough to scrub a floor. And if she was going out, she was going out without her shoes.

After the brief, objective glance, his gaze was drawn irresistibly back to her face. Classic, naked and undeniably sensuous. The mouth alone would make a man's blood move. Blake ignored what he considered an automatic sexual pull.

"Blake Cocharan to see Ms. Lyndon."

Summer's left brow rose—a sign of surprise. Then her lips curved slightly—a sign of pleasure.

Plump, he wasn't, she observed. Hard and lean— racketball, tennis, swimming. He was obviously a man more prone to these than lingering over executive lunches. Balding, no. His hair was rich black and thick. It was styled well, with slight natural waves that added to the attractiveness of a cool, sensual face. A sweep of cheekbones, a firm line of chin. She liked the look of the former that spoke of strength, and the latter, just barely cleft, that spoke of charm. Black brows were almost straight over clear, water-blue eyes. His mouth was a bit long but beautifully shaped. His nose was very straight—the sort she'd always thought was made to be looked down. Perhaps she'd been right about the outward trimmings—the Italian shoes, and so forth—but, Summer admitted, she'd been off the mark with the man.

The assessment didn't take her long—three, perhaps four, seconds. But her mouth curved more. Blake couldn't take his eyes off it. It was a mouth a man, if he breathed, wanted to taste. "Please come in, Mr. Cocharan." Summer stepped back, swinging the door wider in invitation. "It's very considerate of you to agree to meet here. Please have a seat. I'm afraid I'm in the middle of something in the kitchen." She smiled, gestured and disappeared.

Blake opened his mouth—he wasn't used to being brushed off by servants—then closed it again. He had enough time to be tolerant. As he set down his briefcase he glanced around the room. There were fringed lamps, a curved sofa in plush blue velvet, a fussily carved cherrywood table. Aubusson carpets—two—softly faded in blues and grays—were spread over the floors. A Ming vase. Potpourri in what was certainly a Dresden compote.

The room had no order; it was a mix of European periods and styles that should never have suited, but was instantly attractive. He saw that a pedestal table at the far end of the room was covered with jumbled typewritten pages and handwritten notes. Street sounds drifted in through the window. Chopin floated from the stereo.

As he stood there, drawing it in, he was abruptly certain there was no one in the apartment but himself and the woman who had opened the door. Summer Lyndon? Fascinated with the idea, and with the aroma creeping from the kitchen, Blake crossed the room.

Six pastry shells, just touched with gold and moisture, sat on a rack. One by one Summer filled them to overflowing with what appeared to be some rich white cream. When Blake glanced at her face he saw the concentration, the seriousness and intensity he might have associated with a brain surgeon. It should have amused him. Yet somehow, with the strains of Chopin pouring through the kitchen speakers, with those delicate, slim-fingered hands arranging the cream in mounds, he was fascinated.

She dipped a fork in a pan and dribbled what he guessed was warmed caramel over the cream. It ran lavishly down the sides and gelled. He doubted that it was humanly possible not to lust after just one taste. Again, one by one, she scooped up the tarts and placed them on a plate lined with a lacy paper doily. When the last one was arranged, she looked up at Blake.

"Would you like some coffee?" She smiled and the line of concentration between her brows disappeared. The intensity that had seemed to darken her irises lightened.

Blake glanced at the dessert plate and wondered how her waist could be hand-spannable. "Yes, I would."

"It's hot," she told him as she lifted the plate. "Help yourself. I have to run these next door." She was past him and to the doorway of the kitchen before she turned around. "Oh, there're some cookies in the jar, if you like. I'll be right back."

She was gone, and the pastries with her. With a shrug, he turned back to the kitchen, which was a shambles. Summer Lyndon might be a great cook, but she was obviously not a neat one. Still if the scent and look of the pastries had been any indication…

He started to root in the cupboards for a cup, then gave in to temptation. Standing in his Saville Row suit, Blake ran his finger along the edge of the bowl that had held the cream. He laid it on his tongue. With a sigh, his eyes closed. Rich, thick and very French.

He'd dined in the most exclusive restaurants, in some of the wealthiest homes, in dozens of countries all over the world. Logically, practically, honestly, he couldn't say he'd ever tasted better than what he now scooped from the bowl in this woman's kitchen. In deciding to specialize in desserts and pastries, Summer Lyndon had chosen well, he concluded. He felt a momentary regret that she'd taken those rich, fat tarts to someone else. This time when Blake started his search for a cup, he spotted the ceramic cookie jar shaped like a panda.

Normally he wouldn't have been interested. He wasn't a man with a particularly active sweet tooth. But the flavor of the cream lingered on his tongue. What sort of cookie did a woman who created the finest of haute cuisine make? With a cup of English bone china in one hand, Blake lifted off the top of the panda's head. Setting it down, he pulled out a cookie and stared in simple wonder.

No American could mistake that particular munchie. A classic? he mused. A tradition? An Oreo. Blake continued to stare at the chocolate sandwich cookie with its double dose of white center. He turned it over in his hand. The brand was unmistakably stamped into both sides. This from a woman who baked and whipped and glazed for royalty?

A laugh broke from him as he dropped the Oreo back into the panda. Throughout his career he'd had to deal with more than his share of eccentrics. Running a chain of hotels wasn't just a matter of who checked in and who checked out. There were designers, artists, architects, decorators, chefs, musicians, union representatives. Blake considered himself knowledgeable of people. It wouldn't take him long to learn what made Summer tick.

She dashed back into the kitchen just as he was finally pouring the coffee. "I'm sorry to have kept you waiting, Mr. Cocharan. I know it was rude." She smiled, as if she had no doubt she'd be forgiven, as she poured her own coffee. "I had to get those pastries finished for my neighbor. She's having a small engagement tea this afternoon—with prospective in-laws." Her smile turned to a grin and, sipping her black coffee, she plucked the top from the panda. "Did you want a cookie?"

"No. Please, you go ahead."

Taking him at his word, Summer chose one and nibbled. "You know," she said thoughtfully, "these are uniformly excellent for their kind." She gestured with the half cookie she had left. "Shall we go sit down and discuss your proposition?"

She moved fast, he mused with approval. Perhaps he'd at least been on the mark about the no-nonsense attitude. With a nod of acknowledgment, Blake followed her. He was successful in his profession, not because he was a third-generation Cocharan, but because he had a quick and analytical mind. Problems were systematically solved. At the moment, he had to decide just how to approach a woman like Summer Lyndon.

She had a face that belonged in the shade of a tree on the Bois de Boulogne. Very French, very elegant. Her voice had the round, clear tones that spoke unmistakably of European education and upbringing—a wisp of France again but with the discipline of Britain. Her hair was pinned up, a concession to the heat and humidity, he imagined—though she had the windows open, ignoring the available air-conditioning. The studs in her ears were emeralds, round and flawless. There was a good-sized tear in the sleeve of her T-shirt.

Sitting on the couch, she folded her legs under her. Her bare toes were painted with a wild rose enamel, but her fingernails were short and unvarnished. He caught the allure of her scent—a touch of the caramel from the pastries, but under it something unmistakably French, unapologetically sexual.

How did one approach such a woman? Blake reflected. Did he use charm, flattery or figures? She was reputed to be a perfectionist and occasionally a firebrand. She'd refused to cook for an important political figure because he wouldn't fly her personal kitchen equipment to his country. She'd charged a Hollywood celebrity a small fortune to create a twenty-tiered wedding cake extravaganza. And she'd just hand-baked and hand-delivered a plate of pastries to a neighbor for a tea. Blake would much prefer to have the key to her before he made his offer. He knew the advantages of taking a circular route. Indeed some might call it stalking.

"I'm acquainted with your mother," Blake began easily as he continued to gauge the woman beside him.

"Really?" He caught both amusement and affection in the word. "I shouldn't be surprised," she said as she nibbled on the cookie again. "My mother always patronized a Cocharan House when we traveled. I believe I had dinner with your grandfather when I was six or seven." The amusement didn't fade as she sipped at her coffee. "Small world."

An excellent suit, Summer decided, relaxing against the back of the sofa. It was well cut and conservative enough to have gained her father's approval. The form it was molded to was well built and lean enough to have gained her mother's. It was perhaps the combination of the two that drew her interest.

Good God, he is attractive, she thought as she took another considering survey of his face. Not quite smooth, not quite rugged, his power sat well on him. That was something she recognized—in herself and in others. She respected someone who sought and got his own way, as she judged Blake did. She respected herself for the same reason. Attractive, she thought again—but she felt that a man like Blake would be so, regardless of physical appearance.

Her mother would have called him *séduisant,* and accurately so. Summer would have called him dangerous. A difficult combination to resist. She shifted, perhaps unconsciously, to put more distance between them. Business, after all, was business.

"You're familiar then with the standards of a Cocharan House," Blake began. Quite suddenly he wished her scent weren't so alluring or her mouth so tempting. He didn't care to have business muddled with attraction, no matter how pleasant.

"Of course." Summer set down her coffee because

drinking it only seemed to accentuate the odd little flutter in her stomach. "I invariably stay at them myself."

"I've been told your standards of quality are equally high."

This time when Summer smiled there was a hint of arrogance to it. "I'm the very best at what I do because I have no intention of being otherwise."

The first key, Blake decided with satisfaction. Professional vanity. "So my information tells me, Ms. Lyndon. The very best is all that interests me."

"So." Summer propped an elbow on the back of the sofa then rested her head on the palm. "How exactly do I interest you, Mr. Cocharan?" She knew the question was loaded, but couldn't resist. When a woman was constantly taking risks and making experiments in her professional life, the habit often leaked through.

Six separate answers skimmed through his mind, none of which had any bearing on his purpose for being there. Blake set down his coffee. "The restaurants at the Cocharan Houses are renowned for their quality and service. However, recently the restaurant here in our Philadelphia complex seems to be suffering from a lack of both. Frankly, Ms. Lyndon, it's my opinion that the food has become too pedestrian—too boring. I plan to do some remodeling, both in physical structure and in staff."

"Wise. Restaurants, like people, often become too complacent."

"I want the best head chef available." He aimed a level look. "My research tells me that's you."

Summer lifted a brow, not in surprise this time but in consideration. "That's flattering, but I freelance, Mr. Cocharan. And I specialize."

"Specialize, yes, but you do have both experience and knowledge in all areas of haute cuisine. As for the freelancing, you'd be free to continue that to a large extent, at least after the first few months. You'd need to establish your own staff and create your own menu. I don't believe in hiring an expert, then interfering."

She was frowning again—concentration, not annoyance. It was tempting, very tempting. Perhaps it was just the travel weariness from her trip back from Italy, but she'd begun to grow a bit tired—bored?—with the constant demands of flying to any given country to make that one dish. It seemed he'd hit her at the right moment to stir her interest in concentrating on one place, and one kitchen, for a span of time.

It would be interesting work—if he were being truthful about the free hand she'd have—redoing a kitchen and the menu in an old, established and respected hotel. It would take her perhaps six months of intense effort, and then... It was the "and then" that made her hesitate again. If she gave that much time and effort to a full-time job, would she still retain her flair for the spectacular? That, too, was something to consider.

She'd always had a firm policy against committing herself to any one establishment—a wariness of commitments ribboned through all areas of her life. If you locked yourself into something, to someone, you opened yourself to all manner of complications.

Besides, Summer reasoned, if she wanted to affiliate herself with a restaurant, she could open and run her own. She hadn't done it yet because it would tie her too long to one place, attach her too closely to one project. She preferred traveling, creating one superb dish at a time, then moving on. The next country, the next dish. That was her style. Why should she consider altering it now?

"A very flattering offer, Mr. Cocharan—"

"A mutually advantageous one," he interrupted, perceptive enough to catch the beginning of a refusal. With deliberate ease, he tossed out a six-digit annual salary that rendered Summer momentarily speechless—not a simple task.

"And generous," she said when she found her voice again.

"One doesn't get the best unless one's willing to pay for it. I'd like you to think about this, Ms. Lyndon." He reached in his briefcase and pulled out a sheaf of papers. "This is a draft of an agreement. You might like to have your attorney look it over, and of course, points can be negotiated."

She didn't want to look at the damn contract because she could feel, quite tangibly, that she was being maneuvered into a corner—a very plush one. "Mr. Cocharan, I do appreciate your interest, but—"

"After you've thought it over, I'd like to discuss it with you again, perhaps over dinner. Say, Friday?"

Summer narrowed her eyes. The man was a steamroller, she decided. A very attractive, very sleek steamroller. No matter how elegant the machinery, you still got flattened if you were in the path. Haughtiness emanated from her. "I'm sorry, I'm working Friday evening—the governor's charity affair."

"Ah, yes." He smiled, though his stomach had tightened. He had a suddenly vivid, completely wild image of making love to her on the ground of some moist, shadowy forest. That alone nearly made him consider accepting her refusal. And that alone made him all the more determined not to. "I can pick you up there. We can have a late supper."

"Mr. Cocharan," Summer said in a frigid voice, "you're going to have to learn to take no for an answer."

Like hell, he thought grimly, but gave her a rather rueful, rather charming smile. "My apologies, Ms. Lyndon, if I seem to be pressuring you. You were my first choice, you see, and I tend to go with my instincts. However..." Seemingly reluctant, he rose. The knot of tension and anger in Summer's stomach began to loosen. "If your mind's made up..." He plucked the contract from the table and started to slip it into his briefcase. "Perhaps you can give me your opinion on Louis LaPointe."

"LaPointe?" The word whispered through Summer's lips like venom. Very slowly she uncurled from the sofa, then rose, her whole body stiff. "You ask me of LaPointe?" In anger, her French ancestry became more pronounced in her speech.

"I'd appreciate anything you could tell me," Blake went on amiably, knowing full well he'd scored his first real point off her. "Seeing that you and he are associates and—"

With a toss of her head, Summer said something short, rude and to the point in her mother's tongue. The gold flecks in her eyes glimmered. Sherlock Holmes had Professor Moriarty. Superman had Lex Luthor. Summer Lyndon had Louis LaPointe.

"Slimy pig," she grated, reverting to English. "He has the mind of a peanut and the hands of a lumberjack.

You want to know about LaPointe?" She snatched a cigarette from the case on the table, lighting it as she did only when extremely agitated. "He's a peasant. What else is there to know?"

"According to my information, he's one of the five top chefs in Paris." Blake pressed because a good pressure point was an invaluable weapon. "His *Canard en Croûte* is said to be unsurpassable."

"Shoe leather." She all but spat out the words, and Blake had to school every facial muscle to prevent the grin. Professional vanity, he thought again. She had her share. Then as she drew in a deep breath, he had to school the rest of his muscles to hold off a fierce surge of desire. Sensuality—perhaps she had more than her share. "Why are you asking me about LaPointe?"

"I'm flying to Paris next week to meet with him. Since you're refusing my offer—"

"You'll offer this—" she wagged a finger at the contract still in Blake's hand "—to him?"

"Admittedly he's my second choice, but there are those on the board who feel Louis LaPointe is more qualified for the position."

"Is that so?" Her eyes were slits now behind a screen of smoke. She plucked the contract from his hand, then dropped it beside her cooling coffee. "The members of your board are perhaps ignorant?"

"They are," he managed, "perhaps mistaken."

"Indeed." Summer took a drag of her cigarette, then released smoke in a quick stream. She detested the taste. "You can pick me up at nine o'clock on Friday at the governor's kitchen, Mr. Cocharan. We'll discuss this matter further."

"My pleasure, Ms. Lyndon." He inclined his head,

careful to keep his face expressionless until he'd closed
the front door behind him. He laughed his way down
four flights of steps.

Chapter 2

Making a good dessert from scratch isn't a simple matter. Creating a masterpiece from flour, eggs and sugar is something else again. Whenever Summer picked up a bowl or a whisk or beater, she felt it her duty to create a masterpiece. Adequate, as an adjective in conjunction with her work, was the ultimate insult. Adequate, to Summer, was the result achieved by a newlywed with a cookbook first opened the day after the honeymoon. She didn't simply bake, mix or freeze—she conceived, developed and achieved. An architect, an engineer, a scientist did no more, no less. When she'd chosen to study the art of haute cuisine, she hadn't done so lightly, and she hadn't done so without the goal of perfection in mind. Perfection was still what she sought whenever she lifted a spoon.

She'd already spent the better part of her day in the

kitchen of the governor's mansion. Other chefs fussed with soups and sauces—or each other. All of Summer's talent was focused on the creation of the finale, the exquisite mix of tastes and textures, the overall aesthetic beauty of the bombe.

The mold was already lined with the moist cake she'd baked, then systematically sliced into a pattern. This had been done with templates as meticulously as when an engineer designs a bridge. The mousse, a paradise of chocolate and cream, was already inside the dessert's dome. This deceptively simple element had been chilling since early morning. Between the preparations, the mixing, making and building, Summer had been on her feet essentially that long.

Now, she had the beginnings of her bombe on a waist-high table, with a large stainless steel bowl of crushed berries at her elbow. At her firm instructions, Chopin drifted through the kitchen speakers. The first course was already being enjoyed in the dining room. She could ignore the confusion reigning around her. She could shrug off the pressure of having her part of the meal complete and perfect at precisely the right moment. That was all routine. But as she stood there, prepared to begin the next step, her concentration was scattered.

LaPointe, she thought with gritted teeth. Naturally it was anger that had kept her attention from being fully focused all day, the idea of having Louis LaPointe tossed in her face. It hadn't taken Summer long to realize that Blake Cocharan had used the name on purpose. Knowing it, however, didn't make the least bit of difference to her reaction…except perhaps that her venom was spread over two men rather than one.

Oh, he thinks he's very clever, Summer decided, thinking of Blake—as she had too often that week. She took three cleansing breaths as she studied the golden dome in front of her. Asking me, *me,* to give LaPointe a reference. Despicable French swine, she muttered silently, referring to LaPointe. As she scooped up the first berries she decided that Blake must be an equal swine even to be considering dealing with the Frenchman.

She could remember every frustrating, annoying contact she'd had with the beady-eyed, undersized LaPointe. As she carefully coated the outside of the cake with crushed berries, Summer considered giving him a glowing recommendation. It would teach that sneaky American a lesson to find himself stuck with a pompous ass like LaPointe. While her thoughts raged, her hands were delicately smoothing the berries, rounding out and firming the shape.

Behind her one of the assistants dropped a pan with a clatter and a bang and suffered a torrent of abuse. Neither Summer's thoughts nor her hands faltered.

Smug, self-assured jerk, she thought grimly of Blake. In a steady flow, she began layering rich French cream over the berries. Her face, though set in concentration, betrayed anger in the flash in her eyes. A man like him delighted in maneuvering and outmaneuvering. It showed, she thought, in that oh-so-smooth delivery, in that gloss of sophistication. She gave a disdainful little snort as she began to smooth out the cream.

She'd rather have a man with a few rough edges than one so polished that he gleamed. She'd rather have a man who knew how to sweat and bend his back than one with manicured nails and five-hundred-dollar suits. She'd rather have a man who…

Summer stopped smoothing the cream while her thoughts caught up with her consciousness. Since when had she considered having any man, and why, for God's sake, was she using Blake for comparisons? Ridiculous.

The bombe was now a smooth white dome waiting for its coating of rich chocolate. Summer frowned at it as an assistant whisked empty bowls out of her way. She began to blend the frosting in a large mixer as two cooks argued over the thickness of the sauce for the entrée.

For that matter, her thoughts ran on, it was ridiculous how often she'd thought of him the past few days, remembering foolish details… His eyes were almost precisely the shade of the water in the lake on her grandfather's estate in Devon. How pleasant his voice was, deep, with that faint but unmistakable inflection of the American Northeast. How his mouth curved in one fashion when he was amused, and another when he smiled politely.

It was difficult to explain why she'd noticed those things, much less why she'd continued to think of them days afterward. As a rule, she didn't think of a man unless she was with him—and even then she only allowed him a carefully regulated portion of her concentration.

Now, Summer reminded herself as she began to layer on frosting, wasn't the time to think of anything but the bombe. She'd think of Blake when her job was finished, and she'd deal with him over the late supper she'd agreed to. Oh, yes—her mouth set—she'd deal with him.

Blake arrived early deliberately. He wanted to see her work. That was reasonable, even logical. After all, if he were to contract Summer to Cocharan House for a year, he should see firsthand what she was capable of, and how she went about it. It wasn't at all unusual for him to check out potential employees or associates on their own turf. If anything, it was characteristic of him. Good business sense.

He continued to tell himself so, over and over, because there was a lingering doubt as to his own motivations. Perhaps he had left her apartment in high good spirits knowing he'd outmaneuvered her in the first round. Her face, at the mention of her rival LaPointe, had been priceless. And it was her face that he hadn't been able to push out of his mind for nearly a week.

Uncomfortable, he decided as he stepped into the huge, echoing kitchen. The woman made him uncomfortable. He'd like to know the reason why. Knowing the reasons and motivations was essential to him. With them neatly listed, the answer to any problem would eventually follow.

He appreciated beauty—in art, in architecture and certainly in the female form. Summer Lyndon was beautiful. That shouldn't have made him uncomfortable. Intelligence was something he not only appreciated but invariably demanded in anyone he associated with. She was undoubtedly intelligent. No reason for discomfort there. Style was something else he looked for—he'd certainly found it in her.

What was it about her…the eyes? he wondered as he passed two cooks in a heated argument over pressed duck. That odd hazel that wasn't precisely a definable color—those gold flecks that deepened or lightened according to her mood. Very direct, very frank eyes, he mused. Blake respected that. Yet the contrast of moody color that wasn't really a color intrigued him. Perhaps too much.

Sexuality? It was a foolish man who was wary because of a natural feminine sexuality and he'd never considered himself a foolish man. Nor a particularly susceptible one. Yet the first time he'd seen her he'd felt that instant curl of desire, that immediate pull of man for woman. Unusual, he thought dispassionately. Something he'd have to consider carefully—then dispose of. There wasn't room for desire between business associates.

And they would be that, he thought as his lips curved. Blake counted on his own powers of persuasion, and his casual mention of LaPointe to turn Summer Lyndon his way. She was already turning that way, and after tonight, he reflected, then stopped dead. For a moment it felt as though someone had delivered him a very quick, very stunning blow to the base of the spine. He'd only had to look at her.

She was half-hidden by the dessert she worked on. Her face was set, intent. He saw the faint line that might've been temper or concentration run down between her brows. Her eyes were narrowed, the lashes swept down so that the expression was unreadable. Her mouth, that soft, molded mouth that she seemed never to paint, was forming a pout. It was utterly kissable.

She should have looked plain and efficient, all in white. The chef's hat over her neatly bound hair could have given an almost comic touch. Instead she looked outrageously beautiful. Standing there, Blake could hear the Chopin that was her trademark, smell the exotic pungent scents of cooking, feel the tension in the air as temperamental cooks fussed and labored over their creations. All he could think, and think quite clearly, was how she would look naked, in his bed, with only candles to vie with the dark.

Catching himself, Blake shook his head. *Stop it,* he thought with grim amusement. *When you mix business and pleasure, one or both suffers.* That was something Blake invariably avoided without effort. He held the position he did because he could recognize, weigh and dismiss errors before they were ever made. And he could do so with a cold-blooded ruthlessness that was as clean as his looks.

The woman might be as delectable as the concoction she was creating, but that wasn't what he wanted—correction, what he could afford to want—from her. He needed her skill, her name and her brain. That was all. For now, he comforted himself with that thought as he fought back waves of a more insistent and much more basic need.

As he stood, as far outside of the melee as possible, Blake watched her patiently, methodically apply and smooth on layer after layer. There was no hesitation in her hands—something he noticed with approval even as he noted the fine-boned elegant shape of them. There was no lack of confidence in her stance. Looking on, Blake realized that she might have been alone for all the noise and confusion around her mattered.

The woman, he decided, could build her spectacular bombe on the Ben Franklin Parkway at rush hour and never miss a step. Good. He couldn't use some hysterical female who folded under pressure.

Patiently he waited as she completed her work. By the time Summer had the pastry bag filled with white icing and had begun the final decorating, most of the kitchen staff were on hand to watch. The rest of the meal was a fait accompli. There was only the finale now.

On the last swirl, she stepped back. There was a communal sigh of appreciation. Still, she didn't smile as she walked completely around the bombe, checking, rechecking. Perfection. Nothing less was acceptable.

Then Blake saw her eyes clear, her lips curve. At the scattered applause, she grinned and was more than beautiful—she was approachable. He found that disturbed him even more.

"Take it in." With a laugh, she stretched her arms high to work out a dozen stiffened muscles. She decided she could sleep for a week.

"Very impressive."

Arms still high, Summer turned slowly to find herself facing Blake. "Thank you." Her voice was very cool, her eyes wary. Sometime between the berries and the frosting, she'd decided to be very, very careful with Blake Cocharan III. "It's meant to be."

"In looks," he agreed. Glancing down, he saw the large bowl of chocolate frosting that had yet to be removed. He ran his finger around the edge, then licked it off. The taste was enough to melt the hardest hearts. "Fantastic."

She couldn't have prevented the smile—a little boy's trick from a man in an exquisite suit and silk tie. "Naturally," she told him with a little toss of her head. "I only make the fantastic. Which is why you want me— correct, Mr. Cocharan?"

"Mmm." The sound might have been agreement, or it might have been something else. Wisely, both left it at that. "You must be tired, after being on your feet for so long."

"A perceptive man," she murmured, pulling off the chef's hat.

"If you'd like, we'll have supper at my penthouse. It's private, quiet. You'd be comfortable."

She lifted a brow, then sent a quick, distrustful look over his face. Intimate suppers were something to be considered carefully. She might be tired, Summer mused, but she could still hold her own with any man—particularly an American businessman. With a shrug, she pulled off her stained apron. "That's fine. It'll only take me a minute to change."

She left him without a backward glance, but as he watched, she was waylaid by a small man with a dark moustache who grabbed her hand and pressed it dramatically to his lips. Blake didn't have to overhear the words to gauge the intent. He felt a twist of annoyance that, with some effort, he forced into amusement.

The man was speaking rapidly while working his way up Summer's arm. She laughed, shook her head and gently nudged him away. Blake watched the man gaze after her like a forlorn puppy before he clutched his own chef's hat to his heart.

Quite an effect she has on the male of the species, Blake mused. Again dispassionately, he reflected that there was a certain type of woman who drew men without any visible effort. It was an innate…skill, he supposed was the correct term. A skill he didn't admire or condemn, but simply mistrusted. A woman like that could manipulate with the flick of the wrist. On a personal level, he preferred women who were more obvious in their gifts.

He positioned himself well out of the way while the cacophony and confusion of cleaning up began. It was a skill he figured wouldn't hurt in her position as head chef of his Philadelphia Cocharan House.

In nine more than the minute she'd claimed she'd be, Summer strolled back into the kitchen. She'd chosen the thin poppy-colored silk because it was perfectly simple—so simple it had a tendency to cling to every curve and draw every eye. Her arms were bare but for one ornately carved gold bracelet she wore just above the elbow. Drop spiral earrings fell almost to her shoulders. Unbound now, her hair curled a bit around her face from the heat and humidity of the kitchen.

She knew the result was part eccentric, part exotic. Just as she knew it transmitted a primal sexuality. She dressed as she did—from jeans to silks—for her own pleasure and at her own whim. But when she saw the fire, quickly banked, in Blake's eyes she was perversely satisfied.

No iceman, she mused—of course she wasn't interested in him in any personal way. She simply wanted to establish herself as a person, an individual, rather than a name he wanted neatly signed on a contract. Her work clothes were jumbled into a canvas tote she carried in one hand, while over her other shoulder hung a tiny exquisitely beaded purse. In a rather regal gesture, she offered Blake her hand.

"Ready?"

"Of course." Her hand was cool, small and smooth. He thought of streaming sunlight and wet, fragrant grass. Because of it, his voice became cool and pragmatic. "You're lovely."

She couldn't resist. Humor leaped into her eyes. "Of course." For the first time she saw him grin—fast, appealing. Dangerous. In that moment she wasn't quite certain who held the upper hand.

"My driver's waiting outside," Blake told her smoothly. Together they walked from the brightly lit, noisy kitchen out into the moonlit street. "I take it you were satisified with your part of the governor's meal. You didn't choose to stay for the criticism or compliments."

As she stepped into the back of the limo, Summer sent him an incredulous look. "Criticism? The bombe is my specialty, Mr. Cocharan. It's always superb. I need no one to tell me that." She got in the car, smoothed her skirt and crossed her legs.

"Of course," Blake murmured, sliding beside her, "it's a complicated dish." He went on conversationally, "If my memory serves me, it takes hours to prepare properly."

She watched him remove a bottle of champagne from ice and open it with only a muffled pop. "There's very little that can be superb in a short amount of time."

"Very true." Blake poured champagne into two tulip glasses and, handing Summer one, smiled. "To a lengthy association."

Summer gave him a frank look as the streetlights flickered into the car and over his face. A bit Scottish warrior, a bit English aristocrat, she decided. Not a simple combination. Then again, simplicity wasn't always what she looked for. With only a brief hesitation, she touched her glass to his. "Perhaps," she said. "You enjoy your work, Mr. Cocharan?" She sipped, and without looking at the label, identified the vintage of the wine she drank.

"Very much." He watched her as he drank, noting

that she'd done no more than sweep some mascara over her lashes when she'd changed. For an instant he was distracted by the speculation of what her skin would feel like under his fingers. "It's obvious by what I caught of that session in there that you enjoy yours."

"Yes." She smiled, appreciating him and what she thought would be an interesting struggle for power. "I make it a policy to do only what I enjoy. Unless I'm very much mistaken, you have the same policy."

He nodded, knowing he was being baited. "You're very perceptive, Ms. Lyndon."

"Yes." She held her glass out for a refill. "You have excellent taste in wines. Does that extend to other areas?"

His eyes locked on hers as he filled her glass. "All other areas?"

Her mouth curved slowly as she brought the champagne to it. Summer enjoyed the effervescence she could feel just before she tasted it. "Of course. Would it be accurate to say that you're a discriminating man?"

What the hell was she getting at? "If you like," Blake returned smoothly.

"A businessman," she went on. "An executive. Tell me, don't executives…delegate?"

"Often."

"And you? Don't you delegate?"

"That depends."

"I wondered why Blake Cocharan III himself would take the time and trouble to woo a chef into his organization."

He was certain she was laughing at him. More, he was certain she wanted him to know it. With an effort, he suppressed his annoyance. "This project is a personal pet of mine. Since I want only the best for it, I take the time and trouble to acquire the best personally."

"I see." The limo glided smoothly to the curb. Summer handed Blake her empty glass as the driver opened her door. "Then how strange that you would even mention LaPointe if only the best will serve you." With the haughty grace a woman can only be born with, Summer alighted. That, she thought smugly, should poke a few holes in his arrogance.

The Cocharan House of Philadelphia stood only twelve stories and had a weathered brick facade. It had been built to blend and accent the colonial architecture that was the heart of the city. Other buildings might zoom higher, might gleam with modernity, but Blake Cocharan had known what he'd wanted. Elegance, style and discretion. That was Cocharan House. Summer was forced to approve. In a great many things, she preferred the old world to the new.

The lobby was quiet, and if the gold was a bit dull, the rugs a bit soft and faded looking, it was a deliberate and canny choice. Old, established wealth was the ambience. No amount of gloss, gleam or gilt would have been more effective.

Taking Summer's arm, Blake passed through with only a nod here and there to the many "Good evening, Mr. Cocharans" he received. After inserting a key into a private elevator, he led her inside. They were enveloped by silence and smoked glass.

"A lovely place," Summer commented. "It's been years since I've been inside. I'd forgotten." She glanced around the elevator and saw their reflections trapped deep in gray glass. "But don't you find it confining to live in a hotel—to live, that is, where you work?"

"No. Convenient."

A pity, Summer mused. When she wasn't working, she wanted to remove herself from the kitchens and timers. She'd never been one—as her mother and father had been—to bring her work home with her.

The elevator stopped so smoothly that the change was hardly noticeable. The doors slid open silently. "Do you have the entire floor to yourself?"

"There're three guest suites as well as my penthouse," Blake explained as they walked down the hall. "None of them are occupied at the moment." He inserted a key into a single panel of a double oak door then gestured her inside.

The lights were already dimmed. He'd chosen his colors well, she thought as she stepped onto the thick pewter-toned carpet. Grays from silvery pale to smoky dominated in the low, spreading sofa, the chairs, the walls. With the lights low it had a dreamlike effect that was both sensuous and soothing.

It might have been dull, even bland, but there were splashes of color cleverly interspersed. The deep midnight blue of the drapes, the pearl-like tones of the army of cushions lining the sofa, the rich, primal green of an ivy tangling down the rungs of a breakfront. Then there were the glowing colors of the one painting, a French Impressionist that dominated one wall.

There was none of the clutter she would have chosen for herself, but a sense of style she admired immediately. "Unusual, Mr. Cocharan," Summer complimented as she automatically stepped out of her shoes. "And effective."

"Thank you. Another drink, Ms. Lyndon? The bar's fully stocked, or there's champagne if you prefer."

Still determined to come out of the evening on top, Summer strolled to the sofa and sat. She sent him a cool, easy smile. "I always prefer champagne."

While Blake dealt with the bottle and cork, she took an extra moment to study the room again. Not an ordinary man, she decided. Too often ordinary was synonymous with boring. Summer was forced to admit that because she'd associated herself with the bohemian, the eccentric, the creative for most of her life, she'd always thought of people in business as innately boring.

No, Blake Cocharan wouldn't be dull. She almost regretted it. A dull man, no matter how attractive, could be handled with the minimum of effort. Blake was going to be difficult. Particularly since she'd yet to come to a firm decision on his proposition.

"Your champagne, Ms. Lyndon." When she lifted her eyes to his, Blake had to fight back a frown. The look was too measuring, too damn calculating. Just what was the woman up to now? And why in God's name did she look so right, so temptingly right, curled on his sofa with pillows at her back? "You must be hungry," he said, astonished that he needed the defense of words. "If you'd tell me what you'd like, the kitchen will prepare it. Or I can get you a menu, if you'd prefer."

"A menu won't be necessary." She sipped more cold, frothy French champagne. "I'd like a cheeseburger."

Blake watched the silk shift as she nestled into the corner of the sofa. "A what?"

"Cheeseburger," Summer repeated. "With a side order of fries, shoestring." She lifted her glass to examine the color of the liquid. "Do you know, this was a truly exceptional year."

"Ms. Lyndon..." With strained patience, Blake dipped

his hands in his pockets and kept his voice even. "Exactly what game are you playing?"

She sipped slowly, savoring. "Game?"

"Do you seriously want me to believe that you, a gourmet, a Cordon Bleu chef, want to eat a cheeseburger and shoestring fries?"

"I wouldn't have said so otherwise." When her glass was empty, Summer rose to refill it herself. She moved, he noted, lazily, with none of that sharp, almost military motion she'd used when cooking. "Your kitchen does have lean prime beef, doesn't it?"

"Of course." Certain she was trying to annoy him, or make a fool of him, Blake took her arm and turned her to face him. "Why do you want a cheeseburger?"

"Because I like them," she said simply. "I also like tacos and pizza and fried chicken—particularly when someone else is cooking them. That sort of thing is quick, tasty and convenient." She grinned, relaxed by the wine, amused by his reaction. "Do you have a moral objection to junk food, Mr. Cocharan?"

"No, but I'd think you would."

"Ah, I've shattered your image of a gastronomic snob." She laughed, a very appealing, purely feminine sound. "As a chef, I can tell you that rich sauces and heavy creams aren't easy on the digestion either. Besides that, I cook professionally. For long periods of time I'm surrounded by the finest of haute cuisine. Delicacies, foods that have to be prepared with absolute perfection, split-second timing. When I'm not working, I like to relax." She drank champagne again. "I'd prefer a cheeseburger, medium rare, to *Filet aux Champignons* at the moment, if you don't mind."

"Your choice," he muttered and moved the phone to

order. Her explanation had been reasonable, even logical. There was nothing that annoyed him more than having his own style of manuevering used against him.

With her glass in hand, Summer wandered to the window. She liked the looks of a city at night. The buildings rose and spread in the distance and traffic wound its way silently on the intersecting roads. Lights, darkness, shadows.

She couldn't have counted the number of cities she'd been in or viewed from a similar spot, but her favorite remained Paris. Yet she'd chosen to live for long lengths of time in the States—she liked the contrast of people and cultures and attitudes. She liked the ambition and enthusiasm of Americans, which she saw typified in her mother's second husband.

Ambition was something she understood. She had a lot of her own. She understood this to be the reason she looked for men with more creative ability than ambition in her personal relationships. Two competitive, career-oriented people made an uneasy couple. She'd learned that early on watching her own parents with each other, and their subsequent spouses. When she chose permanence in a relationship—something Summer considered was at least a decade away—she wanted someone who understood that her career came first. Any cook, from a child making a peanut butter sandwich to a master chef, had to understand priorities. Summer had understood her own all of her life.

"You like the view?" Blake stood behind her, where he'd been studying her for a full five minutes. Why should she seem different from any other woman he'd ever brought to his home? Why should she seem more elusive, more alluring? And why should her presence alone make it so difficult for him to keep his mind on the business he'd brought her there for?

"Yes." She didn't turn because she realized abruptly just how close he was. It was something she should have sensed before, Summer thought with a slight frown. If she turned, they'd be face-to-face. There'd be a brush of bodies, a meeting of eyes. The quick scramble of nerves made her sip the champagne again. Ridiculous, she told herself. No man made her nervous.

"You've lived here long enough to recognize the points of interest," Blake said easily, while his thoughts centered on how the curve of her neck would taste, would feel under the brush of his lips.

"Of course. I consider myself a Philadelphian when I'm in Philadelphia. I'm told by some of my associates that I've become quite Americanized."

Blake listened to the flow of the European accented voice, drew in the subtle, sexy scent of Paris that was her perfume. The dim light touched on the gold scattered through her hair. Like her eyes, he thought. He had only to turn her around and look at her face to see her sculptured, exotic look. And he wanted, overwhelmingly, to see that face.

"Americanized," Blake murmured. His hands were on her shoulders before he could stop them. The silk slid cool under his palms as he turned her. "No…" His gaze flicked down, over her hair and eyes, and lingered on her mouth. "I think your associates are very much mistaken."

"Do you?" Her fingers had tightened on the stem of her glass, her mouth had heated. Willpower alone kept her voice steady. Her body brushed his once, then twice as he began to draw her closer. Needs, tightly controlled, began to smolder. While her mind raced with the possibilities, Summer tilted her head back and spoke calmly. "What about the business we're here to discuss, Mr. Cocharan?"

"We haven't started on business yet." His mouth hovered over hers for a moment before he shifted to whisper a kiss just under one eyebrow. "And before we do, it might be wise to settle this one point."

Her breathing was clogging, backing up in her lungs. Drawing away was still possible, but she began to wonder why she should consider it. "Point?"

"Your lips—will they taste as exciting as they look?"

Her lashes were fluttering down, her body softening. "Interesting point," she murmured, then tilted her head back in invitation.

Their lips were only a breath apart when the sharp knock sounded at the door. Something cleared in Summer's brain—reason—while her body continued to hum. She smiled, concentrating hard on that one slice of sanity.

"The service in a Cocharan House is invariably excellent."

"Tomorrow," Blake said as he drew reluctantly away, "I'm going to fire my room service manager."

Summer laughed, but took a shaky sip of wine when he left her to answer the door. Close, she thought, letting out a long, steadying breath. Much too close. It was time to steer the evening into business channels and keep it there. She gave herself a moment while the waiter set up the meal on the table.

"Smells wonderful," Summer commented, crossing the room as Blake tipped and dismissed the waiter. Before sitting, she glanced at his meal. Steak, rare, a steaming potato popping out of its skin, buttered asparagus. "Very sensible." She shot him a teasing grin over her shoulder as he held out her chair.

"We can order dessert later."

"Never touch them," she said, tongue in cheek. With a generous hand she spread mustard over her bun. "I read over your contract."

"Did you?" He watched as she cut the burger neatly in two then lifted a half. It shouldn't surprise him, Blake mused. She did, after all, keep Oreos in her cookie jar.

"So did my attorney."

Blake added some ground pepper to his steak before cutting into it. "And?"

"And it seems to be very much in order. Except…" She allowed the word to hang while she took the first bite. Closing her eyes, Summer simply enjoyed.

"Except?" Blake prompted.

"*If* I were to consider such an offer, I'd need considerably more room."

Blake ignored the *if*. She was considering it, and they both knew it. "In what area?"

"Certainly you're aware that I do quite a bit of traveling." Summer dashed salt on the French fries, tasted and approved. "Often it's a matter of two or three days when I go to, say, Venice and prepare a *Gâteau St. Honoré*. Some of my clients book me months in advance. On the other hand, there are some that deal more spontaneously. A few of these—" Summer bit into the cheeseburger again "—I'll accommodate because of personal affection or professional challenge."

"In other words you'd want to fly to Venice or wherever when you felt it necessary." However incongruous he felt the combination was, Blake poured more champagne into her glass while she ate.

"Precisely. Though your offer does have some slight interest for me, it would be impossible, even, I feel, unethical, to turn my back on established clients."

"Understood." She was crafty, Blake thought, but so was he. "I should think a reasonable arrangement could be worked out. You and I could go over your current schedule."

Summer nibbled on a fry, then dusted her fingers on a white linen napkin. "You and I?"

"That would keep it simpler. Then if we agreed to discuss whatever other occasions might crop up during the year on an individual basis…" He smiled as she picked up the second half of her cheeseburger. "I like to think I'm a reasonable man, Ms. Lyndon. And, to be frank, I personally would prefer signing you with my hotel. At the moment, the board's leaning toward LaPointe, but—"

"Why?" The word was a demand and an accusation. Nothing could have pleased Blake more.

"Characteristically, the great chefs are men." She cursed, bluntly and brutally in French. Blake merely nodded. "Yes, exactly. And, through some discreet questioning, we've learned that Monsieur LaPointe is very interested in the position."

"The swine would scramble at a chance to roast chestnuts on a street corner if only to have his picture in the paper." Tossing down her napkin, she rose. "You think perhaps I don't understand your strategy, Mr. Cocharan." The regal lifting of her head accentuated her long, slender neck. Blake remembered quite vividly how that skin had felt under his fingers. "You throw LaPointe in my face thinking that I'll grab your offer as a matter of ego, of pride."

He grinned because she looked magnificent. "Did it work?"

Her eyes narrowed, but her lips wanted badly to curve. "LaPointe is a philistine. *I* am an artist."

"And?"

She knew better than to agree to anything in anger. Knew better, but… "You accommodate my schedule, Mr. Cocharan the Third, and I'll make your restaurant the finest establishment of its kind on the East Coast." And damn it, she could do it. She found she wanted to do it to prove it to both of them.

Blake rose, lifting both glasses. "To your art, mademoiselle." He handed her a glass. "And to my business. May it be a profitable union for both of us."

"To success," she amended, clinking glass to glass. "Which, in the end, is what we both look for."

Chapter 3

Well, I've done it, Summer thought, scowling. She swept back her hair and secured it with two mother-of-pearl combs. Critically she studied her face in the mirror to check her makeup. She'd learned the trick of accenting her best features from her mother. When the occasion called for it, and she was in the mood, Summer exploited the art. Although she felt the face that was reflected at her would do, she frowned anyway.

Whether it had been anger or ego or just plain cussedness, she'd agreed to tie herself to the Cocharan House, and Blake, for the next year. Maybe she did want the challenge of it, but already she was uncomfortable with the long-term commitment and the obligations that went with it.

Three hundred sixty-five days. No, that was too overwhelming, she decided. Fifty-two weeks was hardly a better image. Twelve months. Well, she'd just have to live with it. No, she'd have to do better than that, Summer decided as she wandered back into the studio where she'd be taping a demonstration for public TV. She had to live up to her vow to give the Philadelphia Cocharan House the finest restaurant on the East Coast.

And so she would, she told herself with a flick of her hair over her shoulder. So she damn well would. Then she'd thumb her nose at Blake Cocharan III. The sneak.

He'd manipulated her. Twice, he'd manipulated her. Even though she'd been perfectly aware of it the second time, she'd strolled down the garden path anyway. Why? Summer ran her tongue over her teeth and watched the television crew set up for the taping.

The challenge, she decided, twisting her braided gold chain around one slim finger. It would be a challenge to work with him and stay on top. Competing was her greatest weakness, after all. That was one reason she'd chosen to excel in a career that was characteristically male-dominated. Oh, yes, she liked to compete. Best of all, she liked to win.

Then there was that ripe masculinity of his. Polished manners couldn't hide it. Tailored clothes couldn't cloak it. If she were honest—and she decided she would be for the moment—Summer had to admit she'd enjoy exploring it.

She knew her effect on men. A genetic gift, she'd always thought, from her mother. It was rare that she paid much attention to her own sexuality. Her life was too full of the pressures of her work and the complete relaxation she demanded between clients. But it might be time, Summer mused now, to alter things a bit.

Blake Cocharan III represented a definite challenge.

And how she'd love to shake up that smug male arrogance. How she'd like to pay him back for maneuvering her to precisely where he'd wanted her. As she considered varied ways and means to do just that, Summer idly watched the studio audience file in.

They had the capacity for about fifty, and apparently they'd have a full house this morning. People were talking in undertones, the mumbles and shuffles associated with theaters and churches. The director, a small, excitable man whom Summer had worked with before, hustled from grip to gaffer, light to camera, tossing his arms in gestures that signaled pleasure or dread. Only extremes. When he came over to her, Summer listened to his quick nervous instructions with half an ear. She wasn't thinking of him, nor was she thinking of the vacherin she was to prepare on camera. She was still thinking of the best way to handle Blake Cocharan.

Perhaps she should pursue him, subtly—but not so subtly that he wouldn't notice. Then when his ego was inflated, she'd…she'd totally ignore him. A fascinating idea.

"The first baked shell is in the center storage cabinet."

"Yes, Simon, I know." Summer patted the director's hand while she went over the plan for flaws. It had a big one. She could remember all too clearly that giddy sensation that had swept over her when he'd nearly—just barely—kissed her a few evenings before. If she played the game that way, she just might find herself muddling the rules. So…

"The second is right beneath it."

"Yes, I know." Hadn't she put it there herself to cool after baking? Summer gave the frantic director an absent smile. She could ignore Blake right from the start. Treat him—not with contempt, but with disinterest. The smile became a bit menacing. Her eyes glinted. That should drive him crazy.

"All the ingredients and equipment are exactly where you put them."

"Simon," Summer began kindly, "stop worrying. I can build a vacherin in my sleep."

"We roll tape in five minutes—"

"Where is she!"

Both Summer and Simon looked around at the bellowing voice. Her grin was already forming before she saw its owner. "Carlo!"

"Aha." Dark and wiry and as supple as a snake, Carlo Franconi wound his way around people and over cable to grab Summer and pull her jarringly against his chest. "My little French pastry." Fondly he patted her bottom.

Laughing, she returned the favor. "Carlo, what're you doing in downtown Philadelphia on a Wednesday morning?"

"I was in New York promoting my new book, *Pasta by the Master*." He drew back enough to wiggle his eyebrows at her. "And I said, Carlo, you are just around the corner from the sexiest woman who ever held a pastry bag. So I come."

"Just around the corner," Summer repeated. It was typical of him. If he'd been in Los Angeles, he'd have done the same thing. They'd studied together, cooked together, and perhaps if their friendship had not become so solid and important, they might have slept together. "Let me look at you."

Obligingly, Carlo stepped back to pose. He wore straight, tight jeans that flattered narrow hips, a salmon-colored silk shirt and a cloth fedora that was tilted rakishly over his dark, almond-shaped eyes. An outrageous diamond glinted on his finger. As always, he was beautiful, male and aware of it.

"You look fantastic, Carlo. *Fantastico.*"

"But of course." He ran a finger down the brim of his hat. "And you, my delectable puff pastry—" he took her hands and pressed each palm to his lips "—*esquisita.*"

"But of course." Laughing again, she kissed him full on the mouth. She knew hundreds of people, professionally, socially, but if she'd been asked to name a friend, it would have been Carlo Franconi who'd have come to her mind. "It's good to see you, Carlo. What's it been? Four months? Five? You were in Belgium the last time I was in Italy?"

"Four months and twelve days," he said easily. "But who counts? It's only that I lusted for your Napoleons, your eclairs, your—" he grabbed her again and nibbled on her fingers "—chocolate cake."

"It's vacherin this morning," she said dryly, "and you're welcome to some when the show's over."

"Ah, your meringue. To die for." He grinned wickedly. "I will sit in the front row and cross my eyes at you."

Summer pinched his cheek. "Try to lighten up, Carlo. You're so stuffy."

"Ms. Lyndon, please."

Summer glanced at Simon, whose breathing was becoming shallower as the countdown began. "It's all right, Simon, I'm ready. Get your seat, Carlo, and watch carefully. You might learn something this time."

He said something short and rude and easily translated as they went their separate ways. Relaxed, Sum-

mer stood behind her work surface and watched the
floor director count off the seconds. Easily ignoring
the face Carlo made at her, Summer began the show,
talking directly to the camera.

She took this part of her profession as seriously as
she took creating the royal wedding cake for a European
princess. If she were to teach the average person how
to make something elaborate and exciting, she would
do it well.

She did look exquisite, Carlo thought. Then she
always did. And confident, competent, cool. On one
hand, he was glad to find it true, for he was a man who
disliked things or people who changed too quickly—
particularly if he had nothing to do with it. On the other
hand, he worried about her.

As long as he'd known Summer—good God, had it
been ten years?—she'd never allowed herself a personal
involvement. It was difficult for a volatile, emotional
man like himself to fully understand her quality of reserve, her apparent disinterest in romantic encounters.
She had passion. He'd seen it explode in temper, in joy,
but never had he seen it directed toward a man.

A pity, he thought as he watched her build the meringue rings. A woman, he felt, was wasted without a
man—just as a man was wasted without a woman. He'd
shared himself with many.

Once over kirsch cake and Chablis, she'd loosened
up enough to tell him that she didn't think that men
and women were meant for permanent relationships.
Marriage was an institution too easily dissolved and,
therefore, not an institution at all but a hypocrisy per-
petuated by people who wanted to pretend they could
make commitments. Love was a fickle emotion and,

therefore, untrustworthy. It was something exploited by people as an excuse to act foolishly or unwisely. If she wanted to act foolish, she'd do so without excuses.

At the time, because he'd been on the down end of an affair with a Greek heiress, Carlo had agreed with her. Later, he'd realized that while his agreement had been the temporary result of sour grapes, Summer had meant precisely what she'd said.

A pity, he thought again as Summer took out the previously baked rings from beneath the counter and began to build the shell. If he didn't feel about her as he would about a sister, it would be a pleasure to show her the...appealing side of the man/woman mystique. Ah, well—he settled back—that was for someone else.

Keeping an easy monologue with the camera and the studio audience, Summer went through the stages of the dessert. The completed shell, decorated with strips of more meringue and dotted with candied violets, was popped into an oven. The one that she'd baked and cooled earlier was brought out to complete the final stage. She filled it, arranged the fruit, covered it all with rich raspberry sauce and whipped cream to the murmured approval of her audience. The camera came in for a close-up.

"Brava!" Carlo stood, applauding as the dessert sat tempting and complete on the counter. *"Bravissima!"*

Summer grinned and, pastry bag in hand, took a deep bow as the camera clicked off.

"Brilliant, Ms. Lyndon." Simon rushed up to her, whipping off his earphones as he came. "Just brilliant. And, as always, perfect."

"Thank you, Simon. Shall we serve this to the audience and crew?"

"Yes, yes, good idea." He snapped his fingers at his assistant. "Get some plates and pass this out before we have to clear for the next show. Aerobic dancing," he muttered and dashed off again.

"Beautiful, *cara,*" Carlo told her as he dipped a finger into the whipped cream. "A masterpiece." He took a spoon from the counter and took a hefty serving directly from the vacherin. "Now, I will take you to lunch and you can fill me in on your life. Mine—" he shrugged, still eating "—is so exciting it would take days. Maybe weeks."

"We can grab a slice of pizza around the corner." Summer pulled off her apron and tossed it on the counter. "As it happens, there's something I'd like your advice about."

"Advice?" Though the idea of Summer's asking advice of him, of anyone, stunned him, Carlo only lifted a brow. "Naturally," he said with a silky smile as he drew her along. "Who else would an intelligent woman come to for advice—or for anything—but Carlo?"

"You're such a pig, darling."

"Careful." He slipped on dark glasses and adjusted his hat. "Or you pay for the pizza."

Within moments, Summer was taking her first bite and bracing herself as Carlo zoomed his rented Ferrari into Philadelphia traffic. Carlo managed to steer and eat and shift gears with maniacal skill. "So tell me," he shouted over the boom of the radio, "what's on your mind?"

"I've taken a job," Summer yelled back at him. Her hair whipped across her face and she tossed it back again.

"A job? So, you take lots of jobs?"

"This is different." She shifted, crossing her legs beneath her and turning sideways as she took the next bite. "I've agreed to revamp and manage a hotel restaurant for the next year."

"Hotel restaurant?" Carlo frowned over his slice of pizza as he cut off a station wagon. "What hotel?"

She took a deep sip of soda through a straw. "The Cocharan House here in Philadelphia."

"Ah." His expression cleared. "First class, *cara*. I should never have doubted you."

"A year, Carlo."

"Goes quickly when one has one's health," he finished blithely.

She let the grin come first. "Damn it, Carlo, I painted myself into a corner because, well, I just couldn't resist the idea of trying it and this—this American steamroller tossed LaPointe in my face."

"LaPointe?" Carlo snarled as only an Italian can. "What does that Gallic slug have to do with this?"

Summer licked sauce from her thumb. "I was going to turn down the offer at first, then Blake—that's the steamroller—asked me for my opinion on LaPointe, since he was also being considered for the position."

"And did you give it to him?" Carlo asked with relish.

"I did, and I kept the contract to look it over. The next hitch was that it was a tremendous offer. With the budget I have, I could turn a two-room slum into a gourmet palace." She frowned, not noticing when Carlo zoomed around a compact with little more than wind between metal. "In addition to that, there's Blake himself."

"The steamroller."

"Yes. I can't control the need to get the best of him. He's smart, he's smug and, damn it, he's sexy as hell."

"Oh, yes?"

"I have this tremendous urge to put him in his place."

Carlo breezed through a yellow light as it was turning red. "Which is?"

"Under my thumb." With a laugh, Summer polished off her pizza. "So because of those things, I've locked myself into a year-long commitment. Are you going to eat the rest of that?"

Carlo glanced down to the remains of his pizza, then took a healthy bite. "Yes. And the advice you wanted?"

After drawing through the straw again, Summer discovered she'd hit bottom. "If I'm going to stay sane while locked into a project for a year, I need a diversion." Grinning, she stretched her arms to the sky. "What's the most foolproof way to make Blake Cocharan III crawl?"

"Heartless woman," Carlo said with a smirk. "You don't need my advice for that. You already have men crawling in twenty countries."

"No, I don't."

"You simply don't look behind you, *cara mia*."

Summer frowned, not certain she liked the idea after all. "Turn left at the corner, Carlo, we'll drop in on my new kitchen."

The sights and smells were familiar enough, but within moments, Summer saw a dozen changes she'd make. The lighting was good, she mused as she walked arm-in-arm with Carlo. And the space. But they'd need an eye-level wall-oven there—brick lined. A replacement for the electric oven, and certainly more kitchen help. She glanced around, checking the corners of the ceiling for speakers. None. That, too, would change.

"Not bad, my love." Carlo took down a large chef's knife and checked it for weight and balance. "You have the rudiments here. It's a bit like getting a new toy for Christmas and having to assemble it, *sì?*"

"Hmmm." Absently she picked up a skillet. Stainless steel, she noted and set it down again. The pans would have to be replaced with copper washed with tin. She turned and thudded firmly into Blake's chest.

There was a fraction of a second when she softened, enjoying the sensation of body against body. His scent, sophisticated, slightly aloof, pleased her. Then came the annoyance that she hadn't sensed him behind her as she felt she should have. "Mr. Cocharan." She drew away, masking both the attraction and the annoyance with a polite smile. "Somehow I didn't think to find you here."

"My staff keeps me well informed, Ms. Lyndon. I was told you were here."

The idea of being reported on might have grated, but Summer only nodded. "This is Carlo Franconi," she began. "One of the finest chefs in Italy."

"*The* finest chef in Italy," Carlo corrected, extending his hand. "A pleasure to meet you, Mr. Cocharan. I've often enjoyed the hospitality of your hotels. Your restaurant in Milan makes a very passable linguini."

"Very passable is a great compliment from Carlo," Summer explained. "He doesn't think anyone can make an Italian dish but himself."

"Not think, know." Carlo lifted the lid on a steaming pot and sniffed. "Summer tells me she'll be associated with your restaurant here. You're a fortunate man."

Blake looked down at Summer, glancing at the lean, tanned hand Carlo had placed on her shoulder. Jealousy is a sensation that can be recognized even if it has never been experienced before. Blake didn't care for it, or the cause. "Yes, I am. Since you're here, Ms. Lyndon, you might like to sign the final contract. It would save us both a meeting later."

"All right. Carlo?"

"Go, do your business. They do a rack of lamb over there—it interests me." Without a backward glance, he went to add his two cents.

"Well, he's happy," Summer commented as she walked through the kitchen with Blake.

"Is he in town on business?"

"No, he just wanted to see me."

It was said carelessly, and truthfully, and had the effect of knotting Blake's stomach muscles. So she liked slick Italians, he thought grimly, and slipped a proprietary hand over her arm without being aware of it. That was certainly her business. His was to get her into the kitchens as quickly as possible.

In silence he led her through the lobby and into the hotel offices. Quiet and efficient. Those were brief impressions before she was led into a large, private room that was obviously Blake's.

The colors were bones and creams and browns, the decor a bit more modern than his apartment, but she could recognize his stamp on it. Without being asked, Summer walked over and took a chair. It was hardly past noon, but it occurred to her that she'd been on her feet for almost six consecutive hours.

"Handy that I happened to drop by when you were around," she began, sliding her toes out of her shoes. "It simplifies this contract business. Since I've agreed to do it, we might as well get started." *Then there will be only three hundred and sixty-four days,* she added silently, and sighed.

He didn't like her careless attitude about the contract

any more than he liked her careless affection toward the Italian. Blake walked over to his desk and lifted a packet of papers. When he looked back at her, some of his anger drained. "You look tired, Summer."

The lids she allowed to droop lifted again. His first, his only, use of her given name intrigued her. He said it as though he was thinking of the heat and the storms. She felt her chest tighten and blamed it on fatigue. "I am. I was baking meringue at seven o'clock this morning."

"Coffee?"

"No, thanks. I'm afraid I've overdone that already today." She glanced at the papers he held, then smiled with a trace of self-satisfaction. "Before I sign those, I should warn you I'm going to order some extensive changes in the kitchen."

"One of the essential reasons you're to sign them."

She nodded and held out her hand. "You might not be so amiable when you get the bill."

Taking a pen from a holder on his desk, Blake gave it to her. "I think we're both after the same thing, and would both agree cost is secondary."

"I might think so." With a flourish, she looped her name on the line. "But I'm not signing the checks. So—" she passed the contract back to him "—it's official."

"Yes." He didn't even glance at her signature before he dropped the paper on his desk. "I'd like to take you to dinner tonight."

She rose, though she found her legs a bit reluctant to hold weight again. "We'll have to put the seal on our bargain another time. I'll be entertaining Carlo." Smiling, she held out her hand. "Of course, you're welcome to join us."

"It has nothing to do with business." Blake took her hand, then surprised them both by taking her other one. "And I want to see you alone."

She wasn't ready for this, Summer realized. She was supposed to begin the maneuvers, in her own time, on her own turf. Now she was forced to realign her strategy and to deal with the blood warming just under her skin. Determined not to be outflanked this time, she tilted her head and smiled. "We are alone."

His brow lifted. Was that a challenge, or was she plainly mocking him? Either way, this time, he wasn't going to let it go. Deliberately he drew her into his arms. She fit there smoothly. It was something each of them noticed, something they both found disturbing.

Her eyes were level on his, but he saw, fascinated, that the gold flecks had deepened. Amber now, they seemed to glow against the cloudy, changeable hazel of her irises. Hardly aware of what he did, Blake brushed the hair away from her cheek in a gesture that was as sweet and as intimate as it was uncharacteristic.

Summer fought not to be affected by something so casual. A hundred men had touched her, in greeting, in friendship, in anger and in longing. There was no reason why the mere brush of a fingertip over her skin should have her head spinning. An effort of will kept her from melting into his arms or from jerking away. She remained still, watching him. Waiting.

When his mouth lowered toward hers, she knew she was prepared. The kiss would be different, naturally, because he was different. It would be new because he was new. But that was all. It was still a basic form of communication between man and woman. A touch of lips, a pressure, a testing of another's taste; it was no different from the kiss of the first couple, and so it went through culture and time.

And the moment she experienced that touch of lips, that pressure, that taste, she knew she was mistaken. Different? New? Those words were much too mild. The brush of lips, for it was no more at first, changed the fabric of everything. Her thoughts veered off into a chaos that seemed somehow right. Her body grew hot, from within and without, in the space of a heartbeat. The woman who'd thought she knew exactly what to expect, sighed with the unexpected. And reached out.

"Again," she murmured when his lips hovered a breath from hers. With her hands on either side of his face, she drew him to her, through the smoke and into the fire.

He'd thought she'd be cool and smooth and fragrant. He'd been so sure of it. Perhaps that was why the flare of heat had knocked him back on his heels. Smooth she was. Her skin was like silk when he ran his hands up her back to cup her neck. Fragrant. She had a scent that he would, from that moment on, always associate with woman. But not cool. There was nothing cool about the mouth that clung to his, or the breath that mixed with his as two pairs of lips parted. There was something mindless here. He couldn't grip it, couldn't analyze it, could only experience it.

With a deep, almost feline sound of pleasure, she ran her hands through his hair. God, she'd thought there wasn't a taste she hadn't already known, a texture she hadn't already felt. But his, his was beyond her scope and now, just now, within her reach. Summer wallowed in it and let her lips and tongue draw in the sweetness.

More. She'd never known greed. She'd grown up in a

world of affluence where enough was always available. For the first time in her life, Summer knew true hunger, true need. Those things brought pain, she discovered. A deep well of it that spread from the core. *More.* The thought ran through her mind again with the knowledge that the more she took, the more she would ache for.

Blake felt her stiffen. Not knowing the cause, he tightened his hold. He wanted her now, at once, more than he'd ever wanted or had conceived of wanting any woman. She shifted in his arms, resisting for the first time since he'd drawn her here. Throwing her head back, she looked up into the passion and impatience of Blake's eyes.

"Enough."

"No." His hand was still tangled possessively in her hair. "No, it's not."

"No," she agreed on an unsteady breath. "That's why you have to let me go."

He released her, but didn't back away. "You'll have to explain that."

She had more control now—barely, Summer realized shakily, but it was better than none. It was time to establish the rules—her rules—quickly and precisely. "Blake, you're a businessman, I'm an artist. Each of us has priorities. This—" she took a step back and stood straight "—can't be one of them."

"Want to bet?"

Her eyes narrowed more in surprise than annoyance. Odd that she'd missed the ruthlessness in him. It would be best if she considered that later, when there was some distance between them. "We'll be working together for a specific purpose," she went on smoothly. "But we're two different people with two very different outlooks.

You're interested in a profit, naturally, and in the reputation of your company. I'm interested in creating the proper showcase for my art, and my own reputation. We both want to be successful. Let's not cloud the issue."

"That issue's perfectly clear," Blake countered. "So's this one. I want you."

"Ah." The sound came out slowly. Deliberately she reached for her neglected purse. "Straight and to the point."

"It would be a bit ridiculous to take a more circular route at the moment." Amusement was overtaking frustration. He was grateful for that because it would give him the edge he'd begun to lose the minute he'd tasted her. "You'd have to be unconscious not to realize it."

"And I'm not." Still, she backed away, relying on poise to get her out before she lost whatever slim advantage she had. "But it's your kitchen—and it'll be *my* kitchen—that's my main concern right now. With the amount of money you're paying me, you should be grateful I understand the priorities. I'll have a tentative list of changes and new equipment you'll have to order on Monday."

"Fine. We'll go to dinner Saturday."

Summer paused at the door, turned and shook her head. "No."

"I'll pick you up at eight."

It was rare that anyone ignored a statement she'd made. Rather than temper, Summer tried the patient tone she remembered from her governess. It was bound to infuriate. "Blake, I said no."

If he was infuriated, he concealed it well. Blake merely smiled at her—as one might smile at a fussy child. Two, it seemed, could play the same game with equal skill. "Eight," he repeated and sat on the corner of his desk. "We can even have tacos if you like."

"You're very stubborn."

"Yes, I am."

"So am I."

"Yes, you are. I'll see you Saturday."

She had to put a lot of effort into the glare because she wanted to laugh. In the end, Summer found satisfaction by slamming the door, quite loudly.

Chapter 4

"Incredible nerve," Summer mumbled. She took another bite of her hot dog, scowled and swallowed. "The man has incredible nerve."

"You shouldn't let it affect your appetite, *cara*." Carlo patted her shoulder as they strolled along the sidewalk toward the proud, weathered bricks of Independence Hall.

Summer bit into the hot dog again. When she tossed her head, the sun caught at the ends of her hair and flicked them with gold. "Shut up, Carlo. He's so *arrogant*." With her free hand, she gestured wildly while continuing to munch, almost vengefully, on the dog and bun. "Carlo, I don't take orders from anyone, especially some tailored, polished, American executive with dictatorial tendencies and incredible blue eyes."

Carlo lifted a brow at her description, then shot an

approving look at a leggy blonde in a short pink skirt who passed them. "Of course not, *mi amore*," he said absently, craning his neck to follow the blonde's progress down the street. "This Philadelphia of yours has the most fascinating tourist attractions, *sì?*"

"I make my own decisions, run my own life," Summer grumbled, jerking his arm when she saw where his attention had wandered. "I take requests, Franconi, not orders."

"It's always been so." Carlo gave a last wistful look over his shoulder. Perhaps he could talk Summer into stopping somewhere, a park bench, an outdoor café, where he could get a more…complete view of Philadelphia's attractions. "You must be tired of walking, love," he began.

"I'm definitely not having dinner with him tonight."

"That should teach him to push Summer Lyndon around." The park, Carlo thought, might have the most interesting of possibilities.

She gave him a dangerous stare. "You're amused because you're a man."

"*You're* amused," Carlo corrected, grinning. "And interested."

"I am not."

"Oh, yes, *cara mia,* you are. Why don't we sit so I can take in the…beauty and attractions of your adopted city? After all—" he tipped the brim of his hat at a strolling brunette in brief shorts "—I'm a tourist, *sì?*"

She caught the gleam in his eyes, and the reason for it. After letting out a huff of breath, Summer turned a sharp right. "I'll show you tourist attractions, *amico.*"

"But Summer…" Carlo caught sight of a redhead in

snug jeans walking a poodle. "The view from out here is very educational and uplifting."

"I'll lift you up," she promised and ruthlessly dragged him inside. "The Second Continental Congress met here in 1775, when the building was known as the Pennsylvania State House."

There was an echoing of feet, of voices. A group of schoolchildren flocked by led by a prim, stern-faced teacher wearing practical shoes. "Fascinating," Carlo muttered. "Why don't we go to the park, Summer. It's a beautiful day." For female joggers in tiny shorts and tiny shirts.

"I'd consider myself a poor friend if I didn't give you a brief history lesson before you leave this evening, Carlo." She linked her arm more firmly through his. "It was actually July 8, not July 4, 1776, that the Declaration of Independence was read to the crowd in the yard outside this building."

"Incredible." Hadn't that brunette been heading for the park? "I can't tell you how interesting I find this American history, but some fresh air perhaps—"

"You can't leave Philadelphia without seeing the Liberty Bell." Taking him by the hand, Summer dragged him along. "A symbol of freedom is international, Carlo." She didn't even hear his muttered assent as her thoughts began to swing back to Blake again. "Just what was he trying to prove with that gloss and machismo?" she demanded. "Telling me he'd pick me up at eight after I'd refused to go." Gritting her teeth, she put her hands on her hips and glared at Carlo. "Men—you're all basically the same, aren't you?"

"But no, *carissima*." Amused, he gave her a charming smile and ran his fingers down her cheek. "We are all unique, especially Franconi. There are women in every city of the world who can attest to that."

"Pig," she said bluntly, refusing to be swayed with humor. She sidled closer to him, unconcerned that there was a group of three female college students hanging on every word. "Don't throw your women up to me, you Italian lecher."

"Ah, but, Summer..." He brought her palm to his lips, watching the three young women over it. "The word is...connoisseur."

Her comment was an unladylike snort. "You— men," she corrected, jerking her hand from his, "think of women as something to toy with, enjoy for a while, then disregard. No one's ever going to play that game with me."

Grinning from ear to ear, Carlo took both her hands and kissed them. "Ah, no, no, *cara mia*. A woman, she is like the most exquisite of meals."

Summer's eyes narrowed. As the three girls edged closer she struggled with a grin of her own. "A meal? You dare to compare a woman with a meal?"

"An exquisite one," Carlo reminded her. "One you anticipate with great excitement, one you linger over, savor, even worship."

Her brows arched. "And when your plate's clean, Carlo?"

"It stays in your memory." Touching his thumb and forefinger together, he kissed them dramatically. "Returns in your dreams and keeps you forever searching for an equally sensual experience."

"Very poetic," she said dryly. "But I'm not going to be anyone's entrée."

"No, my Summer, you are the most forbidden of desserts, and therefore, the most desirable." Irrepressible, he winked at the trio of girls. "This Cocharan, do you not think his mouth waters whenever he looks at you?"

Summer gave a short laugh, took two steps away, then stopped. The image had an odd, primitive appeal. Intrigued, she looked back over her shoulder. "Does it?"

Because he knew he'd distracted her, Carlo slipped an arm around her waist and began to lead her from the building. There was still time for fresh air and leggy joggers in the park. Behind them, the three girls muttered in disappointment. "*Cara,* I am a man who has made a study of *amore.* I know what I see in another man's eyes."

Summer fought off a surge of pleasure and shrugged. "You Italians insist on giving a pretty label to basic lust."

With a huge sigh, Carlo led her outside. "Summer, for a woman with French blood, you have no romance."

"Romance belongs in books and movies."

"Romance," Carlo corrected, "belongs everywhere." Though she'd spoken lightly, Carlo understood that she was being perfectly frank. It worried him and, in the way of friend for friend, disappointed him. "You should try candlelight and wine and soft music, Summer. Let yourself experience it. It won't hurt you."

She gave him a strange sidelong smile as they walked. "Won't it?"

"You can trust Carlo like you trust no one else."

"Oh, I do." Laughing again, she swung an arm around his shoulders. "I trust no one else, Franconi."

That too, was the unvarnished truth. Carlo sighed again but spoke with equal lightness. "Then trust yourself, *cara.* Be guided by your own instincts."

"But I do trust myself."

"Do you?" This time it was Carlo who slanted a look at her. "I think you don't trust yourself to be alone with the American."

"With Blake?" He could feel her stiffen with outrage under the arm he still held around her waist. "That's absurd."

"Then why are you so upset about the idea of having a simple dinner with him?"

"Your English is suffering, Carlo. Upset's the wrong word. I'm annoyed." She made herself relax under his arm again, then tilted her chin. "I'm annoyed because he assumed I'd have dinner with him, then continued to assume I would even after I'd refused. It's a normal reaction."

"I believe your reaction to him is very normal. One might say even—ah—basic." He took out his dark glasses and adjusted them meticulously. Perhaps squint lines added character to a face, but he wanted none on his. "I saw what was in your eyes as well that day in the kitchen."

Summer scowled at him, then lifted her chin a bit higher. "You don't know what you're talking about."

"I'm a gourmet," Carlo corrected with a sweep of his free arm. "Of food, yes, but also of love."

"Just stick to your pasta, Franconi."

He only grinned and patted her flank. "*Carissima,* my pasta never sticks."

She uttered a single French word in the most dulcet tones. It was one most commonly seen scrawled in Parisian alleyways. In tune with each other, they walked on, but both were speculating about what would happen that evening at eight.

* * *

It was quite deliberate, well thought out and very satisfying. Summer put on her shabbiest jeans and a faded T-shirt that was unraveled at the hem on one sleeve. She didn't bother with even a pretense of makeup. After seeing Carlo off at the airport, she'd gone through the drive-in window at a local fast-food restaurant and had picked up a cardboard container of fried chicken, complete with French fries and a tiny plastic bowl of coleslaw.

She opened a can of diet soda and flicked the television on to a syndicated rerun of a situation comedy.

Picking up a drumstick, Summer began to nibble. She'd considered dressing to kill, then breezing by him when he came to the door with the careless comment that she had a date. Very self-satisfying. But this way, Summer decided as she propped up her feet, she could be comfortable and insult him at the same time. After a day spent walking around the city while Carlo ogled and flirted with every female between six and sixty, comfort was every bit as important as the insult.

Satisfied with her strategy, Summer settled back and waited for the knock. It wouldn't be long, she mused. If she was any judge of character, she'd peg Blake as a man who was obsessively prompt. And fastidious, she added, taking a pleased survey of her cluttered, comfortably disorganized apartment.

Let's not forget smug, she reminded herself as she polished off the drumstick. He'd arrive in a sleek, tailored suit with the shirt crisp and monogrammed on the cuffs. There wouldn't be a smudge on the Italian leather of his shoes. Not a hair out of place. Pleased, she glanced down at the tattered hem on her oldest jeans. A pity they didn't have a few good holes in them.

Grinning gleefully, she reached for her soda. Holes or not, she certainly didn't look like a woman waiting anxiously to impress a man. And that, Summer concluded, was what a man like Blake expected. Surprising him would give her a great deal of pleasure. Infuriating him would give her even more.

When the knock came, Summer glanced around idly before unfolding her legs. Taking her time, she rose, stretched, then moved to the door.

For the second time, Blake wished he'd had a camera to catch the look of blank astonishment on her face. She said nothing, only stared. With a hint of a smile on his lips, Blake tucked his hands into the pockets of his snug, faded jeans. There was no one, he reflected, whom he'd ever gotten more pleasure out of outwitting. So much so, it was tempting to make a career out of it.

"Dinner ready?" He took an appreciative sniff of the air. "Smells good."

Damn his arrogance—and his perception, Summer thought. How did he always manage to stay one step ahead of her? Except for the fact that he wore tennis shoes—tattered ones—he was dressed almost identically to her. It was only more annoying that he looked every bit as natural, and every bit as attractive, in jeans and a T-shirt as he did in an elegant business suit. With an effort, Summer controlled her temper, and twin surges of humor and desire. The rules might have changed, but the game wasn't over.

"*My* dinner's ready," she told him coolly. "I don't recall inviting you."

"I did say eight."

"I did say no."

"Since you objected to going out—" he took both her hands before breezing inside "—I thought we'd just eat in."

With her hands caught in his, Summer stood in the open doorway. She could order him to leave, she considered. Demand it… And he might. Although she didn't mind being rude, she didn't see much satisfaction in winning a battle so directly. She'd have to find another, more devious, more gratifying method to come out on top.

"You're very persistent, Blake. One might even say pigheaded."

"One might. What's for dinner?"

"Very little." Freeing one hand, Summer gestured toward the take-out box.

Blake lifted a brow. "Your penchant for fast food's very intriguing. Ever thought of opening your own chain—Minute Croissants? Drive Through Pastries?"

She wouldn't be amused. "You're the businessman," she reminded him. "I'm an artist."

"With a teenager's appetite." Strolling over, Blake plucked a drumstick from the box. He settled on the couch, then propped his feet on the coffee table. "Not bad," he decided after the first bite. "No wine?"

No, she didn't want to be amused, was determined not to be, but watching him make himself at home with her dinner, Summer fought off a grin. Maybe her plan to insult him hadn't worked, but there was no telling what the evening might bring. She only needed one opening to give him a good, solid jab. "Diet soda." She sat down and lifted the can. "There's more in the kitchen."

"This is fine." Blake took the drink from her and

sipped. "Is this how one of the greatest dessert chefs spends her evenings?"

Lifting a brow, Summer took the can back from him. "*The* greatest dessert chef spends her evenings as she pleases."

Blake crossed one ankle over the other and studied her. The flecks in her eyes were more subtle this evening— perhaps because she was relaxed. He liked to think he could make them glow again before the night was over. "Yes, I'm sure you do. Does that extend to other areas?"

"Yes." Summer took another piece of chicken before handing Blake a paper napkin. "I've decided your company's tolerable—for the moment."

Watching her, he took another bite. "Have you?"

"That's why you're here eating half my meal." She ignored his chuckle and propped her own feet on the table beside his. There was something cozy about the setting that appealed to her—something intimate that made her wary. She was too cautious a woman to allow herself to forget the effect that one kiss had had on her. She was too stubborn a woman to back down.

"I'm curious about why you insisted on seeing me tonight." A commercial on floor wax flicked across the television screen. Summer glanced at it before turning to Blake. "Why don't you explain?"

He took a plastic fork and sampled the coleslaw. "The professional reason or the personal one?"

He answered a question with a question too often, she decided. It was time to pin him down. "Why don't you take it one at a time?"

How did she eat this stuff? he wondered as he dropped the fork back into the box. When you looked at her you could see her in the most elegant of restaurants—flowers,

French wine, starchily correct waiters. She'd be wearing silk and toying with some exotic dessert.

Summer rubbed the bottom of one bare foot over the top of the other while she took another bite of chicken. Blake smiled even as he asked himself why she attracted him.

"Business first then. We'll be working together closely for several months at least. I think it's wise if we get to know each other—find out how the other works so we can make the proper adjustments when necessary."

"Logical." Summer plucked out a couple of French fries before offering the box to Blake. "It's just as well that you find out up front that I don't make adjustments at all. I work only one way—my way. So...personal?"

He enjoyed her confidence and the complete lack of compromise. He planned to explore the first and undo the second. "Personally, I find you a beautiful, interesting woman." Dipping his hand into the box, he watched her. "I want to take you to bed." When she said nothing, he nibbled on a fry. "And I think we should get to know each other first." Her stare was direct and unblinking. He smiled. "Logical?"

"Yes, and egotistical. You seem to have your share of both qualities. But—" she wiped her fingers on the napkin before she picked up the soda again "—you're honest. I admire honesty in other people." Rising, she looked down at him. "Finished?"

His gaze remained as cool as hers while he handed her the box. "Yeah."

"I happen to have a couple of éclairs in the fridge, if you're interested."

"Supermarket special?"

Her lips curved, slowly, slightly. "No. I do have some standards. They're mine."

"Then I could hardly insult you by turning them down."

This time she laughed. "I'm sure diplomacy's your only motive."

"That, and basic gluttony," he added as she walked away. *She's a cool one,* Blake reflected, thinking back to her reaction, or lack of one, to his statement about taking her to bed. The coolness, the control, intrigued him. Or perhaps more accurately, challenged him.

Was it a veneer? If it was, he'd like the opportunity to strip off the layers. Slowly, he decided, even lazily, until he found the passion beneath. It would be there— he imagined it would be like one of her desserts—dark and forbidden beneath a cool white icing. Before too much time had passed, Blake intended to taste it.

Her hands weren't steady. Summer cursed herself as she opened the refrigerator. He'd shaken her—just as he'd meant to. She only hoped he hadn't been able to see through her off-hand response. Yes, he'd intended to shake her, but he'd said precisely what he'd meant. That she understood. At the moment, she didn't have the time to absorb and dissect her feelings. There was only her first reaction—not shock, not outrage, but a kind of nervous excitement she hadn't experienced in years.

Silly, Summer told herself while she arranged éclairs on two Meissen plates. She wasn't a teenager who de- lighted in fluttery feelings. Nor would she tolerate being informed she was about to become someone's lover. Affairs, she knew, were dangerous, time-consuming and distracting. And there always seemed to be one party who was more involved, therefore, more vulnerable, than the other. She wouldn't allow herself to be in that position.

But the little twinges of nervous excitement remained.

She was going to have to do something about Blake Cocharan, Summer decided as she poured out two cups of coffee. And she was going to have to do it quickly. The problem was—what?

As Summer arranged cups and plates on a tray, she decided to do what she did best under pressure. She'd wing it.

"You're about to have a memorable, sensuous experience."

Blake glanced up at the announcement and watched her come into the room, tray in hand. Desire hit him surprisingly hard, surprisingly fast. It warned him that if he wanted to stay in control, he'd have to play the game with skill.

"My éclairs aren't to be taken lightly," Summer continued. "Nor are they to be eaten with anything less than reverence."

He waited until she sat beside him again before he took a plate. Very skillfully done, he thought again as her scent drifted to him. "I'll do my best."

"Actually—" she brought down the side of her fork and broke off the first bite "—no effort's required. Just taste buds." Unable to resist, Summer brought the fork to his lips.

He watched her, and she him, as she fed him. The light slanted through the window behind them and caught in her eyes. More green now, Blake thought, almost feline. A man, any man, could lose himself trying to define that color, read that expression. The rich cream and flaky pastry melted in his mouth. Exotic, unique, desirable—like its creator. The first taste, like the first kiss, demanded more.

"Incredible," he murmured, and as her lips curved, he wanted them under his.

"Naturally." As she broke off another portion, Blake's hand closed over her wrist. Her pulse scrambled briefly, he could feel it, but her eyes remained cool and level.

"I'll return the favor." He said it quietly, and his fingers stayed lightly on her wrist as he took the fork in his other hand. He moved slowly, deliberately, keeping his eyes on hers, bringing the pastry to her lips, then pausing. He watched them part, saw the tip of her tongue. It would have been so easy to close his mouth over hers just then—from the rapid beat of her pulse under his fingers, he knew there'd be no resistance. Instead, he fed her the éclair, his stomach muscles tightening as he imagined the taste that was even now lying delicately on her tongue.

She'd never felt anything like this. She'd sampled her own cooking countless times, but had never had her senses so heightened. The flavor seemed to fill her mouth. Summer wanted to keep it there, exploring the sensation that had become so unexpectedly, so intensely, sexual. It took a conscious effort to swallow, and another to speak.

"More?" she asked.

His gaze flicked down from her eyes to her mouth then back again. "Always."

A dangerous game. She knew it, but opted to play. And to win. Taking her time, she fed him the next bite. Was the color of his eyes deeper? She didn't think she was imagining it, nor the waves of desire that seemed to pound over her. Did they come from her, or from him?

On the television, someone broke into raucous laughter. Neither of them noticed. It would be wise to step back now, cautiously. Even as the thought passed through her mind, she opened her mouth for the next taste.

Some things exploded on the tongue, others heated it or tantalized. This was a cool, elegant experience, no less sensual than champagne, no less primitive than ripened fruit. Her nerves began to calm, but her awareness intensified. He was wearing some subtle cologne that made her think of the woods in autumn. His eyes were the deep blue of an evening sky. When his knee brushed hers, she felt a warmth that seeped through two layers of material and touched flesh. Moment after moment passed without her being aware that they weren't speaking, only slowly, luxuriously, feeding each other. The intimacy wrapped around her, no less intense, no less exciting than lovemaking. The coffee sat cooling. Shadows spread through the room as the sun went down.

"The last bite," Summer murmured, offering it. "You approve?"

He caught the ends of her hair between his thumb and finger. "Completely."

Her skin tingled, much too pleasantly. Although she didn't shift away, Summer set the fork down with great care. She was feeling soft—too soft. And too vulnerable. "One of my clients has a secret passion for éclairs. Four times a year I go to Brittany and make him two dozen. Last fall he gave me an emerald necklace."

Blake lifted a brow as he twined a strand of her hair around his finger. "Is that a hint?"

"I'm fond of presents," she said easily. "But then, that sort of thing isn't quite ethical between business associates."

As she leaned forward for her coffee, Blake tightened his fingers in her hair and held her still. In the moment her eyes met his, he saw mild surprise and mild annoyance. She didn't like to be held down by anyone. "Our business association is only one level. We're both acutely aware of that by this time."

"Business is the first level, and the first priority."

"Maybe." It was difficult to admit, even to himself, that he was beginning to have doubts about that. "In any case, I haven't any intention of staying at level one."

If she were ever going to handle him, it would have to be now. Summer draped her arm negligently across the back of the sofa and wished her stomach would unknot. "I'm attracted to you. And I think it should be difficult, and interesting, to work around that for the next few months. You said you wanted to understand me. I rarely explain myself, but I'll make an exception." Leaning forward again, she plucked a cigarette from its holder. "Have you a light?"

It was strange how easily she drew feelings from him without warning. Now it was annoyance. Blake took out his lighter and flicked it on. He watched her pull in smoke, then blow it out quickly in a gesture he realized came more from habit than pleasure. "Go on."

"You said you knew my mother," Summer began. "You'd know of her in any case. She's a beautiful, talented, intelligent woman. I love her very much, both as a mother, and as a person who's full of the joy of life. If she has one weakness, it is men."

Summer folded her legs under her and concentrated

on relaxing. "She's had three husbands, and innumerable lovers. She's always certain each relationship is forever. When she's involved with a man, she's blissfully happy. His interests are her interests, his dislikes her dislikes. Naturally, when it ends, she's crushed."

Again, Summer drew on her cigarette. She'd expected him to make some passing comment. When instead, he only listened, only watched, she went further than she'd intended. "My father is a more practical man, and yet he's been through two wives and quite a few discreet affairs. Unlike my mother, who accepts flaws—even enjoys them for a short time—he looks for perfection. Since there is no perfection in people, only in what people create, he's continually disappointed. My mother looks for elation and romance, my father looks for the perfect companion. I don't look for either of those."

"Why don't you tell me what you look for then?"

"Success," she said simply. "Romance has a beginning, so it follows it has an end. A companion demands compromise and patience. I give all my patience to my work, and I have no talent for compromise."

It should have satisfied him, even relieved him. After all, he wanted nothing more than a casual affair, no strings, no commitments. He didn't understand why he wanted to shake the words back down her throat, only knew that he did. "No romance," he said with a nod. "No companionship. That doesn't rule out the fact that you want me, and I want you."

"No." The smoke was leaving a bitter taste in her mouth. As Summer crushed out her cigarette she thought how much their discussion sounded like a negotiation. Yet wasn't that how she preferred things? "I said it would be difficult to work around, but it's also necessary. You want a service from me, Blake, and I agreed to give you that, because I want the experience and the publicity I'll get out of it. But changing the tone and face of your restaurant is going to be a long, complicated process. Combining that with my other commitments, I won't have time for any personal distractions."

"Distractions?" Why should that one word have infuriated him? It did, just as her businesslike dismissal of desire infuriated him. Perhaps she hadn't meant it as a challenge, but he couldn't take it as anything less. "Does this distract you?" He ran his finger down the side of her throat before he cupped the back of her neck.

She could feel the firm pressure of each of his fingers against her skin. And in his eyes, she could see the temper, the need. Both pulled at her. "You're paying me a great deal of money, to do a job, Blake." Her voice was steady. Good. Her heartbeat wasn't. "As a businessman, you should want the complications left to a minimum."

"Complications," he repeated. He drew his other hand through her hair so that her face was tilted back. Summer felt a jolt of excitement shoot down her spine. "Is this—" he brushed his lips over her cheek "—a complication?"

"Yes." Her brain sent out the signal to pull away, but her body refused the command.

"And a distraction?"

He took his mouth on a slow journey to hers, but only nibbled. There was no pressure but the slight grip he kept on the base of her neck with fingers moving slowly, rhythmically over her skin. Summer didn't move away, though she told herself she still could.

She'd never permitted herself to be seduced, and tonight was no different.

Just a sample, she thought. She knew how to taste and judge, then step away from even the most tempting of flavors. Just as she knew how to absorb every drop of pleasure from that one tiny test.

"Yes," she murmured and let her eyes flutter closed. She needed no visual image now, but only the sensations. Warm, soft, moist—his mouth against hers. Firm, strong, persuasive—the fingers against her skin. Subtle, male, intriguing—the scent that clung to him. When he spoke her name, his voice flowed over her like a breeze, one that carried a trace of heat and the hint of a storm.

"How simple do you want it to be, Summer?" It was happening again, he realized. That total involvement he neither looked for nor wanted—the total involvement he couldn't resist. "There's only you and me."

"There's nothing simple about that." Even as she disagreed, her arms were going around him, her mouth was seeking his again.

It was only a kiss. She told herself that as his lips slanted lightly over hers. She could still end it, she was still in control. But first, she wanted just one more taste. Without thinking, she touched the tip of his tongue with hers, to fully explore the flavor. Her own moan sounded softly in her ears as she drew him closer. Body against body, firm and somehow right. This new thought drifted to her even as the sensation concentrated on the play of mouth to mouth.

Why had kisses seemed so basic, so simplistic before this? There were hundreds of pulse points in her body she'd remained unaware of until this moment. There were pleasures deeper, richer than she'd ever imagined that could be drawn out and exploited by the most elemental gesture between a man and a woman. She'd thought she'd known the limits of her own needs, the depth of her own passions...until now. Barely touching her, Blake was tearing something from her that wasn't calm, ordered and disciplined. And when it was totally free, what then?

She found herself at the verge of something she'd never come to before—where emotions commanded her mind completely. A step further and he would have all of her. Not just her body, not just her thoughts, but that most private, most well guarded possession, her heart.

She felt a greed for him and pulled away from it. If she were greedy, if she took, then he would too. He still held her, lightly enough for her to draw back, firmly enough to keep her close. She was breathless, moved. As she struggled to think clearly, Summer decided it would be foolish to try to deny either.

"I think I proved my point," she managed.

"Yours?" Blake countered as he ran a hand up her back. "Or mine?"

She took a deep breath, expelling it slowly. That one small show of emotion had desire clawing at him again. "I've mixed enough ingredients to know that business affairs and personal affairs aren't palatable. On Monday, I go to work for Cocharan. I intend to give you your money's worth. There can't be anything else."

"There's quite a bit else already." He cupped her chin in his hand so that their eyes held steady. Inside he was a mass of aching needs and confusion. With that kiss, that long, slow kiss, he'd all but forgotten his strictest rule. *Keep the emotions harnessed, both in business and in pleasure. Otherwise, you make mistakes that aren't easily rectified.* He needed time, and he realized he needed distance. "We know each other better now," he said after a moment. "When we make love, we'll understand each other."

Summer remained seated when he rose. She wasn't completely sure she could stand. "On Monday," she said in a firmer voice, "we'll be working together. That's all there is between us from this point on."

"When you deal with as many contracts as I do, Summer, you learn that paper is just that: paper. It's not going to make any difference."

He walked to the door thinking he needed some fresh air to clear his head, a drink to settle his nerves. And distance, a great deal of distance, before he forgot everything except the raging need to have her.

With his hand on the knob, Blake turned around for one last look at her. There was something in the way she frowned at him, with her eyes focused and serious, her lips soft in a half pout that made him smile.

"Monday," he told her, and was gone.

Chapter 5

Why in hell couldn't he stop thinking of her? Blake sat at his desk examining the details of a twenty-page contract in preparation for what promised to be a long, tense meeting in the boardroom. He wasn't taking in a single word. Uncharacteristic. He knew it, resented it and could do nothing about it.

For days Summer had been slipping into his mind and crowding out everything else. For a man who took order and self-control for granted, it was nerve-racking.

Logically, there was no reason for his obsession with her. Blake called it obsession, for lack of a better term, but it didn't please him. She was beautiful, he mused as his thoughts drifted further away from clauses and terms. He'd known hundreds of beautiful women. She was intelligent, but intelligent women had been in his life before. Desirable—even now in his neat, quiet office he could feel the first stirrings of need. But he was no stranger to desire.

He enjoyed women, as friends and as lovers. Enjoyment, Blake reflected, was perhaps the key word— he'd never looked for anything deeper in a relationship with a woman. But he wasn't certain it was the proper word to describe what was already between himself and Summer. She moved him—too strongly, too quickly— to the point where his innate control was shaken. No, he didn't enjoy that, but it didn't stop him from wanting more. Why?

Utilizing his customary method of working through a problem, Blake leaned back and, picking up a pen, began to list the possibilities.

Perhaps part of the consistent attraction was the fact that he liked outmaneuvering her. It wasn't easily done, and took quick thinking and careful planning. Up till this point, he'd countered her at every turn. Blake was realistic enough to know that that wouldn't last, but he was human enough to want to try. Just where would they clash next? he wondered. Over business…or over something more personal? In either case he wanted to go head to head with her just as much—well, almost as much—as he wanted to make love with her.

And perhaps another reason was that he knew the attraction was just as strong on her part—yet she continued to refuse it. He admired that strength of will in her. She mistrusted intimacy, he mused. Because of her parents' track record? Yes, partially, he decided. But he didn't think that was all of it. He'd just have to dig a bit deeper to get the whole picture.

He wanted to dig, he realized. For the first time in his life Blake wanted to know a woman completely.

Her thought process, her eccentricities, what made her laugh, what annoyed, what she really wanted for and in her life. Once he knew all there was to know... He couldn't see past that. But he wanted to know her, understand her. And he wanted her as a lover as he'd never wanted anything else.

When the buzzer on his desk sounded, Blake answered it automatically with his thoughts still centering on Summer Lyndon.

"Your father's on his way back, Mr. Cocharan."

Blake glanced down at the contract on his desk and mentally filed it. He still needed an hour with it before the board meeting. "Thanks." Even as he released the intercom button, the door swung open. Blake Cocharan II strolled into the room and took it over.

In build and coloring, he was similar to his son. Exercise and athletics had kept him trim and hard over the years. There were threads of gray in the dark hair that was covered by a white sea captain's hat. But his eyes were young and vibrant. He walked with the easy rolling gait of a man more accustomed to decks than floors. He wore canvas on his sockless feet, and a Swiss watch on his wrist. When he grinned, the lines etched by time and squinting at the sun fanned out from his eyes and mouth. As he stood to greet him, Blake caught the salty, sea-breezy scent he always associated with his father.

"B.C." Their hands clasped, one older and rougher than the other, both firm. "Just passing through?"

"On my way to Tahiti, going to do some sailing." B.C. grinned again, appealingly, as he ran a finger along the brim of his cap. "Want to play hookey and crew for me?"

"Can't. I'm booked solid for the next two weeks."

"You work too hard, boy." In an old habit, B.C. walked over to the bar at the west side of the room and poured himself bourbon, neat.

Blake grinned at his father's back as B.C. tossed down three fingers of liquor. It was still shy of noon. "I came by it honestly."

With a chuckle, B.C. poured a second drink. When it had been his office, he'd stocked only the best bourbon. He was glad his son carried on the tradition. "Maybe—but I learned to play just as hard."

"You paid your dues, B.C."

"Yeah." Twenty-five years of ten-hour days, he reflected. Of hotel rooms, airports and board meetings. "So did the old man—so've you." He turned back to his son. Like looking into a mirror that's twenty years past, he thought, and smiled rather than sighed. "I've told you before, you can't wrap your life up in hotels." He sipped appreciatively at the bourbon this time, then swirled it. "Gives you ulcers."

"Not so far." Sitting again, Blake steepled his fingers, watching his father over them. He knew him too well, had apprenticed under him, watched him wheel and deal. Tahiti might be his destination, but he hadn't stopped off in Philadelphia without a reason. "You came in for the board meeting."

B.C. nodded before he found some salted almonds under the bar. "Have to put in my two cents worth now and again." He popped two nuts in his mouth and bit down with relish. He was always grateful that the teeth were still his and his eyesight was keen. If a man had those, and a forty-foot sloop, he needed little else. "If we buy the Hamilton chain, it's going to mean twenty more hotels, over two thousand more employees. A big step."

Blake lifted a brow. "Too big?"

With a laugh, B.C. dropped down into a chair across from the desk. "I didn't say that, don't think that—and apparently you don't think so either."

"No, I don't." Blake waved away his father's offering of almonds. "Hamilton's an excellent chain, simply mismanaged at this point. The buildings themselves are worth the outlay." He gave his father a mild, knowledgeable look. "You might check out the Hamilton Tahiti while you're there."

Grinning, B.C. leaned back. The boy was sharp, he thought, pleased. But then he came by that honestly, too. "Thought crossed my mind. By the way, your mother sends her love."

"How is she?"

"Up to her neck in a campaign to save another crumbling ruin." The grin widened. "Keeps her off the streets. Going to meet me on the island next week. Hell of a first mate, your mother." He nibbled on another almond, pleased to think of having some time alone with his wife in the tropics. "So, Blake, how's your sex life?"

Too used to his father to be anything but amused, Blake inclined his head. "Adequate, thanks."

With a short laugh, B.C. downed the rest of his drink. "Adequate's a disgrace to the Cocharan name. We do everything in superlatives."

Blake drew out a cigarette. "I've heard stories."

"All true," his father told him, gesturing with the empty glass. "One day I'll have to tell you about this dancer in Bangkok in '39. In the meantime, I've heard you plan to do some face-lifting right here."

"The restaurant." Blake nodded and thought of Summer. "It promises to be...fascinating work."

B.C. caught the tone and began to gently probe. "I can't disagree that the place needs a little glitzing up. So you hired on a French chef to oversee the operation."

"Half French."

"A woman?"

"That's right." Blake blew out smoke, aware which path his father was trying to lead him down.

B.C. stretched out his legs. "Knows her business, does she?"

"I wouldn't have hired her otherwise."

"Young?"

Blake drew on his cigarette and suppressed a smile. "Moderately, I suppose."

"Attractive?"

"That depends on your definition—I wouldn't call her attractive." Too tame a word, Blake thought, much, much too tame. Exotic, alluring—those suited her more. "I can tell you that she's dedicated to her profession, an ambitious perfectionist and that her éclairs…" His thoughts drifted back to that intoxicating interlude. "Her éclairs are an experience not to be missed."

"Her éclairs," B.C. repeated.

"Fantastic." Blake leaned back in his chair. "Absolutely fantastic." He kept the grin under control as his buzzer sounded again.

"Ms. Lyndon is here, Mr. Cochran."

Monday morning, he thought. Business as usual. "Send her in."

"Lyndon." B.C. set down his glass. "That's the cook, isn't it?"

"Chef," Blake corrected. "I'm not sure if she answers to the term 'cook.'"

The knock was brief before Summer walked in. She

carried a slim leather folder in one hand. Her hair was braided and rolled at the nape of her neck so that the hints of gold threaded through the brown. Her suit in a deep plum color was Chanel, simple and exquisite over a high-necked lace blouse that rose to frame her face. The strict professionalism of her attire made Blake instantly speculate on what she wore beneath—something brief, silky and sexy, the same color as her skin.

"Blake." Following her own self-lecture on priorities, Summer held out her hand. Impersonal, business-like and formal. She wasn't going to think about what happened when his mouth touched hers. "I've brought you the list of changes of equipment and suggestions we spoke about."

"Fine." He saw her turn her head as B.C. rose from his chair. And he saw the gleam light his father's eyes as it always did when he was in the company of a beautiful woman. "Summer Lyndon, Blake Cocharan II. B.C., Ms. Lyndon will be managing the kitchen here at the Philadelphia Cocharan House."

"Mr. Cocharan." Summer found her hand enveloped in a large, calloused one. He looks, she realized with a jolt, exactly as Blake will in thirty years. Distinguished, weathered, with that perennial touch of polish. Then B.C. grinned, and she understood that Blake would still be dangerous in three decades.

"B.C.," he corrected, lifting her fingers to his lips. "Welcome to the family."

Summer shot Blake a quick look. "Family?"

"We consider anyone associated with Cocharan House part of the family." B.C. gestured to the chair he'd vacated. "Please, sit down. Let me get you a drink."

"Thank you. Perhaps some Perrier." She watched

B.C. cross the room before she sat and laid the folder on her lap. "I believe you're acquainted with my mother, Monique Dubois."

That stopped him. B.C. turned, the bottle of Perrier still in his hand, the glass in the other still empty. "Monique? You're Monique's girl? I'll be damned."

And so he might be, B.C. thought. Years before— was it nearly twenty now?—during a period of marital upheaval on both sides, he'd had a brief, searing affair with the French actress. They'd parted on amicable terms and he'd reconciled with his wife. But the two weeks with Monique had been…memorable. Now he was in his son's office pouring Perrier for her daughter. Fate, he thought wryly, was a tricky sonofabitch.

If Summer had suspected before that her mother and Blake's father had once been lovers, she was now certain of it. Her thoughts on fate directly mirrored his as she crossed her legs. Like mother, like daughter? she wondered. Oh, no, not in this case. B.C. was still staring at her. For a reason she didn't completely understand, she decided to make it easy for him.

"Mother is a loyal client of Cocharan Houses; she'll stay nowhere else. I've already mentioned to Blake that we once had dinner with your father. He was very gracious."

"When it suits him," B.C. returned, relieved. *She knows,* he concluded before his gaze strayed to Blake's. There he saw a frown of concentration that was all too familiar. *And so will he if I don't watch my step,* B.C. decided. *Hot water,* he mused. *After twenty years I could still be in hot water.* His wife was the love of his life, his best friend, but twenty years wasn't long enough to be safe from a transgression.

"So—" he finished pouring the Perrier, then brought it to her "—you decided against following in your mother's footsteps and became a chef instead."

"I'm sure Blake would agree that following in a parent's footsteps is often treacherous."

Instinct told Blake that it wasn't business she spoke of now. A look passed between his father and Summer that he couldn't comprehend. "It depends where the path leads," Blake countered. "In my case I preferred to look at it as a challenge."

"Blake takes after his grandfather," B.C. put in. "He has that cagey kind of logic."

"Yes," Summer murmured. "I've seen it in action."

"Apparently you made the right choice," B.C. went on. "Blake told me about your éclairs."

Slowly, Summer turned her head until she was facing Blake again. The muscles in her stomach, in her thighs, tightened with the memory. Her voice remained calm and cool. "Did he? Actually, my specialty is the bombe."

Blake met her gaze directly. "A pity you didn't have one available the other night."

There were vibrations there, B.C. thought, that didn't need to bounce off a third party. "Well, I'll let you two get on with your business. I've some people to see before the board meeting. A pleasure meeting you, Summer." He took her hand again and held it as his eyes held hers. "Please, give my best to your mother."

She saw his eyes were like Blake's, in color, in shape, in appeal. Her lips curved. "I will."

"Blake, I'll see you this afternoon."

He only murmured an assent, watching Summer rather than his father. The door closed before he spoke.

"Why do I feel as though there were messages being passed in front of me?"

"I have no idea," Summer said coolly as she lifted the folder. "I'd like you to glance over these papers while I'm here, if you have time." Zipping open the folder, she pulled them out. "That way, if there are any questions or any disagreements, we can get through them now before I begin downstairs."

"All right." Blake picked up the first sheet but studied her over it. "Is that suit supposed to keep me at a distance?"

She sent him a haughty look. "I have no idea what you're talking about."

"Yes, you do. And another time I'd like to peel it off you, layer by layer. But at the moment, we'll play it your way." Without another word, he lowered his gaze to the paper and started to read.

"Arrogant swine," Summer said distinctly. When he didn't even bother to look up she folded her arms over her chest. She wanted a cigarette to give her something to do with her hands, but refused herself the luxury. She would sit like a stone, and when the time came, she would argue for every one of the changes she'd listed. And win every one of them. On that level *she* was in complete control.

She wanted to hate him for realizing she'd worn the elegant, career-oriented suit to set a certain tone. Instead, she had to respect him for being perceptive enough to pick up on small details. She wanted to hate him for making her want so badly with only a look and a few words. It wasn't possible when she'd spent the remainder of the weekend alternately wishing she'd never met him and wishing he'd come back and bring her that excitement again. He was a problem; there was no denying it. She understood that you solved problems one step at a time. Step one, her kitchen—accent on the personal pronoun.

"Two new gas ovens," he murmured as he scanned the sheet. "One electric oven and two more ranges of each kind." Without lowering it, he glanced at her over the top of the page.

"I believe I explained to you before the need for both gas and electric ovens. First, yours are antiquated. Second, in a restaurant of this size the need for two gas ovens is imperative."

"You specify brands."

"Of course, I know what I like to work with."

He only lifted a brow, thinking that procurement was going to grumble. "All new pots and pans?"

"Definitely."

"Perhaps we should have a yard sale," Blake mumbled as he went back to the sheet. He hadn't the vaguest idea what a *sautoir* was or why she required three of them. "And this particular heavy-duty mixer?"

"Essential. The one you have is adequate. I don't accept adequate."

He smothered a laugh as he recalled his father's view on adequate in relation to love lives. "Did you list so much of this in French to confuse me?"

"I listed in French," Summer countered, "because French is correct."

He made an indefinable sound as he passed over the next sheet. "In any case, I've no intention of quibbling over equipment in French or English."

"Good. Because I've no intention of working with

any less than the best." She smiled at him and settled back. First point taken.

Blake flipped over the second sheet and went on to the third. "You intend to rip out the existing counters, have the new ranges built in, add an island and an additional six feet of counter space."

"More efficient," Summer said easily.

"And time-consuming."

"In a hurry? You hired me, Blake, not Minute Chef." His quick grin made her eyes narrow. "My function is to organize your kitchen, which means making it as efficient and creative as I know how. Once the nuts and bolts of that are done, I'll beef up your menu."

"And this—" he flipped through the five typed sheets "—is all necessary for that?"

"I don't bother with anything that isn't necessary when it comes to business. If you don't agree," she said as she rose, "we can terminate the agreement. Hire LaPointe," she suggested, firing up. "You'll have an ostentatious, overpriced, second-rate kitchen that produces equally ostentatious, overpriced and second-rate meals."

"I have to meet this LaPointe," Blake murmured as he stood. "You'll get what you want, Summer." As a satisfied smile formed on her lips, he narrowed his eyes. "And you damn well better deliver what you promised."

The fire leapt back, accenting the gold in her irises. And as he saw it, he wanted.

"I've given you my word. Your middle-class restaurant with its mediocre prime rib and soggy pastries will be serving the finest in haute cuisine within six months."

"Or?"

So he wanted collateral, Summer thought, and heaved a breath. "Or my services for the term of the contract are gratis. Does that satisfy you?"

"Completely." Blake held out a hand. "As I said, you'll have precisely what you've asked for, down to the last egg beater."

"A pleasure doing business with you." Summer tried to draw her hand away and found it caught firm. "Perhaps you don't," she began, "but I have work to do. You'll excuse me?"

"I want to see you."

She let her hand remain passively in his rather than risk a struggle she might lose. "You have seen me."

"Tonight."

"Sorry." She smiled again, though her teeth were beginning to clench. "I have a date."

She felt the quick increase in pressure of his fingers over hers and was perversely pleased. "All right, when?"

"I'll be in the kitchen every day, and some evenings, to oversee the remodeling. You need only ride the elevator down."

He drew her closer, and though the desk remained between them, Summer felt that the ground beneath was a bit less firm. "I want to see you alone," he said quietly. Lifting her hand to his lips, he kissed her fingers slowly, one by one. "Away from here, outside of business hours."

If Blake Cocharan II had been anything like Blake Cocharan III in his youth, Summer could understand how her mother had become so quickly, so heatedly involved. The yearning was there, and the temptation—but she wasn't Monique. In this case, she was determined history would not repeat itself. "I've explained to you why that's not possible. I don't enjoy covering the same ground twice."

"Your pulse is racing," Blake pointed out as he ran a finger across her wrist.

"It generally does when I become annoyed."

"Or aroused."

Tilting her head, she sent him a killing look. "Would you amuse yourself with LaPointe in this way?"

Temper stirred and he suppressed it, knowing she wanted him to be angry. "At the moment, I don't care whether you're a chef or a plumber or a brain surgeon. At the moment," he repeated, "I only care that you're a woman, and one who I desire very much."

She wanted to swallow because her throat had gone dry but fought off the need. "At the moment I *am* a chef with a specific job to do. I'll ask you again to excuse me so I can begin to do it."

This time, Blake thought as he released her hand. But, by God, this time was the last time. "Sooner or later, Summer."

"Perhaps," she agreed as she picked up her leather folder. "Perhaps not." In one quick gesture, she zipped it closed. "Enjoy your day, Blake." As if her legs weren't weak and watery, she strolled to the door and out.

Summer continued to walk calmly through the outer office, over the plush carpet, past the busy secretaries and through the reception area. Once in the elevator, she leaned back against the wall and let out the long, tense breath she'd been holding. Nerves jumping, she began the ride down.

That was over, she told herself. She'd faced him in his office and won every point.

Sooner or later, Summer.

She let out another breath. Almost every point, she corrected. The important thing now was to concentrate on her kitchen, and to keep busy. It wasn't going to help matters if she allowed herself to think of him as she had over the weekend.

As her nerves began to calm, Summer straightened away from the wall. She'd handled herself well, she'd made herself clear and *she'd* walked out on him. All in all, a successful morning. She pressed a hand against her stomach, where a few muscles were still jumping. Damn it, things would be simpler if she didn't want him so badly.

When the doors slid open she stepped out, then wound her way around to the kitchen. In the prelunch bustle, she went unnoticed. She approved of the noise. A quiet kitchen to Summer meant there was no communication. Without that, there was no cooperation. For a moment, she stood just inside the doorway to watch.

She approved of the smells. It was a mixture of lunch-time aromas over the still-lingering odors of breakfast. Bacon, sausage and coffee. She caught the scent of baking chicken, of grilled meat, of cakes fresh from the oven. Narrowing her eyes, she envisioned the room as it would be in a short time. Made to her order. Better, Summer decided with a nod.

"Ms. Lyndon."

Distracted, she frowned up at a big man in white apron and cap. "Yes?"

"I'm Max." His chest expanded, his voice stiffened. "Head chef."

Ego in danger, she thought as she extended a hand. "How do you do, Max. I missed you when I was in last week."

"Mr. Cocharan has instructed me to give you full cooperation during this—transition period."

Marvelous, she thought with an inward moan. Resentment in a kitchen was as difficult to deal with as a deflated soufflé. Left to herself, she might have been able to keep injured feelings to a minimum, but the damage had already been done. She made a mental note to give Blake her opinion of his tact and diplomacy.

"Well, Max, I'd like to go over the proposed structural changes with you, since you know the routine here better than anyone else."

"Structural changes?" he repeated. His full, round face flushed. The moustache over his mouth quivered. She caught the gleam of a single gold tooth. "In *my* kitchen?"

My kitchen, Summer mentally corrected, but smiled. "I'm sure you'll be pleased with the improvements— and the new equipment. You must have found it frustrating trying to create something special with outdated appliances."

"This oven," he said and gestured dramatically toward it, "this range—both have been here since I began at Cocharan. We are none of us outdated."

So much for cooperation, Summer thought wryly. If it was too late for a friendly transition of authority, she'd have to go with the *coup.* "We'll be receiving three new ovens," she began briskly. "Two gas, one electric. The electric will be used exclusively for desserts and pastries. This counter," she continued, walking toward it without looking back to see if Max was following, "will be removed and the ranges I specified built into a new counter—butcher block. The grill remains. There'll be an island here to provide more working area and to make use of what is now essentially wasted space."

"There is no wasted space in my kitchen."

Summer turned and aimed her haughtiest stare. "That isn't a matter for debate. Creativity will be the first priority of this kitchen, efficiency the second. We'll be expected to produce quality meals during the remodeling—difficult but not impossible if everyone makes the necessary adjustments. In the meantime, you and I will go over the current menu with an eye toward adding excitement and flair to what is now pedestrian."

She heard him suck in his breath but continued before he could rage. "Mr. Cocharan contracted me to turn this restaurant into the finest establishment in the city. I fully intend to do just that. Now, I'd like to observe the staff in lunch preparations." Unzipping her leather folder, Summer pulled out a note pad and pen. Without another word she began walking through the busy kitchen.

The staff, she decided after a few moments, was well trained and more orderly than many. Credit Max. Cleanliness was obviously a first priority. Another point for Max. She watched a cook expertly bone a chicken. Not bad, Summer decided. The grill was sizzling, pots steaming. Lifting a lid, she ladeled out a small portion of the soup du jour. She sampled it, holding the taste on her tongue a moment.

"Basil," she said simply, then walked away. Another cook drew apple pies from an oven. The scent was strong and wholesome. Good, she mused, but any experienced grandmother could do the same. What was needed was some pizzazz. People would come to this restaurant for what they wouldn't get at home. Charlottes, Clafouti, flambées.

The structural changes came from her practical side, but the menu—the menu stemmed from her creativity, which was always paramount.

As she surveyed the kitchen, the staff, drew in the smells, absorbed the sounds, Summer felt the first real stirrings of excitement. She would do it, and she would do it for her own satisfaction just as much as in answer to Blake's challenge. When she was finished, this kitchen would bear her mark. It would be different entirely from jetting from one place to the next to create a single memorable dish. This would have continuity, stability. A year from now, five years from now, this kitchen would still retain her touch, her influence.

The thought pleased her more than she'd expected. She'd never looked for continuity, only the flash of an individual triumph. And wouldn't she be behind the scenes here? She might be in the kitchen in Milan or Athens, but the guests in the dining room knew who was preparing the Charlotte Royal. Clients wouldn't come into the restaurant anticipating a Summer Lyndon dessert, but a Cocharan Hotel meal.

Even as she mulled the thought over in her mind, she found it didn't matter. Why, she was still unsure. For now, she only knew the pleasurable excitement of planning. *Think about it later,* she advised herself as she made a final note. There were months to worry about consequences, reasons, pitfalls. She wanted to begin, get elbow deep in a project she now, for whatever reason, considered peculiarly her own.

Slipping her folder under her arm, she walked out. She couldn't wait to start working on menus.

Chapter 6

Russian Beluga Malasol Caviar—that should be available from lunch to late-night dining. All night through room service.

Summer made another scrawled note. During the past two weeks, she'd changed the projected menu a dozen times. After one abortive session with Max, she'd opted to go solo on the task. She knew the ambience she wanted to create, and how to do so through food.

To save herself time, she'd set up a small office in a storage room off the kitchen. There, she could oversee the staff and the beginnings of the remodeling while having enough privacy to work on what was now her pet project.

Avoiding Blake had been easy because she'd kept herself so thoroughly busy. And it appeared he was just as involved in some complicated corporate deal. Buying out another hotel chain, if rumor were fact. Summer had little interest in that, for her concentration focused on items like medallions of veal in champagne sauce.

As long as the remodeling was going on, the staff remained in a constant state of panic or near panic. She'd come to accept that. Most of the kitchens she'd worked in were full of the tension and terror only a cook would understand. Perhaps it was that creative tension, and the terror of failure, that helped form the best meals.

For the most part, she left the staff supervision to Max. She interfered with the routine he'd established as little as possible, incorporating the changes she'd initiated unobtrusively. She'd learned the qualities of diplomacy and power from her father. If it placated Max at all, it wasn't apparent in his attitude toward Summer. That remained icily polite. Summer shrugged this off and concentrated on perfecting the entrées her kitchen would offer.

Calf's Liver Berlinoise. An excellent entrée, not as popular certainly as a broiled filet or prime rib, but excellent. As long as she didn't have to eat it, Summer thought with a smirk as she noted it down.

Once she'd organized the meat and poultry, she'd put her mind to the seafood. And naturally there had to be a cold buffet available twenty-four hours a day through room service. That was something else to work out. Soups, appetizers, salads—all of those had to be considered, decided on and confirmed before she began on the desserts. And at the moment, she'd have traded any of the elegant offerings jotted down in front of her for a cheeseburger on a sesame seed bun and a bag of chips.

"So this is where you've been hiding." Blake leaned against the doorway. He'd just completed a grueling four-hour meeting and had fully intended to go up to his suite for a long shower and a quiet, solitary meal. Instead, he'd found himself heading for the kitchen, and Summer.

She looked as she had the first time he'd seen her— her hair down, her feet bare. On the table in front of her were reams of scrawled-on paper and a half-empty glass of diluted soda. Behind her, boxes were stacked, sacks piled. The room smelled faintly of pine cleaner and cardboard. In her own way, she looked competent and completely in charge.

"Not hiding," she corrected. "Working." Tired, she thought. He looked tired. It showed around the eyes. "Been busy? We haven't seen you down here for the past couple of weeks."

"Busy enough." Stepping inside, he began to poke through her notes.

"Wheeling and dealing from what I hear." She leaned back, realizing all at once that her back ached. "Taking over the Hamilton chain."

He glanced up, then shrugged and looked back at her notes again. "It's a possibility."

"Discreet." She smiled, wishing she weren't quite so glad to see him again. "Well, while you've been playing Monopoly, I've been dealing with more intimate matters." When he glanced at her again, with his brow raised exactly as she'd expected it to be, she laughed. "Food, Blake, is the most basic and personal of desires, no matter what anyone might say to the contrary. For many, eating is a ritual experienced three times a day. It's a chef's job to make each experience memorable."

"For you, eating's a jaunt through adolescence."

"As I said," Summer continued mildly, "food is very personal."

"Agreed." After another glance around the room, he looked back at her. "Summer, it's not necessary for you to work in a storage room. It's a simple matter to set you up in a suite."

She pushed through the papers, looking for her list on poultry. "This is convenient to the kitchen."

"There's not even a window. The place is packed with boxes."

"No distractions." She shrugged. "If I'd wanted a suite, I'd have asked for one. For the moment, this suits me." And it's several hundred feet away from you, she added silently. "Since you're here, you might want to see what I've been doing."

He lifted a sheet of paper that listed appetizers. "*Coquilles St. Jacques, Escargots Bourguignonne, Pâté de Campagne.* Is it too personal a question to ask if you ever eat what you recommend?"

"From time to time, if I trust the chef. You'll see, if you go more thoroughly through my notes, that I want to offer a more sophisticated menu, because the American palate is becoming more sophisticated."

Blake smiled at the term *American,* and the way she said it, before he sat across from her. "Is it?"

"It's been a slow process," she said dryly. "Today, you can find a good food processor in almost every kitchen. With one, and a competent cookbook, even you could make an acceptable mousse."

"Amazing."

"Therefore," she continued, ignoring him, "to lure people into a restaurant where they'll pay, and pay well to be fed, you have to offer them the superb. A few blocks down the street, they can get a wholesome, filling meal for a fraction of what they'll pay in the Cocharan House." Summer folded her hands and rested her chin on them. "So you have to give them a very special ambience, incomparable service and exquisite food." She picked up her soda and sipped. "Personally, I'd rather pick up a take-out pizza and eat it at home, but…" She shrugged.

Blake scanned the next sheet. "Because you like pizza, or you like being alone?"

"Both. Now—"

"Do you stay out of restaurants because you spend so much time in a kitchen behind them or because you simply don't like being in a group?"

She opened her mouth to answer and found she didn't know. Uncomfortable, she toyed with her soda. "You're getting more personal, and off the point."

"I don't think so. You're telling me we have to appeal to people who're becoming sophisticated enough to make dishes that were once almost exclusively professionally prepared, as well as draw in clientele who might prefer a quick, less expensive meal around the corner. You, due to your profession and your taste, fall into both categories. What would a restaurant have to offer not only to bring you in, but to make you want to come back?"

A logical question. Summer frowned at it. She hated logical questions because they left you no choice but to answer. "Privacy," she answered at length. "It isn't an easy thing to accomplish in a restaurant, and of course, not everyone looks for it. Many go out to eat to see and be seen. Some, like myself, prefer at least the illusion of solitude. To accomplish both, you have to have a certain number of tables situated in such a way that they seem removed from the rest."

"Easily enough done with the right lighting, a clever arrangement of foliage."

"The key words are right and clever."

"And privacy is your prerequisite in choosing a restaurant."

"I don't generally eat in them," Summer said with a restless movement of her shoulders. "But if I do, privacy ranks equally with atmosphere, food and service."

"Why?"

She began to push the papers together on her desk and stack them. "That's definitely a personal question."

"Yes." He covered her hands with one of his to still them. "Why?"

She stared at him a moment, certain she wouldn't answer. Then she found herself drawn by the quiet look and the gentle touch. "I suppose it stems back to eating in so many restaurants as a child. And I suppose one of the reasons I first became interested in cooking was as a defense against the interminable ritual of eating out. My mother was—is—of the type who goes out to see and be seen. My father often considered eating out a business. So much of my parents' lives, and therefore mine, was public. I simply prefer my own way."

Now that he was touching her, he wanted more. Now that he was learning of her, he wanted all. He should have known better than to believe it would be otherwise. He'd nearly convinced himself that he had his feelings for her under control. But now, sitting in the cramped storage room with kitchen sounds just outside the door, he wanted her as much—more—than ever.

"I wouldn't consider you an introvert, or a recluse."

"No." She didn't even notice that she'd laced her fingers with his. There was something so comfortable, so right about the gesture. "I simply like to keep my private life just that. Mine and private."

"Yet, in your field, you're quite a celebrity." He shifted and under the table his leg brushed against hers. He felt the warmth glow through him and the need double.

Without thinking, she moved her leg so that it brushed his again. The muscles in her thighs loosened. "Perhaps. Or you might say my desserts are celebrities."

Blake lifted their joined hands and studied them. Hers was shades lighter than his, inches smaller and more narrow. She wore a sapphire, oval, deeply blue in an ornate antique setting that made her fingers look that much more elegant. "Is that what you want?"

She moistened her lips, because when his eyes came back to hers they were intense and as darkly blue as the stone on her hand. "I want to be successful. I want to be considered the very best at what I do."

"Nothing more?"

"No, nothing." Why was she breathless? she asked herself frantically. Young girls got breathless—or romantics. She was neither.

"When you have that?" Blake rose, drawing her to her feet without effort. "What else?"

Because they were standing, she had to angle her head to keep her eyes level with his. "It's enough." As she said it, Summer had her first doubts of the truth of that statement. "What about you?" she countered. "Aren't you looking for success—more success? The finest hotels, the finest restaurants."

"I'm a businessman." Slowly, he walked around the

table until nothing separated them. Their hands were still joined. "I have a standard to maintain or improve. I'm also a man." He reached for her hair, then let it flow through his fingers. "And there're things other than account books I think about."

They were close now. Her body brushed his and caused her skin to hum. She forgot all the rules she'd set out for both of them and reached up to touch his cheek. "What else do you think about?"

"You." His hand was at her waist, then sliding gently up her back as he drew her closer. "I think very much about you, and this."

Lips touched—softly. Eyes remained open and aware. Pulses throbbed. Desire tugged.

Lips parted—slowly. A look said everything there was to say. Pulses hammered. Desire tore free.

She was in his arms, clinging, greedy, burning. Every hour of the past two weeks, all the work, the planning, the rules, melted away under a blaze of passion. If she sensed impatience in him, it only matched her own. The kiss was hard, long, desperate. Body strained against body in exquisite torment.

Tighter. Whether she said the word aloud or merely thought it, he seemed to understand. His arms curved around her, crushing her to him as she wanted to be. She felt the lines and planes of his body mold to hers even as his mouth molded to hers, and somehow she seemed softer than she'd ever imagined herself to be.

Feminine, sultry, delicate, passionate. Was it possible to be all at once? The need grew and expanded—for him—for a taste and touch she'd found nowhere else. The sound she made against his lips came as much from confusion as from pleasure.

Good God, how could a woman take him so far with only a kiss? He was already more than half-mad for her. Control was losing its meaning in a need that was much more imperative. Her skin would slide like silk under his hands—he knew it. He had to feel it.

He slipped a hand under her sweater and found her. Beneath his palm, her heartbeat pounded. Not enough. The thought raced through his mind that it would never be enough. But questions, reason, were for later. Burying his face against her throat he tasted her skin. The scent he remembered lingered there, enticing him further, drawing him closer to the edge where there could be no turning back. The fatigue he'd felt when he'd entered the room vanished. The tension he felt whenever she was near evaporated. At that moment, he considered her completely his without realizing he'd wanted exclusive possession.

Her hair brushed over his face, cloud soft, fragrant. It made him think of Paris, right before the heat of summer took over from spring. But her skin was hot and vibrating, making him envision long humid nights when lovemaking would be slow, endlessly slow. He wanted her there, in the cramped little room where the floor was littered with boxes.

She couldn't think. Summer could feel her bones dissolve and her mind empty. Sensation after sensation poured over her. She could have drowned in them. Yet she wanted more—she could feel her body craving more, wanting all. Storm, thunder, heat. Just once…the longing seeped into her with whispering promises and dark pleasure. She could let herself be his, take him as hers. Just once. And then…

With a moan, she tore her mouth from his and buried

her face against his shoulder. Once with Blake would haunt her for the rest of her life.

"Come upstairs," Blake murmured. Tilting her head back, he ran kisses over her face. "Come up with me where I can make love with you properly. I want you in my bed, Summer. Soft, naked, mine."

"Blake…" She turned her face away and tried to steady her breathing. What had happened to her—when—how? "This is a mistake—for both of us."

"No." Taking her by the shoulders, he kept her facing him. "This is right—for both of us."

"I can't get involved—"

"You already are."

She let out a deep breath. "No further than this. It's already more than I intended."

When she started to back away, he held her firmly in front of him. "I need a reason, Summer, a damn good one."

"You confuse me." Summer blurted it out before she realized it, then swore at the admission. "Damn it, I don't like to be confused."

"And I ache for you." His voice was as impatient as hers, his body as tense. "I don't like to ache."

"We've got a problem," she managed, dragging a hand through her hair.

"I want you." Something in the way he said it made her hand pause in midair and her gaze lift to his. There was nothing casual in those three words. "I want you more than I've ever wanted anyone. I'm not comfortable with that."

"A big problem," she whispered and sat unsteadily on the edge of the table.

"There's one way to solve it."

She managed a smile. "Two ways," she corrected. "And I think mine's the safest."

"Safest." Reaching down, he ran a fingertip over the curve of her cheek. "You want safety, Summer?"

"Yes." It was easily said because she'd discovered it was true. Safety was something she'd never thought about until Blake, because she'd never felt endangered until then. "I've made myself a lot of promises, Blake, set a lot of goals. Instinct tells me you could interfere. I always go with my instincts."

"I've no intention of interfering with your goals."

"Nevertheless, I have a few very strict rules. One of them is never to become intimate with a business associate or a client. In one point of view, you fall into both categories."

"How do you intend to prevent it from happening? Intimacies come in a lot of degrees, Summer. You and I have already reached some of them."

How could she deny it? She wanted to run from it. "We managed to keep out of each other's way for two weeks," she pointed out. "It's simply a matter of continuing to do so. Both of us are very busy at the moment, so it shouldn't be too difficult."

"Eventually one of us is going to break the rules."

And it could be me just as easily as it could be him, she thought. "I can't think about eventually, only about now. I'll stay downstairs and do my job. You stay upstairs and do yours."

"Like hell," Blake muttered and took a step forward. Summer was halfway to her feet when a knock sounded on her door.

"Mr. Cocharan, there's a phone call for you. Your secretary says it's urgent."

Blake controlled his fury. "I'll be there." He gave Summer a long, hard look. "We're not finished."

She waited until he'd reached the door. "I can turn this place into a palace or a greasy spoon," she said quietly. "It's your choice."

Turning around, he measured her. "Blackmail?"

"Insurance," she corrected and smiled. "Play it my way, Blake and everybody's happy."

"Your point, Summer," he acknowledged with a nod. "This time."

When the door closed behind him, she sat again. She may have outmaneuvered him this time, she mused, but the game was far from over.

Summer gave herself another hour before she left her temporary office to go back to the kitchen. Busboys wheeled in and out with trays of dirty dishes. The dishwasher hummed busily. Pots simmered. Someone sang as she basted a chicken. Two hours to the dinner rush. In another hour, the panic and confusion would set in.

It was then, when the scent of food hit her, that Summer realized she hadn't eaten. Deciding to kill two birds with one stone, she began to root through the cupboards. She'd find something for a late lunch, and see just how provisions were organized.

She couldn't complain about the latter. The cupboards were not only well stocked, they were systematically stocked. Max had a number of excellent qualities, she thought. A pity an open mind wasn't among them. She continued to scan shelf after shelf, but the item she was looking for was nowhere to be found.

"Ms. Lyndon?"

Hearing Max's voice behind her, Summer slowly

closed the cabinet door. She didn't have to turn around to see the cold politeness in his eyes or the tight disapproval of his mouth. She was going to have to do something about this situation before long, she decided. But at the moment she was a bit tired, quite a bit hungry and not in the mood to deal with it.

"Yes, Max." She opened the next door and surveyed the stock.

"Perhaps I can help you find what you're looking for."

"Perhaps. Actually, I'm checking to see how well stocked we are while searching out a jar of peanut butter. Apparently—" she closed that door and went on to the next "—we're very well stocked indeed, and very well organized."

"My kitchen is completely organized," Max began stiffly. "Even in the midst of all this—this carpentry."

"The carpentry's almost finished," she said easily. "I think the new ovens are working out well."

"To some, new is always better."

"To some," she countered, "progress is always a death knell. Where do I find the peanut butter, Max? I really want a sandwich."

This time she did turn, in time to see his eyebrows rise and his mouth purse. "Below," he said with a hint of a smirk as he pointed. "We keep such things on hand for the children's menu."

"Good." Unoffended, Summer crouched down and found it. "Would you like to join me?"

"Thank you, no. I have work to do."

"Fine." Summer took two slices of bread and began to spread the peanut butter. "Tomorrow, nine o'clock, you and I will go over the proposed menus in my office."

"I'm very busy at nine."

"No," she corrected mildly. "We're very busy from seven to nine, then things tend to ease off, particularly midweek, until the lunch rush. Nine o'clock," she repeated over his huff of breath. "Excuse me, I have to get some jelly for this."

Leaving Max gritting his teeth, Summer went to one of the large refrigerators. Pompous, narrow-minded ass, she thought as she found a restaurant-sized jar of grape jelly. As long as he continued to be uncooperative and stiff, things were going to be difficult. More than once, she'd expected Max to turn in his resignation—and there were times, though she hated to be so hard line, that she wished he would.

The changes in the kitchen were already making a difference, she thought as she closed the second slice of bread over the jelly and peanut butter. Any fool could see that the extra range, the more efficient equipment, tightened the flow of preparation and improved the quality of food. Annoyed, she bit into her sandwich just as excited chatter broke out behind her.

"Max'll be furious. *Fur-i-ous.*"

"Nothing he can do about it now."

"Except yell and throw things."

Perhaps it was the underlying glee in the last statement that made Summer turn. She saw two cooks huddled over the stove. "What'll Max be furious about?" she asked over another mouthful of sandwich.

The two faces turned to her. Both were flushed either from the heat of the stove or excitement. "Maybe you ought to tell him, Ms. Lyndon," one of the cooks said after a moment of indecision. The glee was still there, she noticed, barely suppressed.

"Tell him what?"

"Julio and Georgia eloped—we just got word from Julio's brother. They took off for Hawaii."

Julio and Georgia? After a quick flip through her mental file, Summer placed them as two cooks who worked the four-to-eleven shift. A glance at her watch told her they were already fifteen minutes late.

"I take it they won't be coming in today."

"They quit." One of the cooks snapped his fingers. "Just like that." He glanced across the room where Max was babying a rack of lamb. "Max'll hit the roof."

"He won't solve anything up there," she murmured. "So we're two short for the dinner shift."

"Three," the second cook corrected. "Charlie called in sick an hour ago."

"Wonderful." Summer finished off her sandwich, then rolled up her sleeves. "Then the rest of us better get to work."

With an apron covering her jeans and sweater, Summer took over one section of the new counter. Perhaps it wasn't her usual style, she mused as she began mixing the first oversized bowl of cake batter, but circumstances called for immediate action. And, she thought as she licked some batter from her knuckle, they damn well better get the stereo speakers in before the end of the week. Summer might bake without Chopin in an emergency once, but she wouldn't do it twice.

She was arranging several layers of Black Forest cake in the oven when Max spoke over her shoulder.

"You're making yourself some dessert now?" he began.

"No." Summer set the timer, then moved back to the counter to start preparations on chocolate mousse. "It seems there's been a wedding and an illness—though I don't think the first has anything to do with the second. We're shorthanded tonight. I'm taking over the desserts, Max, and I don't exchange small talk when I'm working."

"Wedding? What wedding?"

"Julio and Georgia eloped to Hawaii, and Charlie's sick. I have this mousse to deal with at the moment."

"Eloped!" he exploded. "Eloped without my permission?"

She took the time to look over her shoulder. "I suppose Charlie should have checked with you before he got sick as well. Save the hysterics, Max, and have someone peel me some apples. I want to do a *Charlotte de Pommes* after this."

"Now you're changing my menu!" he exploded.

She whirled, fire in her eyes. "I have a dozen different desserts to make in a very short time. I'd advise you to stay out of my way while I do it. I'm not known for graciousness when I'm cooking."

He sucked in his stomach and pulled back his shoulders. "We'll see what Mr. Cocharan has to say about this."

"Terrific. Keep him out of my way, too, for the next three hours or someone's going to end up with a face full of my best whipped cream." Spinning back around, she went to work.

There wasn't time, she couldn't take the time, to study and approve each dessert as it was completed. Later, Summer would think of the hours as assembly line work. At the moment, she was too pressed to think. Julio and Georgia had been the dessert chefs. It was now up to her to do the work of two people in the same amount of time.

She ignored the menu and went with what she knew she could make from memory. The diners that evening were in for a surprise, but as she finished topping the second Black Forest cake, Summer decided it would be a pleasant one. She arranged the cherries quickly, cursing the need to rush. Impossible to create when one was on such a ridiculous timetable, she thought, and muttered bad temperedly under her breath.

By six, the bulk of the baking was done and she concentrated on the finishing touches of a line of desserts designed to satisfy an army. Chocolate icing there, a dab of cream here, a garnish, a spoon of jam or jelly. She was hot, her arms aching. Her once-white apron was streaked and splashed. No one spoke to her, because she wouldn't answer. No one approached her, because she tended to snarl.

Occasionally she would indicate with a wave of her arm a section of dishes that were to be taken away. This was done instantly, and without a sound. If there was talk, it was done in undertones and out of her hearing. None of them had ever seen anything quite like Summer Lyndon on a roll.

"Problems?"

Summer heard Blake speak quietly over her shoulder but didn't turn. "Cars are made this way," she mumbled, "not desserts."

"Early reports from the dining room are more than favorable."

She grunted and rolled out pastry dough for tarts. "The next time I'm in Hawaii, I'm going to look up Julio and Georgia and knock their heads together."

"A bit testy, aren't you?" he murmured and earned

a lethal glare. "And hot." He touched her cheek with a fingertip. "How long have you been at it?"

"Since a bit after four." After shrugging his hand away she began to rapidly cut out pastry shells. Blake watched, surprised. He'd never seen her work quickly before. "Move."

He stepped back but continued to watch her. By his calculations, she'd worked on the menus in the windowless storage room for more than six hours, and had now been on her feet for nearly three. Too small, he thought as a protective urge moved through him. Too delicate.

"Summer, can't someone else take over now? You should rest."

"No one touches my desserts." This was said in such a strong, authoritative voice that the image of a delicate flower vanished. He grinned despite himself.

"Anything I can do?"

"I'll want some champagne in an hour. Dom Perignon, '73."

He nodded as an idea began to form in his mind. She smelled like the desserts lined on the counter in front of her. Tempting, delicious. Since he'd met her, Blake had discovered he possessed a very demanding sweet tooth. "Have you eaten?"

"A sandwich a few hours ago," she said testily. "Do you think I could eat at a time like this?"

He glanced at the sumptuous array of cakes and pastries. He could smell delicately roasted meats, spicy sauces. Blake shook his head. "No, of course not. I'll be back."

Summer muttered something, then fluted the edges of her pastry shells.

Chapter 7

By eight o'clock, Summer was finished, and not in the best of humors. For nearly four hours, she'd whipped, rolled, fluted and baked. Often, she'd spent twice that time, and twice that effort, perfecting one single dish. That was art. This, on the other hand, had been labor, plain and simple.

She felt no flash of triumph, no glow of self-satisfaction, but simply fatigue. An army cook, she thought disdainfully; it was hardly different from producing the quickest and easiest for the masses. At the moment, if she never saw the inside of another egg again, it would be too soon.

"There should be enough made up to get us through the dinner hour, and room service tonight," she told Max briskly as she pulled off her soiled apron. Critically she frowned at a line of fruit tarts. More than one of them were less than perfect in shape. If there'd been time, she'd have discarded them and made others. "I want someone in touch with personnel first thing in the morning to see about hiring two more dessert chefs."

"Mr. Cocharan has already contacted personnel." Max stood stiffly, not wanting to give an inch, though he'd been impressed with how quickly and efficiently she'd avoided what could easily have been a catastrophe. He clung tightly to his resentment, even though he had to admit—to himself—that she baked the best apricot tart he'd ever tasted.

"Fine." Summer ran a hand over the back of her neck. The skin there was damp, the muscles drawn taut. "Nine o'clock tomorrow, Max, in my office. Let's see if we can get organized. I'm going home to soak in a hot tub until morning."

Blake had been leaning against the wall, watching her work. It had been fascinating to see just how quickly the temperamental artist had put her nose to the grindstone and produced.

She'd shown him two things he hadn't expected—a speed and lack of histrionics when she'd been forced to deal with a less than ideal situation, and a calm acceptance of what was obviously a touchy area with Max. However much she played the role of prima donna, when her back was against the wall, she handled herself very well.

When she removed her apron, he stepped forward. "Give you a lift?"

Summer glanced over at him as she pulled the pins from her hair. It fell to her shoulders, tousled, and a bit damp at the ends from the heat. "I have my car."

"And I have mine." The arrogance, with that trace of aloofness, was still there, even when he smiled.

"And a bottle of Dom Perignon, '73. My driver can pick you up in the morning."

She told herself she was only interested in the wine. The cool smile had nothing to do with her decision. "Properly chilled?" she asked, arching her brow. "The champagne, that is."

"Of course."

"You're on, Mr. Cocharan. I never turn down champagne."

"The car's out in the back." He took her hand rather than her arm as she'd expected. Before she could make any counter move, he was leading her from the kitchen. "Would it embarrass you if I said I was very impressed with what you did this evening?"

She was used to accolades, even expected them. Somehow, she couldn't remember ever getting so much pleasure from one before. She moved her shoulders, hoping to lighten her own response. "I make it my business to be impressive. It doesn't embarrass me."

Perhaps if she hadn't been tired, he wouldn't have seen through the glib answer so easily. When they reached his car, Blake turned and took her by the shoulders. "You worked very hard in there."

"Just part of the service."

"No," he corrected, soothing the muscles. "That's not what you were hired for."

"When I signed the contract, that became my kitchen. What goes out of it has to satisfy my standards, my pride."

"Not an easy job."

"You wanted the best."

"Apparently I got it."

She smiled, though she wanted badly just to sit

down. "You definitely got it. Now, you did say something about champagne?"

"Yes, I did." He opened the door for her. "You smell of vanilla."

"I earned it." When she sat, she let out a long, pleasurable sigh. Champagne, she thought, a hot bath with mountains of bubbles, and smooth, cool sheets. In that order. "Chances are," she murmured, "even as we speak, someone in there is taking the first bite of my Black Forest cake."

Blake shut the driver's door, then glanced at her as he started the ignition. "Does it feel odd?" he asked. "Having strangers eat something you spent so much time and care creating?"

"Odd?" Summer stretched back, enjoying the plush luxury of the seat and the view of the dusky sky through the sun roof. "A painter creates on canvas for whoever will look, a composer creates a symphony for whoever will listen."

"True enough." Blake maneuvered his way onto the street and into the traffic. The sun was red and low. The night promised to be clear. "But wouldn't it be more gratifying to be there when your desserts are served?"

She closed her eyes, completely relaxed for the first time in hours. "When one cooks in one's own kitchen for friends, relatives, it can be a pleasure or a duty. Then there might be the satisfaction of watching something you've cooked being appreciated. But again, it's a pleasure or a duty, not a profession."

"You rarely eat what you cook."

"I rarely cook for myself," she countered. "Except the simpler things."

"Why?"

"When you cook for yourself, there's no one there to clean up the mess."

He laughed and turned into a parking lot. "In your own odd way you're a very practical woman."

"In every way I'm a practical woman." Lazily, she opened her eyes. "Why did we stop?"

"Hungry?"

"I'm always hungry after I work." Turning her head, she saw the blue neon sign of a pizza parlor.

"Knowing your tastes by now, I thought you'd find this the perfect accompaniment to the champagne."

She grinned as the fatigue was replaced with the first real stirrings of hunger. "Absolutely perfect."

"Wait here," he told her as he opened the door. "I had someone call ahead and order it when I saw you were nearly finished."

Grateful, and touched, Summer leaned back and closed her eyes again. When was the last time she'd allowed anyone to take care of her? she wondered. If memory served her, the last time she'd been pampered she'd been eight, and cranky with a case of chicken pox. Independence had always been expected of her, by her parents, and by herself. But tonight, this one time, it was a rather sweet feeling to let someone else make the arrangements with her comfort in mind.

And she had to admit, she hadn't expected simple consideration from Blake. Style, yes, credit where credit was due, yes—but not consideration. He'd put in a hard day himself, she thought, remembering how tired he'd looked that afternoon. Still, he'd waited long past the time when he could have had his own dinner in comfort, relaxed in his own way. He'd waited until she was finished.

Surprises, she mused. Blake Cocharan III definitely had some surprises up his sleeve. She'd always been a sucker for them.

When Blake opened the car door, the scent of pizza rolled pleasurably inside. Summer took the box from him, then leaned over and kissed his cheek. "Thanks."

"I should've tried pizza before," he murmured.

She settled back again, letting her eyes close and her lips curve. "Don't forget the champagne. Those are two of my biggest weaknesses."

"I've made a note of it." Blake pulled out of the parking lot and joined the traffic again. Her simple gratitude shouldn't have surprised him. It certainly shouldn't have moved him. He had the feeling she would have had the same low-key, pleased reaction if he'd presented her with a full-length sable or a bracelet of blue-white diamonds. With Summer, it wouldn't be the gift, but the nature of the giving. He found he liked that idea very much. She wasn't a woman who was easily impressed, he mused, yet she was a woman who could be easily pleased.

Summer did something she rarely did unless she was completely alone. She relaxed, fully. Though her eyes were closed, she was no longer sleepy, but aware. She could feel the smooth motion of the car beneath her, hear the rumble of traffic outside the windows. She had only to draw in a breath to smell the tangy scent of sauce and spice. The car was spacious, but she could sense the warmth of Blake's body across the seat.

Pleasant. That was the word that drifted through her mind. So pleasant, there seemed to be no need for caution, for defenses. It was a pity, she reflected, that they weren't driving aimlessly...

Strange, she'd never chosen to do anything aimlessly. And yet, tonight, to drive…along a long, deserted
beach—with the moon full, shining off the water, and
the sand white. You'd be able to hear the surf ebb and
flow, and see the hundreds of stars you so rarely noticed
in the city. You'd smell the salt and feel the spray. The
moist, warm air would flow over your skin.

She felt the car swing off the road, then purr to a
stop. For an extra moment, Summer held on to the fan-
tasy.

"What're you thinking?"

"About the beach," she answered. "Stars." She caught
herself, surprised that she'd indulged in what could only
be termed romanticism. "I'll take the pizza," she said,
straightening. "You can bring the champagne."

He put a hand on her arm, lightly but it stopped her.
Slowly he ran a finger down it. "You like the beach?"

"I never really thought about it." At the moment, she
found she'd like nothing better than to rest her head
against his shoulder and watch waves surge against the
shore. Star counting. Why should she want to indulge
in something so foolish now when she never had before? "For some reason, it just seemed like the night for
it." And she wondered if she were answering his question or her own.

"Since there's no beach, we'll just have to come up
with something else. How's your imagination?"

"Good enough." Quite good enough, Summer
thought, to see where she'd end up if she didn't change
the mood—hers as well as his. "And at the moment, I
imagine the pizza's getting cold, and the champagne
warm." Opening the door, she climbed out with the

box in hand. Once inside the building, Summer started up the stairs.

"Does the elevator ever work?" Blake shifted the bag in his arm and joined her.

"Off and on—mostly it's off. Personally, I don't trust it."

"In that case, why'd you pick the fourth floor?"

She smiled as they rounded the second landing. "I like the view—and the fact that salesmen are usually discouraged when they're faced with more than two flights of steps."

"You could've chosen a more modern building, with a view, a security system and a working elevator."

"I look at modern tools as essential, a new car, well tuned, as imperative." Drawing out her keys, Summer jiggled them lightly as they approached her door. "As to living arrangements, I'm a bit more open-minded. My flat in Paris has temperamental plumbing and the most exquisite cornices I've ever seen."

When she opened the door, the scent of roses was overwhelming. There were a dozen white in a straw basket, a dozen red in a Sevres vase, a dozen yellow in a pottery jug and a dozen pink in Venetian glass.

"Run into a special at the florist's?"

Summer raised her brows as she set the pizza on the dinette. "I never buy flowers for myself. These are from Enrico."

Blake set the bag next to the box and drew out the champagne. "All?"

"He's a bit flamboyant—Enrico Gravanti—you might've heard of him. Italian shoes and bags."

Two hundred million dollars worth of shoes and bags, as Blake recalled. He flicked a finger down a rose petal. "I hadn't heard Gravanti was in town. He normally stays at the Cocharan House."

"No, he's in Rome." As she spoke, Summer went into the kitchen for plates and glasses. "He wired these when I agreed to make the cake for his birthday next month."

"Four dozen roses for a cake?"

"Five," Summer corrected as she came back in. "There's another dozen in the bedroom. They're rather lovely, a kind of peach color." In anticipation, she held out both glasses. "And, after all, it is one of my cakes."

With a nod of acknowledgment, Blake loosened the cork. Air fizzed out while the champagne bubbled toward the lip of the bottle. "So, I take it you'll be going to Italy to bake it."

"I don't intend to ship it air freight." She watched the pale gold liquid rise in the glass as Blake poured. "I should only be in Rome two days, three at most." Raising the glass to her lips, she sipped, eyes closed, senses keen. "Excellent." She sipped again before she opened her eyes and smiled. "I'm starving." After lifting the lid on the box, she breathed deep. "Pepperoni."

"Somehow I thought it suited you."

With a laugh, an easy one, she sat down. "Very perceptive. Shall I serve?"

"Please." And as she began to, Blake flicked on his lighter and set the three staggered-length tapers she had on the table burning. "Champagne and pizza," he said as he turned off the lights. "That demands candlelight, don't you think?"

"If you like." When he sat, Summer lifted her first piece. The cheese was hot enough to make her catch her breath, the sauce tangy. "Mmmm. Wonderful."

"Has it occurred to you that we spend a great deal of our time together eating?"

"Hmm—well, it's something I thoroughly enjoy. I always try to look at eating as a pleasure rather than a physical necessity. It adds something."

"Pounds, usually."

She shrugged and reached for the champagne. "Of course, if one isn't wise enough to take one's pleasure in small doses. Greed is what adds pounds, ruins the complexion and makes one miserable."

"You don't succumb to greed?"

She remembered abruptly that it had been just that, exactly that, that she'd felt for him. But she'd controlled it, Summer reminded herself. She hadn't succumbed. "No." She ate slowly, savoring. "I don't. In my profession, it would be disastrous."

"How do you keep your pleasure in small doses?"

She wasn't sure she trusted the way the question came out. Taking her time, she set a second piece on each plate. "I'd rather have one spoonful of a superb chocolate soufflé than an entire plateful of food that doesn't have flair."

Blake took another bite of pizza. "And this has flair?"

She smiled because it was so obviously not the sort of meal he was used to. "An excellent balance of spices— perhaps just a tad heavy on the oregano—a good marriage of sauce and crust, the proper handling of cheese and the bite of pepperoni. With the proper use of the senses, almost any meal can be memorable."

"With the proper use of the senses," Blake countered, "other things can be memorable."

She reached for her glass again, her eyes laughing over the rim. "We're speaking of food. Taste, of course, is paramount, but appearance…" He linked his hand with hers and she found herself watching him. "Your eyes tell you first of the desire to taste." His face was lean, the eyes a deep blue she found continuously compelling…

"Then a scent teases you, entices you." His was dark, woodsy, tempting…

"You hear the way champagne bubbles into a glass and you want to experience it." Or the way he said her name, quietly.

"After all this," she continued in a voice that was beginning to take on a faint huskiness, a faint trace of feeling, "you have the taste, the texture to explore." And his mouth held a flavor she couldn't forget.

"So—" he lifted her hand and pressed his mouth to the palm "—your advice is to savor every aspect of the experience in order to absorb all the pleasure. Then…" Turning her hand over, he brushed his lips, then the tip of his tongue, over her knuckles. "The most basic of desires becomes unique."

In an arrow-straight line, the heat shot up her arm. "No experience is acceptable otherwise."

"And atmosphere?" Lightly, with just a fingertip, he traced the shape of her ear. "Wouldn't you agree that the proper setting can enhance the same experience? Candlelight, for instance."

Their faces were closer now. She could see the soft shifting light casting shadows, mysteries. "Outside devices can often add more intensity to a mood."

"You could call it romance." He took his fingertip down the length of her jawline.

"You could." Champagne never went to her head, yet her head was light. Slowly, luxuriously, her body was softening. She made an effort to remember why she should allow neither to happen, but no answer came.

"And romance, for some, is another very elemental need."

"For some," he murmured when his lips followed the trail of his fingertip.

"But not for you." He nipped at her lips and found them soft, and warm.

"No, not for me." But her sigh was as soft and warm as her lips.

"A practical woman." He was raising her to her feet so that their bodies could touch.

"Yes." She tilted her head back, inviting the exploration of his lips.

"Candlelight doesn't move you?"

"It's only an attractive device." She curved her arms up his back to bring him closer. "As chefs, we're taught that such things can lend the right mood to our meals."

"And it wouldn't matter if I told you that you were beautiful? In the full sun where your skin's flawless—in candlelight, which turns it to porcelain. It wouldn't matter," he continued as he ran a line of moist heat down her throat, "if I told you you excite me as no other woman ever has? Just looking at you makes me want, touching you drives me mad."

"Words," she managed, though her head was spinning. "I don't need—"

Then his mouth covered hers. The one long, deep kiss made lies of all her practical claims. Tonight, though she'd never wanted such things before, she wanted the romance of soft words, soft lights. She wanted the slow, savoring loving that emptied the mind and made a furnace of the body. Tonight she wanted, and there was only one man. If tomorrow there were consequences, tomorrow was hours away. He was here.

She didn't resist as he lifted her. Tonight, if only for a short while, she'd be fragile, soft. She heard him blow out the candles and the light scent of melted wax followed them toward the bedroom.

Moonlight. The silvery sorcery of moonlight slipped through the windows. Roses. The fragile fragrance of roses floated on the air. Music. The muted magic of Beethoven drifted in from the apartment below.

There was a breeze. Summer felt it whisper over her face as he placed her on the bed. Atmosphere, she thought hazily. If she had planned on a night of lovemaking, she could have set the stage no better. Perhaps… She drew him down to join her… Perhaps it was fate.

She could see his eyes. Deep blue, direct, involving. He watched her while doing no more than tracing the shape of her face, of her lips, with his finger. Had anyone ever shown her that kind of tenderness? Had she ever wanted it?

No. And if the answer was no, the answer had abruptly changed. She wanted this new experience, the sweetness she'd always disregarded, and she wanted the man who would bring her both.

Taking his face in her hands, she studied him. This was the man she would share this one completely private moment with, the one who would soon know her body as well as her vulnerabilities. She might have wavered over the trust, reminded herself of the pitfalls— if she'd been able to resist the need, and the strength, she saw in his eyes.

"Kiss me again," she murmured. "No one's ever made me feel the way you do when you kiss me."

He felt a surge of pleasure, intense, stunning. Lowering his head, he touched his lips to hers, toying with them, watching her as she watched him while their emotions heightened and their need sharpened. Should he have known she'd be even more beautiful in the moonlight, with her hair spread over a pillow? Could he have known that desire for her would be an ache unlike any desire he'd known? Was it still as simple as desire, or had he crossed some line he'd been unaware of? There were no answers now. Answers were for the daylight.

With a moan, he deepened the kiss and felt her body yield beneath his even as her mouth grew avid. Little tongues of passion flickered, still subdued beneath a gentleness they both seemed to need. Odd, because neither of them had needed it before, or often thought to show it.

Her hands were light on his face, over his neck, then slowly combing through his hair. Though his body was hard on hers, there was no demand yet.

Savor me. The thought ran silkily through her mind even as Blake's lips journeyed over her face. Slowly. She'd never known a man with such patience or an arousal so heady. Mouth against mouth, then mouth against skin—each drew her deeper and still deeper into a languor that encompassed both body and mind.

Touch me. And he seemed to understand this fresh need. His hands moved, but still without hurry, over her shoulders, down her sides, then up again to whisper over her breasts—until it was no longer enough for either of them. Then wordlessly they began to undress each other.

Fingers of moonlight fell across exposed flesh—a shoulder, the length of an arm, a lean torso. Luxuriously, Summer ran her hands over Blake's chest and learned the muscle and form. Lazily, he explored the length of her and learned the subtle curves and silk. Even when the last barrier of clothing was drawn away, they didn't rush. So much to touch, taste—and time had no meaning.

The breeze flitted in, but they grew warmer. Wherever her fingers wandered, his flesh would burn, then cool only to burn again. As he took his lips over her, finding pleasure, learning secrets, she began to heat. And demand crept into both of them.

More urgently now, with quick moans, trembling breaths, they took each other further. He hadn't known he could be led, and she'd always refused to be, yet now, one guided the other to the same destination.

Summer felt reality slipping away from her, but had no will to stop it. The music penetrated only faintly into her consciousness, but his murmurs were easily heard. It was his scent, no longer the roses, that titillated. She would feel whatever she was meant to feel, go wherever she was meant to go, as long as he was with her. Along with the strongest physical desire she'd ever known was an emotional need that exploded inside her. She couldn't question it, couldn't refuse it. Her body, mind, heart, ached for him.

With his name trembling on her lips, she took him into her. Then, for both of them, the pleasure was so acute that sanity was forgotten. Sensation—waves, floods, storms—whipped through her. The calm had become a hurricane to revel in. Together, they were swept away.

Had hours passed or minutes? Summer lay in the filtered moonlight and tried to orient herself. She'd never felt quite like this. Sated, exhilarated, exhausted. Once she'd have said it was impossible to be all at once.

She could feel the brush of Blake's hair against her shoulder, the whisper of his breath against her cheek. His scent and hers were mixed now, so that the roses were only an accent. The music had stopped, but she thought she could still hear the echo. His body was pressed into hers, but his weight was a pleasure. She knew, without effort, she could wrap her arms around him and stay just so for the rest of her life. So through the hazy pleasure came the first stirrings of fear.

Oh, God, how far had she gone in such a short time? She'd always been so certain her emotions were perfectly safe. It wasn't the first time she'd been with a man, but she was too aware that it was the first time she'd made love in the true sense of the word.

Mistake. She forced the word into her head even as her heart tried to block it. She had to think, had to be practical. Hadn't she seen what uncontrolled emotions and dreams had done to two intelligent people? Both her parents had spent years moving from relationship to relationship looking for…what?

This, her heart told her, but again she blocked it out. She knew better than to look for something she didn't believe existed. Permanency, commitment—they were illusions. And illusions had no place in her life.

Closing her eyes a moment, she waited for herself to settle. She was a grown woman, sophisticated enough to understand and accept mutual desire that held no strings. *Treat it lightly,* she warned herself. *Don't pretend it's more than it is.*

But she couldn't resist smoothing his hair as she spoke. "Odd how pizza and champagne affect me."

Raising his head, Blake grinned at her. At the moment, he felt he could've taken on the world. "I think it should be your staple diet." He kissed the curve of her shoulder. "It's going to be mine. Want some more?"

"Pizza and champagne?"

Laughing, he nuzzled her neck. "That, too." He shifted, drawing her against his side. It was one more gesture of intimacy that had something inside her trembling.

Set out the rules, Summer told herself. *Do it now, before...before it would be much too easy to forget.*

"I like being with you," she said quietly.

"And I you." He could see the shadows play on the ceiling, hear the muted sound of traffic outside, but he was still saturated with her.

"Now that we've been together like this, it's going to affect our relationship one of two ways."

Puzzled, he turned his head to look at her. "One of two ways?"

"It's either going to increase the tension while we're working, or alleviate it. I'm hoping it alleviates it."

In the darkness he frowned at her. "What happened just now had absolutely nothing to do with business."

"Whatever you and I do together is bound to affect our working relationship." Moistening her lips, she tried to continue in the same light way. "Making love with you was...personal, but tomorrow morning we're back to being associates. This can't change that—I think it'd be a mistake to let it change the tone of our business dealings." Was she rambling? Was she making sense? She wished desperately that he would say something, anything at all. "I think we both knew this was bound to happen. Now that it has, it's cleared the air."

"Cleared the air?" Infuriated, and to his surprise, hurt, he rose on his elbow. "It did a damn sight more than that, Summer. We both know that, too."

"Let's keep it in perspective." How had she begun this so badly? And how could she keep rambling on when she only wanted to curl up next to him and hold on? "We're both unattached adults who're attracted to each other. On that level, we shouldn't expect any more from each other than's reasonable. On a business level, we both have to expect total involvement."

He wanted to push the business level down her throat. Violently. The emotion didn't please him, nor did the sudden realization that he wanted total involvement on a very personal level. With an effort, he controlled the fury. He needed to ask, and answer, some questions for himself—soon. In the meantime, he needed to keep a cool head.

"Summer, I intend to make love with you often, and when I do, business can go to hell." He ran a hand down her side and felt her body respond. If she wanted rules, he thought furiously, he'd give her rules. His. "When we're here, there isn't any hotel or any restaurant. There's just you and me. Back at Cocharan House, we'll be as professional as you want."

She wasn't certain if she wanted to calmly agree with him or scream in protest. She remained silent.

"And now," he continued, drawing her still closer, "I want to make love with you again, then I want to sleep with you. At nine o'clock tomorrow, we'll get back to business."

She might have spoken then, but his mouth touched hers. Tomorrow was hours away.

Chapter 8

Damn, it was frustrating. Blake had heard men complain about women, calling them incomprehensible, contradictory, baffling. Because he'd always found it possible to deal with women on a sensible level, he'd never put much credence in any of it, until Summer. Now, he found himself searching for more adjectives. Rising from his desk, Blake paced to the window and frowned out at his view of the city.

When they'd made love the first time, he realized that he'd never known that a woman could be that soft, that giving. Strong—still strong, yes, but with a fragility that had a man lying in velvet. Had it been his imagination, or had she been totally his in every way one person could belong to another? He'd have sworn that for that space of time she'd thought of nothing but him, wanted nothing but him. And yet, before their bodies had cooled, she'd been so practical, so…unemotional.

Damn, wasn't a man supposed to be grateful for that—a man who wanted the pleasure and companionship of a woman without all the complications? He could remember other relationships where a neat set of rules had proven invaluable, but now…

Below, a couple walked along the sidewalk, their arms slung around each other's shoulders. As he watched he imagined them laughing at something no one else would understand. And as he watched, Blake thought of his own statement of the degrees of intimacy. Instinct told him that he and Summer had shared an intimacy as deep as any two people could experience. Not just a merging of bodies, but a touching, a twining, of thoughts and needs and wants that was absolute. But if his instincts had told him one thing, she had told him another. Which was he to believe?

Frustrating, he thought again and turned away from the window. He couldn't deny that he'd gone to her apartment the night before with the idea of seducing her, and putting an end to the tension between them. But he couldn't deny that he'd been seduced after five minutes alone with her. He couldn't see her and not want to touch her. He couldn't hear her laugh without wanting to taste the curve of her lips. Now that he'd made love with her, he wasn't certain a night would pass without his wanting her again.

There must be a term for what he was experiencing. Blake was always more comfortable when he could label something and therefore file it properly. The most efficient heading, the most logical category. What was it called when you thought of a woman when you should be thinking about something else? What name did you give to this constant edgy feeling?

Love... The word crept up on him, not entirely pleasantly. Good God. Uneasy, Blake sat again and stared at the far wall. He was in love with her. It was just as simple—and just as terrifying—as that. He wanted to be with her, to make her laugh, to make her tremble with desire. He wanted to see her eyes glow with temper, and with passion. He wanted to spend quiet evenings, and wild nights, with her. And he was deadly sure he'd want the same thing twenty years down the road.

Since the first time he'd walked down those four flights of stairs from her apartment, he hadn't thought of another woman. Love, if it could ever be considered logical, was the logical conclusion. And he was stuck with it. Taking out a cigarette, Blake ran his fingers down the length of it. He didn't light it, but continued to stare at the wall.

Now what? he asked himself. He was in love with a woman who'd made herself crystal clear on her feelings about commitments and relationships. She wanted no part of either. He, on the other hand, believed in the permanency, and even the romance, of marriage—though he'd never considered it specifically applying to himself.

Things were different now. He was a man too well ordered, both outwardly and mentally, not to see marriage as the direct result of love. With love, you wanted stability, vows, endurance. He wanted Summer. Blake leaned back in his chair. And he firmly believed there was always a way to get what you wanted.

If he even mentioned the word love, she'd be gone in a flash. Even he wasn't completely comfortable with it as yet. Strategy, he told himself. It was all a matter of strategy—or so he hoped. He simply had to convince her that he was essential to her life, that theirs was the relationship designed to break her set of rules.

Apparently the game was still on—and he still intended to win. Frowning at the wall, he began to work his way through the problem.

Summer was having problems of her own. Four cups of strong black coffee hadn't quite brought her up to maximum working level. Ten hours' sleep suited her well, eight could be tolerated. With less than that, and she'd had a good deal less than that the night before, she edged perilously close to nastiness. Add to that a state of emotional turmoil, and Max's frigid resentment, and it didn't promise to be the most pleasant or productive morning.

"By using one of the traditional French garnitures for the roast of lamb, we'll add something European and attractive to the entrée." Summer folded her hands on some of the scattered papers on her desk. She'd brought a few of Enrico's flowers in and set them in a water glass. They helped cover some of the dusty smell.

"My roast of lamb is perfect as it is."

"For some tastes," Summer said evenly. "For mine it's only adequate. I don't accept adequate." Their eyes warred, violently. As neither gave way, she continued. "I prefer to go with *clamart,* artichoke hearts filled with buttered peas, and potatoes sautéed in butter."

"We've always used watercress and mushrooms."

Meticulously, she changed the angle of a rosebud. The small distraction helped her keep her temper. "Now, we use *clamart.*" Summer noted it down, underlined it, then went on. "As to the prime rib—"

"You will not touch my prime rib."

She started to snap back but managed to grit her teeth instead. It was common knowledge in the kitchen that the prime rib was Max's specialty, one might say his baby. The wisest course was to give in graciously on this point, and hold a hard line on others. Her British heritage of fair play came through.

"The prime rib remains precisely as it is," she told him. "My function here is to improve what needs improving while incorporating the Cocharan House standard." Well said, Summer congratulated herself while Max huffed and subsided. "In addition, we'll keep the New York strip and the filet." Sensing he was mollified, Summer hit him with the poultry entrée. "We'll continue to serve the very simple roast chicken, with the choice of potatoes or rice and the vegetables of the day, but we add pressed duck."

"Pressed duck?" Max blustered. "We have no one on staff who's capable of preparing that dish properly, nor do we have a duck press."

"No, which is why I've ordered one, and why I'm hiring someone who can use it."

"You're bringing someone into my kitchen just for this!"

"I'm bringing someone into *my* kitchen," she corrected, "to prepare the pressed duck and the lamb dish among other things. He's leaving his current job in Chicago to come here because he trusts my judgment. You might begin to do the same." With this, she began to tidy papers. "That's all for today, Max. I'd like you to take along these notes." While the headache began to drum inside her head, she handed him a stack of papers. "If you have any suggestions on what I've listed, please jot them down." She bent back over her work as he rose and strode silently out of the room.

Perhaps she shouldn't have been so abrupt. Summer understood injured feelings and fragile egos. She might have handled it better. Yes, she might have—with a weary sigh, she rubbed her temple—if she wasn't feeling a bit injured and fragile herself. Your own fault, she reminded herself; then propping her elbows on the table, she dropped her head into the cupped hands.

Now that it was tomorrow, she had to face the consequences. She'd broken one of her own primary rules. Never become intimate with a business associate. She should have been able to shrug and say rules were made to be broken, but... It worried her more that it wasn't that particular rule that was causing the turmoil, but another she'd broken. Never let anyone who could really matter get too close. Blake, if she didn't draw in the lines now and hold them, could really matter.

Drinking more coffee and wishing for an aspirin, she began to go over everything again. She was certain she'd been casual enough, and clear enough, the night before over the lack of ties and obligations. But when they'd made love again, nothing she'd said had made sense. She shook her head, trying to block that out. That morning they'd been perfectly at ease with each other—two adults preparing for a workday without any morning-after awkwardness. That's what she wanted.

Too many times, she'd seen her mother glowing and bubbling at the beginning of an affair. This man was *the* man—this man was the most exciting, the most considerate, the most poetic. Until the bloom faded. Summer's belief was that if you didn't glow, you didn't fade, and life was a lot simpler.

Yet she still wanted him.

After a brief knock, one of the kitchen staff stuck his head around her door. "Ms. Lyndon, Mr. Cocharan would like to see you in his office."

Summer finished off her rapidly cooling coffee. "Yes? When?"

"Immediately."

She lifted a brow. No one summoned her immediately. People requested her, at her leisure. "I see." Her smile was icy enough to make the messenger shrink back. "Thank you."

When the door closed again she sat perfectly still. These were working hours, she reflected, and she was under contract. It was reasonable and right that he should ask her to come to his office. That was acceptable. But she was still Summer Lyndon—she went to no one immediately.

She spent the next fifteen minutes deliberately dawdling over her papers before she rose. After strolling through the kitchen, and taking the time to check on the contents of a pot or skillet on the way, she went to an elevator. On the ride up, she glanced at her watch, pleased to note that she'd arrive nearly twenty-five minutes after the call. As the doors opened she flicked a speck of lint from the sleeve of her blouse, then sauntered out.

"Mr. Cocharan would like to speak to me?" She gave the words the intonation of a question as she smiled down at the receptionist.

"Yes, Ms. Lyndon, you're to go right through. He's been waiting."

Unsure if the last statement had been censure or warning, Summer continued down the hall to Blake's door. She gave a peremptory knock before going in. "Good morning, Blake."

When she entered, he set aside the file in front of him and leaned back in his chair. "Have trouble finding an elevator?"

"No." Crossing the room, she chose a chair and settled down. He looked, she thought, as he had the first time she'd come into his office—aloof, aristocratic. This then was the perfect level for them to deal on. "This is one of the few hotels that has elevators one doesn't grow old waiting for."

"You're aware what the term immediately means."

"I'm aware of it. I was busy."

"Perhaps I should make it clear that I don't tolerate being kept waiting by an employee."

"And I'll make two things clear," she tossed back. "I'm not merely an employee, but an artist. Secondly, I don't come at the snap of anyone's fingers."

"It's eleven-twenty," Blake began with a mildness Summer instantly suspected. "On a workday. My signature is at the base of your checks. Therefore, you do answer to me."

The faint, telltale flush crept along her cheekbones. "You'd turn my work into something to be measured in dollars and cents and minute by minute—"

"Business is business," he countered, spreading his hands. "I think you were quite clear on that subject."

She'd maneuvered herself successfully toward that particular corner, and he'd given her a helpful shove into it. As a result, her attitude only became more haughty. "You'll notice I *am* here at present. You're wasting time."

As an ice queen, she was magnificent, Blake thought.

He wondered if she realized how a change of expression, a tone of voice, could alter her image. She could be half a dozen women in the course of a day. Whether she knew it or not, Summer had her mother's talent. "I received another dissatisfied call from Max," he told her flatly.

She arched a brow and looked like royalty about to dispense a beheading. "Yes?"

"He objects—strongly—to some of the proposed changes in the menu. Ah—" Blake glanced down at the pad on his desk "—pressed duck seems to be the current problem, though several others were tossed in around it."

Summer sat straighter in her chair, tilting up her chin. "I believe you contracted me to improve the quality of Cocharan House dining."

"I did."

"That is precisely what I'm doing."

The French was beginning to seep into the intonation of her voice, her eyes were beginning to glow. Despite the fact it annoyed him, she was undeniably at her most attractive this way. "I also contracted you to manage the kitchen—which means you should be able to control your staff."

"Control?" She was up, and the ice queeen was now the enraged artist. Her gestures were broad, her movements dramatic. "I would need a whip and chain to control such a narrow-minded, ill-tempered old man who worries only about his own egocentricities. *His* way is the only way. *His* menu is carved in stone, sacrosanct. Pah!" It was a peculiarly French expletive that would have been ridiculous coming from anyone else. From Summer, it was perfect.

Blake tapped his pen against the edge of his desk while he watched the performance. He was nearly tempted to applaud. "Is this what's known as artistic temperament?"

She drew in a breath. Mockery? Would he dare? "You've yet to see true temperament, *mon ami*."

He only nodded. It was tempting to push her into full gear—but business was business. "Max has worked for Cocharan for over twenty-five years." Blake set down the pen and folded his hands—calm, in direct contrast to Summer's temper. "He's loyal and efficient, and obviously sensitive."

"Sensitive." She nearly spat the word. "I give him his prime rib and his precious chicken, but still, he's not satisfied. I will have my pressed duck and my *clamart*. My menu won't read like something from the corner diner."

He wondered if he recorded the conversation and played it back to her, she'd see the absurdity of it. At the moment, though he had to clear his throat to disguise a chuckle, he doubted it. "Exactly," Blake said and kept his face expressionless. "I've no desire to interfere with the menu. The point is, I've no desire to interfere at all."

Far from mollified, Summer tossed her hair behind her shoulders and glared at him. "Then why do you bother me with these trivialities?"

"These trivialities," he countered, "are your problem, not mine. As manager, part of your function is to do simply that. Manage. If your supervisory chef is consistently dissatisfied, you're not doing your job. You're free to make whatever compromises you think necessary."

"Compromises?" Her whole body stiffened. Again, he thought she looked magnificent. "I don't make compromises."

"Being hardheaded won't bring peace to your kitchen."

She let out her breath in a hiss. "Hardheaded!"

"Exactly. Now, the problem of Max is back in your court. I don't want any more phone calls."

In a low, dangerous voice, she let out a stream of French, and though he was certain it was colloquial, he caught the drift. With a toss of her head, she started toward the door.

"Summer."

She turned, and the stance reminded him of one of the mythical female archers whose aim was killingly true. She wouldn't even wince as her arrow went straight through the heart. Ice queen or warrior, he wanted her. "I want to see you tonight."

Her eyes went to slits. "You dare."

"Now that we've tabled the first issue, it's time to go onto the second. We might have dinner."

"You tabled the first issue," she retorted. "I don't table things so easily. Dinner? Have dinner with your account book. That's what you understand."

He rose and approached her without hurry. "We agreed that when we're away from here, we're not business associates."

"We're not away from here." Her chin was still angled. "I'm standing in your office, where I was summoned."

"You won't be standing in my office tonight."

"I stand wherever I choose tonight."

"So tonight," he continued easily, "we won't be business associates. Weren't those your rules?"

Personal and professional, and that tangible line of demarcation. Yes, that's the way she'd wanted it, but it wasn't as easy for her to make the separation as she'd thought it would be. "Tonight," she said with a shrug, "I may be busy."

Blake glanced at his watch. "It's nearly noon. We might consider this lunch hour." He looked back at her, half smiling. Lifting a hand, he tangled it in her hair. "During lunch hour, there's no business between us, Summer. And tonight, I want to be with you." He touched his lips to one corner of her mouth, then the other. "I want to spend long—" his lips slanted over hers softly "—private hours with you."

She wanted it too, why pretend otherwise? She'd never believed in pretenses, only in defenses. In any event, she'd already decided to handle Max and the kitchen in her own way. Linking her hands around his neck, she smiled back at him. "Then tonight, we'll be together. You'll bring the champagne?"

She was softening, but not yielding. Blake found it infinitely more exciting than submission. "For a price."

Her laugh was wicked and warm. "A price?"

"I want you to do something for me you haven't done before."

She tilted her head, then touched the tip of her tongue to her lip. "Such as?"

"Cook for me."

Surprise lit her eyes before the laughter sprang out again. "Cook for you? Well, that's a much different request from what I expected."

"After dinner I might come up with a few others."

"So you want Summer Lyndon to prepare your dinner." She considered it as she drew away. "Perhaps I will, though such a thing usually costs much more than a bottle of champagne. Once in Houston I prepared a meal for an oil man and his new bride. I was paid in stock certificates. Blue chip."

Blake took her hand and brought it to his lips. "I bought you a pizza. Pepperoni."

"That's true. Eight o'clock then. And I'd advise you to eat a very light lunch today." She reached for the door handle, then glanced over her shoulder with a grin. "You do like *Cervelles Braisées?*"

"I might, if I knew what it was."

Still smiling, she opened the door. "Braised calf's brains. *Au revoir.*"

Blake stared at the door. She'd certainly had the last word that time.

The kitchen smelled of cooking and sounded like a drawing room. Strains of Chopin were muted as Summer rolled the boneless breasts of chicken in flour. On the range, the clarified butter was just beginning to deepen in color. Perfect. Stuffed tomatoes were already prepared and waiting in the refrigerator. Buttered peas were just beginning to simmer. She would sauté the potato balls while she sautéed the *suprêmes.*

Timing, of course, was critical. *Suprêmes de Volaille à Brun* had to be done to the instant, even a minute of overcooking and she would, like any temperamental cook, throw them out in disgust. Hot butter sizzled as she slipped the floured chicken into it.

She heard the knock but remained where she was. "It's open," she called out. Meticulously, she adjusted the heat under the skillet. "I'll take the champagne in here."

"*Chérie,* if I'd only thought to bring some."

Stunned, Summer turned and saw Monique, glorious in midnight black and silver, framed by her kitchen doorway. "Mother!" With the kitchen fork still in her hand, Summer closed the distance and enveloped her mother.

With that part bubbling, part sultry laugh she was famous for, Monique kissed both of Summer's cheeks, then drew her daughter back. "You are surprised, *oui?* I adore surprises."

"I'm astonished," Summer countered. "What're you doing in town?"

Monique glanced toward the range. "At the moment, apparently interrupting the preparations for an intimate *tête à tête.*"

"Oh!" Whipping around, Summer dashed back to the skillet and turned the chicken breasts, not a second too soon. "What I meant was, what are you doing in Philadelphia?" She checked the flame again, and was satisfied. "Didn't you once say you'd never set foot in the town of the hardware king again?"

"Time mellows one," Monique claimed with a characteristic flick of the wrist. "And I wanted to see my daughter. You are not so often in Paris these days."

"No, it doesn't seem so, does it?" Summer split her attention between her mother and her range, something she would have done for no one else. "You look wonderful."

Monique's smooth cheeks dimpled. "I feel wonderful, *mignonne*. In six weeks, I start a new picture."

"A new picture." Carefully Summer pressed a finger to the top of the chicken. When they sprang back, she removed them to a hot platter. "Where?"

"In Hollywood. They have pestered me, and at last I give in." Monique's infectious laugh bubbled out again.

"The script is superb. The director himself came to Paris to woo me. Keil Morrison."

Tall, somewhat gangly, intelligent face, fiftyish. Summer had a clear enough picture from the glossies, and from a party for a reigning box office queen where she'd prepared *île Flottante*. From her mother's tone of voice, Summer knew the answer before she asked the question. "And the director?"

"He, too, is superb. How would you feel about a new step poppa, *chérie?*"

"Resigned," Summer said, then smiled. That was too hard a word. "Pleased, of course, if you're happy, Mother." She began to prepare the brown butter sauce while Monique expounded.

"Oh, but he is brilliant and so sensitive! I've never met a man who so understands a woman. At last, I've found my perfect match. The man who finally brings everything I need and want into my life. The man who makes me feel like a woman."

Nodding, Summer removed the skillet from the heat and stirred in the parsley and lemon juice. "When's the wedding?"

"Last week." Monique smiled brilliantly as Summer glanced up. "We were married quietly in a little churchyard outside Paris. There were doves—a good sign. I tore myself away from Keil because I wanted to tell you in person." Stepping forward, she flashed a thin diamond-crusted band. "Elegant, *oui?* Keil doesn't believe in the—how do you say?—ostentatious."

So, for the moment, neither would Monique DuBois Lyndon Smith Clarion Morrison. She supposed, when the news broke, the glossies and trades would have a field day. Monique would eat up every line of publicity. Summer kissed her mother's cheek. "Be happy, *ma mère*."

"I'm ecstatic. You must come to California and meet my Keil, and then—" She broke off as the knock interrupted her. "Ah, this must be your dinner guest. Shall I answer for you?"

"Please." With the tongue caught between her teeth, Summer poured the sauce over the *suprêmes*. She'd serve them within five minutes or dump them down the sink.

When the door opened, Blake was treated to a slightly more voluptuous, slightly more glossy, version of Summer. The candlelight disguised the years and enhanced the classic features. Her lips curved slowly, in the way her daughter's did, as she offered her hand.

"Hello, Summer is busy in the kitchen. I'm her mother, Monique." She paused a moment as their hands met. "But you are familiar to me, yes. But yes!" she continued before Blake could speak. "The Cocharan House. You are the son—B.C.'s son. We've met before."

"A pleasure to see you again, Mademoiselle Dubois."

"This is odd, *oui?* And amusing. I stay in your hotel while in Philadelphia. Already my bags are checked in and my bed turned down."

"You'll let me know personally if there's anything I can do for you while you stay with us."

"Of course." She studied him in the brief but thorough way a woman of experience has. Like mother, like daughter, she mused. Each had excellent taste. "Please, come in. Summer is putting the finishing touches on your meal. I've always admired her skill in the kitchen. Myself, I'm helpless."

"Diabolically helpless," Summer put in as she entered with the hot platter. "She always made sure she burned things beyond recognition, and therefore, no one asked her to cook."

"An intelligent move, to my thinking," Monique said easily. "And now, I'll leave you to your dinner."

"You're welcome to join us, Mother."

"Sweet." Monique framed Summer's face in her hands and kissed both cheeks again. "But I need my beauty rest after the long flight. Tomorrow, we catch up, *non?* Monsieur Cocharan, we will all have dinner at your wonderful hotel before I go?" In her sweeping way, she was at the door. *"Bon appétit."*

"A spectacular woman," Blake commented.

"Yes." Summer went back to the kitchen for the rest of the meal. "She continually amazes me." After placing the vegetables on the table, she picked up her glass. "She's just taken her fourth husband. Shall we drink to them?"

He began to remove the foil from the bottle, but her tone had him pausing. "A bit cynical?"

"Realistic. In any case, I do wish her happiness." When he removed the cork, she took it and absently waved it under her nose. "And I envy her perennial optimism." After both glasses were filled, Summer touched hers to his. "To the new Mrs. Morrison."

"To optimism," Blake countered before he drank.

"If you like," Summer said with a shrug as she sat. She transferred one of the *suprêmes* from the platter to his plate. "Unfortunately the calf's brains looked poor today, so we have to settle for chicken."

"A pity." The first bite was tender and perfect. "Would you like some time off to spend with your mother while she's in town?"

"No, it's not necessary. Mother'll divide her time between shopping and the health spa during the day. She tells me she's about to begin a new film."

"Really." It only took him a minute to put things together. "Morrison—the director?"

"You're very quick," Summer acknowledged, toasting him.

"Summer." He laid a hand over hers. "Do you object?"

She opened her mouth to answer quickly, then thought it over. "No. No, object isn't the word. Her life's her own. I simply can't understand how or why she continually plunges into relationships, tying herself up into marriages which on the average have lasted 5.2 years apiece. Is the word optimism, I wonder, or gullibility?"

"Monique doesn't strike me as a gullible woman."

"Perhaps it's a synonym for romantic."

"No, but romantic might be synonymous with hope. Her way isn't yours."

Yet we both chose lovers from the same bloodline, Summer reminded herself. Just what would Blake's reaction be to that little gem? Keep the past in the past, Summer advised herself. And concentrate on the moment. She smiled at him. "No, it's not. And how do you find my cooking?"

Perhaps it was best to let the subject die, for a time. He needed to ease her over that block gently. "As I find everything about you," Blake told her. "Magnificent."

She laughed as she began to eat again. "It wouldn't be advisable for you to become too used to it. I rarely prepare meals for only compliments."

"That had occured to me. So I brought what I thought was the proper token."

Summer tasted the wine again. "Yes, the champagne is excellent."

"But an inadequate token for a Summer Lyndon meal."

When she shot him a puzzled look, he reached in his inside pocket and drew out a small thin box.

"Ah, presents." Amused, she accepted the box.

"You mentioned a fondness for them." Blake saw the amusement fade as she opened the box.

Inside were diamonds—elegant, even delicate in the form of a slender bracelet. They lay white and regal against the dark velvet of the box.

She wasn't often overwhelmed. Now, she found herself struggling through waves of astonishment. "The meal's too simple for a token like this," she managed. "If I'd known, I'd've prepared something spectacular."

"I wouldn't have thought art ever simple."

"Perhaps not, but..." She looked up, telling herself she wasn't supposed to be moved by such things. They were only pretty stones after all. But her heart was full. "Blake, it's lovely, exquisite. I think you've taken me too seriously when I talk of payments and gifts. I didn't do this tonight for any reason more than I wanted to do it."

"This made me think of you," he said as if she hadn't spoken. "See how cool and haughty the stones are? But..." He slipped the bracelet out of the box. "If you look closely, if you hold it to light, there's warmth, even fire." As he spoke, he let the bracelet dangle from his fingers so that it caught and glittered with the flames from the candles. At that moment, it might have been alive.

"So many dimensions, from every angle you can see something different. A strong stone, and more elegant than any other." Laying the bracelet over her wrist, he clasped it. His gaze lifted and locked on hers. "I didn't do this tonight for any reason other than I wanted to do it."

She was breathless, vulnerable. Would it be like this every time he looked at her? "You begin to worry me," Summer whispered.

The one quiet statement had the need whipping through him almost out of control. He rose, then, drawing her to her feet, crushed her against him before she could agree or protest. "Good."

His mouth wasn't patient this time. There seemed to be a desperate need to hurry, take all, take everything. Hunger that had nothing to do with the meal still unfinished on the table sped through him. She was every desire, and every answer. Biting off an oath, he pulled her to the floor.

This was the whirlwind. She'd never been here before, trapped, exhilarated. Elated by the speed, trembling from the power, Summer moved with him. There was no patience with clothes this time. They were tugged and pulled and tossed aside until flesh could meet flesh. Hot and eager, her body arched against his. She wanted the wind and the fury that only he could bring her.

As his hands sped over her, she delighted in their firmness, in the strength of each individual finger. Her own demands raged equally. Her mouth raced down his throat, teeth nipping, tongue darting. Each unsteady breath told her that she drove him just as he drove her. There was pleasure in that, she discovered. To give passion, and to have it returned to you. Even though her mind clouded, she knew the instant his control snapped.

He was rough, but she delighted in it. She had taken

him beyond the civilized only by being. His mouth was everywhere, tasting, on a crazed journey from her lips to her breasts—lingering—then lower, still lower, until she caught her breath in astonished excitement.

The world peeled away, the floor, the walls, ceiling, then the sky and the ground itself. She was beyond all that, in some spiraling tunnel where only the senses ruled. Her body had no bounds, and she had no control. She moaned, struggling for a moment to pull it back, but the first peak swept her up, tossing her blindly. Even the illusion of reason shattered.

He wanted her like this. Some dark, primitive part of him needed to know he could bring her to this throbbing, mindless world of sensations. She shuddered beneath him, gasping, yet he continued to drive her up again and again with hands and mouth only. He could see her face in the candlelight—those flickers of passion, of pleasure, of need. She was moist and heated. And he was greedy.

Her skin pulsed under him everywhere he touched. When he touched his mouth to the sensitive curve where thigh meets hip, she arched and moaned his name. The sound of it tore through him, pounding in his blood long after there was silence.

"Tell me you want me," he demanded as he raced up her shuddering body again. "And only me."

"I want you." She could think of nothing. She would have given him anything. "Only you."

They joined in a violence that went on and on, then shattered into a crystal contentment.

She lay beneath him knowing she'd never gather the strength to move. There was barely the strength to breathe. It didn't seem to matter. For the first time, she noticed the floor was hard beneath her, but it didn't inspire her to shift to a more comfortable position. Sighing, she closed her eyes. Without too much effort, she could sleep exactly where she was.

Blake moved, only to draw himself up and take his weight on his own arms. She seemed so fragile suddenly, so completely without defense. He hadn't been gentle with her, yet during the loving, she'd seemed so strong, so full of fire.

He gave himself the enjoyment of looking at her while she half dozed, wearing nothing more than diamonds at her wrist. As he watched, her eyes fluttered open and she watched him, catlike from half-lowered lids. Her lips curved. He grinned at her, then kissed them.

"What's for dessert?"

Chapter 9

Unfortunately, Summer was going to need a phone in her office. She preferred to work undisturbed, and phones had a habit of disturbing, but the final menu was almost completed. She was approaching the practical stage of selective marketing. With so many new things—and difficult-to-come-by items—on the bill of fare, she would have to begin the process of finding the best suppliers. It was a job she would have loved to have delegated, but she trusted her own negotiating skills, and her own intuition, more than anyone else's. When choosing a supplier of the best oysters or okra, you needed both.

After tidying her morning's work, Summer gave the stack of papers a satisfied nod. Her instincts about taking this very different sort of job had been valid. She was doing it, and doing it well. The kitchen remodeling was exactly what she'd envisioned, the staff was well trained—and with her carefully screened and selected additions would be only more so. The two new pastry chefs were better than she'd expected them to be. Julio and Georgia had sent a postcard from Hawaii, and it had been taped, with some honor, to the front of a refrigerator. Summer had only had a moment's temptation to throw darts at it.

She'd interfered very little with the setup in the dining room. The lighting there was excellent, the linen impeccable. The food—her food—alone would be all the refreshing the restaurant required.

Soon, she thought, she'd be able to have the new menus printed. She had only to pin down a few prices first and haggle over terms and delivery hours. The next step was the installation of a phone. Choosing to deal with it immediately, she headed for the door. She entered the kitchen from one end as Monique entered from the other. All work ceased.

It amused Summer, and rather pleased her, that her mother had that stunning effect on people. She could see Max standing, staring, with a kitchen spoon in one hand that dripped sauce unheeded onto the floor. And, of course, Monique knew how to make an entrance. It might be said she was a woman made for entrances.

She smiled slowly—it almost appeared hesitantly—as she stepped in, bringing the scent of Paris and spring with her. Her eyes were more gray than her daughter's and, despite the difference in years and experience, held more innocence. Summer had yet to decide if it was calculated or innate.

"Perhaps someone could help me?"

Six men stepped forward. Max came perilously close

to allowing the stock from the spoon to drip on Monique's shoulder. Summer decided it was time to restore order. "Mother." She brushed her way through the circle of bodies surrounding Monique.

"Ah, Summer, just who I was looking for." Even as she took her daughter's hands, she gave the group of male faces a sweeping smile. "How fascinating. I don't believe I've ever been in a hotel kitchen before. It's so—ah—large, *oui?*"

"Please, Ms. Dubois—madame." Unable to contain himself, Max took Monique's hand. "I'd be honored to show you whatever you'd like to see. Perhaps you'd care to sample some of the soup?"

"How kind." Her smile would have melted chocolate at fifty yards. "Of course, I must see everything where my daughter works."

"Daughter?"

Obviously, Summer mused, Max had heard nothing but violins since Monique walked into the room. "My mother," Summer said clearly, "Monique Dubois. This is Max, who's in charge of the kitchen staff."

Mother? Max thought dumbly. But of course the resemblance was so strong he felt like a fool for not seeing it before. There wasn't a Dubois film he hadn't seen at least three times. "A pleasure." Rather gallantly, he kissed the offered hand. "An honor."

"How comforting to know my daughter works with such a gentleman." Though Summer's lip curled, she said nothing. "And I would love to see everything, just everything—perhaps later today?" she added before Max could begin again. "Now, I must steal Summer away for just a short time. Tell me, would it be possible to have some champagne and caviar delivered to my suite?"

"Caviar isn't on the menu," Summer put in with an arch look at Max. "As yet."

"Oh." Prettily, Monique pouted. "I suppose some pâté, or some cheese would do."

"I'll see to it personally. Right away, madame."

"So kind." With a flutter of lashes, Monique slipped her arm through Summer's and swept from the room.

"Laying it on a bit thick," Summer muttered.

Monique threw back her head and gave a bubbling laugh. "Don't be so British, *chérie.* I just did you an enormous service. I learned from the delightful young Cocharan this morning that not only is my daughter an employee at this very hotel—which you didn't bother to tell me—but that you had a few internal problems in the kitchen."

"I didn't tell you because it's only a temporary arrangement, and because it's been keeping me quite busy. As to the internal problems..."

"In the form of one very large Max." Monique glided into the elevator.

"I can handle them just fine by myself," Summer finished.

"But it doesn't hurt to have him impressed by your parentage." After pressing the button for her floor, Monique turned to study her daughter. "So, I look at you in the light and see that you've grown more lovely. That pleases me. If one must have a grown daughter, one should have a beautiful grown daughter."

Laughing, Summer shook her head. "You're as vain as ever."

"I'll always be vain," Monique said simply. "God

willing I'll always have a reason to be. Now—" she motioned Summer out of the elevator "—I've had my morning coffee and croissants, and my massage. I'm ready to hear about this new job of yours and your new lover. From the look of you, both agree with you."

"I believe it's customary for mothers and daughters to discuss new jobs, but not new lovers."

"Pooh." Monique tossed open the door to her suite. "We were never just mother and daughter, but friends, *n'est-çe pas?* And *chère amies* always discuss new lovers."

"The job," Summer said distinctly as she dropped into a butter-soft daybed and brought up her legs, "is working out quite well. I took it originally because it intrigued me and—well because Blake threw LaPointe up in my face."

"LaPointe? The beady-eyed little man you detest so much? The one who told the Paris papers you were his…"

"Mistress," Summer said violently.

"Ah, yes, such a foolish word, mistress, so antiquated, don't you agree? Unless one considers that mistress is the feminine term for master." Monique smiled serenely as she draped herself on the sofa. "And were you?"

"Certainly not. I wouldn't have let him put his pudgy little hands on me if he'd been half the chef he claims to be."

"You might have sued."

"Then more people would've snickered and said where there's smoke there's fire. The little French swine would've loved that." She was gritting her teeth, so she deliberately relaxed her jaw. "Don't get me started on

LaPointe. It was enough that Blake maneuvered me into this job with him as an edge."

"A very clever man—your Blake, that is."

"He's not my Blake," Summer said pointedly. "He's his own man, just as I'm my own woman. You know I don't believe in that sort of thing." The discreet knock had Monique waving negligently and Summer rising to answer. She thought, as the tray of cheeses and fresh fruit and the bucket of iced champagne was wheeled in, that Max must have dashed around like a madman to have it served so promptly. Summer signed the check with a flourish and dismissed the waiter.

Idly Monique inspected the tray before choosing a single cube of cheese. "But you're in love with him."

Busy with the champagne cork, Summer glanced over. "What?"

"You're in love with the young Cocharan."

The cork exploded out, champagne fizzed and geysered from the bottle. Monique merely lifted her glass to be filled. "I'm not in love with him," Summer said with an underlying desperation her mother recognized.

"One is always in love with one's lover."

"No, one is not." With a bit more control, Summer poured the wine. "Affairs don't have to be romantic and flowery. I'm fond of Blake, I respect him. I consider him an attractive, intelligent man and enjoy his company."

"It's possible to say the same of a brother, or an uncle. Even perhaps an ex-husband," Monique commented. "This is not what I think you feel for Blake."

"I feel passion for him," Summer said impatiently. "Passion is not to be equated with love."

"Ah, Summer." Amused, Monique chose a grape. "You can think with your British mind, but you feel with your French heart. This young Cocharan isn't a man any woman would lightly dismiss."

"Like father like son?" The moment it was said, Summer regretted it.

But Monique only smiled, softly, reminiscently. "It occurred to me. I haven't forgotten B.C."

"Nor he you."

Interested, Monique flipped back from the past. "You've met Blake's father?"

"Briefly. When your name was mentioned he looked as though he'd been struck by lightning."

The soft smile became brilliant. "How flattering. A woman likes to believe she remains in a man's memory long after they part."

"You may be flattered. I can tell you I was damned uncomfortable."

"But why?"

"Mother." Restless, Summer rose again and began to pace. "I was attracted to Blake—very much attracted—and he to me. How do you think I felt when I was talking to his father, and both B.C. and I were thinking about the fact that you'd been lovers? I don't think Blake has any idea. If he did, do you realize how awkward the situation would be?"

"Why?"

On a long breath, Summer turned to her mother again. "B.C. was and is married to Blake's mother. I get the impression Blake's rather fond of his mother, and of his father."

"What does that have to do with it?" Monique's gesture was typically French—a slight shrug, a slight lifting of the hand, palm out. "I was fond of his father too. Listen to me," she continued before Summer could retort. "B.C. was always in love with his wife. I knew that then. We consoled each other, made each other laugh in what was a miserable time for both of us. I'm grateful for it, not ashamed of it. Neither should you be."

"I'm not ashamed." Frustrated, Summer dragged a hand through her hair. "I don't ask you to be, but— damn it, Mother, it's awkward."

"Life often is. You'll remind me there are rules, and so there are." She threw back her head and took on the regal haughtiness her daughter had inherited. "I don't play by the rules, and I don't apologize."

"Mother." Cursing herself, Summer went and knelt beside the couch. "I wasn't criticizing you. It's only that what's right for you, what's good for you, isn't right and good for me."

"You think I don't know that? You think I'd have you live my life?" Monique laid a hand on her daughter's head. "Perhaps I've seen more deep happiness than you've seen. But I've also seen more deep despair. I can't wish you the first without knowing you'd face the second. I want for you only what you wish for yourself."

"Some things you're afraid to wish for."

"No, but some things are more carefully wished for. I will give you some advice." She patted Summer's head, then drew her up to sit on the sofa. "When you were a little girl, I gave you none because small children have always been a mystery to me. When you grew up, you wouldn't have listened to any. Perhaps now we've come to the point between mother and daughter when each understands the other is intelligent."

With a laugh, Summer picked a strawberry from the tray. "All right, I'll listen."

"It does not make you less of a woman to need a

man." When Summer frowned, she continued. "To need one to exist, yes, this is nonsense. To need one to give one scope and importance, this is dishonest. But to need a man, one man, to bring joy and passion? This is life."

"There can be joy and passion in a woman's life without a man."

"Some joy, some passion," Monique agreed. "Why settle for some? What is it that you prove by cutting off what is a natural need? Perhaps it's a foolish woman who takes a different man as a husband, four times. Again, I don't apologize, but only remind you that Summer Lyndon is not Monique Dubois. We look for different things in different ways. But we are both women. I don't regret my choices."

With a sigh, Summer laid her head on her mother's shoulder. "I want to be able to say that for myself. I've always thought I could."

"You're an intelligent woman. What choice you make will be right for you."

"My greatest fear has always been to make a mistake."

"Perhaps your greatest fear is your greatest mistake." She touched Summer's cheek again. "Come, pour me some more champagne. I'll tell you of my Keil."

When Summer returned to the kitchen, her mind was still playing back her conversation with Monique. It was rare that Monique pressed her for details about her personal life, and rarer still for her to offer advice. It was true that most of the hour they'd spent together had been devoted to a listing of Keil Morrison's virtues, but in those first few moments, Monique had said things designed to make Summer think—designed to make her begin to doubt her own list of priorities.

But when she approached the swinging doors leading into the kitchen, and the sounds of the argument met her, she knew her thinking would have to wait.

"My casserole's perfect."

"Too much milk, too little cheese."

"You've never been able to admit that my casseroles are better than yours."

Perhaps the scene was laughable—huge Max and little Charlie, the undersized Korean cook who came no higher than his superior's breastbone. They stood, glaring at each other, while both of them held a solid grip on a spinach casserole. It might have been laughable, Summer thought wearily, if the rest of the kitchen staff hadn't already been choosing up sides while the luncheon orders were ignored.

"Inferior work," Max retorted. He'd yet to forgive Charlie for being out sick three days running.

"Your casseroles are always inferior work. Mine are perfect."

"Too much milk," Max said solidly. "Not enough cheese."

"Problem?" Summer stepped up, lining herself between them.

"This scrawny little man who masquerades as a cook is trying to pass this mass of soggy leaves off as a spinach casserole." Max tried to tug the glass dish away and found that the scrawny little man was surprisingly strong.

"This big lump of dough who calls himself a chef is jealous because I know more about vegetables than he does."

Summer bit down hard on her bottom lip. Damn it, it was funny, but the timing was all wrong. "Perhaps the rest of you might get back to work," she began coolly, "before what clientele we have left in the dining room evacuates to the nearest golden arches for decent service. Now…" She turned back to the two opponents. Any moment, she decided, there'd be bared teeth and snarls. "This, I take it, is the casserole in question."

"The dish is a casserole," Max tossed back. "What's in it is garbage." He tugged again.

"Garbage!" The little cook squealed in outrage, then curled his lip. "Garbage is what you pass off as prime rib. The only thing edible on the plate is the tiny sprig of parsley you part with." He tugged back.

"Gentlemen, might I ask a question?" Without waiting for an answer, she touched a finger to the dish. It was still warm, but cooling fast. "Has anyone tasted the casserole?"

"I don't taste poison." Max gave the dish another yank. "I pour poison down the sink."

"I wouldn't have this—this ox taste one spoonful of my spinach." Charlie yanked right back. "He'd contaminate it."

"All right, children," Summer said in sweet tones that had both men's annoyance turning on her. "Why don't I do the testing?"

Both men eyed each other warily. "Tell him to let go of my spinach," Charlie insisted.

"Max—"

"He lets go first. I'm his superior."

"Charlie—"

"The only thing superior is his weight." And the tug-of-war began again.

Out of patience, Summer tossed up her hands. "All right, *enough!*"

It might have been the shock of having her raise her voice, something she'd never done in the kitchen—or it might have been that the dish itself was becoming slippery from so much handling. Either way, at her word, the dish fell out of both men's hands with force. It struck the edge of the counter, shattering, so that glass flew even before the casserole and its contents hit the floor. In unison, Max and Charlie erupted with abuse and accusations.

Summer, distracted by the pain in her right arm, glanced down and saw the blood begin to seep from a four-inch gash. Amazed, she stared at it for a full three seconds while her mind completely rejected the idea that blood, her blood, could pour out so quickly.

"Excuse me," she managed at length. "Do you think the two of you could finish this round after I stop bleeding to death?"

Charlie looked over, a torrent of abuse trembling on his tongue. Instead, he stared wide-eyed at the wound, then broke into an excited ramble of Korean.

"If you'd stop interfering," Max began, even as he caught sight of the blood running down Summer's arm. He blanched, then to everyone's surprise, moved like lightning. Grabbing a clean cloth, he pressed it against the gash in Summer's arm. "Sit," he ordered and nudged her onto a kitchen stool. "You," he bellowed at no one in particular, "clean up this mess." Already he was fashioning a tourniquet. "Relax," he said to Summer with unaccustomed gentleness. "I want to see how deep it is."

Giddy, she nodded and kept her eyes trained on the steam from a pot across the room. It didn't really hurt so very much, she thought as her vision blurred then refocused. She'd probably imagined all that blood.

"What the hell's going on in here?" She heard Blake's voice vaguely behind her. "You can hear the commotion in here clear out to the dining room." He strode over, intending to give both Summer and Max the choice of unemployment or peaceful coexistence. The red-stained cloth stopped him cold. "Summer?"

"An accident," Max said hurriedly while Summer shook her head to clear it. "The cut's deep—she'll need stitches."

Blake was already grabbing the cloth from Max and pushing him aside. "Summer. How the hell did this happen?"

She focused on his face and registered concern and perhaps temper in his eyes before everything started to swim again. Then she made the mistake of looking down at her arm. "Spinach casserole," she said foolishly before she slid from the stool in a dead faint.

The next thing she heard was an argument. *Isn't this where I came in?* she thought vaguely. It only took her a moment to recognize Blake's voice, but the other, female and dry, was a stranger.

"I'm staying."

"Mr. Cocharan, you aren't a relative. It's against hospital policy for you to remain while we treat Ms. Lyndon. Believe me, it's only a matter of a few stitches."

A few stitches? Summer's stomach rolled. She didn't like to admit it, but when it came to needles—the kind the medical profession liked to poke into flesh—she was a complete coward. And if her sense of smell wasn't playing tricks on her, she knew where she was. The odor of antiseptics was much too recognizable. Perhaps if she just sat up and quietly walked away, no one would notice.

When she did sit up, she found herself in a small, curtained examining room. Her gaze lit on a tray that held all the shiny, terrifying tools of the trade.

Blake caught the movement out of the corner of his eye, and was beside her. "Summer, just relax."

Moistening her lips, she studied the room again. "Hospital?"

"Emergency Room. They're going to fix your arm."

She managed a smile, but kept her gaze locked on the tray. "I'd just as soon not." When she started to swing her legs over the side of the examining table, the doctor was there to stop her.

"Lie still, Ms. Lyndon."

Summer stared back at the tough, lined female face. She had frizzy hair the color of a peach, and wire-rim glasses. Summer gauged her own strength against the doctor's and decided she could win. "I'm going home now," she said simply.

"You're going to lie right there and get that arm sewed up. Now be quiet."

Well, perhaps if she recruited an ally. "Blake?"

"You need stitches, love."

"I don't want them."

"Need," the doctor corrected, briskly. "Nurse!" While she scrubbed her hands in a tiny sink, she looked back over her shoulder. "Mr. Cocharan, you'll have to wait outside."

"No." Summer managed to struggle back into a sitting position. "I don't know you," she told the white-coated woman at the sink. "And I don't know her," she added when the nurse pushed passed the curtains. "If

I'm going to have to sit here while you sew up my arm with cat gut or whatever it is you use, I'm going to have someone here that I know." She tightened her grip on Blake's hand. "I know him." She lay back down but kept the death hold on Blake's hand.

"Very well." Recognizing both a strong will and basic fear, the doctor gave in. "Just turn your head away," she advised. "This won't take long. I've already used yards of cat gut today."

"Blake." Summer took a deep breath and looked straight into his eyes. She wouldn't think about what the two women on the other side of the table were doing to her arm. "I have a confession to make. I don't deal very well with this sort of thing." She swallowed again when she felt the pressure on her skin. "I have to be tranquilized to get through a dental appointment."

Out of the corner of his eye, he saw the doctor take the first stitch. "We almost had to do the same thing for Max." He ran his thumb soothingly over his knuckles. "After this, you could tell him you're going to put in a wood-burning stove and a hearth and he wouldn't give you any trouble."

"A hell of a way to get cooperation." She winced, felt her stomach roll and swallowed desperately. "Talk to me—about anything."

"We should take a weekend, soon, and go to the beach. Some place quiet, right on the ocean."

It was a good image, she struggled to focus on it. "Which ocean?"

"Any one you want. We'll do nothing for three days but lie in the sun, make love."

The young nurse glanced over, and a sigh escaped before the doctor caught her eye.

"As soon as I'm back from Rome. All you have to do is find some little island in the Pacific while I'm gone. I'd like a few palm trees and friendly natives."

"I'll look into it."

"In the meantime," the doctor put in as she snipped off a length of bandage, "keep this dressing dry, have it changed every third day and come back in two weeks to have the stitches removed. A nasty slice," she added, giving the bandage a last professional adjustment. "But you'll live."

Cautiously Summer turned her head. The wound was now covered in the sterile white gauze. It looked neat, trim and somehow competent. The nausea faded instantly. "I thought they made the stitches so they dissolved."

"It's a nice arm." The doctor rinsed off her hands in the sink. "We wouldn't want a scar on it. I'll give you a prescription for some pain pills."

Summer set her jaw. "I won't take them."

With a shrug, the doctor dried her hands. "Suit yourself. Oh, and you might try the Solomon Islands off New Guinea." Whipping back the curtain, she strode out.

"Quite a lady," Summer muttered as Blake helped her off the table. "Terrific bedside manner. I can't think why I don't hire her as my personal physician."

The spunk was back, Blake thought with a grin, but kept a supportive arm around her waist. "She was exactly what you needed. You didn't need any more sympathy, or worry, than you were getting from me."

She frowned up at him as he led her into the parking lot. "When I bleed," she corrected, "I need a great deal of sympathy and worry."

"What you need—" he kissed her forehead before

opening the car door "—is a bed, a dark room and a few hours' rest."

"I'm going back to work," she corrected. "The kitchen's probably chaos, and I have a long list of phone calls to make—as soon as you arrange to have a phone hooked up for me."

"You're going home, to bed."

"I've stopped bleeding," Summer reminded him. "And though I admit I'm a complete baby when it comes to blood and needles and doctors in white coats, that's done now. I'm fine."

"You're pale." He stopped at a light and turned to her. It wasn't entirely clear to him how he'd gotten through the last hour himself. "Your arm's certainly throbbing now, or soon will be. I make it a policy—whenever one of my staff faints on the job, they have the rest of the day off."

"Very liberal and humanitarian of you. I wouldn't have fainted if I hadn't looked."

"Home, Summer."

She sat up, folded her hands and took a deep breath. Her arm *was* throbbing, but she wouldn't have admitted it now for anything. With the new ache, and annoyance, it was easy to forget that she'd clung to his hand a short time before. "Blake, I realize I've mentioned this before, but sometimes it doesn't hurt to reiterate. I don't take orders."

Silence reigned in the car for almost a full minute. Blake turned west, away from Cocharan House and toward Summer's apartment building.

"I'll just take a cab," she said lightly.

"What you'll take is a couple of aspirin, right before I draw the shades and tuck you into bed."

God, that sounded like heaven. Ignoring the image, she set her chin. "Just because I depended on you—a little—while that woman was plying her needle, doesn't mean I need a keeper."

There was a way to convince her to do as he wanted. Blake considered it. Perhaps the direct way was the best way. "I don't suppose you noticed how many stitches she put in your arm."

"No." Summer looked out the window.

"I did. I counted them as she sewed. Fifteen. You didn't notice the size of the needle, either?"

"No." Pressing a hand to her stomach she glared at him. "Dirty pool, Blake."

"If it works…" Then he slipped a hand over hers. "A nap, Summer. I'll stay with you if you like."

How was she supposed to deal with him when he went from being kind, to filthy, to gentle? How was she supposed to deal with herself when all she really wanted was to curl up beside him where she knew it would be safe and warm? "I'll rest." All at once, she felt she needed to, badly, but it no longer had anything to do with her arm. If he continually stirred her emotions like this, the next few months were going to be impossible. "Alone," she finished firmly. "You have enough to do back at the hotel."

When he pulled up in front of her building, she put out a hand to stop him from turning off the engine. "No, you needn't bother to come up. I'll go to bed, I promise." Because she could feel him tense with an objection, she smiled and squeezed his hand. I have to go up alone, she realized. If he came with her now, everything could change. "I'm going to take those aspirin, turn on the stereo and lie down. I'd feel better if you'd go by the kitchen and make certain everything's all right there."

He studied her face. Her skin was pale, her eyes weary. He wanted to stay with her, have her hold onto him for support again. Even as he sat beside her, he could feel the distance she was putting between them. No, he wouldn't allow that—but for now, she needed rest more than she needed him.

"If that's what you want. I'll call you tonight."

Leaning over, she kissed his cheek, then climbed from the car quickly. "Thanks for holding my hand."

Chapter 10

It was beginning to grate on her nerves. It wasn't as though Summer didn't enjoy attention. More than enjoying it, she'd come to expect it as a matter of course in her career. It wasn't as if she didn't enjoy being catered to. That was something she'd developed a taste for early on, growing up in households with servants. But as any good cook knows, sugar has to be dispensed with a careful hand.

Monique had extended her stay a full week, claiming that she couldn't possibly leave Philadelphia while Summer was still recovering from an injury. The more Summer tried to play down the entire incident of her arm and the stitches, the more Monique looked at her with admiration and concern. The more admiration and concern she received, the more Summer worried about that next visit to the doctor.

Though it wasn't in character, Monique had gotten into the habit of coming by Summer's office every day with healing cups of tea and bowls of healthy soup—then standing over her daughter until everything was consumed.

For the first few days, Summer had found it rather sweet—though tea and soup weren't regulars on her diet. As far as she could remember, Monique had always been loving and certainly kind, but never maternal. For this reason alone, Summer drank the tea, ate the soup and swallowed complaints along with them. But as it continued, and as Monique consistently interrupted the final stages of her planning, Summer began to lose patience. She might have been able to tolerate Monique's overreaction and mothering, if it hadn't been for the same treatment by the kitchen staff, headed by Max.

She was permitted to do nothing for herself. If she started to brew a pot of coffee, someone was there, taking over, insisting that she sit and rest. Every day at precisely noon, Max himself brought her in a tray with the luncheon speciality of the day. Poached salmon, lobster soufflé, stuffed eggplant. Summer ate—because like her mother, he hovered over her—while she had visions of a bacon double cheeseburger with a generous side order of onion rings.

Doors were opened for her, concerned looks thrown her way, conciliatory phrases heaped on her until she wanted to scream. Once when she'd been unnerved enough to snap that she had some stitches in her arm, not a terminal illness, she'd been brought yet another soothing cup of tea—with a saucer of plain vanilla cookies.

They were killing her with kindness.

Every time she thought she'd reached her limit, Blake managed to level things for her again. He wasn't callous of her injury or even unkind, but he certainly wasn't treating her as though she were the star attraction at a deathbed.

He had an uncanny instinct for choosing the right time to phone or drop in on the kitchen. He was there, calm when she needed calm, ordered when she yearned for order. He demanded things of her when everyone else insisted she couldn't lift a finger for herself. When he annoyed her, it was in an entirely different way, a way that tested and stretched her abilities rather than smothered them.

And with Blake, Summer didn't have that hampering guilt about letting loose with her temper. She could shout at him knowing she wouldn't see the bottomless patience in his eyes that she saw in Max's. She could be unreasonable and not be worried that his feelings would be hurt like her mother's.

Without realizing it, she began to see him as a pillar of solidity and sense in a world of nonsense. And, for perhaps the first time in her life, she felt an intrinsic need for that pillar.

Along with Blake, Summer had her work to keep her temper and her nerve ends under some kind of control. She poured herself into it. There were long sessions with the printer to design the perfect menu—an elegant slate gray with the words COCHARAN HOUSE embossed on the front—thick creamy parchment paper inside listing her final choices in delicate script. Then there were the room service menus that would go into each unit—not quite so luxurious, perhaps, but Summer saw to it that they were distinguished in their own right.

She talked for hours with suppliers, haggling, demanding and enjoying herself more than she would ever have guessed, until she got precisely the terms she wanted.

It gave her a glow of success—perhaps not the flash she felt on completing some spectacular dish—but a definite glow. She found that in a different way, it was equally satisfying.

And it was unpardonably annoying to be told, after the completion of a particularly long and successful negotiation, that she should take a little nap.

"Chérie." Monique glided into the storage room, just as Summer hung up the phone with the butcher, bearing the inevitable cup of herbal tea. "It's time you had a break. You mustn't push yourself so."

"I'm fine, Mother." Glancing at the tea, Summer sincerely hoped she wouldn't gag. She wanted something carbonated and cold, preferably loaded with caffeine. "I'm just going over the contracts with the suppliers. It's a bit complicated and I've still got one or two calls to make."

If she'd hoped that would be a gentle hint that she needed privacy to work, she was disappointed. "Too complicated when you've already worked so many hours today," Monique insisted and took a seat on the other side of the desk. "You forget, you've had a shock."

"I cut my arm," Summer said with strained patience.

"Fifteen stitches," Monique reminded her, then frowned with disapproval as Summer reached for a cigarette. "Those are so bad for your health, Summer."

"So's nervous tension," she muttered, then doggedly cleared her throat. "Mother, I'm sure Keil's missing you desperately just as you must be missing him. You shouldn't be away from your new husband for so long."

"Ah, yes." Monique sighed and looked dreamily at the ceiling. "For a new bride, a day away from her husband is like a week, a week can be a year." Abruptly, she pressed her hands together, shaking her head. "But my Keil, he is the most understanding of men. He knows I must stay when my daughter needs me."

Summer opened her mouth, then shut it again. Diplomacy, she reminded herself. Tact. "You've been wonderful," she began, a bit guiltily, because it was true. "I can't tell you how much I appreciate all the time, all the trouble, you've taken over this past week or so. But my arm's nearly healed now. I'm really fine. I feel terribly guilty holding you here when you should be enjoying your honeymoon."

With her light, sexy laugh, Monique waved a hand. "My sweet, you'll learn that a honeymoon isn't a time or a trip, but a state of mind. Don't concern yourself with that. Besides, do you think I could leave before they take those nasty stitches out of your arm?"

"Mother—" Summer felt the hitch in her stomach and reached for the tea in defense.

"No, no. I wasn't there for you when the doctor treated you, but—" here, her eyes filled and her lips trembled "—I will be by your side when she removes them—one at a time."

Summer had an all-too-vivid picture of herself lying once again on the examining table, the tough-faced doctor over her. Monique, frail in black, would be standing by, dabbing at her eyes with a lacy handkerchief. She wasn't sure if she wanted to scream, or just drop her head between her knees.

"Mother, you'll have to excuse me. I've just remembered, I have an appointment with Blake in his office."

Without waiting for an answer, Summer dashed from the storage room.

Almost immediately Monique's eyes were dry and her lips curved. Leaning back in her chair, she laughed in delight. Perhaps she hadn't always known just what to do with a daughter when Summer had been a child, but now... Woman to woman, she knew precisely how to nudge her daughter along. And she was nudging her along to Blake, where Monique had no doubt her strong-willed, practical and much-loved daughter belonged.

"À l'amour," she said and lifted the tea in a toast.

It didn't matter to Summer that she didn't have an appointment, only that she see Blake, talk to him and restore her sanity. "I have to see Mr. Cocharan," she said desperately as she pushed right past the receptionist.

"But, Ms. Lyndon—"

Heedless, Summer dashed through the outer office and tossed open his door without knocking. "Blake!"

He lifted a brow, motioned her inside, then continued with his telephone conversation. She looked, he thought, as if she were on the last stages of a manhunt, and on the wrong side of the bloodhounds. His first instinct might have been to comfort, to soothe, but common sense prevailed. It was all too obvious that she was getting enough of that, and detesting it.

Frustrated, she whirled around the room. Nervous energy flowed from her. She stalked to the window, then, restless, turned away from the view. Ultimately she walked to the bar and poured herself a defiant portion of vermouth. The moment she heard the phone click back on the cradle, she turned to him.

"Something has to be done!"

"If you're going to wave that around," he said mildly,

indicating her glass, "you'd better drink some first. It'
be all over you."

Scowling, Summer took a long sip. "Blake, m
mother has to go back to California."

"Oh?" He finished scrawling a memo. "Well, we'
be sorry to see her go."

"*No!* No, she has to go back, but she won't. She i
sists on staying here and nursing me into catatonia. An
Max," she continued before he could comment. "Som
thing has to be done about Max. Today—today it wa
shrimp salad and avocado. I can't take much more." Sh
sucked in a breath, then continued in a dazed ramblin
of complaints. "Charlie looks at me as if I were Joan
Arc, and the rest of the kitchen staff is just as bad—
not worse. They're driving me crazy."

"I can see that."

The tone of voice had her pacing coming to a quic
halt and her eyes narrowing. "Don't aim that cool
amused smile at me."

"Was I smiling?"

"Or that innocent look, either," she snapped back
"You were smiling inside, and nervous breakdowns ar
definitely not funny."

"You're absolutely right." He folded his hands o
the desk. "Why don't you sit down and start from th
beginning."

"Listen—" She dropped into a chair, sipped the ve
mouth, then was up and pacing again. "It's not that
don't appreciate kindness, but there's a saying abou
too much of a good thing."

"I think I've heard that."

Ignoring him, she plunged on. "You can ruin

dessert with too much pampering, too much attention, you know."

He nodded. "The same's sometimes said of a child."

"Just stop trying to be cute, damn it."

"It doesn't seem to take any effort." He smiled. She scowled.

"Are you listening to me?" she demanded.

"Every word."

"I wasn't cut out to be pampered, that's all. My mother—every day it's cup after cup of herbal tea until I have visions of sloshing when I walk. 'You should rest, Summer. You're not strong yet, Summer.' Damn it, I'm strong as an ox!"

He took out a cigarette, enjoying the show. "I'd've said so myself."

"And Max! The man's positively smothering me with good will. Lunch every day, twelve on the dot." With a groan, she pressed a hand against her stomach. "I haven't had a real meal in a week. I keep getting these insane cravings for tacos, but I'm so full of tea and lobster bisque I can't do anything about it. If one more person tells me to put up my feet and rest, I swear, I'm going to punch them right in the mouth."

Blake scrutinized the end of his cigarette. "I'll make sure I don't mention it."

"That's just it, you don't." She spun around the desk, then sat on it directly in front of him. "You're the only one around here who's treated me like a normal person since this ridiculous thing happened. You even shouted at me yesterday. I appreciate that."

"Think nothing of it."

With a half laugh, she took his hand. "I'm serious. I feel foolish enough for being so careless as to let an accident like that happen in my kitchen. You don't constantly remind me of it with pats on the head and concerned looks."

"I understand you." Blake linked his fingers with hers. "I've been making a study of you almost from the first instant we met."

The way he said it had her pulse fluctuating. "I'm not an easy person to understand."

"No?"

"I don't always understand."

"Let me tell you about Summer Lyndon, then." He measured her hand against his before he linked their fingers. "She's a beautiful woman, a bit spoiled from her upbringing and her own success." He smiled when her brows drew together. "She's strong and opinionated and intensely feminine without being calculating. She's ambitious and dedicated with a skill for concentration that reminded me once of a surgeon. And she's romantic, though she'll claim otherwise."

"That's not true," Summer began.

"She listens to Chopin when she works. Even while she chooses to have an office in a storage room, she keeps roses on her desk."

"There're reasons why—"

"Stop interrupting," he told her simply, and with a huff, she subsided. "What fears she has are kept way below the surface because she doesn't like to admit to having any. She's tough enough to hold her own against anyone, and compassionate enough to tolerate an uncomfortable situation rather than hurt someone's feelings. She's controlled, and she's passionate. She has a taste for the best champagne and junk food. There's no one I've known who's annoyed me quite so much, or who I'd trust quite so implicitly."

She let out a long breath. It wasn't the first time he'd put her in a position where words were hard to come by. "Not an entirely admirable woman."

"Not entirely," Blake agreed. "But a fascinating one."

She smiled, then sat on his lap. "I've always wanted to do this," she murmured, snuggling. "Sit on some big corporate executive's lap in an elegant office. I'm suddenly quite sure I'd rather be fascinating than admirable."

"I prefer you that way." He kissed her, but lightly.

"You've chased off my nervous breakdown again."

He brushed at her hair, thinking he was close—very close—to winning her completely. "We aim to please."

"Now if I just didn't have to go back down and face all that sugar." She sighed. "And all those earnestly concerned faces."

"What would you rather do?"

Linking her hands around his neck, she laughed and drew back. "If I could do anything I wanted?"

"Anything."

Thoughtfully she ran her tongue over her teeth then grinned. "I'd like to go to the movies, a perfectly dreadful movie, and eat pounds of buttered popcorn with too much salt."

"Okay." He gave her a friendly slap on the bottom. "Let's go find a dreadful movie."

"You mean now?"

"Right now."

"But it's only four o'clock."

He kissed her, then hauled her to her feet. "It's known as playing hookey. I'll fill you in on the way."

* * *

She made him feel young, foolishly young and irresponsible, sitting in a darkened corner of the theater with a huge barrel of popcorn on his lap and her hand in his. When he looked back over his life, Blake could remember no time when he hadn't felt secure—but irresponsible? Never that. Having a multimillion dollar business behind him had ingrained in him a very demanding sense of obligation. However much he'd benefited growing up, having enough and always the best, there'd always been the unspoken pressure to maintain that standard—for himself, and for the family business.

Because he'd always taken that position seriously, he was a cautious man. Impulsiveness had never been part of his style. But perhaps that was changing a bit—with Summer. He'd had the impulse to give her whatever she'd wanted that afternoon. If it had been a trip to Paris to eat supper at Maxim's, he'd have arranged it then and there. Then again, he should have known that a box of popcorn and a movie were more her style.

It was that style—the contrast of elegance and simplicity—that had drawn him in from the first. He knew, without question, that there would never be another woman who would move him in the same way.

Summer knew it had been days since she had fully relaxed. In fact, she hadn't been able to relax at all since the accident with anyone but Blake. He'd given her support, but more important, he'd given her space. They hadn't been together often over the past week, and she knew Blake was closing the deal with the Hamilton chain. They'd both been busy, preoccupied, pressured, yet when they were alone and away from Cocharan House, they didn't talk business. She knew how hard he'd worked on this purchase—the negotiations, the paperwork, the endless meetings. Yet he'd put all that aside—for her.

Summer leaned toward him. "Sweet."

"Hmm?"

"You," she whispered under the dialogue on the screen. "You're sweet."

"Because I found a dreadful movie?"

With a chuckle, she reached for more popcorn. "It is dreadful, isn't it?"

"Terrible, which is why the theater's nearly empty. I like it this way."

"Antisocial?"

"No, it just makes it easier—" leaning closer, he caught the lobe of her ear between his teeth "—to indulge in this sort of thing."

"Oh." Summer felt the thrill of pleasure start at her toes and climb upward.

"And this sort of thing." He nipped at the cord of her neck, enjoying her quick little intake of breath. "You taste better than the popcorn."

"And it's excellent popcorn." Summer turned her head so that her mouth could find his.

So warm, so right. Summer felt it was almost possible to say that her lips were made to fit his. If she'd believed in such things… If she'd believed in such things, she might have said that they'd been meant to find each other at this stage of their lives. To meet, to clash, to attract, to merge. One man to one woman, enduringly. When they were close, when his lips were heated on hers, she could almost believe it. She wanted to believe it.

He ran a hand down her hair. Soft, fresh. Just the

touch of that and no more could make him want her unreasonably. He never felt stronger than when he was with her. And he never felt more vulnerable. He didn't hear the explosion of sound and music from the speakers. She didn't see the sudden kaleidoscope of color and movement on the screen. Hampered by the small seats, they shifted in an effort to get that much closer.

"Excuse me." The young usher, who had the job until September when school started up again, shifted his feet in the aisle. Then he cleared his throat. "Excuse me."

Glancing up, Blake noticed that the house lights were on and the screen was blank. After a surprised moment, Summer pressed her mouth against his shoulder to muffle a laugh.

"Movie's over," the boy said uncomfortably. "We have to—ah—clear the theater after every show." Glancing at Summer, he decided any man might lose interest in a movie with someone like her around. Then Blake stood, tall, broad shouldered, with that one aloofly raised eyebrow. The boy swallowed. And a lot of guys didn't like to be interrupted.

"Ah—that's the rule, you know. The manager—"

"And reasonable enough," Blake interrupted when he noticed the boy's Adam's apple working.

"We'll just take the popcorn along," Summer said as she rose. She tucked the barrel under one arm and slid her other through Blake's. "Have a nice evening," she told the usher over her shoulder as they walked out.

When they were outside, she burst out laughing. "Poor child, he thought you were going to manhandle him."

"The thought crossed my mind, but only very briefly."

"Long enough for him to get nervous about it." After

climbing into the car, she placed the popcorn in her lap. "You know what he thought, don't you?"

"What?"

"That we were having an illicit affair." Leaning over, she nipped at Blake's ear. "The kind where your wife thinks you're at the office, and my husband thinks I'm shopping."

"Why didn't we go to a motel?"

"That's where we're going now." Nibbling on popcorn again, she sent him a wicked glance. "Though I think in our case we might substitute my apartment."

"I'm willing to be flexible. Summer…" He drew her against his side as they breezed through a light. "Just what was that movie about?"

Laughing, she let her head lay against his shoulder. "I haven't the vaguest idea."

Later, they lay naked in her bed, the curtains open to let in the light, the windows up to let in the breeze. From the apartment below came the repetitive sound of scales being played, a bit unsteadily, on the piano. Perhaps she'd dozed for a short time, because the sunlight seemed softer now, almost rosy. But she wasn't in any hurry for night to fall.

The sheets were warm and wrinkled from their bodies. The air was ripe with supper smells—grilling pork from the piano teacher's apartment, spaghetti sauce from the newlyweds next door. The breeze carried the mix of both, appealingly.

"It's nice," Summer murmured, with her head nestled in the curve of her lover's shoulder. "Just being here like this, knowing that anything there is to do can be done just as well tomorrow. You probably haven't played hookey enough." She was quite sure she hadn't.

"If I did, the business would suffer and the board would begin to grumble. Complaining's one of their favorite things."

Absently, she rubbed the bottom of her foot over the top of one of his. "I haven't asked you about the Hamilton chain because I thought you probably got enough of that at the office, and from the press, but I'd like to know if you got what you wanted."

He thought about reaching for a cigarette then decided it wasn't worth the effort. "I wanted those hotels. As it turned out, the deal satisfied all parties in the end. You can't ask for more than that."

"No." Thoughtfully, she rolled over so that she could look at him directly. Her hair brushed over his chest. "Why did you want them? Is it the acquisition itself, the property or just a matter of enjoying the wheeling and dealing? The strategy of negotiations?"

"It's all of that. Part of the enjoyment in business is setting up deals, working out the flaws, following through until you've gotten what you were aiming for. In some ways it's not that different from art."

"Business isn't art," Summer corrected archly.

"There are parallels. You set up an idea, work out the flaws, then follow through until you've created what you wanted."

"You're being logical again. In art you use the emotion in equal parts with the mind. You can't do that in business." Her shrug was typically French. Somehow she became more French whenever her craft was under discussion. "This is all facts and figures."

"You left out instinct. Facts and figures aren't enough without that."

She frowned, considering. "Perhaps, but you wouldn't follow instinct over a solid set of facts."

"Even a solid set of facts varies according to the circumstances and the players." He was thinking of her now, and himself. Reaching up, he tucked her hair behind her ear. "Instincts are very often more reliable."

And she was thinking of him now, and herself. "Often more," Summer murmured, "but not always more. That leaves room for failure."

"No amount of planning, no amount of facts, precludes failure."

"No." She laid her head on his shoulder again, trying to ward off the little trickle of panic that was trying to creep in.

He ran a hand down her back. She was still so cautious, he thought. A little more time, a little more room—a change of subject. "I have twenty new hotels to oversee, to reorganize," he began. "That means twenty more kitchens that have to be studied and graded. I'll need an expert."

She smiled a little as she lifted her head again. "Twenty is a very demanding and time-consuming number."

"Not for the best."

Tilting her head, she looked down her straight, elegant nose. "Naturally not, but the best is very difficult to come by."

"The best is currently very soft and very naked in my arms."

Her lips curved slowly, the way he most enjoyed them. "Very true. But this, I think, is not a negotiating table."

"You've a better idea how to spend the evening?"

She ran a fingertip along his jawline. "Much better."

He caught her hand in his and, drawing her finger into his mouth, nipped lightly. "Show me."

The idea appealed, and excited. It seemed that whenever they made love she was quickly dominated by her own emotions and his skill. This time, she would set the pace, and in her own time, in her own way, she would destroy the innate control that brought her both admiration and frustration. Just the thought of it sent a thrill racing up her spine.

She brought her mouth close to his, but used her tongue to taste. Slowly, very slowly, she traced his lips. Already she could feel the heat rising. With a lazy sigh, she shifted so that her body moved over his as she trailed kisses down his jaw.

A strong face, she thought, aristocratic but not soft, intelligent, but not cold. It was a face some women would find haughty—until they looked into the eyes. She did so now and saw the intensity, the heat, even the ruthlessness.

"I want you more than I should," she heard herself say. "I have you less than I want."

Before he could speak, she crushed her mouth to his and started the journey for both of them.

He was still throbbing from her words alone. He'd wanted to hear that kind of admission from her; he'd waited to hear it. Just as he'd waited to feel this strong, pure emotion from her. It was that emotion that stripped away all his defenses even as her seeking hands and mouth exploited the weaknesses.

She touched. His skin heated.

She tasted. His blood sang.

She encompassed. His mind swam.

Vulnerable. Blake discovered the new sensation in himself. She made him so. In the soft, lowering light— near dusk—he was trapped in that midnight world of quietly raging powers. Her fingers were cool and very sure as they stroked, enticed. He could feel them slide leisurely over him, pausing to linger while she sighed. And while she sighed, she exploited. His body was weighed down with layer after layer of pleasures—to be seduced so carefully, to be desired so fully.

With long, lengthy, openmouthed kisses, she explored all of him, reveling in the firm masculinity of his body— knowing she would soon rip apart that impenetrable control. She was obsessed with it, and with him. Could it be that now, after she'd made love with him, after she'd begun to understand the powers and weaknesses in his body, she would find even more delight in learning of them again?

There seemed to be no end to the variations of her feelings, to the changes of sensations she could experience when she was with him like this. Each time, every time, was as vital and unique as the first had been. If this was a contradiction to everything she'd ever believed was true about a man and woman, she didn't question it now. She exalted in it.

He was hers. Body and mind—she felt it. Almost tangibly she could sense the polish, the civilized sheen, that was so much a part of him melt away. It was what she wanted.

There was little sanity left. As she roamed over him the need became more primitive, more primal. He wanted more, endlessly more, but the blood was drumming in his head. She was so agile, so relentless. He experienced a wave of pure helplessness for the first time in his life. Her hands were clever—so clever he couldn't hear the quick unsteadiness of her breathing. He could feel her tormenting him exquisitely, but he couldn't see the flickers of passion or depth of desire in her eyes. He was blind and deaf to everything.

Then her mouth was devouring his and everything savage that civilized men restrain tore from him. He was mad for her. In his mind were dark swirling colors, in his ears was a wild rushing like a sea crazed by a storm. Her name ripped from him like an oath as he gripped her, rolling her to her back, enclosing her, possessing her.

And there was nothing but her, to take, to drown in, to ravage and to worship until passion spun from its peak and emptied him.

Chapter 11

"I'm starving."

It was full dark, with no moon to shed any trickle of light into the room. The darkness itself was comfortable and easy. They were still naked and tangled on Summer's bed, but the piano had been silent for an hour. There were no more supper smells in the air. Blake drew her a bit closer and kept his eyes shut, though it wasn't sleep he sought. Somehow in the silence, in the darkness, he felt closer to her.

"I'm starving," Summer repeated, a bit sulkily this time.

"You're the chef."

"Oh, no, not this time." Rising on her elbow, Summer glared at him. She could see the silhouette of his profile, the long line of chin, the straight nose, the sweep of brow. She wanted to kiss all of them again, but knew it was time to make a stand. "It's definitely your turn to cook."

"My turn?" He opened one eye, cautiously. "I could send out for pizza."

"Takes too long." She rolled on top of him to give him a smacking kiss—and a quick jab in the ribs. "I said I was starving. That's an immediate problem."

He folded his arms behind his head. He, too, could see only a silhouette—the drape of her hair, slope of her shoulder, the curve of her breasts. It was enough. "I don't cook."

"Everyone cooks something," she insisted.

"Scrambled eggs," he said, hoping it would discourage her. "That's about it."

"That'll do." Before he could think of anything to change her mind, she was off the bed and switching on the bedside lamp.

"Summer!" He tossed his arm over his eyes to shield them and tried a halfhearted moan. She grinned at that before she turned to the closet to find a robe.

"I have eggs, and a skillet."

"I make very bad eggs."

"That's okay." She found his slacks, shook them out briefly, then tossed them on top of him. "Real hunger makes allowances."

Resigned, Blake put his feet on the floor. "Then I don't expect a critique afterward."

While she waited, he slipped into a pair of brief jockey shorts. They were dark blue, cut low at the waist, high at the thigh. Very sexy, she mused, and very discreet. Strange how such an incidental thing could reflect a personality.

"Cooks like to be cooked for," she told him as he drew on his slacks.

He shrugged into his shirt, leaving it unbuttoned. "Then don't interfere."

"Wouldn't dream of it." Hooking her arm through his, Summer led him to the kitchen. Again, she switched on lights and made him wince. "Make yourself at home," she invited.

"Aren't you going to assist?"

"No, indeed." Summer took the top off the cookie jar and plucked out the familiar sandwich cookie. "I don't work overtime and I never assist."

"Union rules?"

"My rules."

"You're going to eat cookies?" he asked as he rummaged for a bowl. "And eggs?"

"This is just the appetizer," she said with her mouth full. "Want one?"

"I'll pass." Sticking his head in the refrigerator, he found a carton of eggs and a quart of milk.

"You might want to grate a bit of cheese," Summer began, then shrugged when he sent her an arch look. "Sorry. Carry on." Blake broke four eggs into the bowl then added a dollop of milk. "One should measure, you know."

"One shouldn't talk with one's mouth full," he said mildly and began to beat the eggs.

Overbeating them, she thought but managed to restrain herself. But when it came to cooking, willpower wasn't her strong suit. "You haven't heated up the pan, either." Undaunted by being totally ignored, she took another cookie. "I can see you're going to need lessons."

"If you want something to do, make some toast."

Obligingly she took a loaf of bread from the bin and popped two pieces in the toaster. "It's characteristic of cooks to get a bit testy when they're watched, but a good chef has to overcome that—and distractions." She waited until he'd poured the egg mixture into a skillet before going to him. Wrapping her arms around his waist, she pressed her lips to the back of his neck. "All manner of distraction. And you've got the flame up too high."

"Do you like your eggs singed or burned clear through?"

With a laugh, she ran her hands up his bare chest. "Singed is fine. I have a nice little white Bordeaux you might've put in the eggs, but since you didn't, I'll just pour some into glasses." She left him to cook and, by the time Blake had finished the eggs, she had buttered toast on a plate and chilled wine in glasses. "Impressive," Summer decided as she sat at the dinette. "And aromatic."

But it's the eyes that tell you first, he remembered. "Attractive?" He watched as she spooned eggs on her plate.

"Very, and—" she took a first testing bite "—yes, and quite good, all in all. I might consider putting you on the breakfast shift, on a trial basis."

"I might consider the job, if cold cereal were the basic menu."

"You'll have to expand your horizons." She continued to eat, enjoying the hot, simple food on an empty stomach. "I believe you could be quite good at this with a few rudimentary lessons."

"From you?"

She lifted her wine, and her eyes laughed over the rim. "If you like. You certainly couldn't have a better teacher."

Her hair was still rumpled around her face—his hands had done that. Her cheeks were flushed, her eyes bright and flecked with gold. The robe threatened to slip off one shoulder, and left a teasing hint of skin exposed. As passion had stripped away his control, now emotions stripped away all logic.

"I love you, Summer."

She stared at him while the smile faded slowly. What went through her she didn't recognize. It didn't seem to be any one sensation, but a cornucopia of fears, excitement, disbelief and longings. Oddly, no one of them seemed dominant at first, but were so mixed and muddled she tried to grip any one of them and hold on to it. Not knowing what else to do, she set the glass down precisely, then stared at the wine shimmering inside.

"That wasn't a threat." He took her hand, holding it until she looked up at him again. "I don't see how it could come as that much of a surprise to you."

But it had. She expected affection. That was something she could deal with. She understood respect. But love—that was such a fragile word. Such an easily broken word. And something inside her begged for it to be taken from him, cherished, protected. Summer struggled against it.

"Blake, I don't need to hear that sort of thing the way other women do. Please—"

"Maybe you don't." He hadn't started the way he'd intended to, but now that he had, he'd finish. "But I need to say it. I've needed to for a long time now."

She drew her hand from his and nervously picked up her glass again. "I've always thought that words are the first thing that can damage a relationship."

"When they're not said," Blake countered. "It's a lack of words, a lack of meaning, that damages a relationship. This one isn't a word I use casually."

"No." She could believe that. It might have been the belief that had the fear growing stronger. Love, when it was given demanded some kind of return. She wasn't ready—she was sure she wasn't ready. "I think it's best, if we want things to go on as they are, that we—"

"I don't want things to go on as they are," he interrupted. He'd rather have felt annoyance than this panic that was sneaking in. He took a moment, trying to alleviate both. "I want you to marry me."

"No." Summer's own panic became full-blown. She stood quickly, as if that would erase the words, put back the distance. "No, that's impossible."

"It's very possible." He rose too, unwilling to have her draw away from him. "I want you to share my life, my name. I want to share children with you and all the years it takes to watch them grow."

"Stop." She threw up her hand, desperate to halt the words. They were moving her, and she knew it would be too easy to say yes and make that ultimate mistake.

"Why?" Before she could prevent it, he'd taken her face in his hands. The touch was gentle, though there was steel beneath. "Because you're afraid to admit it's something you want, too?"

"No, it's not something I want—it's not something I believe in. Marriage—it's a license that costs a few dollars. A piece of paper. For a few thousand dollars more, you can get a divorce decree. Another piece of paper."

He could feel her trembling and cursed himself for not knowing how to get through. "You know better than that. Marriage is two people who make promises to each other, and who make the effort to keep them. A divorce is giving up."

"I'm not interested in promises." Desperate, she pushed his hands from her face and stepped back. "I don't want any made to me, and I don't want to make any. I'm happy with my life just as it is. I have my career to think of."

"That's not enough for you, and we both know it. You can't tell me you don't feel for me. I can see it. Every time I'm with you it shows in your eyes, more each time." He was handling it badly, but saw no other course open but straight ahead. The closer he came, the further away she drew. "Damn it, Summer, I've waited long enough. If my timing's not as perfect as I wanted it to be, it can't be helped."

"Timing?" She dragged a hand through her hair. "What are you talking about? You've waited?" Dropping her hands, she began to pace the room. "Has this been one of your long-term plans, all neatly thought out, all meticulously outlined? Oh, I can see it." She let out a trembling breath and whirled back to him. It no longer made any difference to her if she were unreasonable. "Did you sit in your office and go over your strategy point by point? Was this the setting up, the looking for flaws, the following through?"

"Don't be ridiculous—"

"Ridiculous?" she tossed back. "No, I think not. You'd play the game well—disarming, confusing, charming, supportive. Patience, you'd have a lot of that. Did you wait until you thought I was at my most vulnerable?" Her breath was heaving now, and the words were tumbling out on each one. "Let me tell you something, Blake, I'm not a hotel chain you can acquire by waiting until the market's ripe."

In a slanted way she'd been killingly accurate. And the accuracy put him on the defensive. "Damn it, Summer, I want to marry you, not acquire you."

"The words are often one and the same, to my way of thinking. Your plan's a little off the mark this time, Blake. No deal. Now, I want you to leave me alone."

"We have a hell of a lot of talking to do."

"No, we have no talking to do, not about this. I work for you, for the term of the contract. That's all."

"Damn the contract." He took her by the shoulders, shaking her once in frustration. "And damn you for being so stubborn. I love you. That's not something you can brush aside as if it doesn't exist."

To their mutual surprise, her eyes filled abruptly, poignantly. "Leave me alone," she managed as the first tears spilled out. "Leave me completely alone."

The tears undermined him as her temper never would have done. "I can't do that." But he released her when he wanted to hold her. "I'll give you some time, maybe we both need time, but we'll have to come back to this."

"Just go away." She never allowed tears in front of anyone. Though she tried to dash them away, others fell quickly. "Go away." On the repetition she turned from him, holding herself stiff until she heard the click of the door.

She looked around, and though he was gone, he was everywhere. Dropping to the couch, she let herself weep and wished she were anywhere else.

* * *

She hadn't come to Rome for the cathedrals or the fountains or the art. Nor had she come for culture or history. As Summer took a wicked cab ride from the airport into the city, she was more grateful for the crowded streets and noise than the antiquity. Perhaps she'd stayed in America too long this time. Europe was fast cars, crumbling ruins and palaces. She needed Europe again, Summer told herself. As she zipped past the Trevi Fountain she thought of Philadelphia.

A few days away, she thought. Just a few days away, doing what she was best at, and everything would fall back into perspective again. She'd made a mistake with Blake—she'd known from the beginning it had been a mistake to get involved. Now it was up to her to break it off, quickly, completely. Before long he'd be grateful to her for preventing him from making an even larger mistake. Marriage—to her. Yes, she imagined he'd be vastly relieved, within even a few weeks.

Summer sat in the back of the cab watching Rome skim by and was more miserable than she'd ever been in her life.

When the cab squealed to a halt at the curb she climbed out. She stood for a moment, a slender woman in white fedora and jacket with a snakeskin bag slung carelessly over one shoulder. She was dressed like a woman of confidence and experience. In her eyes was a child who was lost.

Mechanically she paid off the driver, accepted her bag and his bow, then turned away. It was only just past 10:00 a.m. in Rome, and already hot under a spectacular sky. She remembered she'd left Philadelphia in a thunderstorm. Walking up the steps to an old, distinguished building, she knocked sharply five times. After a reasonable wait, she knocked again, harder.

When the door opened, she looked at the man in the short silk robe. It was embroidered, she noticed, with peacocks. On anyone else it would've looked absurd. His hair was tousled, his eyes half-closed. A night's growth of beard shadowed his chin.

"Hello, Carlo. Wake you up?"

"Summer!" He swallowed the string of Italian abuse that had been on his tongue and grabbed her. "A surprise, *sì?*" He kissed her soundly, twice, then drew her away. "But why do you bring me a surprise at dawn?"

"It's after ten."

"Ten is dawn when you don't begin to sleep until five. But come in, come in. I don't forget you come for Gravanti's birthday."

Outside, Carlo's home was distinguished. Inside it was opulent. Dominated by marble and gold, the entrance hall only demonstrated the beginning of his penchant for the luxurious. They walked through and under arches into a living area crowded with treasures, small and large. Most of them had been given to him by pleased clients—or women. Carlo had a talent for picking lovers who remained amiable even when they were no longer lovers.

There was a brocade at the windows, Oriental carpets on the floor and a Tintoretto on the wall. Two sofas were piled with cushions deep enough to swim in. An alabaster lion, nearly two feet in height, sat beside one. A three-tiered chandelier shot out splinters of refracted light from its crystals.

She ran her finger down a porcelain ewer in delicate Chinese blue and white. "New?"

"Sì."

"Medici?"

"But of course. A gift from a…friend."

"Your friends are always remarkably generous."

He grinned. "But then, so am I."

"Carlo?"

The husky, impatient voice came from up the curving marble stairs. Carlo glanced up, then looked back at Summer and grinned again.

Summer removed her white fedora. "A friend, I take it."

"You'll give me a moment, *cara*." He was heading for the steps as he spoke. "Perhaps you could go into the kitchen, make coffee."

"And stay out of the way," Summer finished as Carlo disappeared upstairs. She started toward the kitchen, then went back to take her suitcase with her. There wasn't any use leaving Carlo with something like luggage to explain to his friend.

The kitchen was as spectacular as the rest of the house and as large as the average hotel room. Summer knew it as well as she knew her own. It was all in ebonies and ivories with what appeared to be acres of counter space. It boasted two ovens, a restaurant-sized refrigerator, two sinks and a dishwasher that could handle the aftermath of an embassy dinner. Carlo Franconi had never been one to do anything in a small way.

Summer opened a cabinet for the coffee beans and grinder. On impulse, she decided to make crêpes. Carlo, she mused, might be just a little while.

When he did come, she was just finishing up at the stove. "Ah, *bella,* you cook for me. I'm honored."

"I had a twinge of guilt about disrupting your morning. Besides—" She slipped crêpes, pregnant with warm apples and cinnamon, onto plates. "I'm hungry." Summer set them on a scrubbed worktable while Carlo pulled up chairs. "I should apologize for coming like this without warning. Was your friend annoyed?"

He flashed a grin as he sat. "You don't give me enough credit."

"Scusi." She passed the small pitcher of cream. "So, we'll be working together for Enrico's birthday."

"My veal, with spaghetti. Enrico has a weakness for my spaghetti. Every Friday, he is in my restaurant eating." Carlo started immediately on the crêpe. "And you make the dessert."

"A birthday cake." Summer drank coffee while her crêpe cooled untouched. Suddenly, she had no appetite for it. "Enrico requested something special, created just for him. Knowing his vanity, and his fondness for chocolate and whipped cream, it was easy to come up with it."

"But the dinner isn't for two more days. You come early?"

She shrugged and toyed with her coffee. "I wanted to spend some time in Europe."

"I see." And he thought he did. She was looking a bit hollow around the eyes. A sign of romantic trouble. "Everything goes well in Philadelphia?"

"The remodeling's done, the new menus printed. I think the kitchen staff is going to do very well. I hired Maurice from Chicago. You remember?"

"Oh, yes, pressed duck."

"It's an exciting menu," she went on. "Just the sort I'd have if I ever decided to have a place of my own. I suppose I developed a bit of respect for you, Carlo, when I started to deal with the paperwork."

"Paperwork." He finished off his crêpes and eyed hers. "Ugly but necessary. You aren't eating, Summer."

"Hmm? No, I guess it's a touch of jet lag." She waved at her plate. "Go ahead."

Taking her at her word, he switched plates. "You solved the problem of Max?"

Absently she touched her arm. The stitches, thank God, were a thing of the past. "We're managing. Mother came to visit for a while. She always makes an impression."

"Monique! So, how is she?"

"Married again," Summer said simply and lifted her coffee. "A director this time, another American."

"She's happy?"

"Naturally." The coffee was strong—stronger than she'd grown used to in America. She thought in frustration that nothing was as it once was for her. "They're starting a film together in another few weeks."

"Perhaps her wisest choice. Someone who would understand her artistic temperament, her needs." He lingered over the perfect melding of spices and fruit. "And how is your American?"

Summer set down her coffee and stared at Carlo. "He wants to marry me."

Carlo choked on a bite of crêpe and grabbed for his cup. "So—congratulations."

"Don't be silly." Unable to sit, she rose, sticking her hands in the pockets of her long, loose jacket. "I'm not going to."

"No?" Going to the stove, Carlo poured them both more coffee. "Why not? You find him unattractive, maybe? Bad tempered, stupid?"

"Of course not." Impatient, she curled and uncurled her fingers inside the jacket pockets. "That has nothing to do with it."

"What has?"

"I've no intention of getting married to anyone. That's one merry-go-round I can do without."

"You don't choose to grab for the brass ring, maybe because you're afraid you'd miss."

She lifted her chin. "Be careful, Carlo."

He shrugged at the icy tone. "You know I say what I think. If you'd wanted to hear something else, you wouldn't have come here."

"I came here because I wanted a few days with a friend, not to discuss marriage."

"You're losing sleep over it."

She'd picked up her cup and now slammed it down again. Coffee spilled over the sides. "It was a long flight and I've been working hard. And, yes, maybe I'm upset over the whole thing," she continued before Carlo could speak. "I hadn't expected this from him, hadn't wanted it. He's an honest man, and I know when he says he loves me and wants to marry me, he means it. For the moment. That doesn't make it any easier to say no."

Her fury didn't unnerve him. Carlo was well used to passionate emotions from women—he preferred them. "And you—how do you feel about him?"

She hesitated, then walked to the window. She could look out on Carlo's garden from there—a quiet, isolated spot that served as a border between the house and the busy streets of Rome. "I have feelings for him,"

Summer murmured. "Stronger feelings than are wise. If anything, they only make it more important that I break things off now. I don't want to hurt him, Carlo, any more than I want to be hurt myself."

"You're so sure love and marriage would hurt?" He put his hands on her shoulders and kneaded them lightly. "When you look so hard at the what-ifs in life, *cara mia,* you miss much living. You have someone who loves you, and though you won't say the words, I think you love him back. Why do you deny yourself?"

"Marriage, Carlo." She turned, her eyes earnest. "It's not for people like us, is it?"

"People like us?"

"We're so wrapped up in what it is we do. We're used to coming and going as we please, when we please. We have no one to answer to, no one to consider but ourselves. Isn't that why you've never married?"

"I could say I'm a generous man, and feel it would be too selfish to limit my gifts to only one woman." She smiled, fully, the way he'd wanted to see her smile. Gently, he brushed the hair away from her face. "But to you, the truth is I've never found anyone who could make my heart tremble. I've looked. If I found her, I'd run for a license and a priest quickly."

With a sigh, she turned back to the window. The flowers were a tapestry of color in the strong sun. "Marriage is a fairy tale, Carlo, full of princes and peasants and toads. I've seen too many of those fairy tales fade."

"We write our own stories, Summer. A woman like you knows that because you've always done so."

"Maybe. But this time I just don't know if I have the courage to turn the next page."

"Take your time. There's no better place to think

about life and love than *Roma*. No better man to think
about them with than Franconi. Tonight, I cook for you.
Linguini—" he kissed the tips of his fingers "—to die
for. You can make me one of your babas—just like when
we were students, *si?*"

Turning back to him, Summer wrapped her arms
around his neck. "You know, Carlo, if I were the mar-
rying kind, I'd take you, for your pasta alone."

He grinned. "*Carissima,* even my pasta is nothing
compared to my—"

"I'm sure," she interrupted dryly. "Why don't you
get dressed and take me shopping? I need to buy something fantastic while I'm in Rome. I haven't given my
mother a wedding present yet."

How could he have been so stupid? Blake flicked
on his lighter and watched the flame cut through the
darkness. It wouldn't be dawn for an hour yet, but he'd
given up on sleep. He'd given up on trying to imagine
what Summer was doing in Rome while he sat wake-
ful in an empty suite of rooms and thought of her. If he
went to Rome...

No, he'd promised himself he'd give her some room,
especially since he'd handled everything so badly. He'd
given them both some room.

More strategy, he thought derisively and drew hard
on the cigarette. Was that what the whole thing was
about? He'd always enjoyed challenges, problems. Summer was certainly both. Was that the reason he wanted
her? If she'd agreed to marry him, he could have congratulated himself on a plan well thought out and perfectly executed. Another Cocharan acquisition. Damn it.

He rose. He paced. Smoke curled from the cigarette

between his fingers, then disappeared into the half-light.
He knew better than that, even if she didn't. If it were
true that he'd treated the whole affair like a problem to
be carefully solved, it was only because that was his
make-up. But he loved her, and if he were sure of anything, it was that she loved him too. How was he going
to get over that wall she'd erected?

Go back to the way things were? Impossible. He
looked out at the city as the darkness began to soften. In
the east, the sky was just beginning to lighten with the
first hints of pink. Suddenly he realized he'd watched
too many sunrises alone. Too much had changed between them now, Blake mused. Too much had been
said. You couldn't take love back and lock it away for
convenience's sake.

He'd stayed away from her for a full week before
she'd gone to Rome. It had been much harder than
he'd imagined it would be, but her tears that night had
pushed him to it. Now he wondered if that had been
yet another mistake. Perhaps if he'd gone to her the
next day...

Shaking his head, he moved away from the window
again. All along, his mistake had been trying to treat
the situation with logic. There wasn't any logic in loving someone, only feelings. Without logic, he lost all
advantage.

Madly in love. Yes, he thought the term very apt. It
was all madness, an incurable madness. If she'd been
with him, he could have shown her. Somehow, when she
came back, he thought violently, he'd take that damn
wall down piece by piece until she was forced to face
the madness, too.

When the phone rang he stared at it. Summer? "Hello."

"Blake?" The voice was a little too sulky, a little too French.

"Yes. Monique?"

"I'm sorry to disturb you, but I always forget how much time is different between west and east. I was just going to bed. You were up?"

"Yes." The sun was slowly rising, the room was pale with light. Most of the city wasn't yet awake, but he was. "Did you have a good trip back to California?"

"I slept almost the whole way. Thank God, because there have been so many parties. So little changes in Hollywood—some of the names, some of the faces. Now, to be chic, one must wear sunglasses on a string. My mother did this, but only to keep from losing them."

He smiled because Monique demanded smiles. "You don't need trends to be chic."

"How flattering." Her voice was very young and very pleased.

"What can I do for you, Monique?"

"Oh, so sweet. First I must tell you how lovely it was to stay in your hotel again. Always the service is impeccable. And Summer's arm, it's better, no?"

"Apparently. She's in Rome."

"Oh, yes, my memory. Well, she was never one to sit too long in one space, my Summer. I saw her only briefly before I left. She seemed…preoccupied."

He felt his stomach muscles knotting, his jaw tightening. Deliberately he relaxed both. "She's been working very hard on the kitchen."

Monique's lips curved. *He gives away nothing, this one,* she thought with approval. "Yes, well I may see her again for a short time. I must ask you a favor, Blake. You were so kind during my visit."

"Whatever I can do."

"The suite where I stayed, I found it so restful, so *agréable*. I wonder if you could reserve it for me again, in two days' time."

"Two days?" His brow creased, but he automatically reached for a pen to jot it down. "You're coming back east?"

"I'm so foolish, so—what is it?—absent-minded, *oui?* I have business to take care of there, and with Summer's accident, it all went out of my head. I must come back and tie up the ends that are loose. And the suite?"

"Of course, I'll see to it."

"*Merci.* And perhaps, I could ask one more thing of you. I will have a small party on Saturday evening—just a few old friends and some wine. I'd be very grateful if you could stop by for a few minutes. Around eight?"

There was nothing he wanted less at the moment than a party. But manners, upbringing and business left him only one answer. Again, he automatically noted down the date and time. "I'd be happy to."

"Marvelous. Till Saturday then, *au revoir.*"

After hanging up the phone, Monique gave a tinkle of laughter. True, she was an actress, not a screenwriter, but she thought her little scenario was brilliant. Yes, absolutely brilliant.

Picking up the phone, she prepared to send a cablegram. To Rome.

Chapter 12

Chérie. Must return to Philadelphia for some unfinished business before filming begins. Will be at Cocharan House in my suite over the weekend. Having a little soirée Saturday evening. Do come. 8:30. A bientôt. Mother.

And just what was she up to? Summer glanced over the cable again as she cruised above the Atlantic. Unfinished business? Summer could think of no business Monique would have in Philadelphia, unless it involved husband number two. But that was ancient history, and Monique always had someone else handle her business dealings. She'd always claimed a good actress was a child at heart and had no head for business. It was another one of her diabolically helpless ways that made it possible for her to do only exactly as she wanted. What

Summer couldn't figure out was why Monique would want to come back east.

With a shrug, Summer slipped the cable back into her bag.

She didn't feel like hassling with people and cocktail talk in just over five hours. The day before, she'd outdone herself with the creation of a birthday cake shaped like Enrico's palatial home outside Rome, and filled with a wickedly wonderful combination of chocolate and cream. It had taken her twelve hours. And for once, at the host's insistence, she'd remained and joined the party for champagne and dessert.

She'd thought it would be good for her. The people, the elegance, the celebratory atmosphere. It had done no more than show her that she didn't want to be in Rome exchanging small talk and drinking wine. She wanted to be home. Home, though it surprised her, was Philadelphia.

She didn't long for Paris and her odd little flat on the Left Bank. She wanted her fourth-floor apartment in Philadelphia, where there were memories of Blake in every corner. However foolish it made her, however unwise or impractical it was, she wanted Blake.

Now, flying home, she found that hadn't changed. It was Blake she wanted to go to when she was on the ground again. It was to Blake she wanted to tell all the foolish stories she'd heard in Enrico's dining room. It was Blake she wanted to hear laugh. It was Blake she wanted to curl up next to now that the nervous energy of the past few days was draining.

Sighing, she tilted her seat back and closed her eyes. But she would do her duty and go to her mother's suite. Perhaps Monique's little party was the perfect diversion. It would give Summer just a bit more time before she faced Blake again. Blake, and the decision she had thought was already made.

B.C. ran a finger around the inside of the snug collar of his shirt and hoped he didn't look as nervous as he felt. Seeing Monique again after all these years— having to introduce Lillian to her. *Monique, my wife, Lillian. Lillian, Monique Dubois, a former lover. Small world, isn't it?*

Though he was a man who appreciated a good joke, this one eluded him.

It seemed there was no statute of limitations on marital transgressions. It was true that he'd only strayed once, and then during an unofficial separation from his wife that had left him angry, bitter and frightened. A crime committed once, was still a crime committed.

He loved Lillian, had always loved her, but he'd never be able to deny that the brief affair with Monique had happened. And he couldn't deny that it had been exciting, passionate and memorable.

They'd never contacted each other again, though once or twice he'd seen her when he was still actively working in the business. Even that had been so long ago.

So, why had she called him now, twenty years later, insisting that he come—with his wife—to her suite at the Philadelphia Cocharan House? He ran his finger around his collar once again. Something was choking him. Monique's only explanation had been that it concerned the happiness of his son and her daughter.

That had left him with the problem of fabricating a reason for coming into town and insisting that Lillian accompany him. That hadn't been a piece of cake, because he'd married a sharp-minded, independent woman, but it was nothing compared with the next ordeal.

"Are you going to fuss with that tie all day?" B.C. jumped as his wife came up behind him. "Easy." With a laugh, she brushed the back of his jacket, smoothing it over his shoulders in a habit that took him back to their honeymoon. "You'd think you'd never spent an evening with a celebrity before. Or is it just French actresses that make you nervous?"

This one French actress, B.C. thought and turned to his wife. She'd always been lovely, not the breath-catching beauty Monique had been, but lovely with the kind of quiet looks that remain lovely through the years. Her pure, rich brunette hair was liberally streaked with gray, but styled in such a way that the contrasting colors enhanced her looks.

Lillian had always had style. She'd been his partner, always, had stood up to him, stood by him. A strong woman. He'd needed a strong woman. She was the best damn first mate a man could ask for. He put his hands on her shoulders and kissed her, quite tenderly.

"I love you, Lily." When she touched his cheek and smiled, he took her hand, feeling like the condemned man walking his last mile. "We'd better go. We'll be late."

Blake hung up the phone in disgust. He was certain Summer would be back that evening. But though he'd called her apartment off and on for over an hour, there'd been no answer. He was out of patience, and in no mood to go down and be sociable in Monique's suite. Much like his father had done, he tugged on his tie.

When all this was over, when she was back, he was going to find a way to convince her to go away with him. He'd find that damn island in the Pacific if that's what it took. He'd *buy* the damn island and set up housekeeping. Build a chain of pizza parlors or fast-food restaurants. Maybe that would satisfy the woman.

Feeling unreasonable, and just a little mean, he strode out of the apartment.

Monique surveyed the suite and nodded. The flowers were a nice touch—not too many, just a few buds here and there to give the rooms a whiff of a garden. A touch—only a touch of romance. The wine was chilling, the glasses sparkling in the subdued lighting. And Max had outdone himself with the hors d'oeuvres, she decided. A little caviar, a little pâté, some miniature quiches—very elegant. She must remember to pay a visit to the kitchen.

As for herself—Monique touched a hand to the chignon at the base of her neck. Not her usual style, but she wanted to add the air of dignity. She felt the evening might call for it. But the black silk pants and off-the-shoulder blouse were sexy and chic. She simply couldn't resist the urge to dress with a bit of flair for the part.

The scene was set, she decided. Now it was only a matter for the players...

The knock came. With a slow smile, Monique went toward the door. Act one was about to begin.

"B.C.!" Her smile was brilliant, her hands thrown out to him. "How wonderful to see you again after all this time."

Her beauty was as stunning as ever. There was no resisting that smile. Though he'd been determined to be very aloof and very polite, his voice warmed. "Monique, you don't look a minute older."

"Always the charmer." She laughed, then kissed his cheek before she turned to the woman beside him. "And you are Lillian. How lovely that we meet at last. B.C. has told me so much of you, I feel we're old friends."

Lillian measured the woman across the threshold and lifted a brow. "Oh?"

No fool, this one, Monique decided instantly, and liked her. "Of course, that was all so long ago, so we must get to know each other all over again. Now please come in. B.C., you'd be kind enough to open a bottle of champagne."

A bundle of nerves, B.C. crossed the room to comply. A drink would be an excellent idea. He'd have preferred bourbon, straight up.

"Of course, I've seen you many times," Lillian began. "I'm sure you haven't made a movie I've missed, Ms. Dubois."

"Monique, please." In a simple, gracious gesture, she plucked a rosebud from a vase and handed it to Lillian. "And I'm flattered. From time to time I would retire, this last occasion has been the longest. But always, going back to the film is like going back to an old lover."

The cork blew out of the bottle like a missile and bounced off the ceiling. Calmly Monique slipped an arm through Lillian's. Inside she was giggling like a girl. "Such an exciting sound, is it not? It always makes me happy to hear champagne being opened. We must have a toast, *n'est-ce pas?*"

She lifted a glass with a flourish, and looked, to Lillian's thinking, just like the character she'd played in *Yesterday's Dream*.

"To fate, I think," Monique decided. "And the strange way it twists us all together." She clinked her glass against B.C.'s, then his wife's, before drinking. "So tell me, you are still enchanted with sailing, B.C.?"

He cleared his throat, no longer certain if he should watch his wife or Monique. Both of them were definitely watching him. "Ah, yes. As a matter of fact, Lillian and I just got back from Tahiti."

"How charming. A perfect place for lovers, *oui?*"

Lillian sipped her wine. "Perfect."

"Et voilà," Monique said when the knock sounded. "The next guest. Please help yourself." It was now Act Two. Having the time of her life, Monique went to answer. "Blake, so kind of you to come, and how charming you look."

"Monique." He took the hand she extended and brought it to his lips even as he calculated just how long it would be before he could make his escape. "Welcome back."

"I must be certain not to wear out the welcome. You'll be surprised by my other guests, I think." With this she gestured inside.

The last two people he'd expected to see in Monique's suite were his parents. He crossed the room and bent to kiss his mother. "Very surprised. I didn't know you were in town."

"We only got in a little while ago." Lillian handed her son a glass of champagne. "We did call your suite, but the phone was busy." Just what stage is this woman setting? Lillian wondered as Monique joined them.

"Families," she said grandly, helping herself to some caviar. "I have a great fondness for them. I must tell you both how I admire your son. The young Cocharan carries on the tradition, is it not so?"

For an instant, only an instant, Lillian's eyes narrowed. She wanted to know just what tradition the French actress referred to.

"We're both very proud of Blake," B.C. said with some relief. "He's not only maintained the Cocharan standard, but expanded it. The Hamilton chain was an excellent move." He toasted his son. "Excellent. How's the turnover in the kitchen going?"

"Very smoothly." And it was the last thing he wanted to discuss. "We start serving from the new menu tomorrow."

"Then we timed our visit well," Lillian put in. "We'll have a chance to test it firsthand."

"Do you know the coincidence?" Monique asked Lillian as she offered the tray of quiches.

"Coincidence?"

"But it is amusing. It is my daughter who now manages your son's kitchen."

"Your daughter." Lillian glanced at her husband. "No, it wasn't mentioned to me."

"She is a superb chef. You would agree, Blake? She often cooks for him," she added with a deliberate smile before he could make any comment.

Lillian held the rosebud under her nose. Interesting. "Really?"

"A charming girl," B.C. put in. "She has your looks, Monique, though I could hardly credit that you had a grown daughter."

"And I was just as surprised when I first met your son." She smiled at him. "Isn't it strange where the years go?"

B.C. cleared his throat and poured more wine.

Weeks before, Blake had wondered what messages had passed between Summer and his father. Now he had no trouble recognizing what wasn't being said between B.C. and Monique. He looked at his mother first and saw her calmly drinking champagne.

His father and Summer's mother? When? he wondered as he tried to digest it. For as long as he could remember, his parents had been devoted, almost inseparable. No—abruptly he remembered a short, turbulent time during his early teens. The house had been full of tension, arguments in undertones. Then B.C. had been gone for two weeks—three? A business trip, his mother had told him, but even then he'd known better. But it had been over so quickly, he'd rarely thought of it since. Now…now he had a definite idea where his father had spent at least some of that time away from home. And with whom.

He caught his father's eye—the uncomfortable, half-defiant look. The man, Blake mused, was certainly paying for a slip in fidelity that was two decades old. He saw Monique smile, slowly. Just what the hell was she trying to stir up?

Almost before the anger could fully form, she laid a hand on his arm. It was a gesture that asked him to wait, to be patient. Then came another knock. "Ah, excuse me. You would pour another glass?" Monique asked B.C. "We have one more guest tonight."

When she opened the door, Monique couldn't have been more pleased with her daughter. The simple jade silk dress was soft, narrow and subtly sexy. It made her slight pallor very romantic. "*Chérie,* so good of you not to disappoint me."

"I can't stay long, Mother, I have to get some sleep." She held out a pink-ribboned box. "But I wanted to bring you a wedding gift."

"So sweet." Monique brushed her lips over Summer's cheek. "And I have something for you. Something I hope you'll always treasure." Stepping aside, she drew Summer in.

Not like this, Summer thought desperately when the first shock of seeing Blake again rippled through her. She'd wanted to be prepared, rested, confident. She didn't want to see him here, now. And his parents—one look at the woman beside Blake and she knew she had to be B.C.'s wife. Nothing else made sense—Monique's kind of sense.

"Your game isn't amusing, Mother," she murmured in French.

"On the contrary, it might be the most important thing I've ever done. B.C.," she said in gay tones, "you've met my daughter, *oui?*"

"Yes, indeed." With a smile, he handed Summer a glass of champagne. "Nice to see you again."

"And Blake's mother," Monique continued. "Lillian, may I present my only child, Summer."

"I'm very pleased to meet you." Lillian took her hand warmly. She wasn't blind and had seen the stunned look that had passed between her son and the actress's daughter. There'd been surprise, longing and uncertainty. If Monique had set the stage for this, Lilian would do her best to help. "I've just been hearing that you're a chef and responsible for the new menu we'll be boasting of tomorrow."

"Yes." She searched for something to say. "Did you enjoy your sailing? Tahiti, wasn't it?"

"We had a marvelous time, even though B.C. tends to become Captain Bligh if you don't watch him."

"Nonsense." He slipped his arm around his wife's shoulders. "This is the only woman I'd ever trust at the wheel of one of my ships."

They adore each other. Summer realized it and found it surprised her. Their marriage was nearing its fortieth year, and obviously hadn't been without storms... yet they adored each other.

"It's rather beautiful, is it not, when a husband and wife can share an interest and yet be—separate people?" Monique beamed at them, then looked at Blake. "You would agree that such things keep a man and woman together, even when they have to struggle through hard times and misunderstandings?"

"I would." He looked directly at Summer. "It's a matter of love, and of respect and perhaps of...optimism."

"Optimism!" Monique clearly found the word perfect. "Yes, this I like. I, of course, am always so— perhaps too much. I've had four husbands, clearly too optimistic." She laughed at herself. "But then, I think I looked always first, and perhaps only, for romance. Would you say, Lillian, that it's a mistake not to look beyond that?"

"We all look for romance, love, passion." She touched her husband's arm lightly, in a gesture so natural neither of them noticed it. "Then of course respect. I suppose I'd have to add two things to that." She looked up at her husband. "Tolerance and tenacity. Marriage needs them all."

She knew. As B.C. saw the look in his wife's eyes he realized she'd always known. For twenty years, she'd known.

"Excellent." Rather pleased with herself, Monique set her gift on the table. "This is the perfect time then to open a gift celebrating my marriage. This time I intend to put all those things into it."

She wanted to leave. Summer told herself it was only a matter of turning around and walking to the door. She stood rooted, with her eyes locked on Blake's.

"Oh, but it's beautiful." Reverently, Monique lifted the tiny hand-crafted merry-go-round from the bed of tissue. The horses were ivory, trimmed in gilt—each one perfect, each one unique. At the turn of the base, it played a romantic Chopin Prelude. "But, darling, how perfect. A carousel to celebrate a marriage. The horses should be named romance, love, tenacity and so forth. I shall treasure it."

"I—" Summer looked at her mother, and suddenly none of the practicalities, none of the mistakes mattered. "Be happy, *ma mére*."

Monique touched her cheek with a fingertip, then brushed it with her lips. "And you, *mignonne*."

B.C. leaned down to whisper in his wife's ear. "You know, don't you?"

Amused, she lifted her glass. "Of course," she answered in an undertone. "You've never been able to keep secrets from me."

"But—"

"I knew then and hated you for almost a day. Do you remember whose fault it was? I don't anymore."

"God, Lily, if you'd known how guilty I was. Tonight, I was nearly suffocating with—"

"Good," she said simply. "Now, you old fool, let's get out of here so these children can iron things out. Monique—" She held out her hand, and as hands met, eyes met, things passed between them that would never have to be said. "Thank you for a lovely evening, and my best wishes to you and your husband."

"And mine to you." With a smile reminiscent of the past, she held out her arms to B.C. *"Au revoir, mon ami."*

He accepted the embrace, feeling like a man who'd just been granted amnesty. He wanted nothing more than to go up to his own suite and show his wife how much he loved her. "Perhaps we'll have lunch tomorrow," he said absently to the room at large. "Good night."

Monique began to giggle as the door shut behind him. "Love, it will always make me laugh. So—" Briskly, she began to rewrap her gift and box it. "My bags are being held for me downstairs and my plane leaves in one hour."

"An hour?" Summer began. "But—"

"My business is done." Tucking the box under her arm, she rose on her toes to kiss Blake. "You have the good fortune of possessing excellent parents." Then she kissed Summer. "And so, my sweet, do you, though they weren't suited to remain husband and wife. The suite is paid for through the night, the champagne's still cold." She glided for the door leaving a trail of Paris in her wake. Pausing in the doorway, she looked back. *"Bon appétit, mes enfants."* Monique considered it one of her very finest exits.

When the door closed, Summer stood where she was, unsure if she wanted to applaud or throw something.

"Quite a performance," Blake commented. "More wine?"

She could be as urbane and casual as he. "All right."

"And how was Rome?"

"Hot."

"And your cake?"

"Magnificent." Lifting her freshly filled glass, she took two steps away. It was always better to talk of the unimportant when so many urgent needs were pressing. "Things running smoothly here?"

"Amazingly so. Though I think everyone'll be relieved that you're here for the first run tomorrow. Tell me—" he sipped his own wine, approving it "—when did you first know that my father and your mother had had an affair?"

That was blunt enough, she thought. Well, she would be equally blunt. "When it was happening. I was only a child, but children are astute. You could say I suspected it then. I was sure of it when I first mentioned my mother's name to your father."

He nodded, remembering the meeting in his office. "Just how much have you let that bother you?"

"It was awkward." Restlessly she moved her shoulders.

"And you were determined not to let history repeat itself."

His perception was too often killingly accurate. "Perhaps."

"But then, in a matter of speaking, it did."

With another attempt at casualness, she spread some caviar on a cracker. "But then, neither of us was married."

As if it were only general cocktail talk, Blake chose a quiche. "You know why your mother did this tonight."

Summer shook her head when he offered the tray. "Monique could never resist a scene of any kind. She set the stage, brought in the players, to show me, I think, that while marriage might not be perfect, it can be durable."

"Was she successful?" When she didn't speak, Blake set down his glass. It was time they stopped hedging, time they stopped speaking in generalities. "There hasn't been an hour since the last time I saw you that I haven't thought of you."

Her eyes met his. Helplessly she shook her head. "Blake, I don't think you should—"

"Damn it, you're going to hear me out. We're good for each other. You can't tell me you don't believe that. Maybe you were right before about the way I planned out my...courtship," he decided for a lack of a better word. "Maybe I was too smug about it, too sure that if I waited for just the right moment, I'd have exactly what I wanted with the least amount of trouble. I had to be sure or I'd've gone insane trying to give you enough time to see just what we could have together."

"I was too hard that night." She wrapped her arms around herself then dropped them to her sides. "I said things because you frightened me. I didn't mean them, not all of them."

"Summer." He touched her cheek. "I meant everything I said that night. I want you now as much as I wanted you the first time."

"I'm here." She stepped closer. "We're alone."

The need twisted inside him. "I want to make love with you, but not until I know what it is you want from me. Do you want only a few nights, a few memories, like our parents had together?"

She turned away then. "I don't know how to explain."

"Tell me how you feel."

She took a moment to steady herself. "All right. When I cook, I take this ingredient and that. I have my own hands, my own skill, and putting these together, I make something perfect. If I don't find it perfect, I toss it out. There's little patience in me." She paused a moment, wondering if he could possibly understand this kind of analogy. "I've thought that if I ever decided to become involved in a relationship, there would be this ingredient and that, and again I'd put them together. But I knew it would never be perfect. So…" She let out a long breath. "I wondered if that too would be something to toss out."

"A relationship isn't something that has to be created in a day, or perfected in a day. Part of the game is to keep working on it. Fifty years still isn't long enough."

"A long time to work on something that'll always be just a little flawed."

"Too much of a challenge?"

She whirled, then stopped. "You know me too well," she murmured. "Too well for my own good. Maybe too well for your own."

"You're wrong," he said quietly. "You are my own good."

Her mouth trembled open, then closed. "Please," she managed, "I want to finish this. When I was in Rome, I tried to tell myself that this was what I wanted—to go back to flying here, there, without anyone to worry about but myself and the next dish I would create. When I was in Rome," she added with a sigh, "I was more miserable than I've ever been in my life."

He couldn't prevent the grin. "Sorry to hear it."

"No, I think you're not." Turning away, she ran her fingertip around and around the rim of a champagne

glass. Since she would only explain once, she wanted
to be certain she explained well. "On the plane, I told
myself that when I came back, we would talk, reason-
ably, logically. We'd work the situation out in the best
manner. In my head, I thought that would be a contin-
uation of our relationship as it was. Intimacy without
strings, which is perhaps not intimacy at all." She lifted
the glass and sipped some of the cold, frothy wine.
"When I walked in here tonight and saw you, I knew
that would be impossible. We can't see each other as
we have been. In the end, that would damage us both."

"You're not walking out of my life."

Turning back, she stood toe-to-toe with him. "I
would, if I could. And damn it, you're not the one who's
stopping me. It's me! None of your planning, none of
your logic could've changed what was inside me. Only
I could change it, only what I feel could change it."

She took his hands. She took a deep breath. "I want
to ride that merry-go-round with you, and I want my
shot at the brass ring."

His hands slid up her arms, into her hair. "Why?
Just tell me why."

"Because sometime between the moment you walked
in my front door and now, I fell in love with you. No
matter how foolish it is, I want to take a chance on that."

"We're going to win." His mouth sought hers, and
when she trembled he knew it was as much from nerves
as passion. Soon they'd face the passion, now he would
soothe the nerves. "If you like, we'll take a trial period."
He began to roam her face with kisses. "We can even
put it in contract form—more practical."

"Trial?" She started to draw away from him, but he
held her close.

"Yes, and if during the trial period either of us wants a divorce, they simply have to wait until the end of the contract term."

Her brows came together. Could he speak of business now? Would he dare? Her chin tilted challengingly. "How long is the contract term?"

"Fifty years."

Laughing, she threw her arms around his neck. "Deal. I want it drawn up tomorrow, in triplicate. But tonight—" she began to nibble on his lips as she ran her hands beneath his jacket "—tonight we're only lovers. Truly lovers now. And the suite is ours till morning."

The kiss was long—it was slow—it was lingering.

"Remind me to send Monique a case of champagne," Blake said as he lifted Summer into his arms.

"Speaking of it…" Leaning over—a bit precariously— she lifted the two half-full glasses from the table. "We shouldn't let it get flat. And later," she continued as he carried her toward the bedroom, "much later, perhaps we can send out for pizza."

* * * * *

TEMPTATION

This book is dedicated with gratitude and affection to Nancy Jackson.

Chapter 1

"If there's one thing I hate," Eden mumbled, "it's six o'clock in the morning."

Sunlight poured through the thinly screened windows of the cabin and fell on the wooden floor, the metal bars of her bunk, and her face. The sound of the morning bell echoed dully in her head. Though she'd known that long, clanging ring for only three days, Eden already hated it.

For one fanciful moment, she buried her face under the pillow, imagining herself cuddled in her big four-poster. The Irish-linen sheets would smell ever-so-slightly of lemon. In her airy pastel bedroom, the curtains would be drawn against the morning, the scent of fresh flowers sweetening the air.

The pillowcase smelled of feathers and detergent.

With a grunt, Eden tossed the pillow to the floor,

then struggled to sit up. Now that the morning bell had stopped, she could hear the cries of a couple of excited crows. From the cabin directly across the compound came a happy blast of rock music. With glazed eyes, she watched Candice Bartholomew bound out of the adjoining bunk. Her sharp-featured pixie's face was split by a grin.

"Morning." Candy's long, clever fingers ran through her thatch of red hair like scoops, causing it to bounce into further disarray. Candy was, Eden had always thought, all bounce. "It's a beautiful day," she announced, in a voice as cheerful as the rest of her. Watching her friend stretch in frilly baby-doll pajamas, Eden gave another noncommittal grunt. She swung her bare legs off the mattress and contemplated the accomplishment of putting her feet on the floor.

"I could grow to hate you." Eden's voice, still husky with sleep, carried the rounded tones of her finishing-school education. Eyes shut, she pushed her own tousled blond hair away from her face.

Grinning, Candy tossed open the cabin door so that she could breathe in the fresh morning air while she studied her friend. The strong summer sunlight shot through Eden's pale hair, making it look fragile where it lay against her forehead and cheeks. Her eyes remained shut. Her slender shoulders slumped, she let out an enormous yawn. Candy wisely said nothing, knowing Eden didn't share her enthusiasm for sunrise.

"It can't be morning," Eden grumbled. "I swear I only lay down five minutes ago." Resting her elbows on her knees, she dropped her face into her hands. Her complexion was creamy, with just a suggestion of rose on the crest of her cheekbones. Her nose was small, with a hint of an upward tilt at the tip. What might have been a coolly aristocratic face was gentled by a full, generous mouth.

Candy took in one last breath of air, then shut the door. "All you need is a shower and some coffee. The first week of camp's the toughest, remember?"

Eden opened wide, lake-blue eyes. "Easy for you to say. You're not the one who fell in the poison ivy."

"Still itching?"

"A little." Because her own foul mood was making her feel guilty, Eden managed a smile. Everything softened, eyes, mouth, voice. "In any case, this is the first time we're the campees instead of the campers." Letting out another fierce yawn, she rose and tugged on a robe. The air coming through the screens was fresh as a daisy, and chilly enough to make Eden's toes curl. She wished she could remember what she'd done with her slippers.

"Try under the bunk," Candy suggested.

Eden bent down and found them. They were embroidered pink silk, hardly practical, but it hadn't seemed worthwhile to invest in another pair. Putting them on gave her an excuse to sit down again. "Do you really think five consecutive summers at Camp Forden for Girls prepared us for this?"

Haunted by her own doubts, Candy clasped her hands together. "Eden, are you having second thoughts?"

Because she recognized distress in the bubbly voice, Eden buried her own doubts. She had both a financial and emotional interest in the newly formed Camp Liberty. Complaining wasn't going to put her on the road to success. With a shake of her head, she walked over to squeeze Candy's shoulder. "What I have is a terminal case of morning crankiness. Let me get that shower, then I'll be ready to face our twenty-seven tenants."

"Eden." Candy stopped her before she closed the bathroom door. "It's going to work, for both of us. I know it."

"I know it, too." Eden closed the bathroom door and leaned against it. She could admit it now, while she was alone. She was scared to death. Her last dime, and her last ray of hope, were tied up in the six cabins, the stables and the cafeteria that were Camp Liberty. What did Eden Carlbough, former Philadelphia socialite, know about managing a girls' summer camp? Just enough to terrify her.

If she failed now, with this, could she pick up the pieces and go on? Would there be any pieces left? Confidence was what was needed, she told herself as she turned the taps on. Once inside the narrow shower stall, she gave the tap optimistically marked HOT another twist. Water, lukewarm, dripped out halfheartedly. Confidence, Eden thought again as she shivered under the miserly spray. Plus some cold hard cash and a whole barrel of luck.

She found the soap and began to lather with the soft-scented French milled she still allowed herself to indulge in. A year ago she would never have considered something as lowly as soap an indulgence.

A year ago.

Eden turned so that the rapidly cooling water hit her back. A year ago she would have risen at eight, had a leisurely, steaming shower, then breakfasted on toast and coffee, perhaps some shirred eggs. Sometime before ten, she would have driven to the library for her volunteer morning. There would have been lunch with

Eric, perhaps at the Deux Cheminées before she gave her afternoon to the museum or one of Aunt Dottie's charities.

The biggest decision she might have made was whether to wear her rose silk suit or her ivory linen. Her evening might have been spent quietly at home, or at one of Philadelphia's elegant dinner parties.

No pressure. No problems. But then, Papa had been alive.

Eden sighed as she rinsed away the last of the lather. The light French scent clung to her even as she dried her skin with the serviceable camp-issue towel. When her father had been alive, she had thought that money was simply something to spend and that time was forever. She had been raised to plan a menu, but not to cook; to run a home, but not to clean it.

Throughout her childhood, she had been carelessly happy with her widowed father in the ageless elegance of their Philadelphia home. There had always been party dresses and cotillions, afternoon teas and riding lessons. The Carlbough name was an old and respected one. The Carlbough money had been a simple fact of life.

How quickly and finally things could change.

Now she was giving riding instructions and juggling columns in a ledger with the vain hope that one and one didn't always make two.

Because the tiny mirror over the tiny sink was dripping with condensation, Eden rubbed it with the towel. She took a miserly dab of the half pot of imported face cream she had left. She was going to make it last through the summer. If *she* lasted through the summer herself, another pot would be her reward.

Eden found the cabin empty when she opened the

bathroom door. If she knew Candy, and after twenty years she certainly did, the redhead would be down with the girls already. How easily she became acclimatized, Eden thought; then she reminded herself it was time she did the same. She took her jeans and her red T-shirt with CAMP LIBERTY emblazoned on the chest, and began to dress. Even as a teenager, Eden had rarely dressed so casually.

She had enjoyed her social life—the parties, the well-chaperoned ski trips to Vermont, the trips to New York for shopping or the theater, the vacations in Europe. The prospect of earning a living had never been considered, by her, or her father. Carlbough women didn't work, they chaired committees.

College years had been spent with the idea of rounding out her education rather than focusing on a career. At twenty-three, Eden was forced to admit she was qualified to do absolutely nothing.

She could have blamed her father. But how could she blame a man who had been so indulgent and loving? She had adored him. She could blame herself for being naive and shortsighted, but she could never blame her father. Even now, a year after his sudden death, she still felt pangs of grief.

She could deal with that. The one thing she had been taught to do, the one thing she felt herself fully qualified to accomplish, was to cover emotion with poise, with control, or with disdain. She could go day after day, week after week through the summer, surrounded by the girls at camp and the counselors Candy had hired, and none of them would know she still mourned her father. Or that her pride had been shattered by Eric Keeton.

Eric, the promising young banker with her father's

firm. Eric, always so charming, so attentive, so suitable. It had been during her last year of college that she had accepted his ring and made her promises to him. And he had made promises to her.

When she discovered the hurt was still there, Eden coated it, layer by layer, with anger. Facing the mirror, she tugged her hair back in a short ponytail, a style her hairdresser would have shuddered at.

It was more practical, Eden told her reflection. She was a practical woman now, and hair waving softly to the shoulders would just have got in the way during the riding lessons she was to give that morning.

For a moment, she pressed her fingers against her eyes. Why were the mornings always the worst? She would wake, expecting to come out of some bad dream and find herself at home again. But it wasn't her home any longer. There were strangers living in it now. Brian Carlbough's death had not been a bad dream, but a horrible, horrible reality.

A sudden heart attack had taken him overnight, leaving Eden stunned with shock and grief. Even before the grief could fade, Eden had been struck with another shock.

There had been lawyers, black-vested lawyers with long, technical monologues. They had had offices that had smelled of old leather and fresh polish. With solemn faces and politely folded hands, they had shattered her world.

Poor investments, she had been told, bad market trends, mortgages, second mortgages, short-term loans. The simple fact had been, once the details had been sifted through, there had been no money.

Brian Carlbough had been a gambler. At the time of

his death, his luck had turned, and he hadn't had time to recoup his losses. His daughter had been forced to liquidate his assets in order to pay off the debts. The house she had grown up in and loved was gone. She had still been numbed by grief when she had found herself without a home or an income. Crashing down on top of that had been Eric's betrayal.

Eden yanked open the cabin door and was met by the balmy morning air of the mountains. The breathtaking view of greening hills and blue sky didn't affect her. She was back in Philadelphia, hearing Eric's calm, reasonable voice.

The scandal, she remembered and began marching toward the big cabin where mess would be served. *His* reputation. *His* career. Everything she had loved had been taken away, but he had only been concerned with how he might be affected.

He had never loved her. Eden jammed her hands into her pockets and kept walking. She'd been a fool not to see it from the beginning. But she'd learned, Eden reminded herself. How she'd learned. It had simply been a merger to Eric, the Carlbough name, the Carlbough money and reputation. When they had been destroyed, he had cut his losses.

Eden slowed her quick pace, realizing she was out of breath, not from exertion but from temper. It would never do to walk into breakfast with her face flushed and her eyes gleaming. Giving herself a moment, she took a few deep breaths and looked around her.

The air was still cool, but by midmorning the sun would be warm and strong. Summer had barely begun.

And it was beautiful. Lining the compound were a half-dozen small cabins with their window flaps open to the morning. The sound of girlish laughter floated through the windows. Along the pathway between cabins four and five was a scattering of anemones. A dogwood, with a few stubborn blooms clinging to it, stood nearby. Above cabin two, a mockingbird chattered.

Beyond the main camp to the west were rolling hills, deeply green. Grazing horses and trees dotted them. There was an openness here, a sense of space which Eden found incredible. Her life had always been focused on the city. Streets, buildings, traffic, people, those had been the familiar. There were times when she felt a quick pang of need for what had been. It was still possible for her to have all that. Aunt Dottie had offered her home and her love. No one would ever know how long and hard Eden had wrestled with the temptation to accept the invitation and let her life drift.

Perhaps gambling was in Eden's blood, too. Why else would she have sunk what ready cash she had had left into a fledgling camp for girls in the hills?

Because she had had to try, Eden reminded herself. She had had to take the risk on her own. She could never go back into the shell of the fragile porcelain doll she had been. Here, centered in such open space, she would take the time to learn about herself. What was inside Eden Carlbough? Maybe, just maybe, by expanding her horizons, she would find her place.

Candy was right. Eden took a long last breath. It was going to work. They were going to make it work.

"Hungry?" Her hair damp from whatever shower she'd popped into, Candy cut across Eden's path.

"Starved." Content, Eden swung a friendly arm around Candy's shoulder. "Where did you run off to?"

"You know me, I can't let any part of this place run

by itself." Like Eden, Candy swept her gaze over the camp. Her expression reflected everything inside her— the love, the fear, the fierce pride. "I was worried about you."

"Candy, I told you, I was just cranky this morning." Eden watched a group of girls rush out of a cabin and head for breakfast.

"Eden, we've been friends since we were six months old. No one knows better than I what you're going through."

No, no one did, and since Candy was the person she loved best, Eden determined to do a better job of concealing the wounds that were still open. "I've put it behind me, Candy."

"Maybe. But I know that the camp was initially my venture, and that I roped you in."

"You didn't rope me in. I wanted to invest. We both know it was a pitifully small amount."

"Not to me. The extra money made it possible for me to include the equestrian program. Then, when you agreed to come in and give riding lessons…"

"Just keeping a close eye on my investment," Eden said lightly. "Next year I won't be a part-time riding instructor and bookkeeper. I'll be a full-fledged counselor. No regrets, Candy." This time she meant it. "It's ours."

"And the bank's."

Eden shrugged that away. "We need this place. You, because it's what you've always wanted to do, always worked and studied toward. Me…" She hesitated, then sighed. "Let's face it, I haven't got anything else. The camp's putting a roof over my head, giving me three meals a day and a goal. I need to prove I can make it."

"People think we're crazy."

The pride came back, with a feeling of recklessness Eden was just learning to savor. "Let them."

With a laugh, Candy tugged at Eden's hair. "Let's eat."

Two hours later, Eden was winding up the day's first riding lesson. This was her specialty, her contribution to the partnership she and Candy had made. It had also been decided to trust Eden with the books, mainly because no one could have been more inept with figures than Candice Bartholomew.

Candy had interviewed and hired a staff of counselors, a nutritionist and a nurse. They hoped to have a pool and a swimming instructor one day, but for now there was supervised swimming and rowing on the lake, arts and crafts, hiking and archery. Candy had spent months refining a program for the summer, while Eden had juggled the profit-and-loss statements. She prayed the money would hold out while Candy ordered supplies.

Unlike Candy, Eden wasn't certain the first week of camp would be the toughest. Her partner had all the training, all the qualifications for running the camp, but Candy also had an optimist's flair for overlooking details like red ink on the books.

Pushing those thoughts aside, Eden signaled from the center of the corral. "That's all for today." She scanned the six young faces under their black riding hats. "You're doing very well."

"When can we gallop, Miss Carlbough?"

"After you learn to trot." She patted one of the horses' flanks. Wouldn't it be lovely, she thought, to gallop off into the hills, riding so fast even memories couldn't follow? Foolish, Eden told herself; she gave her attention back to the girls. "Dismount, then cool down your horses. Remember, they depend on you." The breeze tossed her bangs, and she brushed at them absently. "Remember to put all the tack in its proper place for the next class."

This caused the groans she expected. Riding and playing with the horses was one thing, tidying up afterward was another. Eden considered exerting discipline without causing resentment another accomplishment. Over the past week, she'd learned to link the girls' faces and names. The eleven- and twelve-year-olds in her group had an enthusiasm that kept her on her toes. She'd already separated in her mind the two or three she instructed who had the kind of horse fever she recognized from her own adolescence. It was rewarding, after an hour on her feet in the sun, to answer the rapid-fire questions. Ultimately, one by one, she nudged them toward the stables.

"Eden!" Turning, she spotted Candy hustling toward her. Even from a distance, Eden recognized concern.

"What's happened?"

"We're missing three kids."

"What?" Panic came first, and quickly. Years of training had her pulling it back. "What do you mean, missing?"

"I mean they're nowhere in camp. Roberta Snow, Linda Hopkins and Marcie Jamison." Candy dragged a hand through her hair, a habitual gesture of tension. "Barbara was lining up her group for rowing, and they didn't show. We've looked everywhere."

"We can't panic," Eden said, as much to warn herself as Candy. "Roberta Snow? Isn't she the little brunette who stuck a lizard down one of the other girls' shirts? And the one who set off the morning bell at 3:00 a.m.?"

"Yes, that's her." Candy set her teeth. "The little darling. Judge Harper Snow's granddaughter. If she's skinned her knee, we'll probably face a lawsuit." With a shake of her head, Candy switched to an undertone. "The last anyone saw of her this morning, she was walking east." She pointed a finger, paint-spattered from her early art class. "No one noticed the other girls, but my bet is that they're with her. Darling Roberta is an inveterate leader."

"If she's walking that way, wouldn't she run into that apple orchard?"

"Yeah." Candy shut her eyes. "Oh, yeah. I'm going to have six girls up to their wrists in modeling clay in ten minutes, or I'd go off myself. Eden, I'm almost sure they headed for the orchard. One of the other girls admitted she heard Roberta planning to sneak over there for a few samples. We don't want any trouble with the owner. He's letting us use his lake only because I begged, shamelessly. He wasn't thrilled about having a girls' summer camp for a neighbor."

"Well, he has one," Eden pointed out. "So we'll all have to deal with it. I'm the one most easily spared around here, so I'll go after them."

"I was hoping you'd say that. Seriously, Eden, if they've snuck into that orchard, which I'd bet my last dime they have, we could be in for it. The man made no bones about how he feels about his land and his privacy."

"Three little girls are hardly going to do any damage to a bunch of apple trees." Eden began to walk, with Candy scurrying to keep pace.

"He's Chase Elliot. You know, Elliot Apples? Juice, cider, sauce, jelly, chocolate-covered apple seeds, whatever can be made from an apple, they do it. He made it abundantly clear that he didn't want to find any little girls climbing his trees."

"He won't find them, I will." Leaving Candy behind, Eden swung over a fence.

"Put Roberta on a leash when you catch up to her." Candy watched her disappear through the trees.

Eden followed the path from the camp, pleased when she found a crumpled candy wrapper. Roberta. With a grim smile, Eden picked it up and stuffed it in her pocket. Judge Snow's granddaughter had already earned a reputation for her stash of sweets.

It was warm now, but the path veered through a cool grove of aspens. Sunlight dappled the ground, making the walk, if not her errand, pleasant. Squirrels dashed here and there, confident enough in their own speed not to be alarmed at Eden's intrusion. Once a rabbit darted across her path, and disappeared into the brush with a frantic rustle. Overhead a woodpecker drummed, sending out an echo.

It occurred to Eden that she was more completely alone than she had ever been before. No civilization here. She bent down for another candy wrapper. Well, very little of it.

There were new scents here, earth, animal, vegetation, to be discovered. Wildflowers sprang up, tougher and more resilient than hothouse roses. It pleased her that she was even beginning to be able to recognize a few. They came back, year after year, without pampering, taking what came and thriving on it. They gave her hope. She could find a place here. Had found a place, she corrected herself. Her friends in Philadelphia might think her mad, but she was beginning to enjoy it.

The grove of aspens thinned abruptly, and the sunlight was strong again. She blinked against it, then shielded her eyes as she scanned the Elliot orchards.

Apple trees stretched ahead of her as far as she could see, to the north, south and east. Row after row after row of trees lined the slopes. Some of them were old and gnarled, some young and straight. Instantly she thought of early spring and the overwhelming scent of apple blossoms.

It would be magnificent, she thought as she stepped up to the fence that separated the properties. The fragrance, the pretty white-and-pink blossoms, the freshly green leaves, would be a marvelous sight. Now the leaves were dark and thick, and instead of blossoms, she could see fruit in the trees closest to her. Small, shiny, and green they hung, waiting for the sun to ripen them.

How many times had she eaten applesauce that had begun right here? The idea made her smile as she began to climb the fence. Her vision of an orchard had been a lazy little grove guarded by an old man in overalls. A quaint picture, but nothing as huge and impressive as the reality.

The sound of giggling took her by surprise. Shifting toward the direction of the sound, Eden watched an apple fall from a tree and roll toward her feet. Bending, she picked it up, tossing it away as she walked closer. When she looked up, she spotted three pairs of sneakers beneath the cover of leaves and branches.

"Ladies." Eden spoke coolly and was rewarded by three startled gasps. "Apparently you took a wrong turn on your way to the lake."

Roberta's triangular, freckled face appeared through the leaves. "Hi, Miss Carlbough. Would you like an apple?"

The devil. But even as she thought it, Eden had to tighten her lips against a smile. "Down," she said simply, then stepped closer to the trunk to assist.

They didn't need her. Three agile little bodies scrambled down and dropped lightly onto the ground. In a gesture she knew could be intimidating, Eden lifted her left eyebrow.

"I'm sure you're aware that leaving camp property unsupervised and without permission is against the rules."

"Yes, Miss Carlbough." The response would have been humble if it hadn't been for the gleam in Roberta's eye.

"Since none of you seem interested in rowing today, Mrs. Petrie has a great deal of washing up to be done in the kitchen." Pleased by her own inspiration, Eden decided Candy would approve. "You're to report to Miss Bartholomew, then to Mrs. Petrie for kitchen detail."

Only two of the girls dropped their heads and looked down at the ground.

"Miss Carlbough, do you think it's fair to give us extra kitchen detail?" Roberta, one half-eaten apple still in hand, tilted her pointed chin. "After all, our parents are paying for the camp."

Eden felt her palms grow damp. Judge Snow was a wealthy and powerful man with a reputation for indulging his granddaughter. If the little monster complained... No. Eden took a deep breath and not by a flicker showed her anxiety. She wouldn't be intimidated or blackmailed by a pint-size con artist with apple juice on her chin.

"Yes, your parents are paying for you to be entertained, instructed and disciplined. When they signed you up for Camp Liberty, it was with the understanding that you would obey the rules. But if you prefer, I'd be glad to call your parents and discuss this incident with them."

"No, ma'am." Knowing when to retreat, Roberta smiled charmingly. "We'll be glad to help Mrs. Petrie, and we're sorry for breaking the rules."

And I'm sure you have a bridge I could buy, Eden thought, but she kept her face impassive. "Fine. It's time to start back."

"My hat!" Roberta would have darted back up the tree if Eden hadn't made a lucky grab for her. "I left my hat up there. Please, Miss Carlbough, it's my Phillies cap, and it's autographed and everything."

"You start back. I'll get it. I don't want Miss Bartholomew to worry any longer than necessary."

"We'll apologize."

"See that you do." Eden watched them scramble over the fence. "And no detours," she called out. "Or I keep the cap." One look at Roberta assured her that that bit of blackmail was all that was needed. "Monsters," she murmured as they jogged back into the grove, but the smile finally escaped. Turning back, she studied the tree.

All she had to do was climb up. It had looked simple enough when Roberta and her partners-in-crime had done it. Somehow, it didn't look as simple now. Squaring her shoulders, Eden stepped forward to grab a low-hanging branch. She'd done a little mountain-climbing in Switzerland; how much harder could this be? Pulling herself up, she hooked her foot in the first vee she found. The bark was rough against her palm. Concentrating on her goal, she ignored the scrapes. With both feet secured, she reached for the next branch and began to work her way up. Leaves brushed her cheeks.

She spotted the cap hanging on a short branch, two arms' lengths out of reach. When she made the mistake of looking down, her stomach clenched. So don't look, Eden ordered herself. What you can't see can't hurt you. She hoped.

Eden cautiously inched her way out to the cap. When her fingers made contact with it, she let out a low breath of relief. After setting it on her own head, she found herself looking out, beyond the tree, over the orchard.

Now it was the symmetry that caught her admiration. From her bird's height, she could see the order as well as the beauty. She could just barely glimpse a slice of the lake beyond the aspens. It winked blue in the distance. There were barnlike buildings, and what appeared to be a greenhouse, far off to the right. About a quarter of a mile away, there was a truck, apparently abandoned, on a wide dirt path. In the quiet, birds began to sing again. Turning her head, she saw the bright yellow flash of a butterfly.

The scent of leaves and fruit and earth was tangy, basic. Unable to resist, Eden reached out and plucked a sun-warmed apple.

He'd never miss it, she decided as she bit into the skin. The tart flavor, not quite ripe, shot into her mouth. She shivered at the shock of it, the sensual appeal, then bit again. Delicious, she thought. Exciting. Forbidden fruit usually was, she remembered, but she grinned as she took a third bite.

"What in the devil are you doing?"

She started, almost unseating herself, as the voice

boomed up from below. She swallowed the bite of apple quickly before peering down through the leaves.

He stood with his hands on his hips, narrow, lean, spare. A faded denim workshirt was rolled up past the elbows to show tan and muscle. Warily, Eden brought her eyes to his face. It was tanned like his arms, with the skin drawn tight over bone. His nose was long and not quite straight, his mouth full and firm and frowning. Jet-black and unruly, his hair fell over his brow and curled just beyond the collar of his shirt. Pale, almost translucent green eyes scowled up at her.

An apple, Eden, and now the serpent. The idea ran through her head before she drew herself back.

Wonderful, she thought. She'd been caught pinching apples by the foreman. Since disappearing wasn't an option, she opened her mouth to start a plausible explanation.

"Young lady, do you belong at the camp next door?"

The tone brought on a frown. She might be penniless, she might be scrambling to make a living, but she was still a Carlbough. And a Carlbough could certainly handle an apple foreman. "Yes, that's right. I'd like to—"

"Are you aware that this is private property, and that you're trespassing?"

The color of her eyes deepened, the only outward sign of her embarrassed fury. "Yes, but I—"

"These trees weren't planted for little girls to climb."

"I hardly think—"

"Come down." There was absolute command in his tone. "I'll have to take you back to the camp director."

The temper she had always gently controlled bubbled up until she gave serious consideration to throwing what was left of the apple down on his head. No one, absolutely no one, gave her orders. "That won't be necessary."

"I'll decide what's necessary. Come down here."

She'd come down all right, Eden thought. Then, with a few well-chosen words, he'd be put precisely in his place. Annoyance carried her from branch to branch, leaving no room for thoughts of height or inexperience. The two scrapes she picked up on the trip were hardly felt. Her back was to him as she lowered herself into a vee of the trunk. The pleasure of demolishing him with icy manners would be well worth the embarrassment of having been caught in the wrong place at the wrong time. She imagined him cringing and babbling an incoherent apology.

Then her foot slipped, and her frantic grab for a limb was an inch short of the mark. With a shriek that was equal parts surprise and dismay, she fell backward into space.

The breath whooshed back out of her as she connected with something solid. The tanned, muscled arms she'd seen from above wrapped around her. Momentum carried them both to the ground and, like the apple, they rolled. When the world stopped spinning, Eden found herself beneath a very firm, very long body.

Roberta's cap had flown off and Eden's face, no longer shadowed by the brim, was left unguarded in the sunlight. Chase stared down at her and felt soft breasts yield under him.

"You're not twelve years old," he murmured.

"Certainly not."

Amused now, he shifted his weight, but didn't remove it. "I didn't get a good look at you when you were in the tree." He had time to make up for that now, he decided, and he looked his fill. "You're quite a wind-fall." Carelessly, he brushed stray strands of hair away from her face. His fingertips were as rough against her skin as the bark had been to her palms. "What are you doing in a girls' summer camp?"

"Running it," she said coldly. It wasn't a complete lie. Because it would have bruised her dignity even more to squirm, she settled on sending him an icy look. "Would you mind?"

"Running it?" Since she had dropped out of one of his trees, he had no qualms about ignoring her request. "I met someone. Bartholomew—red hair, appealing face." He scanned Eden's classic features. "You're not her."

"Obviously not." Because his body was too warm, too male, and too close, she sacrificed some dignity by putting her hands to his shoulders. He didn't budge. "I'm her partner. Eden Carlbough."

"Ah, of the Philadelphia Carlboughs."

The humor in his voice was another blow to her pride. Eden combated it with a withering stare. "That's correct."

Intriguing little package, he thought. All manners and breeding. "A pleasure, Miss Carlbough. I'm Chase Elliot of the South Mountain Elliots."

Chapter 2

Perfect, just perfect, Eden thought as she stared up at him. Not the foreman, but the bloody owner. Caught stealing apples by, falling out of trees on and pinned to the ground under, the owner. She took a deep breath.

"How do you do, Mr. Elliot."

She might have been in the front parlor pouring tea, Chase thought; he had to admire her. Then he burst out laughing. "I do just fine, Miss Carlbough. And you?"

He was laughing at her. Even after the scandal and shame she had faced, no one had dared laugh at her. Not to her face. Her lips trembled once before she managed to control them. She wouldn't give the oaf the pleasure of knowing how much he infuriated her.

"I'm quite well, thank you, or will be when you let me up."

City manners, he thought. Socially correct and absolutely meaningless. His own were a bit cruder, but more honest. "In a minute. I'm finding this conversation fascinating."

"Then perhaps we could continue it standing up."

"I'm very comfortable." That wasn't precisely true. The soft, slender lines of her body were causing him some problems. Rather than alleviate them, Chase decided to enjoy them. And her. "So, how are you finding life in the rough?"

He was still laughing at her, without troubling to pretend otherwise. Eden tasted the fury bubbling up in her throat. She swallowed it. "Mr. Elliot—"

"Chase," he interrupted. "I think, under the circumstances, we should dispense with formalities."

Control teetered long enough for her to shove against his shoulders again. It was like pushing rock. "This is ridiculous. You *have* to let me up."

"I rarely have to do anything." His voice was a drawl now, and insolent, but no less imposing than the bellow that had first greeted her. "I've heard a lot about you, Eden Carlbough." And he'd seen the newspaper pictures that he now realized had been just shy of the mark. It was difficult to capture that cool sexuality in two dimensions. "I never expected a Carlbough of Philadelphia to fall out of one of my trees."

Her breathing became unsteady. All the training, the years she'd spent being taught how to coat every emotion with politeness, began to crack. "It was hardly my intention to fall out of one of your trees."

"Wouldn't have fallen out if you hadn't climbed up." He smiled, realizing how glad he was that he'd decided to check this section of the orchard himself.

This couldn't be happening. Eden closed her eyes

a moment and waited for things to fall back into their proper places. She couldn't be lying flat on her back under a stranger. "Mr. Elliot." Her voice was calm and reasonable when she tried it again. "I'd be more than happy to give you a complete explanation if you'd let me up."

"Explanation first."

Her mouth quite simply fell open. "You are the most unbelievably rude and boorish man I have ever met."

"My property," he said simply. "My rules. Let's hear your explanation."

She almost shuddered with the effort to hold back the torrent of abuse that leaped to her tongue. Because of her position, she had to squint up at him. Already a headache was collecting behind her eyes. "Three of my girls wandered away from camp. Unfortunately, they climbed over the fence and onto your property. I found them, ordered them down and sent them back to the camp, where they are being properly disciplined."

"Tar and feathers?"

"I'm sure you'd prefer that, but we settled on extra kitchen detail."

"Seems fair. But that doesn't explain you falling out of my tree and into my arms. Though I've about decided not to complain about that. You smell like Paris." To Eden's amazement, he leaned down and buried his face in her hair. "Wicked nights in Paris."

"Stop it." Now her voice wasn't calm, wasn't disciplined.

Chase felt her heart begin to thud against his own. It ran through his mind that he wanted to do more than sample her scent. But when he lifted his head, her eyes were wide. Along with the awareness in them was a trace of fear.

"Explanation," he said lightly. "That's all I intend to take at the moment."

She could hear her own pulse hammering in her throat. Of its own accord, her gaze fell upon his mouth. Was she mad, or could she almost taste the surge of masculine flavor that would certainly be on his lips? She felt her muscles softening, then instantly stiffened. She might very well be mad. If an explanation was what it took, she'd give it to him and get away. Far away.

"One of the girls…" Her mind veered vengefully to Roberta. "One of them left her cap in the tree."

"So you went up after it." He nodded, accepting her explanation. "That doesn't explain why you were helping yourself to one of my apples."

"It was mealy."

Grinning again, he ran a hand along her jawline. "I doubt that. I'd imagine it was hard and tart and delicious. I had my share of stomachaches from green apples years ago. The pleasure's usually worth the pain."

Something uncomfortably like need was spreading through her. The fear of it chilled both her eyes and voice. "You have your explanation, and your apology."

"I never heard an apology."

She'd be damned, she'd be twice damned if she'd give him one now. Glaring at him, she nearly managed to look regal. "I want you to let me up this instant. You're perfectly free to prosecute if you feel the need for compensation for a couple of worm-filled apples, but for now, I'm tired of your ridiculous backwoods arrogance."

His apples were the best in the state, the best in the

country. But at the moment, he relished the idea of her sinking her pretty white teeth into a worm. "You haven't had a taste of backwoods arrogance yet. Maybe you should."

"You wouldn't dare," she began, only to have the last word muffled by his mouth.

The kiss caught her completely off guard. It was rough and demanding and as tart as the apple had been. Forbidden fruit. To a woman accustomed to coaxing, to requesting, the hard demand left her limp, unable to respond or protest. Then his hands were on her face, his thumbs tracing her jawline. Like the kiss, his palms were hard and thrilling.

He didn't regret it. Though he wasn't a man used to taking from a woman what wasn't offered, he didn't regret it. Not when the fruit was this sweet. Even though she lay very still, he could taste the panicked excitement on her lips. Yes, very sweet, he thought. Very innocent. Very dangerous. He lifted his head the moment she began to struggle.

"Easy," he murmured, still stroking her chin with his thumb. Her eyes were more frantic than furious. "It seems you're not the woman of the world you're reputed to be."

"Let me up." Her voice was shaking now, but she was beyond caring.

Getting to his feet, Chase brought her with him. "Want some help brushing off?"

"You are the most offensive man I've ever met."

"I can believe it. A pity you've been spoiled and pampered for so long." She started to turn away, but he caught her shoulders for one last look. "It should be interesting to see how long you last here without the basics—like hairdressers and butlers."

He's just like everyone else, she thought; she coated her hurt and doubt with disdain. "I'm very late for my next class, Mr. Elliot. If you'll excuse me?"

He lifted his hands from her shoulders, holding the palms out a moment before dropping them. "Try to keep the kids out of the trees," he warned. "A fall can be dangerous."

His smile had insults trembling on her lips. Clamping her tongue between her teeth, Eden scrambled over the fence.

He watched her, enjoying the view until she was swallowed up by the aspens. Glimpsing the cap at his feet, he bent down for it. As good as a calling card, he decided, tucking it into his back pocket.

Eden went through the rest of the day struggling not to think. About anything. She had deliberately avoided telling Candy about her meeting with Chase. In telling of it, she would have to think about it.

The humiliation of being caught up a tree was hard enough to swallow. Still, under other circumstances, she and Candy might have shared a laugh over it. Under any other circumstances.

But more than the humiliation, even more than the anger, were the sensations. She wasn't sure what they were, but each separate sensation she had experienced in the orchard remained fresh and vibrant throughout the day. She couldn't shake them off or cover them over, and she certainly couldn't ignore them. If she understood anything, she understood how important it was for her to close off her feelings before they could grow.

Ridiculous. Eden interrupted her own thoughts. She didn't know Chase Elliot. Moreover, she didn't want to know him. It was true that she couldn't block out what had happened, but she could certainly see that it never happened again.

Over the past year, she had taken control of the reins for the first time in her life. She knew what it was to fumble, what it was to fail, but she also knew she would never fully release those reins again. Disillusionment had toughened her. Perhaps that was the one snatch of silver lining in the cloud.

Because of it, she recognized Chase Elliot as a man who held his own reins, and tightly. She had found him rude and overbearing, but she had also seen his power and authority. She'd had her fill of dominating men. Rough-edged or polished, they were all the same underneath. Since her experience with Eric, Eden's opinion of men in general had reached a low ebb. Her encounter with Chase had done nothing to raise it.

It was annoying that she had to remind herself continually to forget about him.

Learning the camp's routine was enough to occupy her mind. Since she didn't have Candy's years of training and experience in counseling, her responsibilities were relatively few and often mundane, but at least she had the satisfaction of knowing she was more than a spectator. Ambition had become a new vice. If her role as apprentice meant she mucked out stalls and groomed horses, then Eden was determined to have the cleanest stables and the glossiest horses in Pennsylvania. She considered her first blister a badge of accomplishment.

The rush after the dinner bell still intimidated Eden. Twenty-seven girls aged ten to fourteen swarmed the cafeteria. It was one of Eden's new duties to help keep order. Voices were raised on topics that usually ranged from boys to rock stars, then back to boys. With a little luck, there was no jostling or shoving in line. But luck usually required an eagle eye.

Camp Liberty's glossy brochures had promised wholesome food. Tonight's menu included crispy chicken, whipped potatoes and steamed broccoli. Flatware rattled on trays as the girls shuffled, cafeteria-style, down the serving line.

"It's been a good day." Candy stood beside Eden, her eyes shifting back and forth as she managed to watch the entire room at once.

"And nearly over." Even as she said it, Eden realized her back didn't ache quite as much as it had the first couple of days. "I've got two girls in the morning riding session who show real promise. I was hoping I could give them a little extra time a couple of days a week."

"Great, we'll check the schedule." Candy watched one of the counselors convince a camper to put a stem of broccoli on her plate. "I wanted to tell you that you handled Roberta and company beautifully. Kitchen detail was an inspiration."

"Thanks." Eden realized how low her pride had fallen when such a small thing made her glow. "I did have a twinge of guilt about dumping them on Mrs. Petrie."

"The report is they behaved like troopers."

"Roberta?"

"I know." Candy's smile was wry. Both women turned to see the girl in question, already seated and eating daintily. "It's like waiting for the other shoe to drop. Eden, do you remember Marcia Delacroix from Camp Forden?"

"How could I forget?" With the bulk of the campers seated, Eden and Candy joined the line. "She was the one who put the garter snake in Miss Forden's lingerie drawer."

"Yeah." She turned to give Roberta another look. "Do you believe in reincarnation?"

With a laugh, Eden accepted a scoop of potatoes. "Let's just say I'll be checking my underwear." Hefting the tray, she started forward. "You know, Candy, I—" She saw it as if in slow motion. Roberta, the devil's own gleam in her eyes, held her fork vertically, a thick blob of potatoes clinging to the tines. Aim was taken as Roberta pulled back the business end of the fork with an expert flick. Even as Eden opened her mouth, Roberta sent the blob sailing into the hair of the girl across from her. Pandemonium.

Globs of potatoes flew. Girls screamed. More retaliated. In a matter of seconds, floors, tables, chairs and adolescents were coated in a messy layer of white. Like a general leading the way into battle, Candy stepped into the chaos and lifted her whistle. Before she had the chance to blow it, she was hit, right between the eyes.

A shocked silence fell.

With her tray still in her hands, Eden stood, afraid to breathe. One breath, one little breath, she thought, and she would dissolve into helpless laughter. She felt the pressure of a giggle in her lungs as Candy slowly wiped the dollop of potato from the bridge of her nose.

"Young ladies." The two words, delivered in Candy's most ferocious voice, had Eden's breath catching in her throat. "You will finish your meal in silence. Absolute silence. As you finish, you will line up against this wall.

When the dinner hour is over, you will be issued rags, mops and buckets. The mess area will shine tonight."

"Yes, Miss Bartholomew." The acknowledgment came in murmured unison. Only Roberta, her hands folded neatly, her face a picture of innocence, responded in clear tones.

After a long ten seconds of silent staring, Candy walked back to Eden and picked up her tray. "If you laugh," she said in an undertone, "I'll tie your tongue into a square knot."

"Who's laughing?" Eden desperately cleared her throat. "I'm not laughing."

"Yes, you are." Candy sailed, like a steamship, to the head table. "You're just clever enough to do it discreetly."

Eden sat, then carefully smoothed her napkin on her lap. "You've got mashed potatoes in your eyebrows." Candy glared at her, and she lifted her coffee cup to hide a grin behind it. "Actually, it's very becoming. You may have found an alternative to hair gel."

Candy glanced down at the cooling potatoes on her own plate. "Would you like to try some?"

"Now, darling, you're the one who's always telling me we have to set an example." Eden took a satisfying bite of her chicken. "Mrs. Petrie's a gem, isn't she?"

It took the better part of two hours to clean the mess area and to mop up the puddles of water spilled by the inexperienced janitorial crew. By lights-out most of the girls were too tired to loiter. A pleasant late-evening hush covered the camp.

If the mornings were the worst for Eden, the evenings were invariably the best. A long day of physical activity left her comfortably tired and relaxed. The sounds of night birds and insects were becoming familiar. More and more, she looked forward to an hour of solitude with a sky full of stars. There was no theater to dress for, no party to attend. The longer she was away from her former life-style, the less she missed it.

She was growing up, she reflected, and she liked the idea. She supposed maturity meant recognizing what was really important. The camp was important, her friendship with Candy vital. The girls under their care for the summer, even the dastardly Roberta Snow, were what really mattered. She came to realize that even if everything she had once had was handed back to her, she would no longer be able to treat it in the same way.

She had changed. And even though she was certain there were still more changes to come, she liked the new Eden Carlbough. This Eden was independent, not financially, but internally. She'd never realized how dependent she had been on her father, her fiancé, the servants. The new Eden could cope with problems, large ones, small ones. Her hands were no longer elegantly manicured. The nails were neat, but short and rounded, unpainted. Practical, Eden thought as she held one up for inspection. Useful. She liked what she saw.

She continued her nightly ritual by walking to the stables. Inside it was cool and dark, smelling of leather, hay and horses. Just stepping inside helped to cement her confidence. This was her contribution. In most other areas, she still relied on pride and nerve, but here she had skill and knowledge.

She would check each of the six horses, then the tack, before she would consider her duties over for the day. Candy might be able to build a cathedral out of papier-mâché, but she knew nothing about strained tendons or split hooves.

Eden stopped at the first stall to stroke the roan gelding she called Courage. In her hand was a paper bag with six apple halves. It was a nightly ritual the horses had caught on to quickly. Courage leaned his head over the stall door and nuzzled her palm.

"Such a good boy," she murmured as she reached into the bag. "Some of the girls still don't know a bit from a stirrup, but we're going to change that." She held the apple in her palm and let him take it. While he chewed contentedly, Eden stepped into the stall to check him over. He'd been a bargain because of his age and his slight swayback. She hadn't been looking for thoroughbreds, but for dependability and gentleness. Satisfied that his grooming had been thorough, she latched the stall door behind her and went to the next.

Next summer they'd have at least three more mounts. Eden smiled as she worked her way from stall to stall. She wasn't going to question whether there would be a Camp Liberty next summer. There would be, and she'd be part of it. A real part.

She realized that she'd brought little with her other than money and a flair for horses. It was Candy who had the training, Candy who had had the three younger sisters and a family that had possessed more tradition than money. Unlike Eden, Candy had always known she would have to earn her own way and had prepared for it. But Eden was a quick learner. By Camp Liberty's second season, she would be a partner in more than name.

Her ambition was already spiraling upward. In a few years, Camp Liberty would be renowned for its equestrian program. The name Carlbough would be respected again. There might even come a time when her Philadelphia contemporaries would send their children to her. The irony of it pleased her.

After the fifth apple had been devoured, Eden moved to the last stall. Here was Patience, a sweet-tempered, aging mare who would tolerate any kind of ineptitude in a rider as long as she received affection. Sympathetic to old bones and muscles, Eden often spent an extra hour rubbing the mare down with liniment.

"Here you are, sweetheart." As the horse gnawed the apple, Eden lifted each hoof for inspection. "A pretty sketchy job," she mumbled before drawing a hoof pick out of her back pocket. "Let's see, wasn't it little Marcie who rode you last? I suppose this means we have to have a discussion on responsibility." With a sigh, Eden switched to another hoof. "I hate discussions on responsibility. Especially when I'm giving them." Patience snorted sympathetically. "Well, I can't leave all the dirty work to Candy, can I? In any case, I don't think Marcie meant to be inconsiderate. She's still a bit nervous around horses. We'll have to show her what a nice lady you are. There. Want a rubdown?" After sticking the pick back in her pocket, Eden rested her cheek against the mare's neck. "Oh, me too, Patience. A nice long massage with some scented oil. You can just lie there with your eyes closed while all the kinks are worked out, then your skin feels so soft, your muscles so supple." With a quick laugh, Eden drew away. "Well, since you can't oblige me, I'll oblige you. Just let me get the liniment."

Giving the mare a final pat, she turned. Her breath caught on a gasp.

Chase Elliot leaned against the open stall door. Shadows fell across his face, deepening its hollows. In the dim light, his eyes were like sea foam. She would have taken a step backward in retreat, but the mare blocked her way. He smiled at her predicament.

That triggered her pride. She could be grateful for that. It had thrown her that, in the shadowed light, he was even more attractive, more…compelling than he had been in the sun. Not handsome, she amended quickly. Certainly not in the smooth, conventional sense, the sense she had always gauged men's looks by before. Everything about him was fundamental. Not simple, she thought. No, not simple, but basic. Basic, like his kiss that morning. Warmth prickled along her skin.

"I'd be happy to help you with the massage." He smiled again. "Yours, or the mare's."

"No, thank you." She became aware that she was even more disheveled than she had been at their first meeting, and that she smelled, all too obviously, of horse. "Is there something I can do for you, Mr. Elliot?"

He liked her style, Chase decided. She might be standing in a stall that could use a bit of cleaning, but she was still the lady of the drawing room. "You've got a good stock here. A bit on the mature side, but solid."

Eden had to ward off a surge of pleasure. His opinion hardly mattered. "Thank you. I'm sure you didn't come to look over the horses."

"No." But he stepped inside the stall. The mare shifted to accommodate him. "Apparently you know your way around them." He lifted a hand to run it down the mare's neck. There was a simple gold ring on his right hand. Eden recognized its age and value, as well as the strength of the man who wore it.

"Apparently." There was no way past him, so she linked her fingers together and waited. "Mr. Elliot, you haven't told me what you're doing here."

Chase's lips twitched as he continued to stroke the mare. Miss Philadelphia was nervous, he thought. She covered it well enough with frigid manners, but her nerves were jumping. It pleased him to know that she hadn't been able to brush off that quick, impulsive kiss any more than he had. "No, I haven't." Before she could avoid it, he reached down for her hand. An opal gleamed dully in the shadowed light, nestled in a circle of diamond chips that promised to catch heat and fire.

"Wrong hand for an engagement ring." He discovered that the fact pleased him, perhaps more than it should have. "I'd heard you and Eric Keeton were to be married last spring. Apparently it didn't come off."

She would like to have sworn, shouted, yelled. That's what *he* wanted, Eden told herself, letting her hand lie passive in his. "No, it didn't. Mr. Elliot, for a, let's say, country squire, you have boundless curiosity about Philadelphia gossip. Don't your apples keep you busy enough?"

He had to admire anyone who could shoot straight and smile. "I manage to eke out a bit of free time. Actually, I was interested because Keeton's a family connection."

"He is not."

There, he'd ruffled her. For the first time since her initial surprise, she was really looking at him. Take a good look, Chase thought. You won't see any resemblance. "Distant, certainly." Capturing her other hand, he turned the palms up. "My grandmother was a Winthrop, and a cousin of his grandmother. Your Philadelphia hands have a couple of blisters. You should take care."

"A Winthrop?" Eden was surprised enough at the name to forget her hands.

"We've thinned the blood a bit in the last few generations." She should be wearing gloves, he thought, as he touched a blister with his thumb. "Still, I'd expected an invitation and was curious why you dumped him."

"I didn't dump him." The words came out like poisoned honey. "But to satisfy your curiosity, and to use your own crude phrase, he dumped me. Now if you'd give me back my hands, I could finish for the day."

Chase obliged, but continued to block her way out of the stall. "I'd never considered Eric bright, but I'd never thought him stupid."

"What a delightful compliment. Please excuse me, Mr. Elliot."

"Not a compliment." Chase brushed at the bangs over her forehead. "Just an observation."

"Stop touching me."

"Touching's a habit of mine. I like your hair, Eden. It's soft, but it goes its own way."

"A veritable bouquet of compliments." She managed one small step backward. He had her pulse thudding again. She didn't want to be touched, not physically, not emotionally, not by anyone. Instinct warned her how easily he could do both. "Mr. Elliot—"

"Chase."

"Chase." She acknowledged this with a regal nod. "The morning bell goes off at six. I still have several things to do tonight, so if there's a purpose in your being here, could we get to it?"

"I came to bring you back your hat." Reaching into his back pocket, he pulled out the Phillies cap.

"I see." One more black mark against Roberta. "It's not mine, but I'd be happy to return it to its owner. Thank you for troubling."

"You were wearing it when you fell out of my tree." Chase ignored her outstretched hand and dropped the cap on her head. "Fits, too."

"As I've already explained—"

Eden's frigid retort was interrupted by the sound of running feet. "Miss Carlbough! Miss Carlbough!" Roberta, in an angelic pink nightgown and bare feet, skidded to a halt at the open stall. Beaming, she stared up at Chase. Her adolescent heart melted. "Hi."

"Hi."

"Roberta." Voice stern, teeth nearly clenched, Eden stepped forward. "It's almost an hour past lights-out."

"I know, Miss Carlbough. I'm sorry." When she smiled, Eden thought you could almost believe it. "I just couldn't get to sleep because I kept thinking about my cap. You promised I could have it back, but you never gave it to me. I helped Mrs. Petrie. Honest, you can ask. There were millions of pans, too. I even peeled potatoes, and—"

"Roberta!" The sharp tone was enough for the moment. "Mr. Elliot was kind enough to return your hat." Whipping it off her own head, Eden thrust it into the girl's hands. "I believe you should thank him, as well as apologize for trespassing."

"Gee, thanks." She treated him to a dazzling smile. "Are those your trees, really?"

"Yeah." With a fingertip, Chase adjusted the brim of her hat. He had a weakness for black sheep and recognized a kindred soul in Roberta.

"I think they're great. Your apples tasted a whole lot better than the ones we get at home."

"Roberta."

The quiet warning had the girl rolling her eyes, which only Chase could see. "I'm sorry I didn't show the proper respect for your property." Roberta turned her head to see whether Eden approved of the apology.

"Very nice, Roberta. Now straight back to bed."

"Yes, ma'am." She shot a last look at Chase. Her little heart fluttered. Crushing the cap down on her head, she raced to the door.

"Roberta." She whipped back around at the sound of Chase's voice. He grinned at her. "See you around."

"Yeah, see you." In love, Roberta floated off to her cabin. When the stable door slammed at her back, all Eden could manage was a sigh.

"It's no use," Chase commented.

"What isn't?"

"Pretending you don't get a kick out of her. A kid like that makes you feel good."

"You wouldn't be so sure of that if you'd seen what she can do with mashed potatoes." But Eden gave in enough to smile. "She's a monster, but an appealing one. Still, I have to admit, if we had twenty-seven Robertas in camp this summer, I'd end up in a padded room."

"Certain people just breed excitement."

Eden remembered the dinner hour. "Some call it chaos."

"Life flattens out quickly without a little chaos."

She looked at him, realizing she'd dropped her guard

enough to have an actual conversation. And realizing as well that they'd stopped talking about Roberta. The stables suddenly seemed very quiet. "Well, now that we've gotten that settled, I think—"

He took a step forward. She took a step back. A smile played around his lips again as he reached for her hand. Eden bumped solidly into the mare before she managed to raise her free hand to his chest.

"What do you want?" Why was she whispering, and why was the whisper so tremulous?

He wasn't sure what he wanted. Once, quickly, he scanned her face before bringing his gaze back to hers with a jolt. Or perhaps he was. "To walk with you in the moonlight, I think. To listen to the owls hoot and wait for the nightingale."

The shadows had merged. The mare stood quietly, breathing softly. His hand was in Eden's hair now, as if it belonged there. "I have to go in." But she didn't move.

"Eden and the apple," he murmured. "I can't tell you how tempting I've found that combination. Come with me. We'll walk."

"No." Something was building inside her, too quickly. She knew he was touching more than her hand, more than her hair. He was reaching for something he should not have known existed.

"Sooner or later." He'd always been a patient man. He could wait for her the way he waited for a new tree to bear fruit. His fingers slid down to her throat, stroking once. He felt her quick shudder, heard the unsteady indrawn breath. "I'll be back, Eden."

"It won't make any difference."

Smiling, he brought her hand to his lips, turning it palm up. "I'll still be back."

She listened to his footsteps, to the creak of the door as he opened it, then shut it again.

Chapter 3

The camp was developing its own routine. Eden adjusted hers to it. Early hours, long, physical days and basic food were both a solace and a challenge. The confidence she'd once had to work at became real.

There were nights during the first month of summer that she fell into her bunk certain she would never be able to get up in the morning. Her muscles ached from rowing, riding and endless hiking. Her head spun from weekly encounters with ledgers and account books. But in the morning the sun would rise, and so would she.

Every day it became easier. She was young and healthy. The daily regimented exercise hardened muscles only touched on by occasional games of tennis. The weight she had lost over the months since her father's death gradually came back, so that her look of fragility faded.

To her surprise, she developed a genuine affection for the girls. They became individuals, not simply a group to be coped with or income on the books. It surprised her more to find that same affection returned.

Right from the start, Eden had been certain the girls would love Candy. Everyone did. She was warm, funny, talented. The most Eden had hoped for, for herself, was to be tolerated and respected. The day Marcie had brought her a clutch of wildflowers, Eden had been too stunned to do more than stammer a thank-you. Then there had been the afternoon she had given Linda Hopkins an extra half hour in the corral. After her first gallop, Linda had thrown herself into Eden's arms for a fierce and delightful hug.

So the camp had changed her life, in so many more ways than she'd expected.

The summer grew hot with July. Girls darted around the compound in shorts. Dips in the lake became a glorious luxury. Doors and windows stayed open at night to catch even the slightest breeze. Roberta found a garter snake and terrorized her cabin mates. Bees buzzed around the wildflowers and stings became common.

Days merged together, content, but never dull, so that it seemed possible that summer could last forever. As the time passed, Eden began to believe that Chase had forgotten his promise, or threat, to come back. She'd been careful to stay well within the borders of the camp herself. Though once or twice she'd been tempted to wander toward the orchards, she stayed away.

It didn't make sense for her to still be tense and uneasy. She could tell herself he'd only been a brief annoyance. Yet every time she went into the stables in the evening, she caught herself listening. And waiting.

* * *

Late in the evening, with the heat still shimmering, Eden stretched out on her bunk, fully dressed. Bribed by the promise of a bonfire the following night, the campers had quieted down early. Relaxed and pleasantly weary, Eden pictured it. Hot dogs flaming on sharpened sticks, marshmallows toasting, the blaze flickering heat over her face and sending smoke billowing skyward. Eden found herself looking forward to the evening every bit as much as the youngest camper. With her head pillowed on her folded arms, she stared up at the ceiling while Candy paced.

"I'm sure we could do it, Eden."

"Hmm?"

"The dance." Gesturing with the clipboard she was carrying, Candy stopped at the foot of the bunk. "The dance I've been talking about having for the girls. Remember?"

"Of course." Eden forced her mind back to business. "What about it?"

"I think we should go ahead with it. In fact, if it works out, I think it should be an annual event." Even after she plopped herself down on Eden's bed, her enthusiasm continued to bounce around the room. "The boys' camp is only twenty miles from here. I'm sure they'd go for it."

"Probably." A dance. That would mean refreshments for somewhere close to a hundred, not to mention music, decorations. She thought first of the red ink in the ledger, then about how much the girls would enjoy it. There had to be a way around the red ink. "I guess there'd be room in the mess area if we moved the tables."

"Exactly. And most of the girls have records with

them. We could have the boys bring some, too." She began to scrawl on her clipboard. "We can make the decorations ourselves."

"We'd have to keep the refreshments simple," Eden put in before Candy's enthusiasm could run away with her. "Cookies, punch, that sort of thing."

"We can plan it for the last week of camp. Kind of a celebrational send-off."

The last week of camp. How strange, when the first week had been so wearing, that the thought of it ending brought on both panic and regret. No, summer wouldn't last forever. In September there would be the challenge of finding a new job, a new goal. She wouldn't be going back to a teaching job as Candy was, but to want ads and résumés.

"Eden? Eden, what do you think?"

"About what?"

"About planning the dance for the last week of camp?"

"I think we'd better clear it with the boys' camp first."

"Honey, are you okay?" Leaning forward, Candy took Eden's hand. "Are you worried about going back home in a few weeks?"

"No. Concerned." She gave Candy's hand a squeeze. "Just concerned."

"I meant it when I told you not to worry about a job right away. My salary takes care of the rent on the apartment, and I still have a little piece of the nest egg my grandmother left me."

"I love you, Candy. You're the best friend I've ever had."

"The reverse holds true, Eden."

"For that reason, there's no way I'm going to sit around while you work to pay the rent and put dinner on the table. It's enough that you've let me move in with you."

"Eden, you know I'm a lot happier sharing my apartment with you than I was living alone. If you look at it as a favor, you're going to feel pressured, and that's ridiculous. Besides, for the past few months, you were taking care of fixing all the meals."

"Only a small portion of which were edible."

"True." Candy grinned. "But I didn't have to cook. Listen, give yourself a little space. You'll need some time to find out what it is you want to do."

"What I want to do is work." With a laugh, Eden lay back on the bed again. "Surprise. I really want to work, to keep busy, to earn a living. The past few weeks have shown me how much I enjoy taking care of myself. I'm banking on getting a job at a riding stable. Maybe even the one I used to board my horse at. And if that doesn't pan out—" She shrugged her shoulders. "I'll find something else."

"You will." Candy set the clipboard aside. "And next year, we'll have more girls, a bigger staff and maybe even a profit."

"Next year, I'm going to know how to make a hurricane lamp out of a tuna can."

"And a pillow out of two washcloths."

"And pot holders."

Candy remembered Eden's one mangled attempt. "Well, maybe you should take it slow."

"There's going to be no stopping me. In the meantime, I'll contact the camp director over at—what's the name, Hawk's Nest?"

"Eagle Rock," Candy corrected her, laughing. "It'll be fun for us, too, Eden. They have counselors. *Male* counselors." Sighing, she stretched her arms to the ceiling. "Do you know how long it's been since I've spoken with a man?"

"You talked to the electrician just last week."

"He was a hundred and two. I'm talking about a man who still has all his hair and teeth." She touched her tongue to her upper lip. "Not all of us have passed the time holding hands with a man in the stables."

Eden plumped up her excuse for a pillow. "I wasn't holding hands. I explained to you."

"Roberta Snow, master spy, gave an entirely different story. With her, it appears to be love at first sight."

Eden examined the pad of callus on the ridge of her palm. "I'm sure she'll survive."

"Well, what about you?"

"I'll survive, too."

"No, I mean, aren't you interested?" After folding her legs under her, Candy leaned forward. "Remember, darling, I got a good look at the man when I was negotiating for the use of his lake. I don't think there's a woman alive who wouldn't sweat a bit after a look at those spooky green eyes."

"I never sweat."

Chuckling, Candy leaned back. "Eden, you're talking to the one who loves you best. The man was interested enough to track you down in the stables. Think of the possibilities."

"It's possible that he was returning Roberta's cap."

"And it's possible that pigs fly. Haven't you been tempted to wander over by the orchard, just once?"

"No." Only a hundred times. "Seen one apple tree, you've seen them all."

"The same doesn't hold true for an apple grower who's about six-two, with a hundred and ninety well-placed pounds and one of the most fascinating faces this side of the Mississippi." Concern edged into her voice. She had watched her friend suffer and had been helpless to do more than offer emotional support. "Have fun, Eden. You deserve it."

"I don't think Chase Elliot falls into the category of fun." Danger, she thought. Excitement, sexuality and, oh yes, temptation. Tossing her legs over the bunk, Eden walked to the window. Moths were flapping at the screen.

"You're gun-shy."

"Maybe."

"Honey, you can't use Eric as a yardstick."

"I'm not." With a sigh, she turned back. "I'm not pining or brooding over him, either."

The quick shrug was Candy's way of dismissing someone she considered a weasel. "That's because you were never really in love with him."

"I was going to marry him."

"Because it seemed the proper thing to do. I know you, Eden, like no one else. Everything was very simple and easy with Eric. It all fit—click, click, click."

Amused, Eden shook her head. "Is something wrong with that?"

"Everything's wrong with that. Love makes you giddy and foolish and achy. You never felt any of that with Eric." She spoke from the experience of a woman who'd fallen in love, and out again, a dozen times before she'd hit twenty. "You would have married him, and maybe you would even have been content. His tastes were compatible with yours. His family mixed well with yours."

Amusement fled. "You make it sound so cold."

"It was. But you're not." Candy raised her hands, hoping she hadn't gone too far. "Eden, you were raised a certain way, to be a certain way; then the roof collapsed. I can only guess at how traumatic that was. You've picked yourself up, but still you've closed pieces of yourself off. Isn't it time you put the past behind you, really behind you?"

"I've been trying."

"I know, and you've made a good start, with the camp, with your outlook. Maybe it's time you started looking for a little more, just for yourself."

"A man?"

"Some companionship, some sharing, some affection. You're too smart to think that you need a man to make things work, but to cut them off because one acted like a weasel isn't the answer, either." She rubbed at a streak of red paint on her fingernail. "I guess I still believe that everyone needs someone."

"Maybe you're right. Right now I'm too busy pasting myself back together and enjoying the results. I'm not ready for complications. Especially when they're six foot two."

"You were always the romantic one, Eden. Remember the poetry you used to write?"

"We were children." Restless, Eden moved her shoulders. "I had to grow up."

"Growing up doesn't mean you have to stop dreaming." Candy rose. "We've started one dream here, together. I want to see you have other dreams."

"When the time's right." Touched, Eden kissed Candy's cheek. "We'll have your dance and charm your counselors."

"We could invite some neighbors, just to round things out."

"Don't press your luck." Laughing, Eden turned toward the door. "I'm going for a walk before I check on the horses. Leave the light on low, will you?"

The air was still, but not quiet. The first nights Eden had spent in the hills, the country quiet had disturbed her. Now, she could hear and appreciate the night music. The chorus of crickets in soprano, the tenor crying of an owl, the occasional bass lowing of the cows on a farm half a mile away all merged into a symphony accompanied by the rustling of small animals in the brush. The three-quarter moon and a galaxy of stars added soft light and dramatic shadows. The erratic yellow beams of an army of fireflies was a nightly light show.

As she strolled toward the lake, she heard the rushing song of peepers over the softer sound of lapping water. The air smelled as steamy as it felt, so she rounded the edge of the lake toward the cooler cover of trees.

With her mind on her conversation with Candy, Eden bent to pluck a black-eyed Susan. Twisting the stem between her fingers, she watched the petals revolve around the dark center.

Had she been a romantic? There had been poetry, dreamy, optimistic poetry, often revolving around love. Troubadour love, she thought now. The sort that meant long, wistful glances, sterling sacrifices and purity. Romantic, but unrealistic, Eden admitted. She hadn't written any poetry in a long time.

Not since she had met Eric, Eden realized. She had

gone from dreamy young girl to proper young woman, exchanging verses for silver patterns. Now both the dreamy girl and the proper woman were gone.

That was for the best, Eden decided, and she tossed her flower onto the surface of the lake. She watched it float lazily.

Candy had been right. It had not been a matter of love with Eric, but of fulfilling expectations. When he had turned his back on her, he had broken not her heart, but her pride. She was still repairing it.

Eric had given her a suitable diamond, sent her roses at the proper times and had never been at a loss for a clever compliment. That wasn't romance, Eden mused, and it certainly wasn't love. Perhaps she'd never really understood either.

Was romance white knights and pure maidens? Was it Chopin and soft lights? Was it the top of the Ferris wheel? Maybe she'd prefer the last after all. With a quiet laugh, Eden wrapped her arms around herself and held her face up to the stars.

"You should do that more often."

She whirled, one hand pressing against her throat. Chase stood a few feet away at the edge of the trees, the edge of the shadows. It flashed through her mind that this was the third time she had seen him and the third time he had taken her by surprise. It was a habit she wanted to break.

"Do you practice startling people, or is it a natural gift?"

"I can't remember it happening much before you." The fact was, he hadn't come up on her, but she on him. He'd been walking since dusk, and had stopped on the banks of the lake to watch the water and to think of her. "You've been getting some sun." Her hair seemed lighter, more fragile against the honeyed tone of her skin. He wanted to touch it, to see if it was still as soft and fragrant.

"Most of the work is outdoors." It amazed her that she had to fight the urge to turn and run. There was something mystical, even fanciful, about meeting him here in the moonlight, by the water. Almost as if it had been fated.

"You should wear a hat." He said it absently, distracted by the pounding of his own heart. She might have been an illusion, long slender arms and legs gleaming in the moonlight, her hair loose and drenched with it. She wore white. Even the simple shorts and shirt seemed to glimmer. "I'd wondered if you walked here."

He stepped out of the shadows. The monotonous song of the crickets seemed to reach a crescendo. "I thought it might be cooler."

"Some." He moved closer. "I've always been fond of hot nights."

"The cabins tend to get stuffy." Uneasy, she glanced back and discovered she had walked farther than she'd intended. The camp, with its comforting lights and company, was very far away. "I didn't realize I'd crossed over onto your property."

"I'm only a tyrant about my trees." She was less of an illusion up close, more of a woman. "You were laughing before. What were you thinking of?"

Her mouth was dry. Even as she backed away, he seemed to be closer. "Ferris wheels."

"Ferris wheels? Do you like the drop?" Satisfying his own need, he reached for her hair. "Or the climb?"

At his touch, her stomach shot down to her knees.
"I have to get back."

"Let's walk."

To walk with you in the moonlight. Eden thought of
his words, and of fate. "No, I can't. It's late."

"Must be all of nine-thirty." Amused, he took her
hand, then immediately turned it over. There was a
hardening ridge of calluses on the pad beneath her fingers. "You've been working."

"Some people make a living that way."

"Don't get testy." He turned her hand back to run a
thumb over her knuckles. Was it a talent of his, Eden
wondered, to touch a woman in the most casual of ways
and send her blood pounding? "You could wear gloves,"
Chase went on, "and keep your Philadelphia hands."

"I'm not in Philadelphia." She drew her hand away.
Chase simply took her other one. "And since I'm pitch-
ing hay rather than serving tea, it hardly seems to matter."

"You'll be serving tea again." He could see her,
seated in some fussy parlor, wearing pink silk and holding a china pot. But, for the moment, her hand was
warm in his. "The moon's on the water. Look."

Compelled, she turned her head. There were such
things as moonbeams. They gilded the dark water of
the lake and silvered the trees. She remembered some
old legend about three women, the moonspinners, who
spun the moon on spindles. More romance. But even
the new, practical Eden couldn't resist.

"It's lovely. The moon seems so close."

"Some things aren't as close as they seem; others
aren't so far away."

He began to walk. Because he still had her hand,

and because he intrigued her, Eden walked with him. "I suppose you've always lived here." Just small talk, she told herself. She didn't really care.

"For the most part. This has always been headquarters for the business." He turned to look down at her. "The house is over a hundred years old. You might find it interesting."

She thought of her home and of the generations of Carlboughs who had lived there. And of the strangers who lived there now. "I like old houses."

"Are things going well at camp?"

She wouldn't think of the books. "The girls keep us busy." Her laugh came again, low and easy. "That's an understatement. We'll just say their energy level is amazing."

"How's Roberta?"

"Incorrigible."

"I'm glad to hear it."

"Last night she painted one of the girls while the girl was asleep."

"Painted?"

Eden's laugh came again, low and easy. "The little darling must have copped a couple of pots of paint from the art area."

"Our Roberta's inventive."

"To say the least. She told me she thought it might be interesting to be the first woman chief justice."

He smiled at that. Imagination and ambition were the qualities he most admired. "She'll probably do it."

"I know. It's terrifying."

"Let's sit. You can see the stars better."

Stars? She'd nearly forgotten who she was with and why she had wanted to avoid being with him. "I don't think I—" Before she'd gotten the sentence out, he'd tugged her down on a soft, grassy rise. "One wonders why you bother to ask."

"Manners," he said easily as he slipped an arm around her shoulders. Even as she stiffened, he relaxed. "Look at the sky. How often do you notice it in the city?"

Unable to resist, she tilted her face up. The sky was an inky black backdrop for countless pinpoints of lights. They spread, winking, shivering, overhead with a glory that made Eden's throat ache just in the looking. "It isn't the same sky that's over the city."

"Same sky, Eden. It's people who change." He stretched out on his back, crossing his legs. "There's Cassiopeia."

"Where?" Curious, Eden searched, but saw only stars without pattern.

"You can see her better from here." He pulled her closer to him, and before she could protest, he was pointing. "There she is. Looks like a W this time of year."

"Yes!" Delighted, she reached for his wrist and outlined the constellation herself. "I've never been able to find anything in the sky."

"You have to look first. There's Pegasus." Chase shifted his arm. "He has a hundred and sixty-six stars you can view with the naked eye. See? He's flying straight up."

Eyes narrowed, she concentrated on finding the pattern. Moonlight splashed on her face. "Oh yes, I see." She shifted a bit closer to guide his hand again. "I named my first pony Pegasus. Sometimes I'd imagine he sprouted wings and flew. Show me another."

He was looking at her, at the way the stars reflected in her eyes, at the way her mouth softened so generously with a smile. "Orion," he murmured.

"Where?"

"He stands with his sword behind him and his shield lifted in front. And a red star, thousands of times brighter than the sun, is the shoulder of his sword arm."

"Where is he? I—" Eden turned her head and looked directly into Chase's eyes. She forgot the stars and the moonlight and the soft, sweet grass beneath her. The hand on his wrist tightened until the rhythm of his pulse was the rhythm of hers.

Her muscles contracted and held as she braced for the kiss. But his lips merely brushed against her temple. Warmth spread through her as softly as the scent of honeysuckle spread through the air. She heard an owl call out to the night, to the stars, or to a lover.

"What are we doing here?" she managed.

"Enjoying each other." Without rushing, his lips moved over her face.

Enjoying? That was much too mild a word for what was burning through her. No one had ever made her feel like this, so weak and hot, so strong and desperate. His lips were soft, the hand that rested on the side of her face was hard. Beneath his, her heart began to gallop uncontrolled. Eden's fingers slipped off the reins.

She turned her head with a moan and found his mouth with hers. Her arms went around him, holding him close as her lips parted in demand. In all her life she had never known true hunger, not until now. This was breathless, painful, glorious.

He'd never expected such unchecked passion. He'd been prepared to go slowly, gently, as the innocence he'd felt in her required. Now she was moving under him, her fingers pressing and kneading the muscles of his back, her mouth hot and willing on his. The patience that was so much a part of him drowned in need.

Such new, such exciting sensations. Her body gave as his pressed hard against it. Gods and goddesses of the sky guarded them. He smelled of the grass and the earth, and he tasted of fire. Night sounds roared in her head, and her own sigh was only a dim echo when his lips slid down to her throat.

Murmuring his name, Eden combed her fingers through his hair. He wanted to touch her, all of her. He wanted to take her now. When her hand came to rest on his face, he covered it with his own and felt the smooth stone of her ring.

There was so much more he needed to know. So little he was sure of. Desire, for the moment, couldn't be enough. Who was she? He lifted his head to look down at her. Who the hell was she, and why was she driving him mad?

Pulling himself back, he tried to find solid ground. "You're full of surprises, Eden Carlbough of the Philadelphia Carlboughs."

For a moment, she could only stare. She'd had her ride on the Ferris wheel, a wild, dizzying ride. Somewhere along the line, she'd been tossed off to spiral madly in the air. Now she'd hit the ground, hard. "Let me up."

"I can't figure you, Eden."

"You aren't required to." She wanted to weep, to curl up into a ball and weep, but she couldn't focus on the reason. Anger was clearer. "I asked you to let me up."

He rose, holding out a hand to help her. Ignoring it,

Eden got to her feet. "I've always felt it was more constructive to shout when you're angry."

She shot him one glittering look. Humiliation. It was something she'd sworn she would never feel again. "I'm sure you do. If you'll excuse me."

"Damn it." He caught her arm and swung her back to face him. "Something was happening here tonight. I'm not fool enough to deny that, but I want to know what I'm getting into."

"We were enjoying each other. Wasn't that your term?" Nothing more, Eden repeated over and over in her head. Nothing more than a moment's enjoyment. "We've finished now, so good night."

"We're far from finished. That's what worries me."

"I'd say that's your problem, Chase." But a ripple of fear—of anticipation—raced through her, because she knew he was right.

"Yeah, it's my problem." My God, how had he passed so quickly from curiosity to attraction to blazing need? "And because it is, I've got a question. I want to know why Eden Carlbough is playing at camp for the summer rather than cruising the Greek Isles. I want to know why she's cleaning out stables instead of matching silver patterns and planning dinner parties as Mrs. Eric Keeton."

"My business." Her voice rose. The new Eden wasn't as good as the old one at controlling emotion. "But if you're so curious, why don't you call one of your family connections? I'm sure any of them would be delighted to give you all the details."

"I'm asking you."

"I don't owe you any explanations." She jerked her arm away and stood trembling with rage. "I don't owe you a damn thing."

"Maybe not." His temper had cooled his passion and cleared his head. "But I want to know who I'm making love with."

"That won't be an issue, I promise you."

"We're going to finish what we started here, Eden." Without stepping closer, he had her arm again. The touch was far from gentle, far from patient. "That I promise you."

"Consider it finished."

To her surprise and fury, he only smiled. His hand eased on her arm to one lingering caress. Helpless against her response, she shivered. "We both know better than that." He touched a finger to her lips, as if reminding her what tastes he'd left there. "Think of me."

He slipped back into the shadows.

Chapter 4

It was a perfect night for a bonfire. Only a few wispy clouds dragged across the moon, shadowing it, then freeing it. The heat of the day eased with sunset, and the air was balmy, freshened by a calm, steady breeze.

The pile of twigs and sticks that had been gathered throughout the day had been stacked, tepeelike, in a field to the east of the main compound. In the clearing, it rose from a wide base to the height of a man. Every one of the girls had contributed to the making of it, just as every one of them circled around the bonfire now, waiting for the fire to catch and blaze. An army of hot dogs and marshmallows was laid out on a picnic table. Stacked like swords were dozens of cleaned and sharpened sticks. Nearby was the garden hose with a tub full of water, for safety's sake.

Candy held up a long kitchen match, drawing out

the drama as the girls began to cheer. "The first annual bonfire at Camp Liberty is about to begin. Secure your hot dogs to your sticks, ladies, and prepare to roast."

Amid the giggles and gasps, Candy struck the match, then held it to the dry kindling at the base. Wood crackled. Flames licked, searched for more fuel, and spread around and around, following the circle of starter fluid. As they watched, fire began its journey up and up. Eden applauded with the rest.

"Fabulous!" Even as she watched, smoke began to billow. Its scent was the scent of autumn, and that was still a summer away. "I was terrified we wouldn't get it started."

"You're looking at an expert." Catching her tongue between her teeth, Candy speared a hot dog with a sharpened stick. Behind her, the bonfire glowed red at the center. "The only thing I was worried about was rain. But just look at those stars. It's perfect."

Eden tilted her head back. Without effort, without thought, she found Pegasus. He was riding the night sky just as he'd been riding it twenty-four hours before. One day, one night. How could so much have happened? Standing with her face lifted to the breeze and her hands growing warm from the fire, she wondered if she had really experienced that wild, turbulent moment with Chase.

She had. The memories were too ripe, too real for dreams. The moment had happened, and all the feelings and sensations that had grown from it. Deliberately she turned her gaze to a riot of patternless stars.

It didn't change what she remembered, or what she still felt. The moment had happened, she thought again, and it had passed. Yet, somehow, she wasn't certain it was over.

"Why does everything seem different here, Candy?"

"Everything *is* different here." Candy took a deep breath, drawing in the scents of smoke, drying grass and roasting meat. "Isn't it marvelous? No stuffy parlors, no boring dinner parties, no endless piano recitals. Want a hot dog?"

Because her mouth was watering, Eden accepted the partially blackened wiener. "You simplify things, Candy." Eden ran a thin line of ketchup along the meat and stuck it in a bun. "I wish I could."

"You will once you stop thinking you're letting down the Carlbough name by enjoying a hot dog by a bonfire." When Eden's mouth dropped open, Candy gave her a friendly pat. "You ought to try the marshmallows," she advised before she wandered off to find another stick.

Is that what she was doing? Eden wondered, chewing automatically. Maybe, in a way that wasn't quite as basic as Candy had said, it was. After all, she had been the one who had sold the house that had been in the family for four generations. In the end, it had been she who had inventoried the silver and china, the paintings and the jewelry for auction. So, in the end, it had been she who had liquidated the Carlbough tradition to pay off debts and to start a new life.

Necessary. No matter how the practical Eden accepted the necessity, the grieving Eden still felt the loss, and the guilt.

With a sigh, Eden stepped back. The scene that played out in front of her was like a memory from her own childhood. She could see the column of gray smoke rising toward the sky, twirling and curling. At the core of the tower of wood, the fire was fiercely gold and greedy. The smell of outdoor cooking was strong and summery, as it had been during her own weeks at Camp Forden for Girls. For a moment, there was regret that she couldn't step back into those memories of a time when life was simple and problems were things for parents to fix.

"Miss Carlbough."

Brought out of a half-formed dream, Eden glanced down at Roberta. "Hello, Roberta. Are you having fun?"

"It's super!" Roberta's enthusiasm was evident from the smear of ketchup on her chin. "Don't you like bonfires?"

"Yes, I do." Smiling, she looked back at the crackling wood, one hand dropping automatically to Roberta's shoulder. "I like them a lot."

"I thought you looked sort of sad, so I made you a marshmallow."

The offering dripped, black and shriveled, from the end of a stick. Eden felt her throat close up the same way it had when another girl had offered her a clutch of wildflowers. "Thanks, Roberta. I wasn't sad really, I was just remembering." Gingerly, Eden pulled the melted, mangled marshmallow from the stick. Half of it plopped to the ground on the way to her mouth.

"They're tricky," Roberta observed. "I'll make you another one."

Left with the charred outer hull, Eden swallowed valiantly. "You don't have to bother, Roberta."

"Oh, I don't mind." She looked up at Eden with a glowing, generous grin. Somehow, all her past crimes didn't seem so important. "I like to do it. I thought camp was going to be boring, but it's not. Especially the horses. Miss Carlbough…" Roberta looked down at the ground and seemed to draw her courage out of her toes. "I guess I'm not as good as Linda with the horses, but I wondered if maybe you could—well, if I could spend some more time at the stables."

"Of course you can, Roberta." Eden rubbed her thumb and forefinger together, trying fruitlessly to rid herself of the goo. "And you don't even have to bribe me with marshmallows."

"Really?"

"Yes, really." Amused despite herself, Eden ruffled Roberta's hair. "Miss Bartholomew and I will work it into your schedule."

"Gee, thanks, Miss Carlbough."

"But you'll have to work on your posting."

Roberta's nose wrinkled only a little. "Okay. But I wish we could do stuff like barrel racing. I've seen it on TV."

"Well, I don't know about that, but you might progress to small jumps before the end of camp."

Eden had the pleasure of seeing Roberta's eyes saucer with pleasure. "No fooling?"

"No fooling. As long as you work on your posting."

"I will. And I'll be better than Linda, too. Wow, jumps." She spun in an awkward pirouette. "Thanks a lot, Miss Carlbough. Thanks a lot."

She was off in a streak, undoubtedly to spread the word. If Eden knew Roberta, and she was beginning to, she was certain the girl would soon have talked herself into a gold medal for equestrian prowess at the next Olympic Games.

But, as she watched Roberta spin from group to

group, Eden realized she wasn't thinking of the past any longer; nor was she regretting. She was smiling. As one of the counselors began to strum a guitar, Eden licked marshmallow goop from her fingers.

"Need some help with that?"

With her fingers still in her mouth, Eden turned. She should have known he'd come. Perhaps, in her secret thoughts, she had hoped he would. Now she found herself thrusting her still-sticky fingers behind her back.

He wondered if she knew how lovely she looked, with the fire at her back and her hair loose on her shoulders. There was a frown on her face now, but he hadn't missed that one quick flash of pleasure. If he kissed her now, would he taste that sweet, sugary flavor she had been licking from her fingers? Through it would he find that simmering, waiting heat he'd tasted once before? The muscles in his stomach tightened, even as he dipped his thumbs into his pockets and looked away from her toward the fire.

"Nice night for a bonfire."

"Candy claims she arranged it that way." Confident there was enough distance between them, and that there were enough people around them, Eden allowed herself to relax. "We weren't expecting any company."

"I spotted your smoke."

That made her glance up and realize how far the smoke might travel. "I hope it didn't worry you. We notified the fire department." Three girls streaked by behind them. Chase glanced their way and had them lapsing into giggles. Eden caught her tongue in her cheek. "How long did it take you to perfect it?"

With a half smile, Chase turned back to her. "What?"

"The deadly charm that has females crumpling at your feet?"

"Oh, that." He grinned at her. "I was born with it."

The laugh came out before she could stop it. To cover her lapse, Eden crossed her arms and took a step backward. "It's getting warm."

"We used to have a bonfire on the farm every Halloween. My father would carve the biggest pumpkin in the patch and stuff some overalls and a flannel shirt with straw. One year he dressed himself up as the Headless Horseman and gave every kid in the neighborhood a thrill." Watching the fire, he remembered and wondered why until tonight he hadn't thought of continuing the tradition. "My mother would give each of the kids a caramel apple, then we'd sit around the fire and tell ghost stories until we'd scared ourselves silly. Looking back, I think my father got a bigger kick out of it than any of us kids."

She could see it, just as he described, and had to smile again. For her, Halloween had been tidy costume parties where she'd dressed as a princess or ballerina. Though the memories were still lovely, she couldn't help wishing she'd seen one of the bonfires and the Headless Horseman.

"When we were planning tonight, I was as excited as any of the girls. I guess that sounds foolish."

"No, it sounds promising." He put a hand to her cheek, turning her slightly toward him. Though she stiffened, her skin was warm and soft. "Did you think of me?"

There it was again—that feeling of drowning, of floating, of going under for the third time. "I've been busy." She told herself to move away, but her legs didn't respond. The sound of singing and strumming seemed to be coming from off in the distance, with melody and lyrics she couldn't quite remember. The only thing that was close and real was his hand on her cheek.

"I-it was nice of you to drop by," she began, struggling to find solid ground again.

"Am I being dismissed?" He moved his hand casually from her cheek to her hair.

"I'm sure you have better things to do." His fingertip skimmed the back of her neck and set every nerve end trembling. "Stop."

The smoke billowed up over her head. Light and shadow created by the fire danced over her face and in her eyes. He'd thought of her, Chase reminded himself. Too much. Now he could only think what it would be like to make love with her near the heat of the fire, with the scent of smoke, and night closing in.

"You haven't walked by the lake."

"I told you, I've been busy." Why couldn't she make her voice firm and cool? "I have a responsibility to the girls, and the camp, and—"

"Yourself?" How badly he wanted to walk with her again, to study the stars and talk. How badly he wanted to taste that passion and that innocence again. "I'm a very patient man, Eden. You can only avoid me for so long."

"Longer than you think," she murmured, letting out a sigh of relief as she spotted Roberta making a beeline for them.

"Hi!" Delighted with the quick fluttering of her heart, Roberta beamed up at Chase.

"Hi, Roberta," he said. She was thrilled that he'd remembered her name. He gave her a smile, and his attention, without releasing Eden's hair. "You're taking better care of your cap, I see."

She laughed and pushed up the brim. "Miss Carlbough said if I wandered into your orchard again, she'd hold my cap for ransom. But if you invited us to come on a tour, that would be educational, wouldn't it?"

"Roberta." Why was it the child was always one step ahead of everyone else? Eden lifted her brow in a quelling look.

"Well, Miss Bartholomew said we should think of interesting things." Roberta put her most innocent look to good use. "And I think the apple trees are interesting."

"Thanks." Chase thought he heard Eden's teeth clench. "We'll give it some thought."

"Okay." Satisfied, Roberta stuck out a wrinkled black tube. "I made you a hot dog. You have to have a hot dog at a bonfire."

"Looks terrific." Accepting it, he pleased Roberta by taking a generous bite. "Thanks." Only Chase and his stomach knew that the meat was still cold on the inside.

"I got some marshmallows and sticks, too." She handed them over. "It's more fun to do it yourself, I guess." Because she was on the border between childhood and womanhood, Roberta picked up easily on the vibrations around her. "If you two want to be alone, you know, to kiss and stuff, no one's in the stables."

"Roberta!" Eden pulled out her best camp director's voice. "That will do."

"Well, my parents like to be alone sometimes." Undaunted, she grinned at Chase. "Maybe I'll see you around."

"You can count on it, kid." As Roberta danced off toward a group of girls, Chase turned back. The moment he took a step toward her, Eden extended her skewered marshmallow toward the fire. "Want to go kiss and stuff?"

It was the heat of the fire that stung her cheeks with color, Eden assured herself. "I suppose you think it would be terribly amusing for Roberta to go home and report that one of the camp directors spent her time in the stables with a man. That would do a lot for Camp Liberty's reputation."

"You're right. You should come to my place."

"Go away, Chase."

"I haven't finished my hot dog. Have dinner with me."

"I've had a hot dog already, thank you."

"I'll make sure hot dogs aren't on the menu. We can talk about it tomorrow."

"We will not talk about it tomorrow." It was anger that made her breathless, just as it was anger that made her unwise enough to turn toward him. "We will not talk about anything tomorrow."

"Okay. We won't talk." To show how reasonable he was, he bent down and closed the conversation, his mouth covering hers. He wasn't holding her, but it took her brain several long, lazy seconds before it accepted the order to back away.

"Don't you have any sense of propriety?" she managed in a strangled voice.

"Not much." He made up his mind, looking down at her eyes, dazed and as blue as his lake, that he wasn't going to take no for an answer—to any question. "We'll make it about nine tomorrow morning at the entrance to the orchard."

"Make what?"

"The tour." He grinned and handed her his stick. "It'll be educational."

Though she was in an open field, Eden felt her back press into a corner. "We have no intention of disrupting your routine."

"No problem. I'll pass it on to your co-director before I go back. That way, you'll be sure to be coordinated."

Eden took a long breath. "You think you're very clever, don't you?"

"Thorough, just thorough, Eden. By the way, your marshmallow's on fire."

With his hands in his pockets, he strolled off while she blew furiously on the flaming ball.

She'd hoped for rain but was disappointed. The morning dawned warm and sunny. She'd hoped for support but was faced with Candy's enthusiasm for a field trip through one of the most prestigious apple orchards in the country. The girls were naturally delighted with any shift in schedule, so as they walked as a group the short distance to the Elliot farm, Eden found herself separated from the excitement.

"You could try not to look as though you're walking to the guillotine." Candy plucked a scrawny blue flower from the side of the road and stuck it in her hair. "This is a wonderful opportunity—for the girls," she added quickly.

"You managed to convince me of that, or else I wouldn't be here."

"Grumpy."

"I'm not grumpy," Eden countered. "I'm annoyed at being manipulated."

"Just a small piece of advice." Picking another

flower, Candy twirled it. "If I'd been manipulated by a man, I'd make certain he believed it was my idea in the first place. Don't you think it would throw him off if you walked up to the gates with a cheery smile and boundless enthusiasm?"

"Maybe." Eden mulled the idea over until her lips began to curve. "Yes, maybe."

"There now. With a little practice, you'll find out that deviousness is much better in some cases than dignity."

"I wouldn't have needed either if you'd let me stay behind."

"Darling, unless I miss my guess, a certain apple baron would have plucked you up from whatever corner you'd chosen to hide in, tossed you over his wonderfully broad shoulder and dragged you along on our little tour, like it or not." Pausing, Candy let a sigh escape. "Now that I think about it, that would have been more exciting."

Because she was well able to picture it herself, Eden's mood hardened again. "At least I thought I could count on support from my best friend."

"And you can. Absolutely." With easy affection, Candy draped an arm over Eden's shoulder. "Though why you think you need my support when you have a gorgeous man giving you smoldering kisses, I can't imagine."

"That's just it!" Because several young heads turned when she raised her voice, Eden fought for calm again. "He had no business pulling something like that in front of everyone."

"I suppose it is more fun in private."

"Keep this up, and you may find that garter snake in your underwear yet."

"Just ask him if he's got a brother, or a cousin. Even an uncle. Ah, here we are," she continued before Eden could reply. "Now smile and be charming, just like you were taught."

"You're going to pay for this," Eden promised her in an undertone. "I don't know how, I don't know when, but you'll pay."

They brought the group to a halt when the road forked. On the left were stone pillars topped with an arching wrought-iron sign that read ELLIOT. Sloping away from the pillars was a wall a foot thick and high as a man. It was old and sturdy, proving to Eden that the penchant for privacy hadn't begun with Chase.

The entrance road, smooth and well-maintained, ribboned back over the crest of a hill before it disappeared. Along the road were trees, not apple but oak, older and sturdier than the wall.

It was the continuity that drew her, the same symmetry she had seen and admired in the groves. The stone, the trees, even the road, had been there for generations. Looking, Eden understood his pride in them. She, too, had once had a legacy.

Then he strode from behind the wall and she fought back even that small sense of a common ground.

In a T-shirt and jeans, he looked lean and capable. There was a faint sheen of sweat on his arms that made her realize he'd already been working that morning. Drawn against her will, she dropped her gaze to his hands, hands that were hard and competent and unbearably gentle on a woman's skin.

"Morning, ladies." He swung the gates open for them.

"Oh Lord, he's something," Eden heard one of the

counselors mumble. Remembering Candy's advice, she straightened her shoulders and fixed on her most cheerful smile.

"This is Mr. Elliot, girls. He owns the orchards we'll tour today. Thank you for inviting us, Mr. Elliot."

"My pleasure—Miss Carlbough."

The girlish murmurs of agreement became babbles of excitement as a dog sauntered to Chase's side. His fur was the color of apricots and glistened as though it had been polished in the sunlight. The big, sad eyes studied the group of girls before the dog pressed against Chase's leg. Eden had time to think that a smaller man might have been toppled. The dog was no less than three feet high at the shoulder. More of a young lion than a house pet, she thought. When he settled to sit at Chase's feet, Chase didn't have to bend to lay a hand on the dog's head.

"This is Squat. Believe it or not, he was the runt of his litter. He's a little shy."

Candy gave a sigh of relief when she saw the enormous tail thump the ground. "But friendly, right?"

"Squat's a pushover for females." His gaze circled the group. "Especially so many pretty ones. He was hoping he could join the tour."

"He's neat." Roberta made up her mind instantly. Walking forward, she gave the dog's head a casual pat. "I'll walk with you, Squat."

Agreeable, the dog rose to lead the way.

There was more to the business of apples than Eden had imagined. It wasn't all trees and plump fruit to be plucked and piled into baskets for market. Harvesting wasn't limited to autumn with the variety of types that were planted. The season, Chase explained, had been extended into months, from early summer to late fall.

They weren't just used for eating and baking. Even cores and peelings were put to use for cider, or dried and shipped to Europe for certain champagnes. As they walked, the scent of ripening fruit filled the air, making more than one mouth water.

The Tree of Life, Eden thought as the scent tempted her. Forbidden fruit. She kept herself surrounded by girls and tried to remember that the tour was educational.

He explained that the quick-maturing trees were planted in the forty-foot spaces between the slow growers, then cut out when the space was needed. A practical business, she remembered, organized, with a high level of utility and little waste. Still, it had the romance of apple blossoms in spring.

Masses of laborers harvested the summer fruit. While they watched the men and machines at work, Chase answered questions.

"They don't look ripe," Roberta commented.

"They're full-size." Chase rested a hand on her shoulder as he chose an apple. "The changes that take place after the fruit's reached maturity are mainly chemical. It goes on without the tree. The fruit's hard, but the seeds are brown. Look." Using a pocketknife with casual skill, he cut the fruit in half. "The apples we harvest now are superior to the ones that hang longer." Reading Roberta's expression correctly, Chase tossed her half the fruit. The other half Squat took in one yawning bite.

"Maybe you'd like to pick some yourself." The reaction was positive, and Chase reached up to demonstrate. "Twist the fruit off the stem. You don't want to break the twig and lose bearing wood."

Before Eden could react, the girls had scattered to nearby trees. She was facing Chase. Perhaps it was the way his lips curved. Perhaps it was the way his eyes seemed so content to rest on hers, but her mind went instantly and completely blank.

"You have a fascinating business." She could have kicked herself for the inanity of it.

"I like it."

"I, ah…" There must be a question, an intelligent question, she could ask. "I suppose you ship the fruit quickly to avoid spoilage."

He doubted that either of them gave two hoots about apples at the moment, but he was willing to play the game. "It's stored right after picking at thirty-two degrees Fahrenheit. I like your hair pulled back like that. It makes me want to tug on the string and watch it fall all over your shoulders."

Her pulse began to sing, but she pretended she hadn't heard. "I'm sure you have various tests to determine quality."

"We look for richness." Slowly, he turned the fruit over in his hand, but his gaze roamed to her mouth. "Flavor." He watched her lips part as if to taste. "Firmness," he murmured, as he circled her throat with his free hand. "Tenderness."

Her breath seemed to concentrate, to sweeten into the sound of a sigh. It was almost too late when she bit it off. "It would be best if we stuck to the subject at hand."

"Which subject?" His thumb traced along her jawline.

"Apples."

"I'd like to make love with you in the orchards, Eden, with the sun warm on your face and the grass soft at your back."

It terrified her that she could almost taste what it would be like, to be with him, alone. "If you'll excuse me."

"Eden." He took her hand, knowing he was pushing too hard, too fast, but unable to stop himself. "I want you. Maybe too much."

Though his voice was low, hardly more than a whisper, she felt her nerves jangling. "You should know you can't say those things to me here, now. If the children—"

"Have dinner with me."

"No." On this, she told herself she would stand firm. She would not be manipulated. She would not be maneuvered. "I have a job, Chase, one that runs virtually twenty-four hours a day for the next few weeks. Even if I wanted to have dinner with you, which I don't, it would be impossible."

He considered all this reasonable. But then, a great many smoke screens were. "Are you afraid to be alone with me? Really alone."

The truth was plain and simple. She ignored it. "You flatter yourself."

"I doubt a couple hours out of an evening would disrupt the camp's routine, or yours."

"You don't know anything about the camp's routine."

"I know that between your partner and the counselors, the girls are more than adequately supervised. And I know that your last riding lesson is at four o'clock."

"How did you—"

"I asked Roberta," he said easily. "She told me you have supper at six, then a planned activity or free time from seven to nine. Lights-out is at ten. You usually spend your time after supper with the horses. And sometimes you ride out at night when you think everyone's asleep."

She opened her mouth, then shut it again, having no idea what to say. She had thought those rides exclusively hers, exclusively private.

"Why do you ride out alone at night, Eden?"

"Because I enjoy it."

"Then tonight you can enjoy having dinner with me."

She tried to remember there were girls beneath the trees around them. She tried to remember that a display of temper was most embarrassing for the person who lost control. "Perhaps you have some difficulty understanding a polite refusal. Why don't we try this? The last place I want to be tonight, or at any other time, is with you."

He moved his shoulders before he took a step closer. "I guess we can just settle all this now. Here."

"You wouldn't…" She didn't bother to finish the thought. By now she knew very well what he would dare. One quick look around showed her that Roberta and Marcie were leaning against the trunk of a tree, happily munching apples and enjoying the show. "All right, stop it." So much for not being manipulated. "I have no idea why you insist on having dinner with someone who finds you so annoying."

"Me, either. We'll discuss it tonight. Seven-thirty." Tossing Eden the apple, he strolled over toward Roberta.

Eden hefted the fruit. She even went so far as to draw a mental bull's-eye on the back of his head. With a sound of disgust, she took a hefty bite instead.

Chapter 5

Vengefully, Eden dragged a brush through her hair. Despite the harsh treatment, it sprang back softly to wisp around her face and wave to her shoulders. She wouldn't go to any trouble as she had for other dates and dinners, but leave it loose and unstyled. Though he was undoubtedly too hardheaded to notice that sort of female subtlety.

She didn't bother with jewelry, except for the simple pearl studs she often wore around camp. In an effort to look cool, even prim, she wore a high-necked white blouse, regretting only the lace at the cuffs. Matching it with a white skirt, she tried for an icy look. The result was an innocent fragility she couldn't detect in the one small mirror on the wall.

Intending on making it plain that she had gone to no trouble for Chase's benefit, she almost ignored makeup.

Grumbling to herself, Eden picked up her blusher. Basic feminine vanity, she admitted; then she added a touch of clear gloss to her lips. There was, after all, a giant step between not fussing and looking like a hag. She was reaching for her bottle of perfume before she stopped herself. No, that was definitely fussing. He would get soap, and soap only. She turned away from the mirror just as Candy swung through the cabin door.

"Wow." Stopping in the doorway, Candy took a long, critical look. "You look terrific."

"I do?" Brow creased, Eden turned back to the mirror. "Terrific wasn't exactly what I was shooting for. I wanted something along the lines of prim."

"You couldn't look prim if you wore sackcloth and ashes, any more than I could look delicate even with lace at my wrists."

With a sound of disgust, Eden tugged at the offending lace. "I knew it. I just knew it was a mistake. Maybe I can rip it off."

"Don't you dare." Laughing, Candy bounded into the room to stop Eden from destroying her blouse. "Besides, it isn't the clothes that are important. It's the attitude, right?"

Eden gave the lace a last tug. "Right. Candy, are you sure everything's going to be under control here? I could still make excuses."

"Everything's already under control." Candy flopped down on her bunk, then began to peel the banana she held. "In fact, things are great. I've just taken a five-minute break to see you off and stuff my face." She took a big bite to prove her point. "Then," she continued over a mouthful of banana, "we're getting together in the mess area to take an inventory of our record collection for the dance. The girls want some practice time before the big night."

"You could probably use extra supervision."

Candy waved her half-eaten banana. "Everyone's going to be in the same four walls for the next couple of hours. You go enjoy your dinner and stop worrying. Where are you going?"

"I don't know." She stuffed some tissue in her bag. "And I really don't care."

"Come on, after nearly six weeks of wholesome but god-awful boring food, aren't you just a little excited about the prospect of oysters Rockefeller or escargots?"

"No." She began to clasp and unclasp her bag. "I'm only going because it was simpler than creating a scene."

Candy broke off a last bite of banana. "Certainly knows how to get his own way, doesn't he?"

"That's about to end." Eden closed her purse with a snap. "Tonight."

At the sound of an approaching car, Candy propped herself up on an elbow. She noticed Eden nervously biting her lower lip, but she only gestured toward the door with her banana peel. "Well, good luck."

Eden caught the grin and paused, her hand on the screen door. "Whose side are you on, anyway?"

"Yours, Eden." Candy stretched, and prepared to go rock and roll. "Always."

"I'll be back early."

Candy grinned, wisely saying nothing as the screen door slammed shut.

However hard Eden might have tried to look remote, icy, disinterested, the breath clogged up in Chase's lungs the moment she stepped outside. They were still an hour from twilight, and the sun's last rays shot through her hair. Her skirt swirled around bare legs honey-toned after long days outdoors. Her chin was lifted, perhaps in anger, perhaps in defiance. He could only see the elegant line of her throat.

The same slowly drumming need rose up inside him the moment she stepped onto the grass.

She'd expected him to look less...dangerous in more formal attire. Eden discovered she had underestimated him again. The muscles in his arms and shoulders weren't so much restricted as enhanced by the sports jacket. The shirt, either by design or good fortune, matched his eyes and was left open at the throat. Slowly and easily he smiled at her, and her lips curved in automatic response.

"I imagined you looking like this." In truth, he hadn't been sure she would come, or what he might have done if she had locked herself away in one of the cabins and refused to see him. "I'm glad you didn't disappoint me."

Feeling her resolve weaken, Eden made an effort to draw back. "I made a bargain," she began, only to fall silent when he handed her a bunch of anemones freshly picked from the side of the road. He wasn't supposed to be sweet, she reminded herself. She wasn't supposed to be vulnerable to sweetness. Still, unable to resist, she buried her face in the flowers.

That was a picture he would carry with him forever, Chase realized. Eden, with wildflowers clutched in both hands; her eyes, touched with both pleasure and confusion, watching him over the petals.

"Thank you."

"You're welcome." Taking one of her hands, he brought it to his lips. She should have pulled away. She knew she should. Yet there was something so simple, so right in the moment—as if she recognized it from some long-ago dream. Bemused, Eden took a step closer, but the sound of giggling brought her out of the spell.

Immediately she tried to pull her hand away. "The girls." She glanced around quickly enough to catch the fielder's cap as it disappeared around the corner of the building.

"Well, then, we wouldn't want to disappoint them?" Turning her hand over, Chase pressed a kiss to her palm. Eden felt the heat spread.

"You're being deliberately difficult." But she closed her hand as if to capture the sensation and hold it.

"Yes." He smiled, but resisted the impulse to draw her into his arms and enjoy the promise he'd seen so briefly in her eyes.

"If you'd let me go, I'd like to put the flowers in water."

"I'll do it." Candy left her post by the door and came outside. Even Eden's glare didn't wipe the smile from her face. "They're lovely, aren't they? Have a good time."

"We'll do that." Chase linked his fingers with Eden's and drew her toward his car. She told herself the sun had been in her eyes. Why else would she have missed the low-slung white Lamborghini parked beside the cabin. She settled herself in the passenger's seat with a warning to herself not to relax.

The moment the engine sprang to life, there was a chorus of goodbyes. Every girl and counselor had lined up to wave them off. Eden disguised a chuckle with a cough.

"It seems this is one of the camp's highlights this summer."

Chase lifted a hand out of the open window to wave back. "Let's see if we can make it one of ours."

Something in his tone made her glance over just long enough to catch that devil of a smile. Eden made up her mind then and there. No, she wouldn't relax, but she'd be damned if she'd be intimidated either. "All right." She leaned back in her seat, prepared to make the best of a bad deal. "I haven't had a meal that wasn't served on a tray in weeks."

"I'll cancel the trays."

"I'd appreciate it." She laughed, then assured herself that laughing wasn't really relaxing. "Stop me if I start stacking the silverware." The breeze blowing in the open window was warm and as fresh as the flowers Chase had brought her. Eden allowed herself the pleasure of lifting her face to it. "This is nice, especially when I was expecting a pickup truck."

"Even country bumpkins can appreciate a well-made machine."

"That's not what I meant." Ready with an apology, she turned, but saw he was smiling. "I suppose you wouldn't care if it was."

"I know what I am, what I want and what I can do." As he took a curve he slowed. His eyes met hers briefly. "But the opinions of certain people always matter. In any case, I prefer the mountains to traffic jams. What do you prefer, Eden?"

"I haven't decided." That was true, she realized with a jolt. In a matter of weeks her priorities, and her hopes, had changed direction. Musing on that, she almost missed the arching ELLIOT sign when Chase turned between the columns. "Where are we going?"

"To dinner."

"In the orchard?"

"In my house." With that he changed gears and had the car cruising up the gravel drive.

Eden tried to ignore the little twist of apprehension she felt. True, this wasn't the crowded, and safe, restaurant she had imagined. She'd shared private dinners before, hadn't she? She'd been raised from the cradle to know how to handle any social situation. But the apprehension remained. Dinner alone with Chase wouldn't be, couldn't possibly be, like any other experience.

Even as she was working out a polite protest, the car crested the hill. The house rose into view.

It was stone. She couldn't know it was local stone, quarried from the mountains. She saw only that it was old, beautifully weathered. At first glance, it gave the appearance of being gray, but on a closer look colors glimmered through. Amber, russet, tints of green and umber. The sun was still high enough to make the chips of mica and quartz glisten. There were three stories, with the second overhanging the first by a skirting balcony. Eden could see flashes of red and buttercup yellow from the pots of geraniums and marigolds. She caught the scent of lavender even before she saw the rock garden.

A wide, sweeping stone stairway, worn slightly in the center, led to double glass doors of diamond panes. A redwood barrel was filled with pansies that nodded in the early evening breeze.

It was nothing like what she had expected, and yet…

the house, and everything about it, was instantly recognizable.

His own nervousness caught Chase off guard. Eden said nothing when he stopped the car, still nothing when he got out to round the hood and open her door. It mattered, more than he had ever imagined it could, what she thought, what she said, what she felt about his home.

She held her hand out for his in a gesture he knew was automatic. Then she stood beside him, looking at what was his, what had been his even before his birth. Tension lodged in the back of his neck.

"Oh, Chase, it's beautiful." She lifted her free hand to shield her eyes from the sun behind the house. "No wonder you love it."

"My great-grandfather built it." The tension had dissolved without his being aware of it. "He even helped quarry the stone. He wanted something that would last and that would carry a piece of him as long as it did."

She thought of the home that had been her family's for generations, feeling the too-familiar burning behind her eyes. She'd lost that. Sold it. The need to tell him was almost stronger than pride, because in that moment she thought he might understand.

He felt her change in mood even before he glanced down and saw the glint of tears in her eyes. "What is it, Eden?"

"Nothing." No, she couldn't tell him. Some wounds were best left hidden. Private. "I was just thinking how important some traditions are."

"You still miss your father."

"Yes." Her eyes were dry now, the moment past. "I'd love to see inside."

He hesitated a moment, knowing there had been

more and that she'd been close to sharing it with him. He could wait, Chase told himself, though his patience was beginning to fray. He would have to wait until she took that step toward him rather than away from him.

With her hand still in his, he climbed the steps to the door. On the other side lay a mountain of apricot fur known as Squat. Even after Chase opened the door, the mound continued to snore.

"Are you sure you should have such a vicious watch-dog unchained?"

"My theory is most burglars wouldn't have the nerve to step over him." Catching Eden around the waist, Chase lifted her up and over.

The stone insulated well against the heat, so the hall was cool and comfortable. High, beamed ceilings gave the illusion of unlimited space. A Monet landscape caught her eye, but before she could comment on it, Chase was leading her through a set of mahogany doors.

The room was cozily square, with window seats recessed into the east and west walls. Instantly Eden could imagine the charm of watching the sun rise or set. Comfort was the theme of the room, with its range of blues from the palest aqua to the deepest indigo. Hand-hooked rugs set off the American antiques. There were fresh flowers here, too, spilling out of a Revere Ware bowl. It was a touch she hadn't expected from a bachelor, particularly one who worked with his hands.

Thoughtful, she crossed the room to the west window. The slanting sun cast long shadows over the buildings he had taken them through that morning. She remembered the conveyor belts, the busy sorters and packers, the noise. Behind her was a small, elegant room with pewter bowls and wild roses.

Peace and challenge, she realized, and she sighed without knowing why. "I imagine it's lovely when the sun starts to drop."

"It's my favorite view." His voice came from directly behind her, but for once she didn't stiffen when he rested his hands on her shoulders. He tried to tell himself it was just coincidence that she had chosen to look out that window, but he could almost believe that his own need for her to see and understand had guided her there. It wouldn't be wise to forget who she was and how she chose to live. "There's no Symphony Hall or Rodin Museum."

His fingers gently massaged the curve of her shoulders. But his voice wasn't as patient. Curious, she turned. His hands shifted to let her slide through, then settled on her shoulders again. "I don't imagine they're missed. If they were, you could visit, then come back to this." Without thinking, she lifted her hand to brush the hair from his forehead. Even as she caught herself, his hand closed around her wrist. "Chase, I—"

"Too late," he murmured; then he kissed each of her fingers, one by one. "Too late for you. Too late for me."

She couldn't allow herself to believe that. She couldn't accept the softening and opening of her emotions. How badly she wanted to let him in, to trust again, to need again. How terrifying it was to be vulnerable. "Please don't do this. It's a mistake for both of us."

"You're probably right." He was almost sure of it himself. But he brushed his lips over the pulse that hammered in her wrist. He didn't give a damn. "Everyone's entitled to one enormous mistake."

"Don't kiss me now." She lifted a hand but only curled her fingers into his shirt. "I can't think."

"One has nothing to do with the other."

When his mouth touched hers, it was soft, seeking. *Too late.* The words echoed in her head even as she lifted her hands to his face and let herself go. This is what she had wanted, no matter how many arguments she had posed, no matter how many defenses she had built. She wanted to be held against him, to sink into a dream that had no end.

He felt her fingers stream through his hair and had to force himself not to rush her. Desire, tensed and hungry, had to be held back until it was tempered with acceptance and trust. In his heart he had already acknowledged that she was more than the challenge he had first considered her. She was more than the summer fling he might have preferred. But as her slim, soft body pressed against his, as her warm, willing mouth opened for him, he could only think of how he wanted her, now, when the sun was beginning to sink toward the distant peaks to the west.

"Chase." It was the wild, drumming beat of her heart that frightened her most. She was trembling. Eden could feel it start somewhere deep inside and spread out until it became a stunning combination of panic and excitement. How could she fight the first and give in to the second? "Chase, please."

He had to draw himself back, inch by painful inch. He hadn't meant to take either of them so far, so fast. Yet perhaps he had, he thought as he ran a hand down her hair. Perhaps he had wanted to push them both toward an answer that still seemed just out of reach.

"The sun's going down." His hands weren't quite steady when he turned her toward the window again. "Before long, the light will change."

She could only be grateful that he was giving her time to regain her composure. Later she would realize how much it probably had cost him.

They stood a moment in silence, watching the first tints of rose spread above the mountains. A loud, rasping cough had her already-tense nerves jolting.

"S'cuze me."

The man in the doorway had a grizzled beard that trailed down to the first button of his red checked shirt. Though he was hardly taller than Eden, his bulk gave the impression of power. The folds and lines in his face all but obscured his dark eyes. Then he grinned, and she caught the glint of a gold tooth.

So this was the little lady who had the boss running around in circles. Deciding she was prettier than a barrelful of prime apples, he nodded to her by way of greeting. "Supper's ready. Unless you want to eat it cold, you best be moving along."

"Eden Carlbough, Delaney." Chase only lifted a brow, knowing Delaney had already sized up the situation. "He cooks and I don't, which is why I haven't fired him yet."

This brought on a cackle. "He hasn't fired me because I wiped his nose and tied his shoes."

"We could add that that was close to thirty years ago."

She recognized both affection and exasperation. It pleased her to know someone could exasperate Chase Elliot. "It's nice to meet you, Mr. Delaney."

"Delaney, ma'am. Just Delaney." Still grinning, he pulled on his beard. "Mighty pretty," he said to Chase. "It's smarter to think of settling down with someone who isn't an eyesore at breakfast. Supper's going to get cold," he added. Then he was gone.

Though Eden had remained politely silent during Delaney's statement, it took only one look at Chase's face to engender a stream of laughter. The sound made Chase think more seriously about gagging Delaney with his own beard.

"I'm glad you're amused."

"Delighted. It's the first time I've ever seen you speechless. And I can't help being pleased not to be considered an eyesore." Then she disarmed him by offering him her hand. "Supper's going to get cold."

Instead of the dining room, Chase led her out to a jalousied porch. Two paddle fans circled overhead, making the most of the breeze that crept in the slanted windows. A wind chime jingled cheerfully between baskets of fuchsia.

"Your home is one surprise after another," Eden commented as she studied the plump love seats and the glass-and-wicker table. "Every room seems fashioned for relaxation and stunning views."

The table was set with colorful stoneware. Though the sun had yet to drop behind the peaks, two tapers were already burning. There was a single wild rose beside her plate.

Romance, she thought. This was the romance she had once dreamed of. This was the romance she must now be very wary of. But, wary or not, she picked up the flower and smiled at him. "Thank you."

"Did you want one, too?" As she laughed, Chase drew back her chair.

"Sit down. Sit down. Eat while it's hot." Despite his bulk, Delaney bustled into the room. In his large hands was an enormous tray. Because she realized how easily she could be mowed down, Eden obeyed. "Hope you got an appetite. You could use a little plumping up, missy. Then, I've always preferred a bit of healthy meat on female bones."

As he spoke, he began to serve an exquisite seafood salad. "Made my special, Chicken Delaney. It'll keep under the covers if you two don't dawdle over the salad. Apple pie's on the hot plate, biscuits in the warmer." He stuck a bottle of wine unceremoniously in an ice bucket. "That's the fancy wine you wanted." Standing back, he took a narrowed-eyed glance around before snorting with satisfaction. "I'm going home. Don't let my chicken get cold." Wiping his hands on his jeans, he marched to the door and let it swing shut behind him.

"Delaney has amazing style, doesn't he?" Chase took the wine from the bucket to pour two glasses.

"Amazing," Eden agreed, finding it amazing enough that those gnarled hands had created anything as lovely as the salad in front of her.

"He makes the best biscuits in Pennsylvania." Chase lifted his glass and toasted her. "And I'd put his Beef Wellington up against anyone's."

"Beef Wellington?" With a shake of her head, Eden sipped her wine. It was cool, just a shade tart. "I hope you'll take it the right way when I say he looks more like the type who could charcoal a steak over a backyard grill." She dipped her fork in the salad and sampled it. "But..."

"Appearances can be deceiving," Chase finished for her, pleased with the way her eyes half shut as she tasted. "Delaney's been cooking here as long as I can remember. He lives in a little cottage my grandfather helped him build about forty years ago. Nose-wiping and shoe-tying aside, he's part of the family."

She only nodded, looking down at her plate for a moment as she remembered how difficult it had been to tell her longtime servants she was selling out. Perhaps they had never been as familiar or as informal as Chase's Delaney, but they, too, had been part of the family.

It was there again, that dim candle glow of grief he'd seen in her eyes before. Wanting only to help, he reached over to touch her hand. "Eden?"

Quickly, almost too quickly, she moved her hand and began to eat again. "This is wonderful. I have an aunt back home who would shanghai your Delaney after the first forkful."

Home, he thought, backing off automatically. Philadelphia was still home.

The Chicken Delaney lived up to its name. As the sun set, the meal passed easily, even though they disagreed on almost every subject.

She read Keats and he read Christie. She preferred Bach and he Haggard, but it didn't seem to matter as the glass walls filtered the rosy light of approaching twilight. The candles burned lower. The wine shimmered in crystal, inviting one more sip. Close and clear and quick came the two-tone call of a quail.

"That's a lovely sound." Her sigh was easy and content. "If things are quiet at camp, we can hear the birds in the evening. There's a whippoorwill who's taken to singing right outside the cabin window. You can almost set your watch by her."

"Most of us are creatures of habit," he murmured. He wondered about her, what habits she had, what habits she had changed. Taking her hand, he turned it up.

The ridge of callus had hardened. "You didn't take my advice."

"About what?"

"Wearing gloves."

"It didn't seem worth it. Besides..." Letting the words trail off, she lifted her wine.

"Besides?"

"Having calluses means I did something to earn them." She blurted it out, then sat swearing at herself and waiting for him to laugh.

He didn't. Instead he sat silently, passing his thumb over the toughened skin and watching her. "Will you go back?"

"Go back?"

"To Philadelphia."

It was foolish to tell him how hard she'd tried not to think about that. Instead, she answered as the practical Eden was supposed to. "The camp closes down the last week in August. Where else would I go?"

"Where else?" he agreed, but when he released her hand she felt a sense of loss rather than relief. "Maybe there comes a time in everyone's life when they have to take a hard look at the options." He rose, and her hands balled into fists. He took a step toward her, and her heart rose up to her throat. "I'll be back."

Alone, she let out a long, shaky breath. What had she been expecting? she asked herself. What had she been hoping for? Her legs weren't quite steady when she rose, but it could have been the wine. But wine would have made her warm, and she felt a chill. To ward it off, she rubbed her arms with her hands. The sky was a quiet, deepening blue but for a halo of scarlet along the horizon. She concentrated on that, trying not to imagine how it would look when the stars came out.

Maybe they would look at the stars together again. They could look, picking out the patterns, and she would again feel that click that meant her needs and dreams were meshing. With his.

Pressing a hand to her lips, she struggled to block off that train of thought. It was only that the evening had been lovelier than she had imagined. It was only that they had more in common than she had believed possible. It was only that he had a gentleness inside him that softened parts of her when she least expected it. And when he kissed her, she felt as though she had the world pulsing in the palm of her hand.

No. Uneasy, she wrapped her hands around her forearms and squeezed. She was romanticizing again, spinning daydreams when she had no business dreaming at all. She was just beginning to sort out her life, to make her own place. It wasn't possible that she was looking to him to be any part of it.

She heard the music then, something low and unfamiliar that nonetheless had tiny shivers working their way up her spine. She had to leave, she thought quickly. And right away. She had let the atmosphere get to her. The house, the sunset, the wine. Him. Hearing his footsteps, she turned. She would tell him she had to get back. She would thank him for the evening, and...escape.

When he came back into the room, she was standing beside the table so that the candlelight flickered over her skin. Dusk swirled behind her with its smoky magic. The scent of wild roses from the bush outside the window seemed to sigh into the room. He wondered, if he touched her now, if she would simply dissolve in his hands.

"Chase, I think I'd better—"

"Shh." She wouldn't dissolve, he told himself as he went to her. She was real, and so was he. One hand captured hers, the other slipping around her waist. After one moment of resistance, she began to move with him. "One of the pleasures of country music is dancing to it."

"I, ah, I don't know the song." But it felt so good, so very good, to sway with him while darkness fell.

"It's about a man, a woman and passion. The best songs are."

She shut her eyes. She could feel the brush of his jacket against her cheek, the firm press of his hand at her waist. He smelled of soap, but nothing a woman would use. This had a tang that was essentially masculine. Wanting to taste, she moved her head so that her lips rested against his neck.

His pulse beat there, quick, surprising her. Forgetting caution, she nestled closer and felt its sudden rise in speed. As her own raced to match it, she gave a murmur of pleasure and traced it with the tip of her tongue.

He started to draw her away. He meant to. When he'd left her, he'd promised himself that he would slow the pace to one they could both handle. But now she was cuddled against him, her body swaying, her fingers straying to his neck, and her mouth… With an oath, Chase dragged her closer and gave in to hunger.

The kiss was instantly torrid, instantly urgent. And somehow, though she had never experienced anything like it, instantly familiar. Her head tilted back in surrender. Her lips parted. Here and now, she wanted the fire and passion that had only been hinted at.

Perhaps he lowered her to the love seat, perhaps she drew him to it, but they were wrapped together, pressed against the cushions. An owl hooted once, then twice, then gave them silence.

He'd wanted to believe she could be this generous. He'd wanted to believe his lips would touch hers and find unrestricted sweetness. Now his mind spun with it. Whatever he had wanted, whatever he had dreamed of, was less, so much less than what he now held in his arms.

He stroked a hand down her body and met trembling response. With a moan, she arched against him. Through the sheer fabric of her blouse, he could feel the heat rising to her skin, enticing him to touch again and yet again.

He released the first button of her blouse, then the second, following the course with his lips. She shivered with anticipation. Her lace cuffs brushed against his cheeks as she lifted her hands to his hair. It seemed her body was filling, flooding with sensations she'd once only imagined. Now they were so real and so clear that she could feel each one as it layered over the next.

The pillows at her back were soft. His body was hard and hot. The breeze that jingled the wind chime overhead was freshened with flowers. Behind her closed eyes came the flicker and glow of candlelight. In teams of thousands, the cicadas began to sing. But more thrilling, more intense, was the sound of her name whispering from him as he pressed his lips against her skin.

Suddenly, searing, his mouth took hers again. In the kiss she could taste everything, his need, his desire, the passion that teetered on the edge of sanity. As her own madness hovered, she felt her senses swimming with him. And she moaned with the ecstasy of falling in love.

For one brief moment, she rose on it, thrilled with the knowledge that she had found him. The dream and the reality were both here. She had only to close them both in her arms and watch them become one.

Then the terror of it fell on her. She couldn't let it be real. How could she risk it? Once she had given her trust and her promise, if not her heart. And she had been betrayed. If it happened again, she would never recover. If it happened with Chase, she wouldn't want to.

"Chase, no more." She turned her face away and tried to clear her head. "Please, this has to stop."

Her taste was still exploding in his mouth. Beneath his, her body was trembling with a need he knew matched his own. "Eden, for God's sake." With an effort that all but drained him, he lifted his head to look down at her. She was afraid. He recognized her fear immediately and struggled to hold back his own needs. "I won't hurt you."

That almost undid her. He meant it, she was sure, but that didn't mean it wouldn't happen. "Chase, this isn't right for me. For either of us."

"Isn't it?" Tension knotted in his stomach as he drew her toward him. "Can you tell me you didn't feel how right it was a minute ago?"

"No." It was both confusion and fear that had her dragging her hands through her hair. "But this isn't what I want. I need you to understand that this can't be what I want. Not now."

"You're asking a hell of a lot."

"Maybe. But there isn't any choice."

That infuriated him. She was the one who had taken

his choice away, simply by existing. He hadn't asked her to fall into his life. He hadn't asked her to become the focus of it before he had a chance for a second breath. She'd given in to him to the point where he was half-mad for her. Now she was drawing away. And asking him to understand.

"We'll play it your way." His tone chilled as he drew away from her.

She shuddered, recognizing instantly that his anger could be lethal. "It's not a game."

"No? Well, in any case, you play it well."

She pressed her lips together, understanding that she deserved at least a part of the lash. "Please, don't spoil what happened."

He walked to the table and, lifting his glass, studied the wine. "What did happen?"

I fell in love with you. Rather than answer him, she began to button her blouse with nerveless fingers.

"I'll tell you." He tossed back the remaining wine, but it didn't soothe him. "Not for the first time in our fascinating relationship, you blew hot and cold without any apparent reason. It makes me wonder if Eric backed out of the marriage out of self-defense."

He saw her fingers freeze on the top button of her blouse. Even in the dim light, he could watch the color wash out of her face. Very carefully, he set his glass down again. "I'm sorry, Eden. That was uncalled-for."

The fight for control and composure was a hard war, but she won. She made her fingers move until the button was in place, then, slowly, she rose. "Since you're so interested, I'll tell you that Eric jilted me for more practical reasons. I appreciate the meal, Chase. It was lovely. Please thank Delaney for me."

"Damn it, Eden."

When he started forward, her body tightened like a bow. "If you could do one thing for me, it would be to take me back now and say nothing. Absolutely nothing."

Turning, she walked away from the candlelight.

Chapter 6

During the first weeks of August, the camp was plagued with one calamity after another. The first was an epidemic of poison ivy. Within twenty-four hours, ten of the girls and three of the counselors were coated with calamine lotion. The sticky heat did nothing to make the itching more bearable.

Just as the rashes started to fade came three solid days of rain. As the camp was transformed into a muddy mire, outdoor activities were canceled. Tempers soared. Eden broke up two hair-pulling battles in one day. Then, as luck would have it, lightning hit one of the trees and distracted the girls from their boredom.

By the time the sun came out, they had enough pot holders, key chains, wallets and pillows to open their own craft shop.

Men with Jeeps and chain saws came to clear away

the debris from the tree. Eden wrote out a check and prayed the last crisis was over.

It was doubtful the check had even been cashed when the secondhand restaurant stove she and Candy had bought stopped working. In the three days the parts were on order, cooking was done in true camp style—around an open fire.

The gelding, Courage, developed an infection that settled in his lungs. Everyone in camp worried about him and fussed over him and pampered him. The vet dosed him with penicillin. Eden spent three sleepless nights in the stables, nursing him and waiting for the crisis to pass.

Eventually the horse's appetite improved, the mud in the compound dried and the stove was back in working order. Eden told herself that the worst had to be over as the camp's routine picked up again.

Yet oddly, the lull brought out a restlessness she'd been able to ignore while the worst was happening. At dusk, she wandered to the stables with her sackful of apples. It wasn't hard to give a little extra attention to Courage. He'd gotten used to being pampered during his illness. Eden slipped him a carrot to go with the apple.

Still, as she worked her way down the stalls, she found the old routine didn't keep her mind occupied. The emergencies over the past couple of weeks had kept her too busy to take a second breath, much less think. Now, with calm settling again, thinking was unavoidable.

She could remember her evening with Chase as if it had been the night before. Every word spoken, every touch, every gesture, was locked in her mind as it had been when it had been happening. The rushing, tumbling sensation of falling in love was just as vital now, and just as frightening.

She hadn't been prepared for it. Her life had always been a series of preparations and resulting actions. Even her engagement had been a quiet step along a well-paved road. Since then, she'd learned to handle the detours and the roadblocks. But Chase was a sudden one-way street that hadn't been on any map.

It didn't matter, she told herself as she finished Patience's rubdown. She would navigate this and swing herself back in the proper direction. Having her choices taken away at this point in her life wasn't something she would tolerate. Not even when the lack of choice seemed so alluring and so right.

"I thought I'd find you here." Candy leaned against the stall door to give the mare a pat. "How was Courage tonight?"

"Good." Eden walked to the little sink in the corner to wash liniment from her hands. "I don't think we have to worry about him anymore."

"I'm glad to know that you'll be using your bunk instead of a pile of hay."

Eden pressed both hands to the small of her back and stretched. No demanding set of tennis had ever brought on this kind of ache. Strangely enough, she liked it. "I never thought I'd actually look forward to sleeping in that bunk."

"Well, now that you're not worried about the gelding, I can tell you I'm worried about you."

"Me?" Eden looked for a towel and, not finding one, dried her hands on her jeans. "Why?"

"You're pushing yourself too hard."

"Don't be silly. I'm barely pulling my weight."

"That stopped being even close to the truth the second week of camp." Now that she'd decided to speak up, Candy took a deep breath. "Damn it, Eden, you're exhausted."

"Tired," Eden corrected her. "Which is nothing a few hours on that miserable bunk won't cure."

"Look, it's okay if you want to avoid the issue with everyone else, even with yourself. But don't do it with me."

It wasn't often Candy's voice took on that firm, nononsense tone. Eden lifted a brow and nodded. "All right, what is the issue?"

"Chase Elliot," Candy stated, and she saw Eden freeze up. "I didn't hound you with questions the night you came back from dinner."

"And I appreciate that."

"Well, don't, because I'm asking now."

"We had dinner, talked a bit about books and music, then he brought me back."

Candy closed the stall door with a creak. "I thought I was your friend."

"Oh, Candy, you know you are." With a sigh, Eden closed her eyes a moment. "All right, we did exactly what I said we did, but somewhere between the talk and the ride home, things got a little out of hand."

"What sort of things?"

Eden found she didn't even have the energy to laugh. "I've never known you to pry."

"I've never known you to settle comfortably into depression."

"Am I?" Eden blew her bangs out of her eyes. "God, maybe I am."

"Let's just say that you've jumped from one problem

to the next in order to avoid fixing one of your own."
Taking a step closer, Candy drew Eden down on a small
bench. "So let's talk."

"I'm not sure I can." Linking her hands, Eden looked
down at them. The opal ring that had once been her
mother's winked back at her. "I promised myself after
Papa died and everything was in such a mess that I
would handle things and find the best way to solve the
problems. I've needed to solve them myself."

"That doesn't mean you can't lean on a friend."

"I've leaned on you so much I'm surprised you can
walk upright."

"I'll let you know when I start limping. Eden, unless my memory's faulty, we've taken turns leaning on
each other since before either of us could walk. Tell me
about Chase."

"He scares me." With a long breath, Eden leaned
back against the wall. "Everything's happening so fast,
and everything I feel seems so intense." Dropping the
last of her guard, she turned her face to Candy's. "If
things had worked out differently, I'd be married to another man right now. How can I even think I might be
in love with someone else so soon?"

"You're not going to tell me you think you're fickle."
The last thing Eden had expected was Candy's bright,
bubbling laughter, but that was what echoed off the stable walls. "Eden, I'm the fickle one, remember? You've
always been loyal to a fault. Wait, I can see you're getting annoyed, so let's take this logically." Candy crossed
her ankles and began to count off on her fingers.

"First, you were engaged to Eric—the slime—
because of all the reasons we've discussed before.

It seemed the proper thing to do. Were you in love with him?"

"No, but I thought—"

"Irrelevant. No is the answer. Second, he showed his true colors, the engagement's been off for months, and you've met a fascinating, attractive man. Now, let's even take it a step further." Warming up to the subject, Candy shifted on the bench. "Suppose—God forbid—that you had actually been madly in love with Eric. After he had shown himself to be a snake, your heart would have been broken. With time and effort, you would have pulled yourself back together. Right?"

"I certainly like to think so."

"So we agree."

"Marginally."

That was enough for Candy. "Then, heart restored, if you'd met a fascinating and attractive man, you would have been equally free to fall for him. Either way, you're in the clear." Satisfied, Candy rose and dusted her palms on her jeans. "So what's the problem?"

Not certain she could explain, or even make sense of it herself, Eden looked down at her hands. "Because I've learned something. Love is a commitment, it's total involvement, promises, compromises. I'm not sure I can give those things to anyone yet. And if I were, I don't know if Chase feels at all the same way."

"Eden, your instincts must tell you he does."

With a shake of her head, she rose. She did feel better having said it all out loud, but that didn't change the bottom line. "I've learned not to trust my instincts, but to be realistic. Which is why I'm going to go hit the account books."

"Oh, Eden, give it a break."

"Unfortunately, I had to give it a break during the poison ivy, the lightning, the stove breakdown and the vet visits." Hooking her arm through Candy's, she started to walk toward the door. "You were right, and talking it out helped, but practicality is still the order of the day."

"Meaning checks and balances."

"Right. I'd really like to get to it. The advantage is I can frazzle my brain until the bunk really does feel like a feather bed."

Candy pushed open the door, then squared her shoulders. "I'll help."

"Thanks, but I'd like to finish them before Christmas."

"Oh, low blow, Eden."

"But true." She latched the door behind them. "Don't worry about me, Candy. Talking about it cleared my head a bit."

"Doing something about it would be better, but it's a start. Don't work too late."

"A couple of hours," Eden promised.

The office, as Eden arrogantly called it, was a small side room off the kitchen. After switching on the gooseneck lamp on the metal army-surplus desk, she adjusted the screen, flap up. As an afterthought, she switched the transistor radio on the corner of the desk to a classical station. The quiet, familiar melodies would go a long way toward calming her.

Still, as always, she drew in a deep breath as she took her seat behind the desk. Here, she knew too well, things were black-and-white. There were no multiple choices, no softening the rules as there could be in other areas of the camp. Figures were figures and facts were facts. It was up to her to tally them.

Opening the drawers, she pulled out invoices, the business checkbook and the ledger. She began systematically sorting and entering as the tape spilled out of the adding machine at her elbow.

Within twenty minutes, she knew the worst. The additional expenses of the past two weeks had stretched their capital to the limit. No matter how many ways Eden worked the numbers, the answer was the same. They weren't dead broke, but painfully close to it. Wearily, she rubbed the bridge of her nose between her thumb and forefinger.

They could still make it, she told herself. She pressed her hand down on the pile of papers, letting her palm cover the checks and balances. By the skin of their teeth, she thought, but they could still make it. If there were no more unexpected expenses. And if, she continued, the pile seeming to grow under her hand, she and Candy lived frugally over the winter. She imagined the pile growing another six inches under her restraining hand. If they got the necessary enrollments for the next season, everything would turn around.

Curling her fingers around the papers, she let out a long breath. If one of those *if*s fell through, she still had some jewelry that could be sold.

The lamplight fell across her opal-and-diamond ring, but she looked away, feeling guilty at even considering selling it. But she would. If her other choices were taken away, she would. What she wouldn't do was give up.

The tears began so unexpectedly that they fell onto the blotter before she knew she had shed them. Even as she wiped them away, new ones formed. There was no one to see, no one to hear. Giving in, Eden laid her head on the piles of bills and let the tears come.

They wouldn't change anything. With tears would come no fresh ideas or brilliant answers, but she let them come anyway. Quite simply, her strength had run out.

He found her like that, weeping almost soundlessly over the neat stacks of paper. At first Chase only stood there, with the door not quite shut at his back. She looked so helpless, so utterly spent. He wanted to go to her, but held himself back. He understood that the tears would be private. She wouldn't want to share them, particularly not with him. And yet, even as he told himself to step back, he moved toward her.

"Eden."

Her head shot up at the sound of her name. Her eyes were drenched, but he saw both shock and humiliation in them before she began to dry her cheeks with the backs of her hands.

"What are you doing here?"

"I wanted to see you." It sounded simple enough, but didn't come close to what was moving inside him. He wanted to go to her, to gather her close and fix whatever was wrong. He stuck his hands in his pockets and remained standing just inside the door. "I just heard about the gelding this morning. Is he worse?"

She shook her head, then struggled to keep her voice calm. "No, he's better. It wasn't as serious as we thought it might be."

"That's good." Frustrated by his inability to think of something less inane, he began to pace. How could he offer comfort when she wouldn't share the problem? Her eyes were dry now, but he knew it was pride, and pride alone, that held her together. The hell with her pride, he thought. He needed to help.

When he turned back, he saw she had risen from the desk. "Why don't you tell me about it?"

The need to confide in him was so painfully strong that she automatically threw up the customary shield. "There's nothing to tell. It's been a rough couple of weeks. I suppose I'm overtired."

It was more than that, he thought, though she did look exhausted. "The girls getting to you?"

"No, really, the girls are fine."

Frustrated, he looked for another answer. The radio was playing something slow and romantic. Glancing toward it, Chase noticed the open ledger. The tail of adding-machine tape was spilling onto the floor. "Is it money? I could help."

Eden closed the book with a snap. Humiliation was a bitter taste at the back of her throat. At least it dried the last of her tears. "We're fine," she told him in a voice that was even and cool. "If you'd excuse me, I still have some work to do."

Rejection was something Chase had never fully understood until he'd met her. He didn't care for it. Nodding slowly, he searched for patience. "It was meant as an offer, not an insult." He would have turned and left her then, but the marks of weeping and sleeplessness gave her a pale, wounded look. "I'm sorry about the trouble you've been having the past year, Eden. I knew you'd lost your father, but I didn't know about the estate."

She wanted, oh so badly, to reach out, to let him gather her close and give her all the comfort she needed. She wanted to ask him what she should do, and have him give her the answers. But wouldn't that mean that all the months of struggling for self-sufficiency had been for nothing? She straightened her shoulders. "It isn't necessary to be sorry."

"If you had told me yourself, it would have been simpler."

"It didn't concern you."

He didn't so much ignore the stab of hurt as turn it into annoyance. "Didn't it? I felt differently—feel differently. Are you going to stand there and tell me there's nothing between us, Eden?"

She couldn't deny it, but she was far too confused, far too afraid, to try to define the truth. "I don't know how I feel about you, except that I don't want to feel anything. Most of all, I don't want your pity."

The hands in his pockets curled into fists. He didn't know how to handle his own feelings, his own needs. Now she was treating them as though they didn't matter. He could leave, or he could beg. At the moment, Chase saw no choice between the two. "Understanding and pity are different things, Eden. If you don't know that, there's nothing else to say."

Turning, he left her. The screen door swished quietly behind him.

For the next two days, Eden functioned. She gave riding instructions, supervised meals and hiked the hills with groups of girls. She talked and laughed and listened, but the hollowness that had spread inside her when the door had closed at Chase's back remained.

Guilt and regret. Those were the feelings she couldn't shake, no matter how enthusiastically she threw herself into her routine. She'd been wrong. She'd known it even as it was happening, but pride had boxed her in. He had offered to help. He had offered to care, and she'd refused him. If there was a worse kind of selfishness, she couldn't name it.

She'd started to phone him, but hadn't been able to dial the number. It hadn't been pride that had held her back this time. Every apology that formed in her mind was neat and tidy and meaningless. She couldn't bear to give him a stilted apology, nor could she bear the possibility that he wouldn't care.

Whatever had started to grow between them, she had squashed. Whatever might have been, she had cut off before it had begun to flower. How could she explain to Chase that she'd been afraid of being hurt again? How could she tell him that when he'd offered help and understanding she'd been afraid to accept it because it was so easy to be dependent?

She began to ride out alone at night again. Solitude didn't soothe her as it once had; it only reminded her that she had taken steps to insure that she would remain alone. The nights were warm, with the lingering scent of honeysuckle bringing back memories of a night where there had been pictures in the sky. She couldn't look at the stars without thinking of him.

Perhaps that was why she rode to the lake, where the grass was soft and thick. Here she could smell the water and wild blossoms. The horse's hooves were muffled, and she could just hear the rustle of wings in flight— some unseen bird in search of prey or a mate.

Then she saw him.

The moon was on the wane, so he was only a shadow, but she knew he was watching her. Just as she had known, somehow, that she would find him there tonight. Reining in, she let the magic take her. For the moment, even if it were only a moment, she would forget everything but that she loved him. Tomorrow would take care of itself.

She slid from the horse and went to him.

He said nothing. Until she touched him, he wasn't sure she wasn't a dream. In silence, she framed his face in her hands and pressed her lips to his. No dream had ever tasted so warm. No illusion had ever felt so soft.

"Eden—"

With a shake of her head, she cut off his words. There were weeks of emptiness to fill, and no questions that needed answering. Rising on her toes, she kissed him again. The only sound was her sigh as his arms finally came around her. She discovered a bottomless well of giving inside her. Something beyond passion, something beyond desire. Here was comfort, strength and the understanding she had been afraid to accept.

His fingers trailed up to her hair, as if each touch reassured him she was indeed real. When he opened his eyes again, his arms wouldn't be empty, but filled with her. Her cheek rubbed his, smooth skin against a day's growth of beard. With her head nestled in a curve of his shoulder, she watched the wink and blink of fireflies and thought of stars.

They stood in silence while an owl hooted and the horse whinnied in response.

"Why did you come?" He needed an answer, one he could take back with him when she had left him again.

"To see you." She drew away, wanting to see his face. "To be with you."

"Why?"

The magic shimmered and began to dim. With a

sigh, she drew back. Dreams were for sleeping, Eden reminded herself. And questions had to be answered. "I wanted to apologize for the way I behaved before. You were being kind." Searching for words, she turned to pluck a leaf from the tree that shadowed them. "I know how I must have seemed, how I sounded, and I am sorry. It's difficult, still difficult for me to..." Restless, she moved her shoulders. "We were able to muffle most of the publicity after my father died, but there was a great deal of gossip, of speculation and not-so-quiet murmurs."

When he said nothing, she shifted again, uncomfortable. "I suppose I resented all of that more than anything else. It became very important to me to prove myself, that I could manage, even succeed. I realize that I've become sensitive about handling things myself and that when you offered to help, I reacted badly. I apologize for that."

Silence hung another moment before he took a step toward her. Eden thought he moved the way the shadows did. Silently. "That's a nice apology, Eden. Before I accept it, I'd like to ask if the kiss was part of it."

So he wasn't going to make it easy for her. Her chin lifted. She didn't need an easy road any longer. "No."

Then he smiled and circled her throat with his hand. "What was it for then?"

The smile disturbed her more than the touch, though it was the touch she backed away from. Strange how you could take one step and find yourself sunk to the hips. "Does there have to be a reason?" When she walked toward the edge of the lake, she saw an owl swoop low over the water. That was the way she felt, she realized. As if she were skimming along the surface of something that could take her in over her head. "I wanted to kiss you, so I did."

The tension he'd lived with for weeks had vanished, leaving him almost light-headed. He had to resist the urge to scoop her up and carry her home, where he'd begun to understand she belonged. "Do you always do what you want?"

She turned back with a toss of her head. She'd apologized, but the pride remained. "Always."

He grinned, nudging a smile from her. "So do I."

"Then we should understand each other."

He trailed a finger down her cheek. "Remember that."

"I will." Steady again, she moved past him to the gelding. "We're having a dance a week from Saturday. Would you like to come?"

His hand closed over hers on the reins. "Are you asking me for a date?"

Amused, she swung her hair back before settling a foot in the stirrup. "Certainly not. We're short of chaperons."

She bent her leg to give herself a boost into the saddle, but found herself caught at the waist. She dangled in midair for a moment before Chase set her on the ground again, turning her to face him. "Will you dance with me?"

She remembered the last time they had danced and saw from the look in his eyes that he did as well. Her heart fluttered in the back of her dry throat, but she lifted a brow and smiled. "Maybe."

His lips curved, then descended slowly to brush against hers. She felt the world tilt, then steady at an angle only lovers understand. "A week from Saturday," he murmured, then lifted her easily into the saddle. His hand remained over hers another moment. "Miss me."

He stayed by the water until she was gone and the night was silent again.

Chapter 7

The last weeks of summer were hot and long. At night, there was invariably heat lightning and rumbling thunder, but little rain. Eden pushed herself through the days, blocking out the uncertainty of life after September.

She wasn't escaping, she told herself. She was coping with one day at a time. If she had learned one important lesson over the summer, it was that she could indeed make changes, in herself and in her life.

The frightened and defeated woman who had come to Camp Liberty almost as if it were a sanctuary would leave a confident, successful woman who could face the world on her own terms.

Standing in the center of the compound, she ran her hands down her narrow hips before dipping them into the pockets of her shorts. Next summer would be even better, now that they'd faced the pitfalls and learned how to maneuver around them. She knew she was skipping over months of her life, but found she didn't want to dwell on the winter. She didn't want to think of Philadelphia and snowy sidewalks, but of the mountains and what she had made of her life there.

If it had been possible, she would have found a way to stay behind during the off-season. Eden had begun to understand that only necessity and the need for employment were taking her back east. It wasn't her home any longer.

With a shake of her head, Eden pushed away thoughts of December. The sun was hot and bright. She could watch it shimmer on the surface of Chase's lake and think of him.

She wondered what would have happened if she had met him two years earlier when her life had been so ordered and set and mapped-out. Would she have fallen in love with him then? Perhaps it was all a matter of timing; perhaps she would have given him a polite how-do-you-do and forgotten him.

No. Closing her eyes, she could recall vividly every sensation, every emotion he'd brought into her life. Timing had nothing to do with something so overwhelming. No matter when, no matter where, she would have fallen in love with him. Hadn't she fought it all along, only to find her feelings deepening?

But she'd thought herself in love with Eric, too.

She shivered in the bright sun and watched a jay race overhead. Was she so shallow, so cold, that her feelings could shift and change in the blink of an eye? That was what held her back and warned her to be cautious. If Eric hadn't turned his back on her, she would have married him. His ring would be on her finger even now. Eden glanced down at her bare left hand.

But that hadn't been love, she reassured herself. Now she knew what love felt like, what it did to heart and mind and body. And yet… How did he feel? He cared, and he wanted, but she knew enough of love now to understand that wasn't enough. She, too, had once cared and wanted. If Chase was in love with her, there wouldn't be any *before*. Time would begin now.

Don't be a fool, she told herself with a flash of annoyance. That kind of thinking would only make her drift back to dependence. There was a before for both of them, and a future. There was no way of being sure that the future would merge with what she felt today.

But she wanted to be a fool, she realized with a quick, delicious shudder. Even if only for a few weeks, she wanted to absorb and concentrate all those mad feelings. She'd be sensible again. Sensible was for January, when the wind was sharp and the rent had to be paid. In a few days she would dance with him, smile up at him. She would have that one night of the summer to be a fool.

Kicking off her shoes, Eden plucked them up in one hand and ran the rest of the way to the dock. Girls, already separated into groups, were waiting for the signal to row out into the lake.

"Miss Carlbough!" In her camp uniform and her familiar cap, Roberta hopped up and down on the grass near the rowboats. "Watch this." With a quick flurry of motion, she bent over, kicked up her feet and stood on her head. "What do you think?" she demanded through teeth clenched with effort. Her triangular face reddened.

"Incredible."

"I've been practicing." With a grunt, Roberta tumbled onto the grass. "Now, when my mom asks what I did at camp, I can stand on my head and show her."

Eden lifted a brow, hoping Mrs. Snow got a few more details. "I'm sure she'll be impressed."

Still sprawled on the grass, arms splayed out to the sides, Roberta stared up at Eden. She was just old enough to wish that her hair was blond and wavy. "You look real pretty today, Miss Carlbough."

Touched, and more than a little surprised, Eden held out a hand to help Roberta up. "Why, thank you, Roberta. So do you."

"Oh, I'm not pretty, but I'm going to be once I can wear makeup and cover my freckles."

Eden rubbed a thumb over Roberta's cheek. "Lots of boys fall for freckles."

"Maybe." Roberta tucked that away to consider later. "I guess you're soft on Mr. Elliot."

Eden dropped her hand back in her pocket. "Soft on?"

"You know." To demonstrate, Roberta sighed and fluttered her eyes. Eden wasn't sure whether to laugh or give the little monster a shove into the lake.

"That's ridiculous."

"Are you getting married?"

"I haven't the vaguest idea where you come up with such nonsense. Now into the boat. Everyone's ready to go."

"My mom told me people sometimes get married when they're soft on each other."

"I'm sure your mother's quite right." Hoping to close the subject, Eden helped Roberta into their assigned rowboat, where Marcie and Linda were already waiting. "However, in this case, Mr. Elliot and I barely know each other. Everyone hook their life jackets, please."

"Mom said she and Daddy fell in love at first sight." Roberta hooked on the preserver, though she thought it was a pain when she swam so well. "They kiss all the time."

"I'm sure that's nice. Now—"

"I used to think it was kind of gross, but I guess it's okay." Roberta settled into her seat and smiled. "Well, if you decide not to marry Mr. Elliot, maybe I will."

Eden was busy locking in the oars, but she glanced up. "Oh?"

"Yeah. He's got a neat dog and all those apple trees." Roberta adjusted the brim of her cap over her eyes. "And he's kind of pretty." The two girls beside her giggled in agreement.

"That's certainly something to think about." Eden began to row. "Maybe you can discuss the idea with your mother when you get home."

"'Kay. Can I row first?"

Eden could only be grateful that the girl's interest span was as fast-moving as the rest of her. "Fine. You and I will row out. Marcie and Linda can row back."

After a bit of drag and a few grunts, Roberta matched her rhythm to Eden's. As the boat began to glide, it occurred to Eden that she was rowing with the same three girls who had started the adventure in the apple orchard. With a silent chuckle, she settled into sync with Roberta and let her mind drift.

What if she had never gone up in that tree? Absently, she touched her lower lip with her tongue, recalling the taste and feel of Chase. If she had it to do over, would she run in the opposite direction?

Smiling, Eden closed her eyes a moment, so that the sun glowed red under her lids. No, she wouldn't run. Being able to admit it, being able to be sure of it, strengthened her confidence. She wouldn't run from Chase, or from anything else in life.

Perhaps she was soft on him, as Roberta had termed it. Perhaps she could hug that secret to herself for a little while. It would be wonderful if things could be as simple and uncomplicated as Roberta made them. Love equaled marriage, marriage equaled happiness. Sighing, Eden opened her eyes and watched the surface of the lake. For a little while she could believe in poetry and dreams.

Daydreams… They were softer and even more mystical than dreams by night. It had been a long time since Eden had indulged in them. Now the girls were chattering and calling to their friends in the other boats. Someone was singing, deliberately off-key. Eden's arms moved in a steady rhythm as the oars cut smoothly into the water and up into the air again.

So she was floating…dreaming with her eyes open… silk and ivory and lace. The glitter of the sun on water was like candlelight. The call of crows was music to dance by.

She was riding on Pegasus. High in a night sky, his white wings effortlessly cut through the air. She could taste the cool, thin wind that took them through clouds. Her hair was free, flying behind her, twined with flowers. More clouds, castle-like, rose up in the distance, filmy and gray and secret. Their secrets were nothing to her. She had freedom for the first time, full, unlimited freedom.

And he was with her, riding the sky through snatches of light and dark. Higher, still higher they rose, until the earth was only mist beneath them. And the stars were flowers, the white petals of anemones that she could reach out and pick as the whim struck her.

When she turned in his arms, she was his without boundaries. All restrictions, all doubts, had been left behind in the climb.

"Hey, look. It's Squat!"

Eden blinked. The daydream disintegrated. She was in a rowboat, with muscles that were just beginning to ache from exertion. There were no flowers, no stars, only water and sky.

They'd rowed nearly the width of the lake. A portion of Chase's orchard spread back from the shore, and visible was one of the greenhouses he had taken the camp through on the day of the tour. Delighted with the company, Squat dashed back and forth in the shallow water near the lake's edge. His massive paws scattered a flurry of water that coated him until he was a sopping, shaggy mess.

Smiling as the girls called out greetings to the dog, Eden wondered if Chase was home. What did he do with his Sundays? she thought. Did he laze around the house with the paper and cups of coffee? Did he switch on the ball game, or go out for long, solitary drives? Just then, as if to answer her questions, he and Delaney joined the dog on the shore. Across the water, Eden felt the jolt as their eyes met.

Would it always be like that? Always stunning, al-

ways fresh? Always immediate? Inhaling slowly, she
coaxed her pulse back to a normal rate.

"Hey, Mr. Elliot!" Without a thought for the consequences, Roberta dropped her oar and jumped up.
Excitement had her bouncing up and down as the boat
teetered.

"Roberta." Acting by instinct, Eden locked her oars.
"Sit down, you'll turn us over." Eden started to grab
for her hand as the other girls took Roberta's lead and
jumped to their feet.

"Hi, Mr. Elliot!"

The greeting rang out in unison, just before the boat
tipped over.

Eden hit the water headfirst. After the heat of the sun
it seemed shockingly cold, and she surfaced sputtering
with fury. With one hand, she dragged the hair out of
her eyes and focused on the three bobbing heads. The
girls, buoyed by their life jackets, waved unrepentantly
at the trio on shore.

Eden grabbed the edge of the upended boat. "Roberta!"

"Look, Miss Carlbough." Apparently the tone, said
through gritted teeth, passed over the girl's head. "Squat's
coming out."

"Terrific." Treading water, Eden plucked Roberta by
the arm and tried to drag her back to the capsized boat.
"Remember the rules of boating safety. Stay here." Eden
went for the next girl, but twisted her head to see the
dog paddling toward them. Uneasy with his progress,
she looked back toward shore.

Her request that Chase call back his dog caught in
her throat as she spotted his grin. Though she couldn't

hear the words, she saw Delaney turn to him with some remark. It was enough to see Chase throw back his head and laugh. That sound carried.

"Want some help?" he called out.

Eden pulled at the next giggling girl. "Don't put yourself out," she began, then shrieked when Squat laid a wet, friendly nose on her shoulder. Her reaction seemed to amuse everyone, dog included. Squat began to bark enthusiastically in her ear.

Fresh pandemonium broke out as the girls began to splash water at each other and the dog. Eden found herself caught in the crossfire. In the other boats, campers and counselors looked on, grinning or calling out encouraging words. Squat paddled circles around her as she struggled to restore some kind of order.

"All right, ladies. Enough." That earned her a mouthful of lake. "It's time to right the boat."

"Can Squat take a ride with us?" Roberta giggled as he licked water from her face.

"No."

"That hardly seems fair."

Eden nearly submerged before Chase gripped her arm. She'd been too busy trying to restore order and her own dignity to notice that he'd swum the few yards from shore. "He came out to help."

His hair was barely damp, while hers was plastered to her head. Chase hooked an arm around her waist to ease her effort to tread water.

"You'd better right the boat," he said to the girls, who immediately fell to doing so with a vengeance. "Apparently you do better with horses." His voice was soft and amused in Eden's ear.

She started to draw away, but her legs tangled with his. "If you and that monster hadn't been on shore—"

"Delaney?"

"No, not Delaney." Frustrated, Eden pushed at her hair.

"You're beautiful when you're wet. Makes me wonder why I haven't thought of swimming with you before."

"We're not supposed to be swimming, we're supposed to be boating."

"Either way, you're beautiful."

She wouldn't be moved. Even though the girls had already righted the boat, Eden knew she was in over her head. "It's that dog," she began. Even as she said it, the girls were climbing back into the boat and urging Squat to join them.

"Roberta, I said—" Chase gently dunked her. Surfacing, she heard him striking the bargain.

"We'll swim back. You bring Squat. He likes boats."

"I said—" Again, she found herself under water. This time when she came up for air, she gave Chase her full attention. The swing she took at him was slow and sluggish because of the need to tread water.

He caught her fist and kissed it. "Beat you back."

Narrowing her eyes, Eden gave him a shove before striking out after the boat. The water around her ears muffled the sound of Squat's deep barking and the girls' excited cheering. With strong, even strokes, she kept a foot behind the boat and made certain the girls behaved.

Less than twenty feet from shore, Chase caught her by the ankle. Laughing and kicking, Eden found herself tangled in his arms.

"You cheat." As he rose, he swept her off her feet so that her accusation ended in another laugh. His bare chest was cool and wet under her palms. His hair was dripping so that the sunlight was caught in each separate drop of water. "I won."

"Wrong." She should have seen it coming. Without effort, he pitched her back in the lake. Eden landed bottom first. "I won."

Eden stood to shake herself off. Managing to suppress a smile, she nodded toward the whooping girls. "And that, ladies, is a classic example of poor sportsmanship." She reached up to squeeze the water out of her hair, unaware that her shirt clung to every curve. Chase felt his heart stop. She waded toward shore, with the clear lake water clinging to her tanned legs. "Good afternoon, Delaney."

"Ma'am." He gave her a gold, flashing grin. "Nice day for a swim."

"Apparently."

"I was about to pick me some blackberries for jam." He cast his gaze over the three dripping girls. "If I had some help, could be I'd have a jar or so extra for some neighbors."

Before Eden could consent or refuse, all the girls and Squat were jumping circles around her. She had to admit that a ten- or fifteen-minute break would make the row back to camp a little more appealing. "Ten minutes," she told them before turning back to signal to the other boats.

Delaney toddled off, sandwiched between girls who were already barraging him with questions. As they disappeared into a cluster of trees, a startled flock of birds whizzed out. She laughed, turning back to see Chase staring at her.

"You're a strong swimmer."

She had to clear her throat. "I think I've just become more competitive. Maybe I should keep an eye on the girls so—"

"Delaney can handle them." He reached out to brush a bead of water from her jawline. Beneath his gentle touch, she shivered. "Cold?"

More than the sun had taken the lake's chill from her skin. Eden managed to shake her head. "No." But when his hands came to her shoulders, she stepped back.

He wore only cutoffs, faded soft from wear. The shirt he had peeled off before diving into the lake had been tossed carelessly to the ground. "You don't feel cold," he murmured as he stroked his hands down her arms.

"I'm not." She heard the laughter beyond the trees. "I really can't let them stay long. They'll have to change."

Patient, Chase took her hand. "Eden, you're going to end up in the lake again if you keep backing up." He was frightening her. Frustrated, he struggled not to push. It seemed that every time he thought he'd gained her trust, he saw that quick flash of anxiety in her eyes again. He smiled, hoping the need that was roiling inside him didn't show. "Where are your shoes?"

Off-balance, she looked down and stared at her own bare feet. Slowly, her muscles began to relax again. "At the bottom of your lake." Laughing, she shook her wet hair back, nearly destroying him. "Roberta always manages to keep things exciting. Why don't we give them a hand with the berry-picking."

His arm came across her body to take her shoulder before she could move past him. "You're still backing away, Eden." Lifting a hand, he combed his fingers through her sleek, wet hair until they rested at the base of her neck. "It's hard to resist you this way, with your face glowing and your eyes aware and just a bit frightened."

"Chase, don't." She put her hand to his.

"I want to touch you." He shifted so that the full length of her body was against his. "I need to touch you." Through the wet cotton, she could feel the texture of his skin on hers. "Look at me, Eden." The slightest pressure of his fingers brought her face up to his. "How close are you going to let me get?"

She could only shake her head. There weren't any words to describe what she was feeling, what she wanted, what she was still too afraid to need. "Chase, don't do this. Not here, not now." Then she could only moan, as his mouth traveled with a light, lazy touch over her face.

"When?" He had to fight the desire to demand rather than to ask, to take rather than to wait. "Where?" This time the kiss wasn't lazy, but hard, bruising. Eden felt rational thought spiral away even as she groped for an answer. "Don't you think I know what happens to you when we're like this?" His voice thickened as his patience stretched thinner and thinner. "Good God, Eden, I need you. Come with me tonight. Stay with me."

Yes, yes. Oh, yes. How easy it would be to say it, to give in, to give everything without a thought for tomorrow. She clung to him a moment, wanting to believe dreams were possible. He was so solid, so real. But so were her responsibilities.

"Chase, you know I can't." Fighting for rationality, she drew away. "I have to stay at camp."

Before she could move away again, he caught her face in his hands. She thought his eyes had darkened, a stormier green now, with splashes of gold from the sun. "And when summer's over, Eden? What then?"

What then? How could she have the answer, when the answer was so cold, so final? It wasn't what she wanted, but what had to be. If she was to keep her promise to herself, to make her life work, there was only one answer. "Then I'll go back, back to Philadelphia, until next summer."

Only summers? Was that all she was willing to give? It was the panic that surprised him and kept the fury at bay. When she left, his life would be empty. He took her shoulders again, fighting back the panic.

"You'll come to me before you go." It wasn't a question. It wasn't a demand. It was a simple statement. The demand she could have rebelled against; the question she could have refused.

"Chase, what good would it do either of us?"

"You'll come to me before you go," he repeated. Because if she didn't, he'd follow her. There would be no choice.

Chapter 8

Red and white crepe paper streamed from corner to corner, twined together in elongated snakes of color. Balloons, bulging with air from energetic young lungs, were crowded into every available space. Stacked in three uneven towers were all the records deemed fit to play.

Dance night was only a matter of hours away.

Under Candy's eagle eye, tables were carried outside, while others were grouped strategically around the mess area. This simple chore took twice as long as it should have, as girls had to stop every few feet to discuss the most important aspect of the evening: boys.

Although her skills with paint and glue were slim at best, Eden had volunteered for the decorating committee—on the understanding that her duties were limited to hanging and tacking what was already made. In addition to the crepe paper and balloons, there were banners and paper flowers that the more talented members of campers and staff had put together by hand. The best of these was a ten-foot banner dyed Camp Liberty red and splashed with bold letters that spelled out WELCOME TO CAMP LIBERTY'S ANNUAL SUMMER DANCE.

Candy had already taken it for granted that it would be the first of many. In her better moods, Eden hoped she was right. In her crankier ones, she wondered if they could swing a deal with the boys' camp to split the cost of refreshments. For the moment, she pushed both ideas aside, determined to make this dance the best-decorated one in Pennsylvania.

Eden let an argument over which records had priority run its course below her as she climbed a stepladder to secure more streamers. Already, the record player at the far end of the room was blaring music.

It was silly. She told herself that yet again as she realized she was as excited about the evening as any of the girls. She was an adult, here only to plan, supervise and chaperon. Even as she reminded herself of this, her thoughts ran forward to the evening, when the mess area would be filled with people and noise and laughter. Like the girls below her, her thoughts kept circling back to vital matters—like what she should wear.

It was fascinating to realize that this simple end-of-the-summer dance in the mountains was more exciting for her than her own debutante ball. That she had taken lightly, as the next step along the path that had been cleared for her before she was born. This was new, untried and full of possibilities.

It all centered on Chase. Eden was nearly ready to

accept that as a new song blared into life. Since it was one she'd heard dozens of times before, she began to hum along with it. Her ponytail swayed with the movement as she attached another streamer.

"We'll ask Miss Carlbough." Eden heard the voices below, but paid little attention, as she had a tack in her mouth and five feet of crepe paper held together by her thumb. "She always knows, and if she doesn't, she finds out."

She had started to secure the tack, but as the statement drifted up to her, she stopped pushing. Was that really the way the girls saw her? Dependable? With a half laugh, she sent the tack home. To her, the statement was the highest of compliments, a sign of faith.

She'd done what she had set out to do. In three short months, she had accomplished something she had never done in all her years of living. She had made something of herself, by herself. And, perhaps more importantly, for herself.

It wasn't going to stop here. Eden dropped the rest of the tacks into her pocket. The summer might be nearly over, but the challenge wasn't. Whether she was in South Mountain or Philadelphia, she wasn't going to forget what it meant to grow. Twisting on the ladder, she started down to find out what it was the girls had wanted to ask her. On the second rung, she stopped, staring.

The tall, striking woman strode into the mess. The tail of her Hermès scarf crossed the neck of a cerise suit and trailed on behind. Her bone-white hair was perfect, as was the double strand of pearls that lay on her bosom. Tucked in the crook of one arm was a small piece of white fluff known as BooBoo.

"Aunt Dottie!" Delighted, Eden scrambled down from the ladder. In seconds she was enveloped by Dottie's personal scent, an elusive combination of Paris and success. "Oh, it's wonderful to see you." Drawing back from the hug, Eden studied the lovely, strong-boned face. Even now, she could see shadows of her father in the eyes and around the mouth. "You're the last person I expected to see here."

"Darling, have you grown thorns in the country?"

"Thorns? I—oh." Laughing, Eden reached in her pocket. "Thumbtacks. Sorry."

"The hug was worth a few holes." Taking Eden's hand, she stepped back to make her own study. Though her face remained passive, she let out a quiet sigh of relief. No one knew how many restless nights she'd spent worrying over her brother's only child. "You look beautiful. A little thin, but with marvelous color." With Eden's hand still in hers, she glanced around the room. "But darling, what an odd place you've chosen to spend the summer."

"Aunt Dottie." Eden just shook her head. Throughout the weeks and months after her father's death, Dottie had stubbornly refused to accept Eden's decision not to use Dottie's money as a buffer, her home as a refuge. "If I have marvelous color, credit the country air."

"Hmm." Far from convinced, Dottie continued to look around as a new record plopped down to continue the unbroken cycle of music. "I've always considered the south of France country enough."

"Aunt Dottie, tell me what you're doing here. I'm amazed you could even find the place."

"It wasn't difficult. The chauffeur reads a map very

well." Dottie gave the fluff in her arms a light pat. "Boo-Boo and I felt an urge for a drive to the country."

"I see." And she did. Like everyone else she had left behind, Eden knew that her aunt considered her camp venture an impulse. It would take more than one summer to convince Dottie, or anyone else, that she was serious. After all, it had taken her most of the summer to convince herself.

"Yes, and since I was in the neighborhood…" Dottie let that trail off. "What a chic outfit," she commented, taking in Eden's paint-spattered smock and tattered sneakers. "Then, perhaps bohemian's coming back. What do you have there?"

"Crepe paper. It goes with the thumbtacks." Eden extended her hand. BooBoo regally allowed her head to be patted.

"Well, give them both to one of these charming young ladies and come see what I've brought you."

"Brought me?" Obeying automatically, Eden handed over the streamers. "Start these around the tables, will you, Lisa?"

"Do you know," Dottie began as she linked her arm through Eden's, "the nearest town is at least twenty miles from here? That is if one could stretch credibility and call what we passed through a town. There, there, BooBoo, I won't set you down on the nasty ground." She cuddled the dog as they stepped outside. "BooBoo's a bit skittish out of the city, you understand."

"Perfectly."

"Where was I? Oh yes, the town. It had one traffic light and a place called Earl's Lunch. I was almost curious enough to stop and see what one did at Earl's Lunch."

Eden laughed, and leaned over to kiss Dottie's cheek. "One eats a small variety of sandwiches and stale potato chips and coffee while exchanging town gossip."

"Marvelous. Do you go often?"

"Unfortunately, my social life's been a bit limited."

"Well, your surprise might just change all that." Turning, Dottie gestured toward the canary-yellow Rolls parked in the main compound. Eden felt every muscle, every emotion freeze as the man straightened from his easy slouch against the hood.

"Eric."

He smiled, and in a familiar gesture, ran one hand lightly over his hair. Around him, a group of girls had gathered to admire the classic lines of the Rolls and the classic looks of Eric Keeton.

His smile was perfectly angled as he walked toward her. His walk was confident, just a shade too conservative for a swagger. As she watched him, Eden saw him in the clear light of disinterest. His hair, several shades darker than her own, was perfectly styled for the boardroom or the country club. Casual attire, which included pleated slacks and a polo shirt, fit neatly over his rather narrow frame. Hazel eyes, which had a tendency to look bored easily, smiled and warmed now. Though she hadn't offered them, he took both her hands.

"Eden, how marvelous you look."

His hands were soft. Strange, she had forgotten that. Though she didn't bother to remove hers, her voice was cool. "Hello, Eric."

"Lovelier than ever, isn't she, Dottie?" Her stiff greeting didn't seem to disturb him. He gave her hands an intimate little squeeze. "Your aunt was worried about you. She expected you to be thin and wan."

"Fortunately, I'm neither." Now, carefully, deliberately, Eden removed her hands. She would have been greatly pleased, though she had no way of knowing it, that her eyes were as cold as her voice. It was so easy to turn away from him. "Whatever possessed you to drive all this way, Aunt Dottie? You weren't really worried?"

"A tad." Concerned with the ice in her niece's voice, Dottie touched Eden's cheek. "And I did want to see the—the place where you spent the summer."

"I'll give you a tour."

A thin left brow arched in a manner identical to Eden's. "How charming."

"Aunt Dottie!" Red curls bouncing, Candy raced around the side of the building. "I knew it had to be you." Out of breath and grinning broadly, Candy accepted Dottie's embrace. "The girls were talking about a yellow Rolls in the compound. Who else could it have been?"

"As enthusiastic as ever." Dottie's smile was all affection. She might not have always understood Candice Bartholomew, but she had always been fond of her. "I hope you don't mind a surprise visit."

"I love it." Candy bent down to the puff of fur. "Hi, BooBoo." Straightening, she let her gaze drift over Eric. "Hello, Eric." Her voice dropped an easy twenty-five degrees. "Long way from home."

"Candy." Unlike Dottie, he had no fondness for Eden's closest friend. "You seem to have paint all over your hands."

"It's dry," she said, carelessly, and somewhat regretfully. If the paint had been wet, she would have greeted him more personally.

"Eden's offered to take us on a tour." Dottie was well

aware of the hostility. She'd driven hundreds of miles from Philadelphia for one purpose. To help her niece find happiness. If it meant she had to manipulate…so much the better. "I know Eric's dying to look around, but if I could impose on you—" She laid her hand on Candy's. "I'd really love to sit down with a nice cup of tea. BooBoo, too. The drive was a bit tiring."

"Of course." Manners were their own kind of trap. Candy sent Eden a look meant to fortify her. "We'll use the kitchen, if you don't mind the confusion."

"My dear, I thrive on it." With that she turned to smile at Eden and was surprised by the hard, knowing look in Eden's eyes.

"Go right ahead, Aunt Dottie. I'll show Eric what the camp has to offer."

"Eden, I—"

"Go have your tea, darling." She kissed Dottie's cheek. "We'll talk later." She turned, leaving Eric to follow or not. When he fell into step beside her, she began. "We've six sleeping cabins this season, with plans to add two more for next summer. Each cabin has an Indian name to keep it distinct."

As they passed the cabins, she saw that the anemones were still stubbornly blooming. They gave her strength. "Each week, we have a contest for the neatest cabin. The reward is extra riding time, or swimming time, or whatever the girls prefer. Candy and I have a small shower in our cabin. The girls share facilities at the west end of the compound."

"Eden." Eric cupped her elbow in his palm in the same manner he had used when strolling down Broad Street. She gritted her teeth, but didn't protest.

"Yes?" The cool, impersonal look threw him off.

It took him only a moment to decide it meant she was hiding a broken heart.

"What have you been doing with yourself?" He waved his hand in a gesture that took in the compound and the surrounding hills. "Here?"

Holding on to her temper, Eden decided to take the question literally. "We've tried to keep the camp regimented, while still allowing for creativity and fun. Over the past few weeks, we've found that we can adhere fairly tightly to the schedule as long as we make room for fresh ideas and individual needs." Pleased with herself, she dipped her hands into the pockets of her smock. "We're up at six-thirty. Breakfast is at seven sharp. Daily inspection begins at seven-thirty and activities at eight. For the most part, I deal with the horses and stables, but when necessary, I can pitch in and help in other areas."

"Eden." Eric stopped her by gently tightening his fingers on her elbow. Turning to him, she watched the faint breeze ruffle his smooth, fair hair. She thought of the dark confusion of Chase's hair. "It's difficult to believe you've spent your summer camping out in a cabin and overseeing a parade of girls on horseback."

"Is it?" She merely smiled. Of course it was difficult for him. He owned a stable, but he'd never lifted a pitchfork. Rather than resentment, Eden felt a stirring of pity. "Well, there's that, among a few other things such as hiking, smoothing over cases of homesickness and poison ivy, rowing, giving advice on teenage romance and fashion, identifying fifteen different varieties of local wildflowers and seeing that a group of girls has fun. Would you like to see the stables?" She headed off without waiting for his answer.

"Eden." He caught her elbow again. It took all her willpower not to jab it back into his soft stomach. "You're angry. Of course you are, but I—"

"You've always had a fondness for good horseflesh." She swung the stable door open so that he had to back off or get a faceful of wood. "We've two mares and four geldings. One of the mares is past her prime, but I'm thinking of breeding the other. The foals would interest the girls and eventually become part of the riding stock. This is Courage."

"Eden, please. We have to talk."

She stiffened when his hands touched her shoulders. But she was calm, very calm, when she turned and removed them. "I thought we were talking."

He'd heard the ice in her voice before, and he understood it. She was a proud, logical woman. He'd approach her on that level. "We have to talk about us, darling."

"In what context?"

He reached for her hand, giving a small shrug when she drew it away. If she had accepted him without a murmur, he would have been a great deal more surprised. For days now, he'd been planning exactly the proper way to smooth things over. He'd decided on regretful, with a hint of humble thrown in.

"You've every right to be furious with me, every right to want me to suffer."

His tone, soft, quiet, understanding, had her swallowing a ball of heat. Indifference, she reminded herself, disinterest, was the greatest insult she could hand him. "It doesn't really concern me if you suffer or not." That wasn't quite true, she admitted. She wouldn't be averse to seeing him writhe a bit. That was because he had come, she realized. Because he had had the gall to come and assume she'd be waiting.

"Eden, you have to know that I have suffered, suffered a great deal. I would have come before, but I wasn't sure you'd see me."

This was the man she had planned to spend her life with. This was the man she had hoped to have children with. She stared at him now, unsure whether she was in the midst of a comedy or a tragedy. "I'm sorry to hear that, Eric. I don't see any reason why you should have suffered. You were only being practical, after all."

Soothed by her placid attitude, he stepped toward her. "I admit that, rightly or wrongly, I was practical." His hands slid up her arms in an old gesture that made her jaw clench. "These past few months have shown me that there are times when practical matters have to take second place."

"Is that so?" She smiled at him, surprised that he couldn't feel the heat. "What would go first?"

"Personal..." He stroked a finger over her cheek. "Much more personal matters."

"Such as?"

His lips were curved as his mouth lowered. She felt the heat of anger freeze into icy disdain. Did he think her a fool? Could he believe himself so irresistible? Then she nearly did laugh, as she realized the answer to both questions was yes.

She let him kiss her. The touch of his lips left her totally unmoved. It fascinated her that, only a few short months before, his kisses had warmed her. It had been nothing like the volcanic heat she experienced with

Chase, but there had been a comfort and an easy pleasure. That was all she had thought there was meant to be.

Now there was nothing. The absence of feeling in
itself dulled the edge of her fury. She was in control.
Here, as in other areas of her life, she was in control.
Though his lips coaxed, she simply stood, waiting for
him to finish.

When he lifted his head, Eden put her hands on his
arms to draw herself away. It was then she saw Chase
just inside the open stable door.

The sun was at his back, silhouetting him, blinding
her to the expression on his face. Even so, her mouth
was dry as she stared, trying to see through shadow and
sun. When he stepped forward, his eyes were on hers.

Explanations sprang to her tongue, but she could only
shake her head as his gaze slid over her and onto Eric.

"Keeton." Chase nodded, but didn't extend his hand.
He knew if he had the other man's fingers in his he
would take pleasure in breaking them, one by one.

"Elliot." Eric returned the nod. "I'd forgotten. You
have land around here, don't you?"

"A bit." Chase wanted to murder him, right there in
the stables, while Eden watched. Then he would find
it just as satisfying to murder her.

"You must know Eden, then." Eric placed a hand
on her shoulder in a casually possessive movement.
Chase followed the gesture before looking at her again.
Her instinctive move to shrug away Eric's hand was
stopped by the look. Was it anger she saw there, or
was it disgust?

"Yes. Eden and I have run into each other a few

times." He dipped his hands into his pockets as they balled into fists.

"Chase was generous enough to allow us to use his lake." Her right hand groped for her left until they were clasped together. "We had a tour of his orchards." Though pride suffered, her eyes pleaded with him.

"Your land must be very near here." Eric hadn't missed the exchange of looks. His hand leaned more heavily on Eden's shoulder.

"Near enough."

Then they were looking at each other, not at her. Somehow that, more than anything, made her feel as though she'd been shifted to the middle. If there was tension and she was the cause of it, she wanted to be able to speak on her own behalf. But the expression in Chase's eyes only brought confusion. The weight of Eric's hand only brought annoyance. Moving away from Eric, she stepped toward Chase.

"Did you want to see me?"

"Yes." But he'd wanted more than that, a great deal more. Seeing her in Eric's arms had left him feeling both murderous and empty. He wasn't ready to deal with either yet. "It wasn't important."

"Chase—"

"Oh, hello." The warmth in Candy's voice came almost as a shock. She stepped through the doorway with Dottie at her side. "Aunt Dottie, I want you to meet our neighbor, Chase Elliot."

Even as Dottie extended her hand, her eyes were narrowed speculatively. "Elliot? I'm sure I know that name. Yes, yes, didn't we meet several years ago? You're Jessie Winthrop's grandson."

Eden watched his lips curve, his eyes warm, but he

wasn't looking at her. "Yes, I am, and I remember you very well, Mrs. Norfolk. You haven't changed."

Dottie's laugh was low and quick. "It's been fifteen years if it's been a day. I'd say there's been a change or two. You were about a foot shorter at the time." She sized him up approvingly in a matter of ten seconds. "It's apples, isn't it? Yes, of course, it is. Elliot's."

And, oh my God, she realized almost as quickly, I've brought Eric along and jammed up the works. A person would have to have a three-inch layer of steel coating not to feel the shock waves bouncing around the stables.

What could be done, she told herself, could be un-done. Smiling, she looked at her niece. "Candy's been telling me about the social event of the season. Are we all invited?"

"Invited?" Eden struggled to gather her scattered wits. "You mean the dance?" She had to laugh. Her aunt was standing in the stables in Italian shoes and a suit that had cost more than any one of the horses. "Aunt Dottie, you don't intend to stay here?"

"Stay here?" The white brows shot up. "I should say not." She twisted the pearls at her neck as she began to calculate. She didn't intend to bunk down in a cabin, but neither was she about to miss the impending fire-works. "Eric and I are staying at a hotel some miles away, but I'd be heartbroken if you didn't ask us to the party tonight." She put a friendly hand on Chase's arm. "You're coming, aren't you?"

He knew a manipulator when he saw one. "Wouldn't miss it."

"Wonderful." Dottie slid Candy's hand back into the crook of her arm, then patted it. "We're all invited then."

Fumbling, Candy looked from Eric to Eden. "Well, yes, of course, but—"

"Isn't this sweet?" Dottie patted her hand again. "We'll have a delightful time. Don't you think so, Eden?"

"Delightful," Eden agreed, wondering if she could hitch a ride out of town.

Chapter 9

Eden had problems—big problems. But not the least of them were the sixty adolescents in the mess hall. However she handled Eric, however she managed to explain herself to Chase, sixty young bodies couldn't be put on hold.

The boys arrived in vans at eight o'clock. Unless Eden missed her guess, they were every bit as nervous as the girls. Eden remembered her own cotillion days, the uncertainty and the damp palms. The blaring music helped cover some of the awkwardness as the boys' counselors trooped them in.

The refreshment table was loaded. There was enough punch stored in the kitchen to bathe in. Candy gave a brief welcoming speech to set the tone, the banners and the paper flowers waving at her back. A fresh record was set spinning on the turntable. Girls stood on one side of the room, boys on the other.

The biggest problem, naturally, was that no one wanted to go first. Eden had worked that out by making up two bowls of corresponding numbers. Boys picked from one, girls from another. You matched, you danced. It wasn't imaginative, but it was expedient.

When the first dance was half over, she slipped into the kitchen to check on backup refreshments, leaving Candy to supervise and to mingle with the male counselors.

When she returned, the dance floor wasn't as crowded, but this time the partners had chosen for themselves.

"Miss Carlbough?"

Eden turned her head as she bent to place a bowl of chips in an empty space on the long crowded table. Roberta's face was spotless. Her thatch of wild hair had been tamed into a bushy ponytail and tied with a ribbon. She had little turquoise stars in her ears to match a ruffled and not-too-badly-wrinkled blouse. The dusting of freckles over her face had been partially hidden by a layer of powder. Eden imagined she had conned it out of one of the older girls, but let it pass.

"Hi, Roberta." Plucking two pretzels from a bowl, she handed one over. "Aren't you going to dance?"

"Sure." She glanced over her shoulder, confident and patient. "I wanted to talk to you first."

"Oh?" It didn't appear that she needed a pep talk. Eden had already seen the skinny, dark-haired boy Roberta had set her sights on. If Eden was any judge, he didn't stand a chance. "What about?"

"I saw that guy in the Rolls."

Eden's automatic warning not to speak with her mouth full was postponed. "You mean Mr. Keeton?"

"Some of the girls think he's cute."

"Hmm." Eden nibbled on her own pretzel.

"A couple of them said you were soft on him. They think you had a lovers' quarrel, you know, like Romeo and Juliet or something. Now he's come to beg you to forgive him, and you're going to realize that you can't live without him and go off and get married."

The pretzel hung between two fingers as Eden listened. After a moment, she managed to clear her throat. "Well, that's quite a scenario."

"I said it was baloney."

Trying not to laugh, she bit into the pretzel. "Did you?"

"You're smart, all the girls say so." Reaching behind Eden, she took a handful of chips. "I said you were too smart to be soft on the guy in the Rolls, because he's not nearly as neat as Mr. Elliot." Roberta glanced over her shoulder as if in confirmation. "He's shorter, too."

"Yes." Eden had to bite her lip. "Yes, he is."

"He doesn't look like he'd jump in the lake to fool around."

The last statement had Eden trying to imagine Eric diving into the cool waters of the lake half-dressed. Or bringing her a clutch of wildflowers. Or finding pictures in the sky. Her lips curved dreamily. "No, Eric would never do that."

"That's why I knew it was all baloney." Roberta devoured the chips. "When Mr. Elliot comes, I'm going to dance with him, but now I'm going to dance with

Bobby." Shooting Eden a smile, she walked across the room and grabbed the hand of the lanky, dark-haired boy. As Eden had thought, he didn't have a chance.

She watched the dancing, but thought of Chase. It came to her all at once that he was the only man she knew whom she hadn't measured against her father. Comparisons had never occurred to her. She hadn't measured Chase against anyone but had fallen in love with him for himself. Now all she needed was the courage to tell him.

"So this is how young people entertain themselves these days."

Eden turned to find Dottie beside her. For Camp Liberty's summer dance, she had chosen mauve lace. The pearls had been exchanged for a single, sensational ruby. BooBoo had a clip of rhinestones—Eden sincerely hoped they were only rhinestones—secured on top of her head. Feeling a wave of affection, Eden kissed her aunt. "Are you settled into your hotel?"

"So to speak." Accepting a potato chip, Dottie took her own survey. The powder-blue voile was the essence of simplicity with its cap sleeves and high neck, but Dottie approved of the way it depended on the wearer for its style. "Thank God you haven't lost your taste."

Laughing, Eden kissed her again. "I've missed you. I'm so glad you came."

"Are you?" Always discreet, Dottie led her toward the screen door. "I was afraid you weren't exactly thrilled to see me here." She let the screen whoosh shut as they stepped onto the porch. "Particularly with the surprise I brought you."

"I was glad to see you, Aunt Dottie."

"But not Eric."

Eden leaned back on the rail. "Did you think I would be?"

"Yes." She sighed, and brushed at the bodice of her lace. "I suppose I did. It only took five minutes to realize what a mistake I'd made. Darling, I hope you understand I was trying to help."

"Of course I do, and I love you for it."

"I thought that whatever had gone wrong between you would have had time to heal over." Forgetting herself, Dottie offered BooBoo the rest of the chip. "To be honest, the way he's been talking to me, I was sure by bringing him to you I'd be doing the next-best thing to saving your life."

"I can imagine," Eden murmured.

"So much for grand gestures." Dottie moved her shoulders so that the ruby winked. "Eden, you never told me why you two called off the wedding. It was so sudden."

Eden opened her mouth, then closed it again. There was no reason to hurt and infuriate her aunt after all these months. If she told her now, it would be for spite or, worse, for sympathy. Eric was worth neither. "We just realized we weren't suited."

"I always thought differently." There was a loud blast of music and a chorus of laughter. Dottie cast a glance over her shoulder. "Eric seems to think differently, too. He's been to see me several times in recent weeks."

Pushing the heavy fall of hair from her shoulders, Eden walked to the edge of the porch. Perhaps Eric had discovered that the Carlbough name wasn't so badly tarnished after all. It gave her no pleasure to be cynical, but it was the only answer that seemed right. It wouldn't have taken him long to realize that eventually she would come into money again, through inheritances. She swallowed her bitterness as she turned back to her aunt.

"He's mistaken, Aunt Dottie. Believe me when I say he doesn't have any genuine feelings for me. Perhaps he thinks he does," she added, when she saw the frown centered between Dottie's brows. "I'd say it's a matter of habit. I didn't love Eric." Her hands outstretched, she went to take her aunt's. "I never did. It's taken me some time to understand that I was going to marry him for all the wrong reasons—because it was expected, because it was easy. And…" She drew in her breath. "Because I mistakenly thought he was like Papa."

"Oh, darling."

"It was my mistake, so most of it was my fault." Now that it was said, and said aloud, she could accept it. "I always compared the men I dated with Papa. He was the kindest, most caring man I've ever known, but even though I loved and admired him, it was wrong of me to judge other men by him."

"We all loved him, Eden." Dottie drew Eden into her arms. "He was a good man, a loving man. A gambler, but—"

"I don't mind that he was a gambler." Now, when she drew back, Eden could smile. "I know if he hadn't died so suddenly, he'd have come out on top again. But it doesn't matter, Aunt Dottie, because I'm a gambler, too." She turned so that her gesture took in the camp. "I've learned how to make my own stake."

"How like him you are." Dottie was forced to draw a tissue out of her bag. "When you insisted on doing this, even when I first came here today, I could only think my poor little Eden's gone mad. Then I looked, really looked, at your camp, at the girls, at you, and I could see you'd made it work." After one inelegant sniff, she stuffed the tissue back in her bag. "I'm proud of you, Eden. Your father would have been proud of you."

Now it was Eden's eyes that dampened. "Aunt Dottie, I can't tell you how much that means to me. After he died and I had to sell everything, I felt I'd betrayed him, you, everyone."

"No." Dottie cupped Eden's chin in her hand. "What you did took tremendous courage, more than I had. You know how badly I wanted to spare you all of that."

"I know, and I appreciate it, but it had to be this way."

"I think I understand that now. I want you to know that I hurt for you, Eden, but I was never ashamed. Even now, knowing you don't need it, I'll tell you that my house is yours whenever you like."

"Knowing that is enough."

"And I expect this to be the finest camp in the east within five years."

Eden laughed again, and all the weight she'd carried with her since her father's death slipped off her shoulders. "It will be."

With a nod, Dottie took a step along the rail and looked out at the compound. "I do believe you should have a pool. Girls should have regulated, regimented swimming lessons. Splashing in the lake doesn't meet those standards. I'm going to donate one."

Eden's back went up immediately. "Aunt Dottie—"

"In your father's name." Dottie paused and cocked a brow. "Yes, I can see you won't argue with that. If I can donate a wing to a hospital, I can certainly donate a swimming pool in my brother's name to my favor-

ite niece's camp. In fact, my accountant's going to be
thrilled. Now, would you like Eric and me to go?"

Barely recovered from being so neatly maneuvered,
Eden only sighed. "Having Eric here means nothing
now. I want you to stay as long as you like."

"Good. BooBoo and I are enjoying ourselves." Dottie bent down to nuzzle in the dog's fur. "The delightful
thing about BooBoo is that she's so much more tractable
than any of my children were. Eden, one more thing before I go inside and absorb culture. I would swear that
I felt, well, how to put it? One might almost say earth
tremors when I walked into the stables this afternoon.
Are you in love with someone else?"

"Aunt Dottie—"

"Answer enough. I'll just add my complete approval,
not that it matters. BooBoo was quite charmed."

"Are you trying to be eccentric?"

With a smile, Dottie shifted the bundle in her arms.
"When you can't rely on beauty any longer, you have
to fall back on something. Ah, look here." She stepped
aside as the Lamborghini cruised up. Lips pursed, Dottie watched Chase climb out. "Hello again," she called.
"I admire your taste." She gave Eden a quick pat. "Yes,
I do. I think I'll just pop inside and try some punch. It
isn't too dreadful, is it?"

"I made it myself."

"Oh." Dottie rolled her eyes. "Well, I've some gambler in me as well."

Bracing herself, Eden turned toward Chase. "Hello.
I'm glad you could—"

His mouth covered hers so quickly, so completely,
that there wasn't even time for surprise. She might think
of the hard possessiveness of the kiss later, but for now

she just slid her hands up his back so that she could grip his shoulders. Instantly intense, instantly real, instantly right.

She hadn't felt this with Eric. That was what Chase told himself as she melted against him. She'd never felt this with anyone else. And he was going to be damn sure she didn't. Torn between anger and need, he drew her away.

"What—" She had to stop and try again. "What was that for?"

He gathered her hair in his hand to bring her close again. His lips tarried a breath from hers. "As someone once said to me, I wanted to kiss you. Any objections?"

He was daring her. Her chin angled in acceptance. "I can't think of any."

"Mull it over. Get back to me." With that, he propelled her toward the lights and music.

She didn't like to admit that cowardice might be part of the reason she carefully divided her time between the girls and the visiting counselors. Eden told herself it was a matter of courtesy and responsibility. But she knew she needed to have her thoughts well in hand before she spoke privately with Chase again.

She watched him dance with Roberta and wanted to throw herself into his arms and tell him how much she loved him. How big a fool would that make her? He hadn't asked about Eric, so how could she explain? It hummed through her mind that if he hadn't asked, it didn't matter to him. If it didn't matter, he wasn't nearly as involved as she was. Still, she told herself that before the evening was over she would find the time to talk it through with him, whether he wanted to hear it or not.

She just wanted to wait until she was sure she could do a good job of it.

There was no such confusion about the evening in general. The summer dance was a hit. Plans between the camp coordinators were already under way to make it an annual event. Already Candy was bubbling with ideas for more joint ventures.

As always, Eden would let Candy plan and organize; then she would tidy up the details.

By keeping constantly on the move, Eden avoided any direct confrontation with Eric or Chase. Of course they spoke, even danced, but all in the sanctuary of the crowded mess hall. Eric's conversation had been as mild as hers, but there had been something danger-ous in Chase's eyes. It was that, and the memory of that rocketing kiss, that had her postponing the inevitable.

"I guess you like her a lot," Roberta ventured as she saw Chase's gaze wander toward Eden yet again.

"What?" Distracted, Chase looked back at his dance partner.

"Miss Carlbough. You're soft on her. She's so pretty," Roberta added with only the slightest touch of envy. "We voted her the prettiest counselor, even though Miss Allison has more—" She caught herself, realizing sud-denly that you didn't discuss certain parts of a woman's anatomy with a man, even with Mr. Elliot. "More, ah..."

"I get the picture." Charmed, as always, Chase swung her in a quick circle.

"Some of the other girls think Mr. Keeton's a honey."

"Oh?" Chase's smile turned into a sneer as he glanced at the man in question.

"I think his nose is skinny."

"It was almost broken," Chase muttered.

"And his eyes are too close together," Roberta added for good measure. "I like you a lot better."

Touched, and remembering his first crush, Chase tugged on her ponytail to tilt her face to his. "I'm pretty soft on you, too."

From her corner, Eden watched the exchange. She saw Chase bend down and saw Roberta's face explode into smiles. A sigh nearly escaped her before she realized she was allowing herself to be envious of a twelve-year-old. With a shake of her head, she told herself that it was the strain of keeping herself unavailable that was beginning to wear on her. The music never played below loud. Uncountable trips to the kitchen kept the refreshment table full. Boys and girls shouted over the music to make themselves heard.

Five minutes, she told herself. She would steal just five quiet, wonderful minutes by herself.

This time, when she slipped back into the kitchen, she kept going. The moist summer air soothed her the moment she stepped outside. It smelled of grass and honeysuckle. Grateful for the fresh air after the cloying scent of fruit punch, Eden breathed deeply.

Tonight, the moon was only a sliver in the sky. She realized she had seen it change, had watched its waning and waxing more in the past three months than she had in all of her life. This was true of more than the moon. She would never look at anything else exactly the same way again.

She stood for a moment, finding the pictures in the sky that Chase had shown her. With the air warm on her face, she wondered if there would ever be a time when he would show her more.

As she crossed the grass, the light was silvery.

From behind her came the steady murmur of music and voices. She found an old hickory tree and leaned against it, enjoying the solitude and the distance.

This was what warm summer nights were for, she thought. For dreams and wishes. No matter how cold it got during the winter, no matter how far away summer seemed, she would be able to take this night out of her memory and live it again.

The creak and swish of the back door cut through her concentration.

"Eric." She straightened, not bothering to disguise the irritation in her voice.

He came to her until he, too, stood under the hickory. Starlight filtered through the leaves to mix with the shadows. "I've never known you to leave a party."

"I've changed."

"Yes." Her eyes were calm and direct. He shifted uncomfortably. "I've noticed." When he reached out to touch her, she didn't step back. She didn't even feel his touch. "We never finished talking."

"Yes, we did. A long time ago."

"Eden." Moving cautiously, he lifted a finger to trace her jawline. "I've come a long way to see you, to make things right between us."

Eden merely tilted her head to the side. "I'm sorry you were inconvenienced, but there's nothing to make right." Oddly, the anger, even the bitterness, had become diluted. It had started weakening, she knew, when he had kissed her that afternoon. Looking at him now, she felt detached, as if he were someone she'd known only vaguely. "Eric, it's foolish for either of us to drag this out. Let's just leave things alone."

"I admit I was a fool." He blocked her exit, as if by

simply continuing in the same vein he could put things back in the order he wanted. "Eden, I hurt you, and I'm sorry, but I was thinking of you as well as myself."

She wanted to laugh, but found she didn't even have the energy to give him that much. "Of me, Eric? All right, have it your way. Thank you and goodbye."

"Don't be difficult," he said, displaying a first trace of impatience. "You know how difficult it would have been for you to go through with the wedding while the scandal was still fresh in everyone's mind."

That stopped her, more than his hand had. She leaned back against the tree and waited. Yes, there was still a trace of anger, she discovered. It was mild, and buried quite deep, but it was still there. Perhaps it would be best to purge everything from her system. "Scandal. By that I assume you mean my father's poor investments."

"Eden." He moved closer again to put a comforting hand on her arm. "Your position changed so dramatically, so abruptly, when your father died and left you…"

"To earn my own way," she finished for him. "Yes, we can agree on that. My position changed. Over the past few months I've become grateful for that." There was annoyance now, but only as if he were a pesky fly she had to swat away. "I've learned to expect things from myself and to realize money had very little to do with the way I was living."

She saw by his frown that he didn't understand, would never understand the person who had grown up from the ashes of that old life. "You might find this amazing, Eric, but I don't care what anyone thinks about my altered circumstances. For the first time in my life, I have what I want, and I earned it myself."

"You can't expect me to believe that this little camp

is what you want. I know you, Eden." He twined a lock of hair around his finger. "The woman I know would never choose something like this over the life we could have together in Philadelphia."

"You might be right again." Slowly, she reached up to untangle his hand from her hair. "But I'm no longer the woman you knew."

"Don't be ridiculous." For the first time he felt a twinge of panic. The one thing he had never considered was driving hundreds of miles to be humiliated. "Come back to the hotel with me tonight. Tomorrow we can go back to Philadelphia and be married, just as we always planned."

She studied him for a moment, trying to see if there was some lingering affection for her there, some true emotion. No, she decided almost at once. She wished it had been true, for then she could have had some kind of respect for him.

"Why are you doing this? You don't love me. You never did, or you couldn't have turned your back on me when I needed you."

"Eden—"

"No, let me finish. Let's finish this once and for all." She pushed him back a foot with an impatient movement of her hands. "I'm not interested in your apologies or your excuses, Eric. The simple truth is you don't matter to me."

It was said so calmly, so bluntly, that he very nearly believed it. "You know you don't mean that, Eden. We were going to be married."

"Because it was convenient for both of us. For that much, Eric, I'll share the blame with you."

"Let's forget blame, Eden. Let me show you what we can have."

She held him off with a look. "I'm not angry anymore, and I'm not hurt. The simple fact is, Eric, I don't love you, and I don't want you."

For a moment, he was completely silent. When he did speak, Eden was surprised to hear genuine emotion in his voice. "Find someone to replace me so soon, Eden?"

She could almost laugh. He had jilted her almost two steps from the altar, but now he could act out the role of betrayed lover. "This grows more and more absurd, but no, Eric, it wasn't a matter of replacing you, it was a matter of seeing you for what you are. Don't make me explain to you what that is."

"Just how much does Chase Elliot have to do with all of this?"

"How dare you question me?" She started past him, but this time he grabbed her arm, and his grip wasn't gentle. Surprised by his refusal to release her, she stepped back and looked at him again. He was a child, she thought, who had thrown away a toy and was ready to stamp his feet now that he wanted it back and couldn't have it. Because her temper was rising, she fell back on her attitude of icy detachment. "Whatever is or isn't between Chase and me is none of your concern."

This cool, haughty woman was one he recognized. His tone softened. "Everything about you concerns me."

Weary, she could only sigh. "Eric, you're embarrassing yourself."

Before she could rid herself of him again, the screen door opened for a second time.

"Apparently I'm interrupting again." Hands in pockets, Chase stepped down from the porch.

"You seem to be making a habit of it." Eric released Eden, only to step between her and Chase. "You should be able to see that Eden and I are having a private conversation. They do teach manners, even here in the hills, don't they?"

Chase wondered if Eric would appreciate his style of manners. No, he doubted the tidy Philadelphian would appreciate a bloody nose. But then, he didn't give a damn what Eric appreciated. He'd taken two steps forward before Eden realized his intent.

"The conversation's over," she said quickly, stepping between them. She might as well have been invisible. As she had felt herself being shifted to the middle that afternoon, now she felt herself being nudged aside.

"Seems you've had considerable time to say what's on your mind." Chase rocked back on his heels, keeping his eyes on Eric.

"I don't see what business it is of yours how long I speak with my fiancée."

"Fiancée!" Eden's outraged exclamation was also ignored.

"You've let some months slip past you, Keeton." Chase's voice remained mild. His hands remained in his pockets. "Some changes have been made."

"Changes?" This time Eden turned to Chase, with no better results. "What are you talking about?"

Calmly, without giving her a glance, he took her hand. "You promised me a dance."

Instantly, Eric had her other arm. "We haven't finished."

Chase turned back, and for the first time the danger in his eyes was as clear as glass. "Yes, you have. The lady's with me."

Infuriated, Eden yanked herself free of both of them. "Stop it!" She'd had enough of being pulled in two directions without being asked if she wanted to move in either. For the first time in her life, she forgot manners, courtesy and control and did what Chase had once advised. When you're mad, he'd said, yell.

"You are both so *stupid*!" A toss of her head had the hair flying into her eyes to be dragged back impatiently. "How dare you stand here like two half-witted dogs snarling over the same bone? Don't either of you think I'm capable of speaking my own mind, making my own decisions? Well, I've got news for both of you. I can speak my own mind just fine. You." She turned to face Eric. "I meant every word I said to you. Understand? *Every single word.* I tried to phrase things as politely as possible, but if you push, let me warn you, you won't receive the same courtesy again."

"Eden, darling—"

"No, no, no!" She slapped away the hand he held out to her. "You dumped me the moment things got rough. If you think I'll take you back now, after you've shown yourself to be a weak, callous, insensitive—" oh, what was Candy's word? "—weasel," she remembered with relish, "you're crazy. And if you dare, if you *dare* touch me again, I'll knock your caps loose."

God, what a woman, Chase thought. He wondered how soon he could take her into his arms and show her how much he loved her. He'd always thought her beautiful, almost ethereal; now she was a Viking. More than he'd wanted anything in his life, he wanted to hold that passion in his arms and devour it. He was smiling at her when she whirled on him.

"And you." Taking a step closer to Chase, she began

to stab him in the chest with her finger. "You go find someone else to start a common brawl over. I'm not flattered by your Neanderthal attempts at playing at the white knight."

It wasn't quite what he'd had in mind. "For God's sake, Eden, I was—"

"Shut up." She gave him another quick jab. "I can take care of myself, Mr. Macho. And if you think I appreciate your interference in my affairs, you're mistaken. If I wanted some—some muscle-flexing he-man to clean up after me, I'd rent one."

Sucking in a deep breath, she turned to face both of them. "The two of you have behaved with less common sense than those children in there. Just for future reference, I don't find it amusing that two grown men should feel it necessary for their egos to use me as a Ping-Pong ball. I make my own choices, and I've got one for you, so listen carefully. I don't want either one of you."

Turning on her heel, she left them standing under the hickory, staring after her.

Chapter 10

The last day of the session was pandemonium. There was packing and tears and missing shoes. Each cabin gave birth to its own personal crisis. Gear had to be stored until the following summer, and an inventory had to be made of kitchen supplies.

Beds were stripped. Linen was laundered and folded. Eden caught herself sniffling over a pillowcase. Somehow, during the first inventory, they came up short by two blankets and counted five towels more than they'd started with.

Eden decided to leave her personal packing until after the confusion had died down. It even crossed her mind to spend one last night in camp and leave fresh the following morning. She told herself it was more practical, even more responsible, for one of them to stay behind so that a last check could be made of the empty cabins. In truth, she just couldn't let go.

She wasn't ready to admit that. Leaving the laundry area for the stables, she began counting bridles. The only reason she was considering staying behind, she lectured herself, was to make certain all the loose ends were tied up. As she marked numbers on her clipboard, she struggled to block out thoughts of Chase. He certainly had nothing to do with her decision to remain behind. She counted snaffle bits twice, got two different totals, then counted again.

Impossible man. She slashed the pencil over the paper, marking and totaling until she was satisfied. Without pausing, she started a critical study of reins, checking for wear. A good rubbing with saddle soap was in order, she decided. That was one more reason to stay over one more night. But, as it often had during the past week, her confrontation with Chase and Eric ran through her mind.

She had meant everything she'd said. Just reaffirming that satisfied her. Every single word, even though she had shouted it, had come straight from the heart. Even after seven days her indignation, and her resolve, were as fresh as ever.

She had simply been a prize to be fought over, she remembered, as indignation began to simmer toward rage. Is that all a woman was to a man, something to yank against his side and stretch his ego on? Well, that wasn't something she would accept. She had only truly forged her own identity in recent months. That wasn't something she was going to give up, or even dilute, for anyone, for any man.

Fury bubbling, Eden crossed over to inspect the saddles. Eric had never loved her. Now, more than ever, that was crystal clear. Even without love, without caring, he'd wanted to lay some sort of claim. My woman. My property. My *fiancée*! She made a sound, somewhere between disgust and derision, that had one of the horses blowing in response.

If her aunt hadn't taken him away, Eden wasn't sure what she might have done. And, at this point, she was equally unsure she wouldn't have enjoyed it immensely.

But worse, a hundred times worse, was Chase. As she stared into space, her pencil drummed a rapid rat-a-tat-tat on the clipboard. He'd never once spoken of love or affection. There had been no promises asked or given, and yet he'd behaved just as abominably as Eric.

That was where the comparison ended, she admitted, as she pressed the heel of her hand to her brows. She was in love with Chase. Desperately in love. If he'd said a word, if he'd given her a chance to speak, how different things might have been. But now she was discovering that leaving him was infinitely more difficult than it had been to leave Philadelphia.

He hadn't spoken; he hadn't asked. The compromises she might have made for him, and only him, would never be needed now. Whatever might have been was over, she told herself, straightening her shoulders. It was time for new adjustments, new plans and, again, a new life. She had done it once, and she could do it again.

"Plans," she muttered to herself as she studied the clipboard again. There were so many plans to make for the following season. It would be summer again before she knew it.

Her fingers clutched the pencil convulsively. Was that how she would live her life, from summer to summer? Would there only be emptiness in between, emptiness and waiting? How many times would she come back and walk along the lake hoping to see him?

No. This was the mourning period. Eden closed her eyes for a moment and waited for the strength to return. You couldn't adjust and go on unless you'd grieved first. That was something else she had learned. So she would grieve for Chase. Then she would build her life.

"Eden. Eden, are you in there?"

"Right here." Eden turned as Candy rushed into the tack room.

"Oh, thank God."

"What now?"

Candy pressed a hand to her heart as if to push her breath back. "Roberta."

"Roberta?" Her stomach muscles balled like a fist. "Is she hurt?"

"She's gone."

"What do you mean, gone? Did her parents come early?"

"I mean gone." Pacing, Candy began to tug on her hair. "Her bags are all packed and stacked in her cabin. She's nowhere in camp."

"Not again." More annoyed than worried now, Eden tossed the clipboard aside. "Hasn't that child learned anything this summer? Every time I turn around she's off on a little field trip of her own."

"Marcie and Linda claim that she said she had something important to take care of before she left." Candy lifted her hands, then let them fall. "She didn't tell them what she was up to, that I'm sure of. You and I both know that she might only have gone to pick some flowers for her mother, but—"

"We can't take any chances," Eden finished.

"I've got three of the counselors out looking, but I thought you might have some idea where she could have gone before we call out the marines." She paused to catch her breath. "What a way to round out the summer."

Eden closed her eyes a minute to concentrate. Conversations with Roberta scattered through her memory until she focused on one in particular. "Oh, no." Her eyes shot open. "I think I know where she's gone." She was already rushing out of the tack room as Candy loped to keep up.

"Where?"

"I'll need to take the car. It'll be quicker." Thinking fast, Eden dashed to the rear of their cabin, where the secondhand compact was parked under a gnarled pear tree. "I'd swear she's gone to say goodbye to Chase, but make sure the orchard gets checked."

"Already done, but—"

"I'll be back in twenty minutes."

"Eden—"

The gunning of the motor drowned out Candy's words. "Don't worry, I'll bring the little darling back." She set her teeth. "If I have to drag her by her hair."

"Okay, but—" Candy stepped back as the compact shot forward. "Gas," she said with a sigh as Eden drove away. "I don't think there's much gas in the tank."

Eden noticed that the sky was darkening and decided to blame Roberta for that as well. She would have sworn an oath that Roberta had gone to see Chase one last time. A three-mile hike would never have deterred a girl of Roberta's determination.

Eden drove under the arching sign, thinking grimly of what she would say to Roberta once she had her. The pleasure she got from that slid away as the car bucked and sputtered. Eden looked down helplessly as it jolted again, then stopped dead. The needle of the gas gauge registered a flat *E*.

"Damn!" She slapped a hand on the steering wheel, then let out a yelp. Padded steering wheels weren't part of the amenities on cars as old as this one. Nursing her aching wrist, she stepped out of the car just as the first blast of thunder shook the air. As if on cue, a torrent of rain poured down.

For a moment, Eden merely stood beside the stalled car, her throbbing hand at her mouth, while water streamed over her. Her clothes were soaked through in seconds. "Perfect," she mumbled; then, on the heels of that: "Roberta." Casting one furious look skyward, she set off at a jogging run.

Lightning cracked across the sky like a whip. Thunder bellowed in response. Each time, Eden's heart leaped toward her throat. As each step brought her closer to Chase's home, her fear mounted.

What if she'd been wrong? What if Roberta wasn't there, but was caught somewhere in the storm, wet and frightened? What if she was lost or hurt? Her breath began to hitch as anxiety ballooned inside her.

She reached Chase's door, soaked to the skin and terrified.

Her pounding at the door sounded weak against the cannoning thunder. Looking back over her shoulder, Eden could see nothing but a solid wall of rain. If Roberta was out there, somewhere… Whirling back, she pounded with both fists, shouting for good measure.

When Chase opened the door, she nearly tumbled over his feet. He took one look at her soaked, bedraggled figure and knew he'd never seen anything more beautiful in his life. "Well, this is a surprise. Get you a towel?"

Eden grabbed his shirt with both hands. "Roberta," she managed, trying to convey everything with one word.

"She's in the front room." Gently, he pushed the hair out of her eyes. "Relax, Eden, she's fine."

"Oh, thank God." Near tears, Eden pressed her fingers to her eyes. But when she lowered them, her eyes were dry and furious. "I'll murder her. Right here, right now. Quickly."

Before she could carry through with her threat, Chase stepped in front of her. Now that he'd had a good taste of her temper, he no longer underestimated it. "I think I have an idea how you feel, but don't be too rough on her. She came by to propose."

"Just move aside, or I'll take you down with her." She shoved him aside and strode past him. The moment she stood in the doorway, Eden drew a breath. "Roberta." Each syllable was bitten off. The girl on the floor stopped playing with the dog and looked up.

"Oh, hi, Miss Carlbough." She grinned, apparently pleased with the company. After a moment her teeth dropped down to her lower lip. Though perhaps an optimist, Roberta was no fool. "You're all wet, Miss Carlbough."

The low sound deep in Eden's throat had Squat's ears pricking. "Roberta," she said again as she started forward. Squat moved simultaneously. Drawing up short, Eden gave the dog a wary glance. He sat now, his tail thumping, directly between Eden and Roberta. "Call off your dog," she ordered without bothering to look at Chase.

"Oh, Squat wouldn't hurt you." Roberta scurried across the floor to leap lovingly on his neck. Squat's tail thumped even harder. Eden thought for a moment that he was smiling. She was certain she'd gotten a good view of his large white teeth. "He's real friendly," Roberta assured her. "Just hold your hand out and he'll sniff it."

And take it off at the wrist—which was giving her enough trouble as it was. "Roberta," Eden began again, staying where she was. "After all these weeks, aren't you aware of the rules about leaving camp?"

"Yes, ma'am." Roberta hooked an arm around Squat's neck. "But it was important."

"That isn't the point." Eden folded her hands. She was aware of how she looked, how she sounded, and she knew that if she turned her head she would see Chase grinning at her. "Rules have a purpose, Roberta. They aren't made up just to spoil your fun, but to see to order and safety. You've broken one of the most important ones today, and not for the first time. Miss Bartholomew and I are responsible for you. Your parents expect, and rightfully so, that we'll…"

Eden trailed off as Roberta listened, solemn-eyed. She opened her mouth again, prepared to complete the lecture, but only a shuddering breath came out. "Roberta, you scared me to death."

"Gee, I'm sorry, Miss Carlbough." To Eden's surprise, Roberta jumped up and dashed across the room to throw her arms around Eden's waist. "I didn't mean to, really. I guess I didn't think anyone would miss me before I got back."

"Not miss you?" A laugh, a little shaky, whispered out as Eden pressed a kiss to the top of Roberta's head. "You monster, don't you know I've developed radar where you're concerned?"

"Yeah?" Roberta squeezed hard.

"Yeah."

"I am sorry, Miss Carlbough, really I am." She drew back so that her freckled, triangular face was tilted to Eden's. "I just had to see Chase for a minute." She sent Eden an intimate, feminine glance that had Eden looking quickly over at Chase.

"Chase?" Eden repeated, knowing her emphasis on Roberta's use of the first name would get her nowhere.

"We had a personal matter to discuss." Chase dropped down onto the arm of a chair. He wondered if Eden had any idea how protectively she was holding Roberta.

Though it was difficult, Eden managed to display some dignity in her dripping clothes. "I realize it's too much to expect a twelve-year-old to show a consistent sense of responsibility, but I would have expected more from you."

"I called the camp," he said, taking the wind out of her sails. "Apparently I just missed catching you. They know Roberta's safe." Rising, he walked over and grabbed the tail of her T-shirt. A flick of the wrist had water dripping out. "Did you walk over?"

"No." Annoyed that he had done exactly what he should have done, Eden smacked his hand away. "The car…" She hesitated, then decided to lie. "Broke down." She turned to frown at Roberta again. "Right before the storm."

"I'm sorry you got wet," Roberta said again.

"And so you should be."

"Didn't you put gas in the car? It was out, you know."

Before Eden could decide to murder her after all, they were interrupted by the blast of a horn.

"That'll be Delaney." Chase walked to the window to confirm it. "He's going to run Roberta back to camp."

"That's very kind of him." Eden held her hand out for Roberta's. "I appreciate all the trouble."

"Just Roberta." Chase caught Eden's hand before she could get away from him again. Ready and willing, or kicking and screaming, he was holding on to what he needed. "You'd better get out of those wet clothes before you come down with something."

"As soon as I get back to camp."

"My mother says you catch a chill if your feet stay wet." Roberta gave Squat a parting hug. "See you next year," she said to Chase, and for the first time Eden saw a hint of shyness. "You really will write?"

"Yeah." Chase bent down, tilted her head and kissed both cheeks. "I really will write."

Her freckles all but vanished under her blush. Turning, she threw herself into Eden's arms again. "I'll miss you, Miss Carlbough."

"Oh, Roberta, I'll miss you, too."

"I'm coming back next year and bringing my cousin. Everyone says we're so much alike we should be sisters."

"Oh," Eden managed weakly. "Wonderful." She hoped one winter was enough time to recharge.

"This was the best summer ever." Roberta gave one last squeeze as tears began to cloud Eden's eyes. "Bye!"

The front door was slamming behind her before Eden had taken the first step. "Roberta—"

"It was my best summer ever, too." Chase took her free hand before she could try for the door.

"Chase, let me go. I have to get back."

"Dry clothes. Though, as I may have mentioned before, you look wonderful wet and dripping."

"I'm not staying," she said, even as he tugged her toward the stairs.

"Since I just heard Delaney pull off, and your car's out of gas, I'd say you are." Because she was shivering now, he hurried her up. "And you're leaving puddles on the floor."

"Sorry." He propelled her through his bedroom. Eden had a fleeting impression of quiet colors and a brass bed before she was nudged into the adjoining bath. "Chase, this is very nice of you, but if you could just drive me back—"

"After you've had a hot shower and changed."

A hot shower. He could have offered her sable and emeralds and not tempted her half so much. Eden hadn't had a hot shower since the first week of June. "No, I really think I should get back."

But the door was already closing behind him.

Eden stared at it; then, her lower lip caught between her teeth, she looked back at the tub. Nothing she'd ever seen in her life had seemed so beautiful, so desirable. It took her less than ten seconds to give in.

"Since I'm here anyway…" she mumbled, and began to peel out of her clothes.

The first sizzle of hot spray stole her breath. Then, with a sigh of pure greed, she luxuriated in it. It was sinful, she thought as the water sluiced over her head. It was heaven.

Fifteen minutes later, she turned the taps off, but not

without regret. On the rack beside the tub was a thick, thirsty bath towel. She wrapped herself in it and decided it was nearly as good as the shower. Then she noticed her clothes were gone.

For a moment, she only frowned at the empty rail where she'd hung them. Then she gripped the towel tighter. He must have come in and taken them while she was in the shower. Lips pursed, Eden studied the frosted glass doors and wondered how opaque they really were.

Be practical, she told herself. Chase had come in and taken her clothes because they needed to be dried. He was simply being a considerate host. Still, her nerves drummed a bit as she lifted the navy-blue robe from the hook on the back of the door.

It was his, of course. His scent clung to the material so that she felt he was all but in the room with her as she drew it on. It was warm and thick, but she shivered once as she secured the belt.

It was practical, she reminded herself. The robe was nothing more than an adequate covering until her clothes were dry again. But she tilted her head so that her chin rubbed along the collar.

Fighting off the mood, she took the towel and rubbed the mist away from the mirror. What she saw was enough to erase any romantic fantasies from her mind. True, the hot water from the shower had brought some color to her cheeks, but she hadn't even a trace of mascara left to darken her lashes. With the color of the robe to enhance them, her eyes dominated her face. She looked as though she'd been saved just before going under for the third time. Her hair was wet, curling in little tendrils around her face. Eden dragged a hand through it a few times, but couldn't bring it to order without a brush.

Charming, she thought before she pulled the door open. In Chase's bedroom she paused, wanting to look, wanting even more to touch something that belonged to him. With a shake of her head, she hurried through the bedroom and down the stairs. It was only when she stopped in the doorway of the front room and saw him that her nerves returned in full force.

He looked so right, so at ease in his workshirt and jeans as he stood in front of a nineteenth-century cabinet pouring brandy from a crystal decanter. She'd come to realize that it was his contradictions, as much as anything else, that appealed to her. At the moment, reasons didn't matter. She loved him. Now she had to get through this last encounter before burying herself in the winter months.

He turned and saw her. He'd known she was there, had felt her there, but had needed a moment. When he'd come into the bath to take her wet clothes, she'd been humming. He'd only seen a shadow of her behind the glass but had wanted, more than he could remember wanting anything, to push the barrier aside and take her. To hold her with her skin wet and warm, her eyes huge and aware.

He wanted her as much, as sharply, now as she stood in the doorway dwarfed by his robe.

So he'd taken a moment, for the simple reason that he had to be sure he could speak.

"Better?"

"Yes, thanks." Her hand reached automatically for the lapels of the robe and fidgeted there. He crossed the room to offer her a snifter.

"Drink. This should ward off the danger of wet feet."

As she took the glass, Chase closed the doors at her back. Eden found herself gripping the snifter with both hands. She lifted it slowly, hoping the brandy would clear her head.

"I'm sorry about all this." She made certain her tone was as polite and as distant as she could manage. She kept her back to the doors.

"No trouble." He wanted to shake her. "Why don't you sit down?"

"No, I'm fine." But when he continued to stand in front of her, she felt it necessary to move. She walked to the window, where the rain was still pouring from the sky. "I don't suppose this can keep up for long."

"No, it can't." The amusement he was beginning to feel came out in his voice. Wary, Eden turned back to him. "In fact, I'm amazed it's gone on this long." Setting his brandy aside, he went to her. "It's time we stopped it, Eden. Time you stopped backing away."

She gave a quick shake of her head and skirted around him. "I don't know what you mean."

"The hell you don't." He was behind her quickly, and there was nowhere to run. He took the snifter from her nerveless fingers before turning her to face him again. Slowly, deliberately, he gathered her hair in his hands, drawing it back until her face was unframed. There was a flash of fear in her eyes, but beneath it, waiting, was the need he'd wanted to see.

"We stood here once before, and I told you then it was too late."

The sun had been streaming through the glass then. Now the rain was lashing against it. As she stood there,

Eden felt past and present overlap. "We stood here once before, and you kissed me."

His mouth found hers. Like the storm, the kiss was fierce and urgent. He'd expected hesitation and found demand. He'd expected fear and found passion. Drawing her closer, he found hunger and need and shimmering desire. What he had yet to find, what he discovered he needed most, was acceptance.

Trust me. He wanted to shout it at her, but her hands were in his hair, entangling him and pulling him to her.

The rain beat against the windowpanes. Thunder walked across the sky. Eden was whirling in her own private storm. She wanted him, wanted to feel him peeling the robe from her shoulders and touching her. She wanted that first delirious sensation of skin meeting skin. She wanted to give her love to him where it could be alive and free, but knew she had to keep it locked inside, secret, lonely.

"Chase. We can't go on like this." She turned her head away. "I can't go on like this. I have to leave. People are waiting for me."

"You're not going anywhere. Not this time." He slid a hand up her throat. His patience was at an end.

She sensed it and backed away. "Candy will be wondering where I am. I'd like to have my clothes now."

"No."

"No?"

"No," he said again as he lifted his brandy. "Candy won't be wondering where you are, because I phoned her and told her you weren't coming back. She said you weren't to worry, that things were under control. And no—" he sipped his brandy "—you can't have your clothes. Can I get you something else?"

"You phoned her?" All the fear, all the anxiety, drained away to make room for temper. Her eyes darkened, losing their fragility. Chase almost smiled. He loved the cool woman, the nervous one, the determined one, but he adored the Viking.

"Yeah. Got a problem with that?"

"Where did you possibly get the idea that you had a right to make my decisions for me?" She pushed a hand, covered by the cuff of his robe, against his chest. "You had no business calling Candy, or anyone else. More, you had no business assuming that I'd stay here with you."

"I'm not assuming anything. You are staying here. With me."

"Guess again." This time, when she shoved, there was enough power behind it to take him back a step. He knew that if he hadn't already been mad about her, he would have fallen in love at that moment. "God, but I'm sick to death of dealing with overbearing, dictatorial men who think all they have to do is want something to have it."

"You're not dealing with Eric now, Eden." His voice was soft, perhaps a shade too soft. "You're not dealing with other men, but with me. Only me."

"Wrong again, because I'm through dealing with you. Give me my clothes."

He set the snifter down very carefully. "No."

Her mouth would have fallen open if her jaw hadn't been clenched so tightly. "All right, I'll walk back in this." Ready to carry out her threat, she marched to the door and yanked it open. Squat lay across the threshold. As they spotted each other, he rose on his haunches with what Eden was certain was a leer. She took one more step, then, cursing herself for a coward, turned back.

"Are you going to call off that beast?"

Chase looked down at Squat, knowing the dog would do nothing more dangerous than slobber on her bare feet. Hooking his thumb in his pocket, he smiled. "He's had his shots."

"Terrific." With her mind set on one purpose, she strode to the window. "I'll go out this way then." Kneeling on the window seat, she began to struggle with the sash. When Chase caught her around the waist, she turned on him.

"Take your hands off me. I said I was leaving, and I meant it." She took a swing, surprising them both when it landed hard in his gut. "Here, you want your robe back. I don't need it. I'll walk the three miles naked." To prove her point, she began fighting the knot at the belt.

"I wouldn't do that." As much for his sake as hers, he caught her hands. "If you do, we won't spend much time talking this through."

"I'm not spending any time at all." She squirmed until they both went down on the cushions of the window seat. "I don't have anything else to say to you." She managed to kick until the robe was hitched up to her thighs. "Except that you have the manners of a pig, and I can't wait until I'm hundreds of miles away from you. I decided the other night, when I was given the choice between a boring fool and a hardheaded clod, that I'd rather join a convent. Now take your hands off me, or I swear, I'll hurt you. No one, but no one, pushes me around."

With that, she put all her energy into one last shove. It sent them both tumbling off the cushions and onto the floor. As he had done once before, Chase rolled with her until he had her pinned beneath him. He stared at her now as he had then, while she fought to get her breath back.

"Oh God, Eden, I love you." Laughing at them both, he crushed his lips to hers.

She didn't fight the kiss. She didn't even move, though her fingers stiffened under his. Each breath took such an effort that she thought her heart had slowed down to nothing. When she could speak again, she did so carefully.

"I'd appreciate it if you'd say that again."

"I love you." He watched her eyes close and felt that quick twinge of panic. "Listen to me, Eden. I know you've been hurt, but you have to trust me. I've watched you take charge of your life this summer. It hasn't been the easiest thing I've ever done to stand back and give you the space you needed to do that."

She opened her eyes again. Her heart wasn't beating at a slow rhythm now, but seemed capable of bursting out of her chest. "Was that what you were doing?"

"I understood that you needed to prove something to yourself. And I think I knew that until you had, you wouldn't be ready to share whatever that was with me."

"Chase—"

"Don't say anything yet." He brought her hand to his lips. "Eden, I know you're used to certain things, a certain way of life. If that's what you need, I'll find a way to give it to you. But if you give me a chance, I can make you happy here."

She swallowed, afraid of misunderstanding. "Chase, are you saying you'd move back to Philadelphia if I asked you to?"

"I'm saying I'd move anywhere if it was important to you, but I'm not letting you go back alone, Eden. Summers aren't enough."

Her breath came out quietly. "What do you want from me?"

"Everything." He pressed his lips to her hand again, but his eyes were no longer calm. "A lifetime, starting now. Love, arguments, children. Marry me, Eden. Give me six months to make you happy here. If I can't, we'll go anywhere you like. Just don't back away."

"I'm not backing away." Her fingers entwined with his. "And I don't want to be anyplace but here."

She saw the change in his eyes even as his fingers tightened on hers. "If I touch you now, there's no going back."

"You've already told me it was too late." She drew him down to her. Passion and promises merged as they strained closer. She felt again that she had the world in the palm of her hand and held it tightly. "Don't ever let me go. Oh, Chase, I could feel my heart breaking when I thought of leaving here today, leaving you when I loved you so much."

"You wouldn't have gotten far."

Her lips curved at that. Perhaps, in some areas, she could accept a trace of arrogance. "You'd have come after me?"

"I'd have come after you so fast I'd have been there before you."

She felt pleasure grow, and glow. "And begged?"

His brow lifted at the glint in her eyes. "Let's just say I'd have left little doubt as to how much I wanted you."

"And crawled," she said, twining her arms around

his neck. "I'm almost sorry I missed that. Maybe you could do it now."

He took a quick nip at her ear. "Don't press your luck."

Laughing, she held on. "One day this will be gray," she murmured as she trailed her fingers through his hair. "And I still won't be able to keep my hands out of it." She drew his head back to look at him, and this time there was no laughter, only love. "I've waited for you all my life."

He buried his face in her throat, fighting back the need to make her his, then and there. With Eden it would be perfect, it would be everything dreams were made of. He drew away to trace the line of her cheekbone. "You know, I wanted to murder Eric when I saw him with his hands on you."

"I didn't know how to explain when I saw you there. Then, later…" Her brow arched. "Well, you behaved very badly."

"You were magnificent. You scared Eric to death."

"And you?"

"You only made me want you more." He tasted her again, feeling the wild, sweet thrill only she had ever brought to him. "I had plans to kidnap you from camp. Bless Roberta for making it easy."

"I hope she's not upset you're going to marry me instead. You have a neat dog, and you're kind of cute." She pressed her lips to the sensitive area just below his ear.

"She understood perfectly. In fact, she approves."

Eden stopped her lazy exploration of his throat. "Approves? You mean you told her you were going to marry me?"

"Sure I did."

"Before you asked me?"

Grinning, Chase leaned down to nip at her bottom lip. "I figured Squat and I could convince you."

"And if I'd said no?"

"You didn't."

"There's still time to change my mind." He touched his lips to hers again, letting them linger and warm. "Well," she said with a sigh, "maybe just this once I'll let you get away with it."

* * * * *